FIERC
GIR

BOOKS BY EMMA TALLON

Runaway Girl

Dangerous Girl

Boss Girl

FIERCE GIRL

EMMA TALLON

bookouture

Published by Bookouture in 2019

An imprint of StoryFire Ltd.

Carmelite House
50 Victoria Embankment
London EC4Y 0DZ

www.bookouture.com

ISBN: 978-1-78681-804-1
eBook ISBN: 978-1-78681-803-4

Every word I write, every hour I work, it will always be for the little love of my life – Christian

PROLOGUE

Grasping the ornate wooden pillar that hid her from view, she stifled a gasp. Horror filled her eyes and her heart as the consequences of what she'd just heard registered in her brain. She had to get out of here – fast. Without thinking, she stepped back and her foot sent a loose stone chip rattling off into the void behind her.

There was a pause.

'Who's there?' he roared as he hurtled towards her blindly in the dark.

With no other option, she turned and ran full pelt down the long, wide hallway behind her. The darkness swallowed her up and she was momentarily grateful for its cover.

This was short-lived and terror shot through her with force as she heard the thumps of his heavy tread picking up the pace behind her. 'Shit,' she muttered, shooting a fearful glance over her shoulder. He was there, his hulking dark mass almost upon her. Survival instinct kicked in and she pushed forward with everything she had. Blood roared through her ears and her heart hammered against her chest as she gasped for breath in a panic. Could she outrun him? She didn't fancy her chances, but it was her only hope if she was going to make it out of this alive. If he caught her, if he saw her face, she was dead.

Dread filled her veins as he gained on her. The gap began to close and her blood turned to ice. No one could help her now. No one even knew she was here.

CHAPTER ONE

Anna's eyes were glazed as she stood in front of the wall of bright flowers, her mind lost in darker places. It took the florist a few attempts to catch her attention. 'Hello? Hello? Miss Davis?'

Anna blinked back into the present and turned to face the kindly older man with his receding grey hair and his warm friendly face. She quickly forced a smile. 'Sorry, I was miles away.'

'I can see that. Are you OK?' he asked, genuine concern in his voice. He liked this young woman; she had become a regular at his shop over the last couple of months.

'I'm fine,' Anna replied. 'Just distracted. You've got some gorgeous colours in this week; I love these deep purple ones.'

'But you won't be going for them though, will you?' He chuckled. 'You'll be going for the peach long-stemmed roses again today, I presume? Shall I make them up for you?'

'Yes, please, that would be lovely,' Anna replied. They were Tanya's favourite. Anna had been putting fresh flowers by her bedside every few days since she'd entered the hospital. Two months had gone by and Tanya still hadn't woken from her coma. After being shot by Anna's boyfriend Freddie's psychotic brother Michael and being left by her ex to bleed to death, she had been in a bad way when they'd finally got her the medical help she needed. It had been touch and go, but she'd pulled through the initial emergency surgery. Only she hadn't woken up afterwards.

Anna eyed the purple flowers again. 'And actually I will take a bunch of the purple today too.' They would brighten up the office a bit. Which happened to be where she was spending most of her time these days.

'Righto,' he said cheerfully. 'Would you like me to mix in a few lilies with them? They go together beautifully.'

Lilies. The flower of death.

Anna shivered. 'No thank you, just the purple ones.' She turned away while he put the bunches together and stared out the window. *Death.* Anna mulled the word over in her mind. It was a subject that was never far from her thoughts these days. Not after what she had done.

'Here you go. Hope your friend's doing OK today.' The cheerful man gave her a warm smile as he passed her the pretty bouquets. Anna returned it tiredly as she handed over the money.

'Thanks. Me too.'

Turning on her heel Anna walked out onto the busy street and stared across the road at the large, imposing hospital. She took a deep breath and made her way over.

As the lift doors opened and she made her way down the long corridor towards Tanya's private room, Anna could sense a difference in the atmosphere. Her senses pricked up, suddenly alert. *What's going on?* The nurses seemed tense, and she could see people coming in and out of the room. She picked up her pace, her heart jumping up into her mouth. *What's happened? Is Tanya OK? Has she...* She didn't dare finish the thought.

Anna's heels clacked loudly on the hard floor as she raced down the hall. The doctors had said Tanya was stable, but that the longer she stayed in the coma, the more damage would be caused to her brain function. What if something major was now impaired? What if she'd been under so long that her brain had stopped telling her lungs to breathe? Would they catch something like that in time? They'd said themselves that they wouldn't know what they were dealing with until it happened, that every case was different.

Her thoughts terrifying her, Anna ran the last few metres to the room and burst in, grasping the doorframe with one hand to steady herself. Three surprised faces turned to her – a doctor she knew and two nurses that she didn't.

'What's going on?' Her voice trembled slightly and she steadied it. 'Is she alright?' Anna's glance flickered from face to face, finally resting on Tanya's. She still lay where she always did, but something was different.

'Her tubes – where are they? Why have you taken her tubes out?' Anna rushed over to the bed.

'Anna.' Dr Javid held his hands out and gave her a reassuring smile. 'It's OK. There's no need to worry. In fact, if anything, there is cause for celebration.'

'What?' Anna frowned. Her heart wanted to soar, but she forced it to stay grounded. She couldn't bear the disappointment if she'd read his words wrongly.

Anna saw movement in her peripheral vision and looked down. She gasped as she saw Tanya's hand limply reach for hers.

'Hey,' Tanya croaked weakly.

Anna looked down at her best friend's pale face to find her eyes blinking open. Tanya was alive. Not only was she alive but she was awake and talking. Her best friend was back. She hadn't got her killed. Anna glanced at the doctor, back to Tanya and promptly burst into tears.

'Oh my God,' she sobbed. 'Oh my God, you're OK.'

*

Freddie pulled the lapels of his suit jacket further up his neck. It had been a mild entry to winter so far, but the warmer days were now definitely behind them. A cold blanket had descended over London and he felt it seeping into his bones. Stepping off the busy Soho street and into one of his massage parlours, Freddie was glad to be out of it.

The bell tinkled and Linda bustled out from the back. 'Heaven Sent mass— Oh! Hello, love,' she greeted Freddie warmly. 'Didn't expect to see you here today – everything OK?' Her brow furrowed in concern. *Had one of the girls pissed off the boss?*

'Everything's fine, Linda, just need to talk to you about something. Can we go out the back?' Freddie asked.

''Course. Come through; I'll get the kettle on.'

Freddie followed Linda's tiny frame through the doorway and down a long hallway with multiple doors leading off it. As usual, muffled groans and sounds of excitement escaped as they passed. Freddie had tried to make the rooms as soundproof as possible, but there was only so much he could achieve without going to stupid and expensive lengths.

Soon enough they were shut inside Linda's cosy office with steaming cups of tea. Linda placed a plate of biscuits between them and waited to see what Freddie had to say. She'd been managing this place for years, past her peak in terms of servicing the clients but with enough experience and a shrewd-enough head to still be of great value to her boss. The parlour had thrived under her management and she was proud of it.

'How's things been?' Freddie asked.

'Great, as always. The girls are doing well, the regulars keep coming, new faces showing up all the time. Some days we're so full up we have to send people away.' A flash of annoyance crossed her face. 'Which I hate to do, but sometimes there's nothing else for it, if the diary is full. I thought about creating a waiting list but the couple of punters I mentioned it to weren't keen. I did say I'd be discreet, say it was a dentist appointment or something, but it still worried them too much. Too risky that the wives will figure it out, I suppose.'

Freddie nodded. He knew another parlour had tried the same thing with the same result. Men didn't want their seedy side hobbies to spill into their day-to-day lives, not even under the pretence of something else.

'That's actually what I wanted to talk to you about,' he said. 'The two flats above next door finally came up for lease and I've managed to secure them.'

'Oh!' Linda's eyes widened. This was interesting news indeed.

'The flats have access to a hall which opens out onto the street right next to us, as you know. I'm planning on knocking through the waiting area down here to the bottom of the stairs, then knocking through the first flat upstairs to link it up. I'll have to have the walls moved about a bit but not that much.'

'Are you allowed to do that?' she asked.

'No,' Freddie answered.

Linda shrugged. 'So, what are you thinking? Those flats are quite big, aren't they?'

'Yeah. I want to expand the services. At the moment, it's all just rub and tug here, but I'd like to make the upstairs a bit more upmarket. Small, but select and catering to different tastes. I think you'll find a lot of the regulars will move onto the higher-end services, which leaves the downstairs free to bring in more trade off the street.'

Freddie put his tea down and leaned forward, painting the picture with his hands. 'At the moment, I know the first flat gets used as the girls' rest area and storage. The girls can still have the smaller room and the kitchen for their breaks, but the other two rooms will be knocked through and made into a lounge bar. This is where the higher-end customers will come, have a drink, be wooed by whoever's time they're paying for. The two flats will be broken up into rooms for the services. I want to make a couple of them more specialist. Fetishes. Nothing violent, of course.'

Freddie didn't stand for any violence against the girls. Unlike most bosses in his game, he treated them with fairness and respect. And in return he expected the same from them. 'You'll focus your time and attentions up there, making sure everyone is happy and things run smoothly.'

'What about downstairs?' Linda asked. 'This place don't run itself – it needs a firm hand and a keen eye.'

'I know. Which is why I wanted to talk to you about bringing Carla in as assistant manager under you. With the expansion, you can't run it on your own, and I think she'd be a good candidate.'

Linda paused and gave Freddie a look. 'Well, yeah, she's a good girl,' she replied. 'She'd be perfect, but have you talked to her about it?' Linda wasn't sure the younger woman would accept when she found out she'd have to come back here.

Eighteen months earlier, Carla had worked as one of the girls in the parlour. She'd been a particular favourite of Michael's, Freddie's younger brother. One day she had disappeared without a word and they'd later learned that Michael had chained her up in an abandoned house and left her to die. She'd been there for days before she was found.

Freddie had moved her to another one of his parlours after she had fully recovered. She hadn't been keen on returning to this one, even with Michael out of the country. But Michael was dead now. The only way he would be coming back for her now was in her dreams. And Carla had proven to be both loyal and hardworking, two things Freddie valued greatly. They were two traits that he needed to see in whoever was going to help Linda manage this expansion.

'I think I can convince her to come back,' Freddie said with confidence. 'This promotion would be good for her and I can't think of anyone better suited.'

'OK then, see what she says.' Linda lifted her teacup in a toast. Freddie chinked it with his own. 'To Heaven Sent becoming the biggest, sauciest place in Soho.'

CHAPTER TWO

Anna marched towards the small hospital room with a spring in her step and a genuine smile spread across her face for once. She didn't often smile these days, but she had good cause today. Tanya had been exhausted when she first awoke and had needed to go back to sleep almost immediately. Anna had been terrified that she might be slipping back into the coma, but the doctors had assured her that this was perfectly normal. She'd left Tanya to rest and had impatiently waited a whole twenty-four hours, as Dr Javid had suggested, before she came back to visit again.

As she approached the open door, she saw that Tanya's bed had been tilted so that she was in a half-sitting position. She still looked as white as a sheet, her face as haunted as if she was just back from the front line of a war, but she was here. She was alive and awake, and right now that was all that mattered.

'Oh my God, it's still just so amazing to see you up like this,' Anna gushed, unable to contain her emotions. She took a deep breath and reminded herself not to overwhelm her friend. 'How are you feeling?'

'Like I've been shot and lying in a coma for two months,' Tanya said drily, her voice still hoarse. She grinned, softening her words.

'Funny that,' Anna joked. She sat down on the edge of the bed and squeezed Tanya's hand. 'It really is so good to have you back. You have no idea how much I missed you.'

'Oh, I think I do,' Tanya croaked, pulling herself up the bed a bit more. The movement was painstakingly slow.

'I nearly went out of my mind when you disappeared. We had no idea what was happening, whether you were dead or hurt.'

'Well…' Anna cleared her throat and swallowed down the feeling of anxiety Tanya's words brought back. 'Let's just agree not to get abducted or shot again any time soon, shall we?'

'Deal. What you got there?' Tanya pointed at the gift bag in Anna's hand.

'All your favourite snacks, seeing as you can't come home yet.' Anna passed it over.

'Ah man, I wish I could eat those. They've got me on a strict diet. Some bullshit about my body having to be eased back in after being drip fed for so long.' She waved her hand dismissively with a look of disgust. 'Apparently, although it contained no solids, it was a full coverage diet to give me everything I needed. Fuckers didn't bother including any cherry vodka though, did they?'

Anna hid a smile. This was the Tanya she'd missed. 'So, what have they said?' she asked.

Before Tanya could answer, Dr Javid walked into the room. 'Ah, Anna's here. Perfect. I thought I heard the nurses say you had a visitor. This will save me running through everything twice.' He closed the door behind him, shutting out the hum of general activity beyond it. Placing the thick file he was holding on the side table, he sat down on the vacant chair beside the bed.

'Tanya, I want to talk you through the next stage of your recovery. As you know, you've been in that coma for a very long time and this has led to a couple of things that are going to take some work to get back on top of.'

He paused and addressed Anna. 'Since Tanya woke up yesterday, we've been running various tests and scans to see what the damage is. I can honestly say that for someone who has been under this long, we have the best outcome we could have hoped for.'

He turned back to Tanya. 'So, don't be too disheartened. You already know your muscles have deteriorated greatly, and I know finding out that you can't yet support your own weight has been hard. But that is not permanent. It's just because your muscles haven't been used at all in so long. The next step will be to transfer you to an inpatient physical rehabilitation centre, where you can work on getting back to your normal strength again.'

Anna and Tanya exchanged glances and Dr Javid quickly tried to reassure them.

'Please don't be alarmed; it's not as awful as it sounds. The one I have referred you to is a fantastic place and the staff there are some of the best.'

'Is this not something she can do here?' Anna asked.

'I'm afraid not. We're not equipped for that sort of care. The unit is over at St Pancras Hospital. It really is the best place for you to carry out your rehab. They have specialists and therapists there to see you through every step of the way. Now, there is another thing that I need to talk to you about.' He took a deep breath. 'Currently, your short-term memory isn't functioning the way it should. We picked this up during routine tests yesterday, so then ran an MRI this morning to see if this was caused by anything we hadn't picked up.'

'Like what?' Anna asked.

'It could have been a few things – a ruptured aneurysm, a small stroke – but we didn't find any physical cause,' he replied.

'So what does that mean?' Anna asked with a frown. 'How sure are you that there's even a problem? I mean, she's just come out of a coma – perhaps she's just a bit forgetful.'

Dr Javid nodded sympathetically. He understood how hard it was for loved ones to be told there was something wrong. He turned to Tanya, who had remained unusually quiet during their exchange.

'Tanya, do you remember me putting you through the MRI machine this morning?'

She slowly shook her head. 'No,' she said. 'I don't think I do.'

'Tanya's long-term memory is unaffected. She knows who she is, what she does, everything before the incident. She remembers most of what happened to her and some of the last twenty-four hours but not much, as this information resides in her short-term memory. That side of things is currently fuzzy and stilted at best,' Dr Javid explained.

'Well,' Anna floundered, not sure what to say. 'Shit.' She ran her hand through her long, dark hair, pushing it back off her face.

'The good thing is,' Dr Javid pushed forward, 'the fact that we didn't find a physical cause indicates that this is a temporary condition. If there was evidence of a stroke or physical trauma to the head then we could have been looking at long-term amnesia.' He shifted his weight. 'In patients who have been through serious mental trauma such as yourself, it is often a psychological blockage. It's like the brain shuts down certain parts of itself, in order to avoid coping with what it's been through until it feels it is better positioned to do so.'

'So, what do I do then? Change batteries? Flick the on switch? How do I turn my brain back on?' Tanya asked, her tone frustrated.

'All the other areas of your brain are working perfectly, and that's something to celebrate. I've had coma patients wake up in a shorter time than you who have lost speech ability or who have developed severe disabilities. You are very lucky,' he stressed. 'And as far as getting your short-term memory back, it will be a process. But with some psychotherapy to work through what it is that's holding you back, you will return to normal eventually. There are some fantastic psychotherapists at the rehab centre who will work with you on that side of things, alongside your physical therapy.'

'Therapists? That want to go inside *my* head?' Tanya turned to Anna in horror. 'Just kill me. Do it. Put the pillow over my face. I won't struggle.'

Anna laughed. 'Oh, come on, it won't be that bad. And you know what, maybe it's what you need,' she said gently. 'You were shot, Tan. That's a lot to process.'

Tanya pursed her lips. She was too tired to argue, and what would be the point anyway? She needed her memory back, even if she didn't like what she had to do to get it.

CHAPTER THREE

Placing the rucksack on the doorstep, Freddie knocked and then turned, walking briskly away from the small terraced house and back into the darkness of the early winter's evening. He jogged across the road a few metres down, where he joined his brother Paul in the parked Mercedes. They waited in silence until, a few seconds later, the door opened.

A thin, middle-aged woman peered out while drying her hands on a tea towel. Her brow furrowed in confusion, as she looked for whoever had knocked. She'd almost closed the door again when the bag caught her eye. She froze and stared at it a moment, before searching the darkness again. After some hesitation, she picked it up and took it inside, quickly closing the door behind her.

Paul started the engine and they pulled away down the road. The woman had been John Fraser's wife, a detective inspector Freddie had had on his payroll for years. Freddie didn't usually like bent coppers. They didn't stand for anything, weren't loyal to anyone. That wasn't something he could respect. But John had been different. Sure, he'd been playing both sides, but he had a strict code of his own, a set of morals by which he led his life whichever side of the line he was standing on at the time. And Freddie had trusted him.

It had been John who had pushed Freddie out of the way of the bullet his other brother had shot at him. If John hadn't pushed him, he'd have died that night. Michael had been nothing if not a perfect marksman. But the bullet had found a mark anyway. John had taken the hit, saving Freddie's life and giving his in return. It was something that Freddie would never forget.

The media storm that followed the series of events that night had been intense, no one quite able to understand how it had all unfolded. Freddie had stayed away from the situation to give it time to die down.

Freddie owed John his life but that wasn't a debt he could pay, so now he repaid him in the only way he could. Money. The bag he'd just left on the doorstep held enough to set John's wife and children up for life. It wouldn't replace the husband and father they had lost, but at least it would help ease other areas of their lives.

This was the way it was in their world. Bent coppers and straight criminals alike, if you worked for the Tylers, you took big risks. There was always a chance of ending up behind bars and sometimes, as happened to John, there was a chance you wouldn't come home from a job. Everyone knew what they were getting themselves into, but they also knew that should the worst outcome happen, their families would be looked after. That was their insurance policy.

Freddie sighed heavily. Paul glanced sideways at his brother as he drove.

'What's eating ya?' he asked.

'Nothing out of the ordinary,' Freddie replied.

'How's Anna? She getting any better?' Paul's tone was concerned.

'Still the same. She's working through it, just needs time. I'm hoping now Tanya's come round that might make a difference.'

That night had changed everyone's lives forever and not for the better. Fraser was dead, Tanya had ended up in her coma, Paul and Freddie had had to say goodbye to their brother and Anna had been the one to pull the trigger. Her first kill.

Freddie could still see her face in his mind, the horror at what she had done as the bullet smashed through Michael's brain. She'd had no choice, something he reminded her of over and over, but still she felt deep guilt. This, mixed up with her grief at losing their baby, had been too much for her to handle. Her expression had remained haunted ever since, her body becoming an empty vessel as she mentally sunk into a place where no one else could follow.

She'd held it together for the clubs, always professional. She'd let Freddie be there for her, but she had held back whenever he tried to get close to her. Anna had dressed, walked and talked the same way she always did, but she wasn't the same. His Anna, the Anna he loved more than anyone else in the world, wasn't in there right now.

Freddie wanted her back more than anything, and he kept telling himself that she just needed time. But deep down he wasn't sure if she was able to come back from this and it worried him deeply. He knew that it was his fault. If it wasn't for him, Michael would never have kidnapped her. She never would have lost the baby and she would never have had to take a life. Freddie knew deep down that it was he who'd unwittingly led this beautiful, intelligent, good-hearted woman down the path of mental destruction. And he hated himself for it.

'It's only been two months,' Paul said. 'Give her time. She ain't like you and me. But she'll get there.'

Freddie nodded. He knew what Paul meant. They'd had a difficult start in the world. Freddie had turned to this way of life out of necessity and had hardened himself from a very early age. They all had. None of them enjoyed the darker side, but they were able to shut themselves off from it emotionally, when they needed to. Anna was not equipped with the mental hardness to do the same.

'Did you get in touch with Rio? Get that last message sent out?' Freddie changed the subject.

'I did, but Dave said he thinks they're starting to cotton on. There's more questions coming through,' Paul replied.

'Well, that's to be expected. It was never a permanent solution.' Freddie bit a nail as he thought about his next move. 'Just keep it going as planned for now. When it reaches a natural end, we'll go from there. Tell Dave to make sure it ghosts though, when they do go searching for a trail.'

'Will do. It's had a good run. I'm surprised they haven't suspected before now,' Paul said.

'Smoke and mirrors. It's often the simplest plan that works the best,' Freddie replied.

'Where do you want dropping?' Paul asked. 'You got anything more to do tonight?'

'Nah, just drop me at Club Anya.'

CHAPTER FOUR

Anna toyed with the pen in front of her absent-mindedly, the shift plans she was working on forgotten. The dull thud of music came through the office door from the club beyond but she didn't hear it, lost in thought. The loud beep and vibration of her phone as a message pinged through made her jump. Back in the present, she picked up her mobile. It was Drew, one of the comedians from the other club. She'd been paying him to help her manage the place part-time since Tanya had been in hospital, finding the workload to be too much to handle on her own. She had no idea how Tanya had managed it when she'd been kidnapped.

Mark Paulton has cancelled for tonight. What do you want me to do?

Anna thought about it for a second before replying.

Cody Shaw is after more spots, ask him to cover.

She locked the phone and picked up the shift plans again. They didn't really need to be done yet, but she liked to keep ahead of herself where possible. Especially at the moment. Work took her mind off things; it was a welcome distraction.

As she began to plan, there was a knock on the door, and she looked up as it opened. Freddie walked in with a warm smile.

'Hey, how's it going?' he said, sitting down opposite her at the desk.

'Yeah, good. Just sorting out paperwork, nothing particularly interesting,' she replied. 'How's your night been?'

'Quiet, about to head home. Thought I might try to convince you to leave early and join me,' Freddie said, testing the water. He waited for her response, pretty sure he already knew the answer. Anna had been hiding in her work as much as she could since she had been cleared from hospital herself, following the miscarriage.

'I don't know,' she replied, her tone unsure. 'There's so much to be done.'

'Carl's out front; he won't mind locking up. You aren't busy tonight,' Freddie pushed.

'I know, but he's been doing so much lately…'

'Not as much as you have. You can't keep doing everything on your own, Anna. You're burning the candle at both ends – you're going to burn out.' Freddie looked at her with genuine concern.

He never usually tried to involve himself in Anna's work or influence her decisions; she was a fiercely independent person and he respected that. He'd always admired how hard-working Anna was, but she was taking things to the extreme at the moment and it was beginning to show. Dark circles ringed her eyes and her clothes hung loose where she had lost weight. She was careful to make sure her hair and make-up was immaculate each day, but he could see the signs of strain beyond that. There were some things she couldn't hide.

Anna bit back the sharp retort that almost shot out. She knew Freddie was right. She was finding any excuse she could to be at work, either here or at The Last Laugh. And it wasn't hard to find excuses, with Tanya off the scene. There was always something to be done. But Freddie was right, she was running herself into the ground. She could feel it throughout her body, which ached to lie down and sleep. But she was scared to sleep. She was terrified of letting herself lie down before she'd reached the point at which she was so exhausted she'd pass out within seconds. Because if she wasn't at that point, she either lay awake thinking about everything that had happened or she dreamed that she was back there.

She looked at the ruggedly handsome man opposite. His hazel-green eyes, which had mesmerised her from the moment they met, bored into her with such love and concern that she could have cried. This man, this hardened criminal who was feared and respected throughout London, would do anything for her. Her eyes roamed over him, his strong jaw, down to the muscular shoulders and broad chest underneath his perfectly tailored suit. Longing stirred inside her to be close to him. They hadn't been intimate since she'd lost the baby.

At first it had been out of necessity while she allowed her body to heal. Freddie hadn't pressed, his priority being her safety. But as she'd cocooned herself away behind her wall of fear and guilt, it had continued. She knew it was down to her, but she hadn't been able to find the drive to be intimate with Freddie since. Now though, as he sat there in front of her, she wanted to be with him again. She needed him. Perhaps it was the worry of Tanya's coma being lifted, or perhaps time was beginning to work its healing magic, but either way she didn't care.

'OK,' she answered. 'Let's go home.' She stood up and grabbed her jacket.

Freddie was surprised. He hadn't expected it to be that easy. 'OK then.' He opened the door. 'Let's go.'

Anna walked out and slipped her hand into his. Nothing was OK in the world, but the one solid constant was her relationship with Freddie. It was one thing she could control. She needed to work on getting them back to where they had been. Even if she wasn't the same person anymore.

CHAPTER FIVE

Seamus whistled a happy tune as he walked down the busy street towards the bookies. The skies were blue, the sun was shining and he'd just come from his morning training at the ring with Robbie. He couldn't be happier.

Seamus knew he had landed on his feet when the Tylers had taken him into the firm. He was able to do the thing he loved most every day and got paid well for running errands and helping Freddie out whenever he needed a man he could trust. He'd certainly seen some sights since he'd started and faced all sorts of danger, but Seamus wasn't someone who was easily rattled, so he took most of it in his stride. Sure, there was some dirty work involved, but he had never been someone who shied away from things like that.

He remembered something his dad had once said to him: 'Son, this life is going to throw shit at you whatever you do. You can either let it hit you in the eye, or you can catch it and use it to feed your garden of life.' Craig had come out with all sorts of odd analogies over the years, but this one had stuck with his son.

Jogging the last few metres, Seamus entered the betting shop and smiled at the cashier before walking through to the rooms at the back. He knocked on the office door and waited for the invitation to enter.

'Alright, mate?' Sammy greeted him as he closed the door.

Seamus zipped up his hoodie to the top and rubbed his hands together. No one could ever understand why Sammy insisted on having the air con turned to such an Arctic setting in his office.

'I'm good thanks, and ye'self?' Seamus's thick Irish accent was as cheery as his smile.

'Blinding mate, blinding,' Sammy's deep tone boomed around the room. 'How's training going?'

'Well, I think,' Seamus replied.

'Good, good. We've got a match coming up in three weeks. You need to start prepping for the weigh-in. Middleweight, I'd put my bets on you going up with Joe Cleaves, but if you can get to light middleweight my guess would be either Ricky Leathers or Roman Hunter.'

Seamus nodded seriously. 'Gotcha. I'll do me best to get to light middle. What's the craic?'

'I think we'll have you win this one. You're still a wildcard to a lot of the punters; everyone's betting on who they know at the moment. But we'll see how the bets go, once you're announced.'

'Grand,' Seamus replied.

There was a knock at the door and a young woman popped her head round. 'I've got the results data, Mr Barker.'

'Thanks, Carrie.' Sammy took the papers from her and she exited with a polite nod.

Sammy cast his eye over the first couple of pages and raised his eyebrows. 'Weird. Hardly any bets on the Tottenham game yesterday. They're usually a whole report on their own.' He put them down and turned back to Seamus.

Seamus frowned and sat forward. 'What game was that, you said?'

'Tottenham–Man City,' Sammy replied, after glancing back at the sheet.

'Spurs didn't play yesterday. There was no match, especially with Man City – I'm sure of it,' Seamus replied, shaking his head in certainty. He was an avid follower of football and a Tottenham fan to boot. There was no way he wouldn't have known they were playing.

'What do you mean?' Sammy sat up straighter. 'There had to be – it's on the system.'

Seamus shrugged and shook his head again. 'I don't know why it's there, but I'm one hundred per cent sure there was no match. I'd have watched it.'

Sammy opened the laptop on the desk in front of him and clicked onto Google. He searched for the game but sure enough there was no record of it anywhere. His frown deepened. 'What the hell?'

Picking up the reports, he looked more carefully at the bets. Overall, they had been out of pocket by about three grand. It wasn't this which struck him as odd; they were in the gambling game and sometimes you lost. But what was odd was the fact there had only been a handful of bets and all but one of them were winners. His lips formed a hard line and thunder flashed across his face.

'We've been fucking done,' he said finally.

'How?' Seamus asked.

'I don't know. But I'm sure as hell going to find out.'

*

Anna wheeled Tanya into her new room at the physical rehab unit and looked around. It was nice enough, as far as hospital rooms went. The curtains were a bright yellow, matching the blankets on the standard hospital bed, there was a flatscreen on the wall and a few framed prints of daffodils and other wildflowers. A door led into the en suite and Anna peeked in. She made a mental note to bring Tanya some decent toiletries.

'So, this is nice,' she said cheerily. 'I mean, it's not The Ritz, but it's clean and bright…' She trailed off, noticing the stony look on Tanya's face. 'I'll sneak you in some vodka tomorrow,' she said, resignedly.

Tanya grinned. 'Now that's the best idea you've had all day.'

The nurse who had shown them around the unit came bustling back in behind them with another nurse. 'Sorry about that, just had to grab Janet here to help me get you settled in. Now, are you able to support your weight at all yet, or shall we just lift you in?'

'I can support myself with help, just not strong enough to stand alone yet,' Tanya replied, looking away. She hated being an invalid. Relying on other people for anything at all was hard for her, let alone having to rely on them for absolutely everything.

Anna turned away and busied herself with unpacking Tanya's things while they got her up onto the bed. She knew her friend didn't want to be seen like this. After everything was put away, she returned to Tanya's bedside, where the nurses were tucking the blanket in by her sides. She was sat up and fully dressed, but Anna could see the journey had taken its toll. She looked wiped out.

'Now, lunch is in about an hour; we'll bring it through. I'll leave you to get settled in. Press the button if you need anything.' The nurse pointed at the button on the side of the bed and then bustled out.

Anna got up and closed the door so that they could talk in peace. Tanya looked miserable, and she felt a stab of intense guilt.

'I'm sorry,' she said, sitting on the chair next to the bed. She looked around. 'It's my fault, all of it. It's my fault you're having to go through this.'

Tanya frowned and reached for her hand. 'No, it's not, Anna. It's not anyone's fault except Michael's. He was the one who took us, and he was the one who shot me. Me being in here now, that's all on him.' She stared off into the distance. 'I still can't believe he did it. I knew him as a kid, for God's sake – we all did. I just can't believe he could do that in cold blood.'

Tanya swallowed and Anna noticed her hand shaking slightly. It was still fresh, all of it, to Tanya. It was still fresh to all of them.

'Then again, there's a lot I can't believe about everything that happened.' Pain flitted across Tanya's face and Anna squeezed her hand harder.

'Don't think about that now. Let's just focus on getting your strength up. I've been without you for long enough, Tan. The clubs have too.'

Tanya's attention was hooked at the mention of the clubs and she gave Anna a wan smile.

'We need you back. I don't have your flair, as Carl loves to remind me.'

'There's no way he'd say that to you,' Tanya scoffed.

'Well, no, not exactly, but I can tell it's what he's thinking. I'm not even allowed to taste his new cocktails – he's been saving them for you.'

'Now that's definitely something to get better for,' Tanya said enthusiastically. 'As soon as I'm well we are going to have a proper night on the town. Well, in the club. I ain't paying for somewhere else when we have the best mixologist in London.'

Anna laughed and nodded. 'We really do. We should probably let him have that title too.'

Tanya smiled but it faltered as her brow creased in pain. Her hand moved to her stomach and the little colour she still had drained from her face. 'Yeah, we should,' she breathed.

Anna tried not to make too much of a fuss. She knew that wasn't what Tanya wanted. Tanya had always been a proud, independent woman who couldn't bear to be seen as weak. Making a fuss would just embarrass her.

Anna cleared her throat. 'So, I have some things to do. I'll leave you to get settled.'

Tanya nodded. Anna leaned over and kissed her friend on the cheek. 'Get some rest, OK? I'll be back tomorrow.'

'With cherry vodka,' Tanya reminded her.

'With cherry vodka,' Anna confirmed.

Tanya's eyes shut tiredly and Anna slipped out, closing the door behind her. She leaned her head against it for a moment. Helpless frustration coursed through her as she wished for the hundredth time that she could take the pain and suffering away from her best friend. But she couldn't. Only time could do that.

Taking a deep breath, she straightened up and pushed back her hair. As she strode towards the exit she slid back into her mental armour and prepared to face the world again.

CHAPTER SIX

Freddie marched into the bookies with Paul hot on his heels. He didn't wait to knock, just walked straight into the office. Sammy's voice had sounded grim when he'd called, which wasn't something Freddie often heard. Sammy was one of the calmest people in the business; nothing fazed him. For him to sound so angry, it must be serious.

'What's 'appening?' he asked, cutting straight to the point. It was just the three of them now, Seamus having left for the daily jobs he was paid by the Tylers to do. Sammy's expression was dark.

'Someone's had us over. There was a game on the system that never took place. Only a few bets placed, obviously by the people in the know. Taken us for three grand,' Sammy said.

'What?' Freddie asked, his tone incredulous. 'How've they done that? And who the *fuck* would be stupid enough to do that in one of *our* bookies?'

'I have no idea, but it gets worse.' Sammy slid a pile of report sheets across the desk and Freddie sat down to have a look. 'I only came across this by chance. Seamus was here and pointed out that Tottenham weren't playing yesterday. After I called you, I had a look through past reports and found a handful of others that had a similarly small list of bets. I pulled them up and researched the games – none of them happened either. Each one has taken us for between a grand and four, but never higher than four. From these alone, we're down by about seventeen grand in the last two months.'

Freddie's eyes widened in surprise. That was no small scam. Someone was somehow placing fake games into their own system and raking in the money from the results. He glanced at Paul, who was scratching his head and looking flummoxed.

'Right.' Freddie wiped his hand down his face. 'From now on you're going to have to check the games manually each morning and again at lunchtime to see if any more fake ones pop up. Give a hard copy list of all the genuine games to the cashiers, tell them not to pay out on any that aren't on it. If you see one come up, call me straight away. We need to get Bill in. Maybe he can trace them back through the system.'

'I'll text him now, get him to come over ASAP,' Paul said.

'Fuckers,' Freddie said, shaking his head. 'Can you keep going back and find out if there are any more? Let me know when you've found them all.'

'Will do,' Sammy replied. He was fuming. He couldn't believe this had been happening under his nose all this time. Seventeen grand was a lot of money, certainly enough that he'd make sure whoever had taken it would pay dearly. But it wasn't so large an amount that they would have seen a dip in the overall books. There hadn't been any red flags, no reason to go looking for issues. They took a vast amount of money each week, both over the counter and online. Siphoned off over two months like that, it wasn't noticeable. 'I'm sorry, Fred. I keep a tight ship here, but I never thought for a second I'd have to watch for something like this.'

'It's OK, Sammy, no one would. You couldn't have predicted that.' Freddie was quick to reassure his friend. Sammy had been running the bookies for years with great efficiency.

'It's all football games. Which is probably another reason I didn't see it,' Sammy replied. He wasn't a football fan; the game bored him. He much preferred following the boxing matches, like Freddie. He shook his head and swore under his breath. He was royally pissed off.

'Don't worry about it.' Freddie's expression turned hard. 'We'll work out how they did this when Bill gets here. Then we'll nail those bastards and make them wish they'd never set eyes on this place.'

*

Joe Luciano paced back and forth across the plush red carpet in his office. He cracked his knuckles and let out a long, heavy breath. 'It's not him.'

'Are you sure, boss?' one of the men lounging in the comfortable chairs around the edge of the room asked in his thick New York drawl.

'I'm certain. I asked if he'd been in touch with Uncle Albert since he'd been in town. The response said no but that he was planning to be.' Joe stopped pacing and faced the man who had spoken. 'We don't have an Uncle Albert in Mexico.'

There was a murmur of understanding. 'Then who the hell is this guy sending the messages?' the man asked, with a frown.

'I don't know, Tino. That's what we need to find out. I've sent men out looking, but so far they've come back with nothing. It's like we're dealing with a ghost. The number we were given for him is dead – it was a burner. We got nothing down there.'

For the last two months, no one had seen Frank Gambino. At first when they didn't hear from him, they had been worried, but then a message came through from him in Mexico. He claimed he was setting up a new venture down there and that he and his men would be there until it was up and running. This hadn't been a problem, Frank had left other perfectly capable men in charge of his day-to-day dealings in New York when he'd left for England, but as time stretched on, Joe had become suspicious. Every message he sent with a question came back with a vague answer, and it wasn't like Frank to be so uninterested in his businesses back home, even if he was tied up with something new. Eventually he had posed the trap question and his suspicions had been confirmed. He had stopped texting and sent men down to try to track the number. But his silence must have tipped off whoever was sending the messages, as since then the phone had been unreachable.

'So, where's Frank now?' Tino asked. 'This is not good.'

'No, it's not,' Joe replied, grinding his teeth. He was angry and worried. Like himself, Frank was one of the heads of the Five Families. He was a very important person and absolutely off the table to mess with. Someone was playing a very dangerous game indeed. 'The last we know that we definitely heard from him was in London. I've asked Lynette to find out if he ever left. If he didn't, which I'm beginning to suspect, then that's where we start looking.'

As if on cue there was a knock on the door and a small blonde head poked around as it opened.

'Mr Luciano?' she asked.

'Come in, Lynette. What did you find?'

'Nothing, Mr Luciano. As far as our contact can see, his passport hasn't been used on any flights or other means of travel to get out of England,' she replied.

'Thank you.'

Joe sighed and rubbed his forehead as Lynette closed the door again. 'Right, boys…' He looked around at the men in the room with a hard stare. 'I think it's time we leave our Big Apple and visit the Big Smoke.'

CHAPTER SEVEN

Tanya squeezed her eyes shut for a second against the sharp, stabbing pains in her stomach. The doctors had told her that the pain was a good thing – it meant the muscles that had been torn were starting to heal. This knowledge didn't make it any easier though, and she wished she was still allowed the stronger painkillers.

She stared up at the ceiling and listened to the soft beeps and murmurs of hospital life outside her room. She couldn't wait until she was allowed home. However nice they tried to make it, it was dismal here. Closing her eyes, she tried to drift off into sleep.

The door opened and clicked shut again. Someone was in the room. Most likely a nurse on their rounds. Tanya didn't feel like making small talk, so she kept her eyes closed and waited for them to leave. After a minute or so she realised that whoever was in the room hadn't moved from their spot by the door. She frowned and decided to take a look, curiosity getting the better of her.

Blinking, she focused her gaze on the figure by the door and her eyes widened in shock.

'Hello, Tanya,' came the quiet greeting.

Her mouth gaped open and she pulled herself half-upright in the bed, ignoring the pain. The pair stared at each other for what seemed to Tanya like an eternity, as every emotion possible seemed to course through her. Eventually she found her voice.

'What the hell are you doing here?' she asked heavily.

*

Sophie twisted and twirled in the air, from one suspended ring to the next. The lights flashed and the deep rhythmic beat of the music resounded through the club. Every table was full, and all eyes were on the talented dancer and her lithe, scantily clad body. This was who they were there to see, the biggest act of the evening.

Anna paused as she came out of the office and watched her for a moment. With an approving nod, she signalled to one of the bar staff to get her another drink. She perched on a stool at the quiet end of the bar and waited. Carl finished serving and wandered over.

'It's a busy one tonight,' he remarked.

'It always is when Sophie performs,' Anna replied.

'True.' Carl nodded. 'How are you anyway? Didn't think you'd be in.' He eyed her subtly. She looked tired and worn, as she often did lately. He had put it down to the stress of Tanya being in the coma and had hoped that now she was awake, Anna might give herself a bit of a break. But she was still as tense as ever, still throwing herself into the clubs at every opportunity. Half of him wanted to ask what was haunting her so much, but he knew better than to actually voice the question. The details he'd been given of the night Tanya got shot were vague at best. He knew that he hadn't been told the full story and that there would be good reason for that, and so he kept his counsel.

'I'm fine.' The answer was robotic, rehearsed. 'Just had some things to tie up, didn't want to leave it overnight,' Anna said, averting her gaze.

Carl didn't respond, just nodded as he busied himself with polishing the empty glass in his hand.

Anna's drink arrived and she took it with a smile of thanks to the barman. 'OK, well I'll be in the back if you need me.'

Walking away from the main club area and into her office, Anna closed the door and the loud music dulled to a muffled beat in the background. She sighed and rolled her shoulders, trying to release the tension that seemed to be permanently present.

She sat down at the table and took a sip of her drink. Her gaze wandered to a picture of her and Freddie in a small frame. It was her favourite photo of the two of them. She smiled fondly at the memory. It had been at a party. They'd been laughing and having fun and Thea, Freddie's sister, had snapped the candid picture.

Anna's smile faded as she thought about how carefree she'd felt back then. Nowadays she just felt disconnected and anxious. Guilt and horror were her constant companions whenever she let her mind wander, and although there were always people around her, she had never felt so alone. She loved Freddie with all her heart, but he couldn't understand how she felt. He had a resilience when it came to this sort of thing that she didn't and never would.

Her hands began to shake and she clasped them together, trying to make them stop. This was what she spent all her time trying to avoid. The PTSD. She knew it was that; she didn't need a psychologist to tell her. She woke up in cold sweats screaming, flashbacks and panic attacks happened at the most inconvenient of times and she didn't feel anything like herself anymore. This was the only thing that seemed to help, throwing herself into work.

Anna opened her laptop and stared at the screen, trying to work out what she needed to do. It was no use though – her brain was all jumbled up.

She felt the weight of the gun in her hand, the cold, unyielding metal beneath her fingers. She saw the look in Michael's eyes as he realised she was going to do it, the shock and panic. She saw the youth in his face, how many years of life there were still ahead of him.

BANG.

Anna jumped up from the desk, holding her head between her hands. 'No, no, no. Come on.' She gritted her teeth and forced herself to breathe deeply and slowly. The dark hallway of the farmhouse faded away and she was back in her office. She opened her eyes and focused on the sounds of the busy club around her.

She couldn't do this; work wasn't going to save her sanity tonight. Grabbing her jacket, Anna closed the laptop. She needed to try walking it off.

*

Bill leaned forward in his chair facing Freddie and rested his forearms on his thighs. 'They've hacked in through an invisible back door in the system. Whether they've stumbled across it by chance or planted it there themselves I can't tell, but that's how they've done it. Each ghost game was set up in the middle of the night after closing; obviously they must assume this is when they're least likely to be disturbed. Different days each time.'

'Fuckers,' Freddie spat, shaking his head. 'Can you track them?' He lit a cigarette and offered one to Bill, who took one and nodded his thanks.

'Not yet,' Bill replied. He paused to light up and took a deep drag, blew out a plume of smoke and rested back in his seat. 'The back door is hidden in code; I can't see it at the moment. I need to be in the system at the same time they are to be able to find it. Once I've got a lock on it, then I can start trying to trace it back to the source.'

'I see.' Freddie sighed in exasperation.

'Look, they're pulling one every week or two, so they're bound to come on soon. They only come on between 1 a.m. and 4 a.m., so we have a window. I'll just have to stake them out the old-fashioned way.' Bill didn't relish the idea but there was no other way. He quietly resigned himself to the fact he wouldn't be getting much sleep for a while.

'I'll make sure you're well compensated for it,' Freddie said.

Bill chuckled. 'I know you will, mate.'

Freddie poured two large whiskies and passed one of the glasses to Bill. They were in Freddie's office in Club CoCo, where he conducted most of his business. Freddie swirled the deep amber liquid in the cut crystal glass and then knocked it back, savouring the burn as it hit the back of his throat.

There was a knock at the door.

'Come in,' Freddie commanded.

The door opened and a tall man in his thirties with a thick mop of blonde hair walked in with a smile. 'Alright, boss? Hope I'm not disturbing you.'

'Not at all, Gavin – what's up?' Freddie replied.

'Just got next month's rotas here for you to check and sign off on. Other than that, all is fine and dandy,' he said cheerfully.

'Don't worry about that; I trust your judgement. Go ahead with it.' Freddie waved him away.

'Great, I'll send them out. Catch you later.' Gavin gave an enthusiastic salute and disappeared back through to the club.

Bill raised his eyebrows at Freddie. 'Fine and dandy? He swallowed a *Mary Poppins* DVD or something?'

Freddie laughed. 'Yeah, he's a bit odd, but he's good at his job. I hired him to manage the club for me full-time. Finally bit the bullet.'

Club CoCo had become more and more popular in recent months and eventually Freddie had realised that he had no choice but to invest in a few more permanent staff members. The previous manager had moved abroad with his wife and, for a while, Freddie had left the day-to-day running to the rest of the long-term bar staff, but this wasn't enough anymore. His only other option was to run the place himself, and that was an idea he wasn't keen on. Aside from the fact he'd only invested in this club as somewhere through which to launder money, he thoroughly enjoyed running his various other businesses and didn't want to be tied down in just one place.

Gavin had been hired as the general manager and a young woman called Holly had come on board as the new marketing and PR manager. She had impressed Freddie already, hosting various different events and making sure the club got decent coverage online. Their VIP tables were fully booked every night now and the influx in business made Freddie realise he should have recruited for these positions a long time ago.

Bill stubbed out his cigarette in the ashtray on the table between them. 'By the way,' he said, his tone serious. 'I heard through the grapevine that Joe Luciano is coming over in the next few days. He knows the messages were faked. He's looking for answers.'

'Yeah, I heard,' Freddie replied soberly. 'I'm working on something, but I need some time.' He bit his lip. 'Don't worry about it. But let me know if you hear any more.'

'I will, Fred. He's got nothing at the moment, but he does know you met with Frank. Frank had told him of the arrangements before he came over, but from what I can tell that's all he knows.'

'Thanks, Bill. That's useful.'

The pair fell into silence, each caught up in their own thoughts. Freddie stubbed out his cigarette with precision and watched the last curls of smoke rise up into the air. There was a storm coming, and it was going to be a big one. He just hoped he had time to build a steadfast shelter for himself and his men before it hit.

CHAPTER EIGHT

Anna felt guilty as she walked towards Tanya's room in the rehab centre. She hadn't made it in the day before, as she was too exhausted from another broken night's sleep. It was a fair excuse, she reasoned, but she still felt bad. She was Tanya's only regular visitor.

As she reached the door, the apology rose to her lips. 'I'm so sorry, Tan, I was so knackered yesterday…' she trailed off as she realised Tanya wasn't alone. 'Oh, hello,' she said with a polite smile.

An older woman was seated in a chair right next to Tanya's and they both looked up as Anna walked in. Anna frowned slightly. The woman seemed familiar but she couldn't think why. She shrugged mentally. Tanya must have made friends with another patient.

'Anna, you're here.' Tanya's voice bubbled with nervous excitement. Her eyes darted from Anna, to the older woman and back to Anna again. 'I've got someone to introduce to you. This' – she gestured towards the woman in the chair – 'is my mum. Rosie.'

'What?' Anna said faintly. She blinked, confused. That was the last thing she had been expecting. But it did explain why she looked familiar; there were more than a few similarities between the two now that she looked closely.

'My mum,' Tanya repeated. 'She, well… obviously we haven't spoken in years, but recently she's been trying to track me down, and she found out I was in here. So she came yesterday and asked to speak to me, and then, well… we've been doing a lot of catching up.'

'Wow,' Anna managed. 'That's… unexpected.' She tried to hide the concern from her expression as she plastered on a fake smile for Rosie.

'Yeah, it was a bit,' Tanya replied with a light laugh. 'But it's a good thing.' She nodded as she spoke. 'It's been too long.'

'It has,' replied Rosie in the deep, gravelly voice of a heavy smoker. 'So nice to meet you, Anna. I've heard a lot about you.'

Likewise, Anna thought caustically, but she kept the retort to herself and shook Rosie's outstretched hand instead. With both seats in the room taken up, Anna perched on the bed, feeling awkward. From various heart to hearts over the years, Anna knew that Rosie had treated Tanya appallingly as a child. She'd destroyed her childhood with systemic abuse, both mental and physical. Tanya had run away the moment she had been old enough to look after herself. She hadn't seen Rosie since.

How could Tanya let her back into her life so easily now?

Rosie was staring at her and Anna looked away, feeling uncomfortable under the scrutiny of the other woman's piercing green eyes.

'So, I guess there's been a lot to catch up on after all these years,' Anna said.

'Oh indeed,' Rosie said. 'It's been a blessing to my ears to hear how well my beautiful daughter has done. The clubs, the properties – what achievements! I'm so proud.'

Tanya blushed bright red at the compliments and her eyes sparkled, full of emotion. 'Thanks, Mum,' she said. 'That really means a lot.'

Yes, and I bet she realises that too, Anna thought darkly. Rosie's comments filled Anna with disgust. Who was this woman to say she was proud of Tanya? She hadn't been any sort of mother. Tanya had built her life up in spite of Rosie, not because of her. She hadn't earned the right to be proud.

Tanya hadn't often spoken of her mother over the years that they had been friends, but when she had, the stories had shocked

Anna. Tales of being pinched and slapped, thrown out in the cold and left hungry as she was made to watch her mother eat. Rosie had torn her down in any way she could, telling her she was worthless, ugly, unlovable. She'd kept her from having friends or enjoying her childhood. Even when Tanya had been old enough to work, Rosie had greedily stolen all her money and given her nothing back. It was no surprise to Anna to hear that Tanya had run away to start afresh as soon as she was old enough. Yet here Rosie was, acting like she was mother of the year and doting on Tanya as though she cared. Anna didn't trust it one bit.

'She's done incredibly well,' Anna conceded. 'And all on her own too.' She stared levelly at Rosie as she spoke and saw a glint of recognition in the other woman's eye.

'Yes, well. I wish I had been able to find her sooner, but it wasn't to be. I tried over the years but got nowhere. You cut all ties; I had nothing to go on,' she said to Tanya, a touch of accusation in her tone.

'I know I did. I'm sorry.' Tanya squeezed her mother's hand and Anna had to stop her mouth from gaping open.

Tanya's sorry? What for?

'But I'm here now. And I'm not going anywhere.' Rosie smiled at Tanya, her eyes crinkling at the sides, showing her age. 'Other than the coffee machine, of course. Can I get you girls one?'

'Oh, yes please, Mum. Anna?' Tanya asked.

'Sure, just a flat white. Thanks.' She managed a tight smile at Rosie as she walked out the room.

The door shut behind her and Anna waited a few seconds to make sure she was definitely out of earshot before she took the seat next to Tanya.

'Tanya, what's going on? Why is she here?' Anna frowned in concern and confusion.

Tanya sighed. 'I was as surprised as you, trust me. I never thought I'd see her face again in this lifetime. But yesterday she walked in, burst into tears and told me she'd been looking for me for years and couldn't believe she'd finally found me.' Tanya held out her hands and shrugged. 'You could have knocked me down with a feather, I was that shocked. I didn't know what to think at first. I've always felt so resentful towards her. She started talking and I just listened. She told me how terrible she felt about how bad our relationship had been when I was young. She explained how it was a lot to do with her alcoholism and that she never forgave herself for pushing me away.'

Tanya twisted the material from the blanket on her lap in her hands. 'It was hard, I won't lie, hearing that. But all this time I've assumed she hated me and didn't want me, and now I can see it's not as simple as that. She was ill.'

'But how has that changed anything? She still treated you that way for your entire childhood, and surely if she was an alcoholic then, she still is now,' Anna said gently.

'No.' Tanya shook her head. 'She's changed. After I left, she realised how bad she'd got. She went to AA, got sober and never looked back.'

Anna raised a sceptical eyebrow. 'So does she still go to group now?'

'Sort of. When she joined AA, she made friends with some people who run church groups for people like her who are lonely and struggle with addiction. She started going to one of those and now all these years on, she actually runs them. She runs three groups a week.'

'Well, that sounds…' Anna sighed and rubbed her head. 'How do you know this is all true? If there's one thing we know about alcoholics it's that they'll happily lie to get what they need.'

'She's my mum, Anna,' Tanya replied sharply. 'Look, I know she hasn't been mother of the century, but she's here. She found me. She didn't need to do that if she didn't want to, if she didn't care. She has no need to lie and no reason to be here other than the fact she wants to reconnect with me. This must have been really hard for her. I could easily have told her to jog on.'

'I guess.' Tanya had a point; Anna couldn't deny that. But it still didn't sit right for some reason. *Why now?*

Tanya frowned and looked down to her hands. 'I've never had a mum, Anna. Not really. Not even when I was with her. But that's what she's trying to be now. So I'd really appreciate if you can give her a chance.'

Anna sat back. 'Of course,' she eventually replied. 'Of course,' she said more strongly. She forced a smile. 'She's *your* family and it's *your* call to make. Just know that I'm here if you want to talk about it.'

'Thank you.' Tanya gave her a warm smile.

The door opened and Rosie entered, balancing the three cups of coffee.

'Here we go, girls,' she said, handing one to each of them.

Anna took her coffee and moved back to her perch on the side of the bed, so that Rosie could sit down. She smiled her thanks and sipped at the hot drink as Tanya and her mother resumed their conversation. She studied the woman, still unsure what to make of her. Her hair was dulled by age but still held the warm auburn tones that Tanya had inherited. Her figure was slim, her clothes a little young for her age but not remarkably so. But it was her eyes that interested Anna the most. They both had the same bright green eyes, except on Tanya they seemed to sparkle full of life, and on Rosie they appeared cold and unyielding.

Sipping again at the coffee, Anna watched her over the brim of the cup. There was something not right about this sudden appearance. Something niggled in the bottom of her stomach. She was going to find out why Rosie was really back in her daughter's life.

CHAPTER NINE

Freddie stepped over the rubble at the base of the large hole in the wall. It had been knocked through from the massage parlour to the stairs leading to the flats above. He glanced up towards the noise of tools at work and then beckoned the young woman behind to follow him up the staircase.

'Mr Tyler,' one of the workmen greeted him, and they all tipped their hard hats in respect.

Freddie nodded back. 'Carry on, boys, I'm just 'aving a look around.' He led Carla through to a quieter room where they were alone and began to outline his plans for the place.

'So, you and Linda can work out yourselves who's best suited where and how the responsibilities fall. You'll be the assistant manager. You'll be on a salary rather than commission from the punters.'

Carla nodded her understanding, taking it all in. 'So, I won't be working with punters directly anymore?' she asked.

'That's up to you. If you want to carry on, you can, but out of hours. This job would come first. This place don't run itself, especially now we're expanding. You'll need to help Linda run things, look after the girls, keep everything and everyone in order. And that's harder than it sounds; you've worked here, you've seen how it can get.'

'Yeah, I know what you mean,' Carla agreed. She looked around and took a deep breath as she considered it. It was a golden opportunity for her – she knew that.

Not many toms got the chance to move into a more professional role. More often they only had a few years to ply their trade in upmarket places like this, before they were no longer young and attractive enough and were sent on their way. From then on it was street corners or cheaper, dirtier knocking shops where they were not properly protected by their pimps and were worn out for pennies until they were too old for even that.

This was a real opportunity to set her future on a better course, and Carla knew she'd be stupid to look this gift horse in the mouth. But one thing still held her back, something she couldn't ignore.

'What if he comes back for me? I know he left the country; I heard the rumours. But what if he comes back and finds me here? He don't know where I live now or where I work since you moved me. That's kept me safe till now.' Carla hugged herself in a subconsciously defensive gesture. It wasn't lost on Freddie.

'Listen, Carla—' He sighed and looked over her shoulder to make sure no one was loitering and listening nearby. 'You're a good girl. I know you know the score and that you can keep your mouth shut. I value that. Especially after all that happened. That's why I'm offering you this position above anyone else. And that's why I also trust you to keep what I'm about to say between us.'

Carla nodded.

Freddie lowered his voice. 'He ain't coming back, Carla. He can't. He's six feet under. He won't be hurting anyone anymore.'

Carla gasped. Freddie looked away and locked his jaw as the familiar wave of grief washed over him. 'That won't be a rumour you'll have heard, nor do I want it to ever join the rumour mill. Understand?'

Carla nodded again. 'Yeah, of course. No one will ever hear that from me.'

'Good. Because I need people to think he's still in South America. OK? But now you know' – he turned to look at her – 'that should put your demons to rest.'

'Thank you, Freddie,' Carla said quietly. She felt relief flood through her and a weight lift from her shoulders that she hadn't even realised was still there. Maybe now she could stop sleeping with one eye open and a knife under her pillow. Perhaps now she could live her life without being in constant fear that her nightmare wasn't over. Because it was. Michael would never come back to finish what he'd started. She could begin a new chapter as a free woman, and this job was the perfect start.

Looking around with fresh eyes, Carla could see what Freddie was planning to do. And it would work. She and Linda could make this place shine. She smiled, the action lighting up her pretty face. 'OK. Let's do it. When do you want me to start?'

'Tomorrow,' Freddie replied. He was pleased she'd accepted and was glad he'd made the decision to tell her. Carla had more than proved her loyalty to him and her ability to keep a secret. 'Just turn up here tomorrow lunchtime to meet Linda and she'll fill you in on all the details.'

'OK.' Carla followed Freddie back down the stairs and out of the noisy building.

'Catch you later then,' Freddie said, closing the door behind them.

'Catch you later, oh and Freddie?' Carla caught his attention before he walked away. 'Thanks,' she said, her tone sincere. 'I really appreciate all you've done for me, you know. I'll work hard here.'

'I know you will,' Freddie replied. He walked back to his car happy with the new arrangement.

He slipped into the black Mercedes. If only everything else was running so smoothly, he'd be a happy man. But it wasn't. Anna was still lost in her own personal darkness and he had no idea how to pull her back. He had a ghost to catch, the scammer in the betting system and now the threat of the Mafia arriving was about to become a very real problem indeed.

He pulled out onto the busy London street and pushed down on the accelerator. There was a lot to do before they were out of the woods.

CHAPTER TEN

Freddie and Anna stepped out of the car and he placed a hand on the small of her back as they walked up the garden path to Mollie's house, locking the car over his shoulder.

'What did we get her again?' Freddie asked. He usually bought his mother's birthday presents himself, but this year he'd been so distracted he'd run out of time. Luckily Anna had been organised enough to notice and sort something out.

'A set of Waterford crystal glasses and a spa weekend for her and Angie,' Anna said quietly as they reached the front door. She shifted the weight of the package onto one arm and smoothed down the front of her red dress before they entered.

'Great, thanks for that,' Freddie replied appreciatively.

'Any time,' Anna answered, returning a warm look. Things might not all be rosy right now, but the bond between them still remained strong. They were a team through thick and thin.

The room was packed with friends and family and the party looked to be in full swing. Upbeat background music sounded from the corner of the living room and balloons were taped up everywhere. *Thea's doing*, Freddie thought.

Bill and his wife Amy were chatting to Seamus near the door to the kitchen. Dean, Reggie and some of Freddie's other men nodded their respect across the room. Angie and a couple of Mollie's other girlfriends cackled away at some joke in the comfortable chairs around the coffee table. Paul was in deep conversation with

Arthur, Anna's father, and her mother Leslie hurried over with a beaming smile on her face as she clocked the pair walking in.

'There you are!' she exclaimed. 'I was wondering when you were going to get here.' She hugged Anna and Freddie and absent-mindedly tidied a stray lock of her daughter's hair. 'Let me get you a drink. Mollie won't let me help with anything even though she's the birthday girl, so that will give me something to do. I'll be back in a moment.' Leslie drifted off towards the kitchen, leaving a waft of her perfume in her wake.

Thea and Paul's boyfriend James walked into the room with plates of savoury pastries that Mollie had no doubt spent days cooking and began to hand them around. As they reached Freddie and Anna, Thea pulled a face of relief.

'Thank God you're here. Maybe you can get her out of the bloody kitchen and in here to enjoy her party. She's doing my nut in,' she said.

Freddie was about to reply when Bill tried to catch his attention. 'Er' – he tilted his head to signal that he'd be over shortly – 'I just need to—'

'Don't worry,' Anna cut in. 'I'll go speak to Mollie. She'll come out when she knows you're here.'

'Thanks.' Freddie walked off, and Anna followed Thea and James back into the kitchen.

Mollie was all in a flap, wringing her hands in the air as she stared down at the heavily laden table. 'My pies. I forgot to put in my bloody pies,' she cried.

'What pies?' Thea asked, her tone exasperated. 'There's enough here to feed two armies; you don't need any more pies, for God's sake, woman.'

'My lemon pies, Thea,' Mollie replied with a withering look. 'These are all savoury. The lemon meringue pies were the only sweet things I made. What are people going to think?'

'They're going to think you're a terrible host, talk about you behind your back for the next ten years and never come to a party here again,' Thea replied, her flat tone dripping with sarcasm.

'Well, if it helps' – James quickly stepped in – 'that tin I gave you earlier holds a rather large lemon drizzle cake. Made to your recipe.' He smiled hopefully and slowly guided her away from Thea.

'Thank you, James,' Mollie said, shooting one last disapproving look towards Thea. 'That would be perfect to add to the table. Hello, love.' Mollie suddenly noticed Anna and grinned warmly. 'Is Freddie with you?'

'He's just in the other room talking to Bill,' Anna replied, kissing Mollie on the cheek. 'Here, this is for you.' She handed her the gift she was still carrying.

'Oh, thank you, you didn't have to get me anything.' Mollie blushed and put it down on the side table next to a couple of other unopened gifts. 'I'll open them later if you don't mind. I need to make sure everything is ready before they all come through.'

James reappeared from the pantry with the cake tin and opened it to show Mollie.

'Oh, that smells lovely, James, it really does. You've developed a right knack for those, since I started teaching you.'

Paul walked in to see what was going on and joined the little group in the kitchen. Mollie turned to him. 'Have you tasted your James's baking lately?'

'Er, yes, Mum, I have as it happens.' His crooked grin lit up his rugged face.

'He's a keeper, son. Cakes like that, you want to make an honest man out of him soon,' Mollie said, with a naughty glint in her eye.

'Oh, Mum, leave off,' Paul replied, laughing nervously.

'Well, you do. Freddie does an' all,' she said, gesturing towards Anna. 'I'm not getting any younger you know. I want grandchildren.'

A sudden silence fell across the room. Paul looked down to the floor awkwardly. James glanced at Anna in concern then quickly looked away, not wanting to draw unwanted attention to her. Thea's wide eyes darted between Anna and her mother, who was now frowning in confusion. She quickly stepped forward.

'Let's get that cake out on the table before people start trying to eat the furniture instead, yeah? You can't invite them all over and then leave them to starve, you know,' Thea added, knowing her comment would hit the mark.

'As if I ever have or would, you cheeky mare.' Mollie tutted and turned away to find a serving dish for the cake. 'Now, where did I put that big plate?'

Anna's expression didn't change; not one flicker of emotion passed across her still face. She stared ahead through the window to the garden, her eyes empty and cold. Thea watched her and shivered. Two minutes ago, it was almost like she was normal again – she'd been smiling and talking. Now it was like there was no one there, her face nothing but an empty mask.

Mollie didn't know about what had happened. They had decided as a family to keep the whole story from her. She missed her youngest son dearly but was comforted by the thought that he'd started a new life in South America. She didn't need the heartache of knowing he was dead, or that he'd caused the death of her unborn grandchild and had tried to kill Freddie. That would kill her.

Anna ignored everyone around her. She couldn't bear to look at the sympathy she knew would be in their faces. They didn't know what to say to her. There were no words that made any of it any better. The cold stone that habitually lay in her stomach these days returned and she swallowed. What had happened had happened. The world kept turning and she needed to find a way to move on. Or at least be more convincing in pretending that she had.

Leslie walked into the kitchen and the tension in the room was broken. 'Ah, there you are. Sorry, I got held up talking to Amy.

Such a lovely girl. Well, woman,' she corrected herself. 'Here you go.' She handed Anna a glass of champagne.

Anna took a deep breath and turned to her mother with a fixed smile. 'Lovely. Just what I needed. Come on, I haven't spoken to Dad yet.'

Anna ushered her mother out of the kitchen and back into the busy lounge. She pushed the sadness down deep inside of her. Deeper and deeper until once again she felt nothing at all.

*

Freddie turned his shoulder to the rest of the room so that he and Bill were half-facing the wall.

'So, has there been any activity at all?' he asked quietly.

'Not a dicky bird so far. But it won't be long. There's no chance they're done. They've had a taste of it now. It's easy money for them, same formula over and over. I'd say it will be a few more days and we'll see them on there. I'll keep watching. We'll get the little fuckers eventually,' Bill said.

'Is there any way they can tell that you're there?' Freddie asked.

'Nah, I'm not active in the system; I'm just watching it. Nothing for them to see,' Bill replied, shaking his head.

'Good, good.' Freddie nodded. 'Keep me up to date.'

Freddie straightened his jacket and moved on to talk to some of the other guests. His easy smile belied the frustration he felt underneath. He couldn't wait to get his hands on the fuckers that were rinsing the bookies.

As he walked through the room he saw Anna come out of the kitchen. He paused. She was smiling but he could see the tension in her stance that had not been there when they walked in. Her rosy cheeks had drained to a cold white and her expression was vacant again. His heart dropped. He had thought she was doing OK today. What the hell had happened?

CHAPTER ELEVEN

The small private plane landed smoothly on the tarmac at London City airport. Joe watched the ice clinking rapidly against the glass full of whisky in his hand and waited for the rumbling of wheels on the runway to desist. As they slowed to a full stop, he lifted the glass and swiftly swallowed the contents. He glared out the small window at the grey skies and dull surroundings. He hated England and resented having to be here now. When he found out who was responsible for his need to visit, they were going to pay big time.

Standing up, he smoothed the front of his exquisitely tailored suit jacket and held his arms out for one of his men to slide his long winter coat on. As he passed the flight attendant, he flicked a coin into the air and watched as she caught it.

'That one's for you, sweetheart,' he said. He watched as her eyes widened in surprise before he walked out of the small hatch and down the stairs. It was a gold sovereign. He liked gold. It was easier to store than actual money. It was also a brilliant way to launder dirty money.

Joe stopped at the bottom and clicked his fingers. His men, Tino, Al and Johnny, moved aside behind him to make way for a slight, serious-looking man with a balding head and a short, trim moustache. He carried a royal blue bag in his arms, complete with a seal linked to an emblem that showed the world that it was a diplomatic pouch.

'Go ahead. Meet me at the hotel in an hour. Any problems, you know what to do,' Joe instructed.

The other man nodded. 'No problem.' He marched off, holding his head high, as if he meant business.

'You sure you didn't just want to get a gun here, boss?' Tino asked, flicking away the cocktail stick he'd just been using to dig food out of his teeth. 'I know a guy who knows a guy.'

'No. I want *my* gun,' Joe growled. 'If I'm putting a bullet in someone's brain, I want that bullet to fly with feeling. A man needs to have a connection to a weapon, Tino. Otherwise we're all just savages in this messed-up world.'

He walked off. Tino exchanged a glance with Al and shrugged.

They moved through security swiftly and without pause. There was nothing in their luggage that would give cause for concern. Joe's gun was the only illegal item that had been brought into the country, and that was already on its way to the hotel. That was the beauty of having diplomats on the payroll. Their bags were immune from any form of inspection upon arrival.

Joe stepped outside, took a deep breath and looked around.

'I'm just letting the driver know to come around,' Johnny said, texting on his phone. Joe nodded in response. 'Where do you want to go?'

'The Dorchester.' He narrowed his eyes and a dark expression crossed his face. 'We'll get settled in, ask some questions. Maybe they'll be able to tell us when Frank checked out.' *Or maybe they can tell us something more,* he thought.

Frank had disappeared off the face of the earth and nobody seemed to know a thing. But Frank was one of the five heads of the Mafia, one of the most powerful men in the world. This disappearance was not going to go unchecked. Joe was going to find out what happened and when he did, whoever was responsible was going to pay a very heavy price.

*

Tanya eased herself back into the wheelchair the nurse was holding steady for her. She closed her eyes and blew out a long breath. It had been a tough session, but she was getting there.

'You did really well today. You should be proud of that,' Zoe, her physio, said with a smile. 'You're nearly there now. Not far off at all.'

'Yeah? I'm not sure I'm quite there yet. That's taken everything out of me,' Tanya admitted.

'You've been ploughing through physical therapy for two hours straight. I'd say most people should be tired after that, hun,' Zoe replied.

'Well, I wasn't exactly super fit before I got shot and left for dead, so I'll take that,' Tanya said with a grin.

'I still can't believe they haven't found the mugger yet. It's awful how slack our justice system has got, it really is,' Zoe said, shaking her head sadly.

'Yeah, well. It was a really quiet area, not even any cameras, so they didn't have much to go on, I guess.' Tanya shrugged, sticking to the story Freddie had set up for her. It was much easier than having to admit she was at the farm and having to answer all the questions that would come with that. She ran her hands through her long red hair and pulled it up off her neck to cool herself down.

Letting the thick wavy locks drop back down around her shoulders, she allowed Zoe to start pushing her back towards her room. She didn't need the wheelchair anymore, not really, but when she became tired like this, the nurses preferred to wheel her back to make sure they didn't push her too far.

'Honestly, I think within a week you'll be strong enough to go home and continue your recovery there,' Zoe said as she pushed her along.

'Really?' Tanya asked, feeling her hopes lift. 'That soon?'

'Yes, I think so. I can't promise, but at the rate you're going, it looks that way. You're walking pretty well now; it's more just building your muscles up.'

'What about, you know, my memory thing?' Tanya asked awkwardly. She had been going for daily sessions to a psychotherapist, but it hadn't been helping much so far. She knew this was mainly her own fault though.

Tanya had not been open to talking about her feelings on the shooting or about any of the events in her personal life leading up to it. The doctor had told her that talking it out might release the mental block her brain had built, but how could she talk about the shooting or her ex Tom? All the facts surrounding the incident were fake. She couldn't tell the truth, and Tom was all mixed up in that too. He had betrayed her that day, her and the people she loved, and he'd left her to die with nothing but a few spiteful words. Tanya knew that all of this had messed her up mentally, but a complete stranger who would no doubt take her story straight to the police wasn't the right person to talk it over with.

'Oh, they'll give you outpatient appointments. You can just come in for them,' Zoe replied.

'Great,' Tanya murmured sarcastically.

Zoe glanced down at her patient. She lowered her voice. 'I mean, you don't have to go to them. Don't say that came from me, of course, but they aren't mandatory. They can't force you to go if you don't want to once you're discharged.'

'Oh.' Tanya raised her eyebrows. 'Well, that's good to know.'

'There you are!' Rosie came round the corner. 'I was just coming to find you, saw you weren't in your room.'

'Just finished up with Zoe,' Tanya said.

Rosie glanced at Zoe and gave a tight smile. 'I can take my daughter from here,' she said.

'Sure. See you tomorrow then, Tanya,' Zoe said with a wave.

Rosie pushed Tanya down the hall before she could respond. She put her half-raised hand back down on her lap and closed her mouth.

'Guess what I've got in me bag?' Rosie said conspiratorially.

'What?' Tanya could tell it was some sort of food from the smell.

'Maccy D's.' She giggled. 'I bet you're gagging for some naughty food after all the healthy stuff they pump you with in here, eh?'

Tanya smiled and tried to look excited. Rosie was still trying to impress her and she didn't want to discourage that. She wasn't much for fast food, preferring to keep a close eye on her figure, but the odd meal wouldn't hurt.

'Thanks, Mum,' she said. It felt so strange calling Rosie 'Mum', but in a good way. After all these years without her, hating her even, it felt so good to be forming this relationship with her again. Or rather, for the first time.

They had never had this even when she had been small. She couldn't remember one instance in her childhood where her mum had treated her to a McDonald's. Not like all the other mums. She felt the familiar stab of hurt and anger pierce her chest at the memories, but she swallowed them down. She needed to try to focus on their future, not their past.

'So, how's things with you today?' Tanya moved the conversation on. 'How did your church group go last night?'

'Oh brilliant,' Rosie enthused as they reached Tanya's room. She set the wheelchair by the table and closed the door. 'Ron was back in last night. I think he's making some real progress now. He's made friends with a few of us.' She came back to the table and laid the hot greasy food out on the takeaway bag.

Rosie had spoken about Ron a few times. A man who'd joined her church group a few weeks ago, lonely after losing his wife to cancer.

'How old is Ron?' Tanya asked, popping a chip in her mouth.

'I'd say about fifty-five maybe?' Rosie bit into her burger.

'You talk about him a lot,' Tanya replied with a glint in her eye. 'I wonder if maybe you'd like to be more than just his friend.'

Rosie snorted between munches. 'Ha, not likely!' she said indignantly. 'He's far too old for me.'

'No, he's not. You're what, fifty-one?' Tanya replied.

'Yeah, well.' Rosie swallowed her mouthful. 'I like 'em younger, don't I? I've still got it, I'll have you know. I'm a MILF.' She winked saucily and Tanya laughed, shaking her head.

'Ah, Mum, you crack me up. OK, well we'll leave poor Ron to the grannies of the group then, shall we?'

'Indeed.' Rosie smiled. 'What about you, anyway? What's happening in your love life?' she asked.

'Oh, well—' Tanya wiped the grease off her hands with a paper napkin. She hadn't told her mother about Tom. She hadn't told her anything much, except a vague overview of the fake mugging story. She looked up at Rosie and felt the overwhelming urge to tell her the truth. She was her mother, after all. 'I've had a bit of a bad run with men. The last one in particular.'

'Go on.' Rosie's expression grew concerned.

'It's all sort of tied in with me getting shot really.' Tanya glanced towards the door. 'Listen, what I tell you now must stay between us,' she said seriously.

'Of course,' Rosie replied. 'You can tell me anything, Tanya.'

Tanya nodded. 'It wasn't a mugging, when I got shot. The person who shot me was someone I knew and it was all part of a very mixed-up situation.'

'Oh my God,' Rosie said, raising her eyebrows.

'Yeah, it's fine. That's been dealt with. I won't go into detail but my ex was sort of involved. He went behind my back and Anna's and Freddie's and was giving this guy information. He was working with him and when I was shot' – Tanya took a deep breath as her voice began to wobble – 'he found me. Later. I'd been in there a while and was bleeding out.'

Tanya looked down at her hands. They had begun to shake. She swallowed. The memory of Tom, of what he'd done to her, tore her up inside. It was something she pushed away every time it snuck into her thoughts. But this time she let it stay. She wanted to tell her mum.

'He found me there and I thought he'd come to help me. I thought he'd been looking for me. But it turns out he wasn't. And instead—' Her voice faltered as the memory of his face flashed across her mind. The hatred and bitterness that radiated from it had been powerful. There was no love, no remorse.

'Instead of helping me,' she pushed forward, 'he told me I deserved it. And then he walked away and left me to die.'

'Christ.' Rosie reached across the table and took Tanya's hands in hers. 'That must have felt terrible.'

'Yeah, it wasn't my favourite day,' Tanya replied, blinking away the tears that were threatening to fall.

'And you were actually together when he did this to you?' Rosie asked.

'Yeah. Well, sort of. We were going through a rough patch. We'd been together about a year and then we'd sort of broken up. I had a lot going on and I was really stressed and just needed some space. I guess that rejection was part of it for him. I left him alone, so he left me to die.' Tanya pulled a face. 'But anyway, he's gone now. He had the sense to leave before Freddie found him.'

Rosie shook her head sadly. 'Well, clearly he wasn't the one for you, Tanya. And clearly he didn't succeed. Because here you are.' She squeezed Tanya's hands. 'You're here and you're fighting, and we're going to get you back home and back to your life in no time. He didn't succeed in taking anything from you.'

'Except my short-term memory,' Tanya said. 'But who wants to remember two hours of physio anyway, right?'

Rosie's head snapped up and her eyes widened.

'What?' Tanya frowned, feeling self-conscious.

'What you just said,' Rosie replied.

'My short-term… Oh!' Tanya's face opened up in surprise. 'I remember, I've just done two hours of physio!' Her voice rose in excitement. 'I remember!'

'What did you have for breakfast?' Rosie asked.

'Muesli!' Tanya cried. 'With… with… ugh.' She dropped her head into her hands. 'I can't remember.'

'But that's progress,' Rosie said with a smile. 'That's definitely progress. You wait here, I'll go get the doctor.'

Rosie hurried off and Tanya picked at the rest of the chips absent-mindedly. It had been hard to talk about Tom but maybe that was what she needed to move forward. She smirked without humour. Perhaps her asshole ex still had his uses after all.

CHAPTER TWELVE

Jimmy Taylor waited impatiently for the last two customers of the night to leave his restaurant. The two lovebirds had taken their time over the last half-bottle of wine and were finally paying the bill. The closed sign had been up on the door for the last forty-five minutes and everyone except himself and the waitress for that section had already left for the night. The kitchens were cleaned down, the takings had been totted up and all that was left to do was give Misha her share of the evening's tips and lock the doors.

Jimmy couldn't get to that point quickly enough this evening. He had things to do, places to be. His gaze flickered towards the door that led up to the two-bedroomed flat above the restaurant, where he lived alone. It was a dingy little abode which needed much more than a lick of paint to bring it up to scratch. But he'd never been one to bother with homemaking and frills. That was a woman's work, and seeing as no woman would touch him with a bargepole, no one had been around to do it. He'd been single pretty much his whole life. With a naturally sour face, a balding head and a tendency to forgo personal hygiene, he wasn't exactly any woman's dream.

The bell above the door tinkled as the couple finally left. Jimmy lifted his hand in a wave and gave them a broad smile. 'Thank you, please come again soon.'

The door closed and the smile was replaced by a miserable sneer. 'Thought they'd never leave,' he muttered.

Misha scurried past him into the kitchen with the two dirty wine glasses and empty bottle. Jimmy reached into his pocket and pulled out her tips. He handed them over as she reappeared.

'Thank you, Mr Taylor,' she said politely.

'No problem. Goodnight.' He swiftly locked the front door behind her as she left.

He turned back towards the door to the stairs with excitement in his eyes but paused before opening it. Tonight there was cause for celebration. And why not? He'd worked hard enough for this, after all. A bottle of brandy was in order. He'd take one from the bar – top shelf. One or two glasses for the road and then he'd take the rest in his suitcase for later. He chuckled to himself as he reached up for it. He strained to reach it, being of shorter stature than most men. But for once, that didn't bother him. Not tonight.

Tonight was the night he was going to change his life for the better. And not before time. He was sick of it. All of it. The restaurant had been handed down to him by his parents and he'd hated every second of it. They had died when he was still young and an uncle had kept it going until he was old enough to take over. He'd run it well enough, but he didn't enjoy it the way his parents had. The money wasn't all that either. And when you had a penchant for gambling like Jimmy did, it didn't even cover expenses.

That was why a few years back he'd taken an opportunity that had been offered. A place on a cocaine distribution tree. Once every couple of weeks someone would drop off a bag of cocaine to him. He had to hold it for a week and then pass it on, getting a grand for his troubles. Naturally he started cutting it with a bit of bicarb and baby powder and kept a chunk back for himself. He dealt it through the restaurant and made another couple of grand off that too. It was a small goldmine. It never lasted though, despite telling himself he should start saving. It always ended up down the bookies.

Over time he'd formed an idea and finally he'd had the balls to put it into motion. He'd lined up his own buyer for the cocaine this week. Instead of passing the parcel down the chain and taking his kickback, he'd handed on a fake parcel barely an hour ago. He'd made sure it was the same weight and size, but it contained nothing but crushed-up paracetamol, baby powder and bicarb. The real stuff was upstairs and his buyer would be arriving any moment now with a neat forty grand for him. He was going to leave this place for good and head out to Nepal. He'd heard that a man could live like a king out there for no more than a hundred pounds a month.

He'd left instructions for his nephew, who had been edging to place himself in line to take over. He could have the restaurant, so long as he placed a percentage of the profit in Jimmy's bank account every month. It would keep him topped up, should he need it over in Nepal.

He was looking forward to this new future he had planned. He could relax out the rest of his days in luxury and maybe see a bit of the world. Plus, hopefully he'd finally find a woman over there who found him attractive. Even if it was only for his wallet. He didn't really care what she saw in him, so long as she cleaned, cooked and opened her legs. Spurred on by this thought, Jimmy skipped up the stairs, taking them two at a time.

Tonight his luck was going to change forever.

Jimmy opened the creaky front door and felt along the wall for the light switch. He found it as the door closed behind him and flicked it on, flooding the place with light. He took a couple of steps forward and then yelped in frightened surprise as he realised there was a man standing across the room from him. Twisting back on himself, he jumped and dropped the bottle of brandy as he caught sight of the second man, now standing between him and the only way out. The bottle smashed on the wooden floor and he groaned in despair as the golden liquid seeped down through the cracks.

'Oh, I wouldn't worry about that. That's definitely not going to be the worst thing you lose tonight,' the first man said, walking towards him.

'Wh-who are you? What are you doing in my flat?' Jimmy's voice quivered. He had a sinking feeling he already knew the answer.

'My name's Freddie, Jimmy. And this is my brother Paul.'

Paul grabbed Jimmy by the arms and roughly pushed him forward, sitting him down on a wooden dining chair that Freddie had pulled out from the round kitchen table in readiness. Jimmy looked up into their faces, scared. He didn't dare try to move. Freddie leaned back on the kitchen table next to him and crossed his arms.

'What do you want?' Jimmy swallowed. His throat suddenly felt very dry.

'What do we want? Honest employees would be a nice start, I guess. Wouldn't you say, Paul?' Freddie asked, raising an eyebrow at his brother.

'Oh, that would be lovely, Fred. Would save us a lot of hassle,' Paul replied, nodding seriously.

'I don't understand. I don't work for anyone. I own this restaurant,' Jimmy blustered.

'Now, see, that's where you're wrong. On both accounts actually. You see' – Freddie turned to face the trembling man – 'the day you accepted the first delivery of cocaine and got paid to watch it, that's the day you started working for me. Sure, not directly, it's a chain for a reason. If one connection breaks it can easily be replaced. And if that connection decides to talk, it only has so much information. Of course you were never going to know who you worked for, Jimmy – that's just good business sense. But I'm the boss. Which means I know *exactly* who works for me.'

Freddie's eyes glinted dangerously and Jimmy shivered. He was in deep shit and he knew it.

He couldn't understand how they knew of his plan though. The guy who took the package would barely have had time to get it back, let alone check it, find it to be fake, call the bosses and get them to travel over here. It didn't make sense. Unless they weren't here about that. Perhaps it was about something else. It was unlikely but he decided to try to bluff it out.

'Well, then it's a pleasure to meet you,' he said, his eyes darting between Paul and Freddie nervously.

The action reminded Freddie of a rat trapped in a corner. 'Is it?' he asked curiously. 'Only if I were you, I'd be shitting myself right now, having found myself to be in a room with the two people I was about to mug off. Wouldn't you, Paul?'

'I would, Fred,' Paul agreed.

'Wh-what?' Jimmy stuttered lamely.

Freddie frowned. 'Surely you haven't forgotten already, Jimmy? Ah, come on now.' Freddie shook his head as though disappointed. 'The deal you set up,' he reminded him sarcastically. 'That one where instead of doing the job that you're already paid *very* well for, you give the next dealer in line a bag full of flour and you sell on the real gear to your own client. Remember? That one.' Freddie stood up and smacked him around the back of the head – hard. 'You're getting forgetful in your old age, Jimmy boy.'

Jimmy whimpered at the blow but bit down on his lip to quieten himself. He was in for it big time and he had never been so scared in his life. He cursed himself for thinking he could pull this off.

'Thing is though, Jimmy,' Freddie continued, pulling a pair of black leather gloves out of his pocket, 'everyone except for you it seems knows who runs things around here. And knowing that, they wouldn't even *think* about the sort of thing you were planning to do. Because people like me and Paul here don't just get to the position we're in by chance. Do we, Paul?'

'No, we certainly don't, Freddie,' he replied, pulling his own pair of leather gloves out. He began putting them on, pushing each finger neatly into place.

'No. We get to where we are by hard fucking graft,' Freddie said, his voice turning hard. He bent down and put his face level to Jimmy's. 'And by making sure people understand that we aren't the sort of people you mess with.'

'Look, I'm sorry, I'm so sorry. I realise that now. I don't know what I was thinking.' The words tumbled out of Jimmy's mouth one after the other in a quivering stream of panic.

'Nah, we don't know what you were thinking either,' Freddie replied. 'But it's too late now for apologies.'

Jimmy eyed the leather gloves and the hard, icy expression on Freddie's face. 'What can I do to make this up to you?' he asked, squirming. 'Perhaps I could lower my price for the cocaine handling?' he asked hopefully. 'As a way of apology for my mistake. And – and you can come to the restaurant any time you like, on the house.'

Freddie threw back his head and laughed.

Paul leaned forward. 'I don't think you heard my brother. He just said it's too late for apologies.'

'You really think that I'd still let you work for me after this?' Freddie asked, his tone incredulous. 'You want to *lower your price*? Mate, it weren't your price to begin with – it was mine. I set it, the same way I set up everything in my business. And as for eating at your restaurant' – he shook his head – 'that ain't going to be your call for much longer either. See I'm going to give you a choice.'

Freddie reached into the inside pocket of his long overcoat and pulled out a butcher's knife at the same time Paul grabbed hold of Jimmy's arm. He slammed it onto the table and pinned it with one hand, holding Jimmy down on the chair with the other. Jimmy squealed and tried to move but Paul was a much larger, stronger man, and he couldn't escape his grip.

'Please, don't!' he yelped, terror written across his face.

'You know, I was reading this article the other day about the different punishments still meted out in different countries for thieving. It was really interesting actually. Did you see it, Paul? In the paper.' Freddie turned his attention to his brother.

'Nah, can't say I did. Sounds like a good read though,' Paul replied calmly, not in the least bit fazed by the man struggling under his grasp.

'Oh, it was. I'll find it for you later. Anyway…' Freddie focused back on Jimmy, who was now crying like a baby and blubbering barely coherent pleas for mercy. 'In Saudi Arabia, they cut off your hand for stealing. And then if you do it again, the opposite foot.'

'Ooh,' Paul reacted. 'Wouldn't want to get caught the second time, would ya?' he said.

'Wouldn't want to be caught the first time personally,' Freddie replied. He lifted the thick blade underneath Jimmy's chin, forcing the man to look up at him. 'But you did get caught. What did you think would happen? You'd have this bright idea, sell to some perfect client and ride off into the sunset with my money?'

'I – I – It…' Jimmy stuttered, not sure how to answer.

'The second you started spreading it about that you wanted a buyer for that amount of coke, alarm bells started ringing. Not just one, but *two* separate people came to tell me about you and your big mouth. You're about as subtle in conducting your business as a brick to the fucking face.' Freddie's lip curled in disgust. 'The man you made a deal with was one of mine. A set-up arranged by Paul here. So, he won't be coming to give you that nice big bag of cash. You'll be getting your just desserts instead,' he said. Freddie lifted the blade and Paul pressed down harder on Jimmy's arm.

'No, please!' Jimmy screamed, tears running down his face. There was a sound of water hitting wood as he pissed himself through the slats of the wooden dining chair. Freddie shook his head in revulsion. Paul repositioned his feet to make sure none of it splashed onto his shoes.

'Not really got the belly for this kind of life, have you, Jimmy?' Freddie barked.

Jimmy shook his head miserably through his sobs.

'Now like I said, I'm going to give you a choice. Either I can cut your hand off and leave and we can call it a day, or' – he leaned down towards Jimmy's face, ignoring the acrid smell coming up from underneath the chair – 'I can break your fingers with a hammer, which in time will heal, and you can sign your restaurant over to me as a thank you for leaving you with all your extremities.'

'What?' Jimmy blinked the tears out of his eyes and looked up at Freddie. Seeing the steely resolve in his face, Jimmy knew he didn't have a third option. There would be no talking himself out of this one.

He didn't want to sign away the restaurant. It was his livelihood, his birthright. He suddenly wished he hadn't taken it all so much for granted. It might not have been much of a life, but it *was* a life all the same. What would he do without it? But then again, what would he do without his hand? He tried to weigh the two up but he couldn't think properly. The coward in him was too scared to even consider the first option.

'OK, I'll give you the restaurant,' he said, hanging his head. 'I just need a few days to—'

'No need,' Freddie cut him off. He put the butcher's knife back into his inside pocket and pulled out a folded document. He spread it on the table in front of Jimmy. 'I've already had the paperwork drawn up. Just sign here and here.' Freddie pointed to the dotted lines that awaited his signature and Paul loosened his grip.

Jimmy swallowed down the bile that rose to the back of his throat. They had planned this from the start, the second they found out about his deal. They must have known he'd choose his own hand over a restaurant. He hadn't stood a chance. Jimmy tried to think of something to say that might save him, but couldn't. What could he say? He hadn't a leg to stand on. He only had himself to blame.

'I'll sign the papers and give you what you want, but only if you leave my hand be. No broken bones – you'll have taken enough,' he said.

'Er, do you think you're the one bartering here?' Freddie asked with a frown. 'I don't remember asking you to make me an offer. I told you that you had a choice.'

'Well, I think—' Jimmy started.

'And that was your first mistake,' Freddie cut him off. He turned to Paul. 'Pin him down. We'll take the hand.'

Paul pushed Jimmy's arm back down on the table and Jimmy yelped in alarm.

'OK, OK, I'll sign. Break the fingers, just don't take my hand,' he begged, tears streaming down his face.

Paul let go again and passed him a pen. They waited in silence as Jimmy shakily signed the two signatures that were required. When he finished he slumped in defeat and Freddie picked up the contract. He glanced at it to make sure it was all in order.

'Thank you, Jimmy. I look forward to checking out my new restaurant. Now…' He refolded the document and slipped it back into his pocket. Paul pulled a hammer out of his own inside pocket and handed it to Freddie. 'Put your hand out on the table and take the rest of your punishment like a man.'

Jimmy sobbed and shook as Paul forced him back into place. Freddie looked at the man before him with contempt. People like him were everything that was wrong with the world. Degenerates who plodded through life taking everything for granted; who tried to skate through a lazy existence off the back of other people's hard work. Well, Jimmy would make a good example for any other snakes looking to take the royal piss. Freddie lifted the hammer high in the air and smashed it down onto Jimmy's pudgy little fingers with all his strength.

No one stole from the Tylers and got away with it. No one.

CHAPTER THIRTEEN

Thea laughed with her friend as they walked out of their usual coffee haunt with takeaway lattes in their hands.

'Oh my God, did you see his face?' her friend Amelia cackled.

'Well, what did he expect?' Thea replied, giggling. 'The guy had a bleedin' man bun, for Christ sake, I was hardly going to go weak at the knees, was I?' She shook her head.

'Some women like that, you know,' Amelia replied, wiping the tears of mirth away.

'Yeah, hippies,' Thea murmured, pulling a face. 'Anyway, I'd best get back. I've got loads of work to do. Thanks for the shopping date.' She rustled her bags and grinned. 'Now I need a good excuse to wear it all.'

'Ooh, I'm sure we'll think of something.' Amelia winked. 'Catch you later, babe.' Juggling her own coffee and bags, Amelia crossed the road and headed off towards the Tube.

Watching her friend's retreating back, Thea stood on the busy pavement for a moment and sipped her coffee thoughtfully. Spotting a bench up ahead, she walked towards it and picked up the pace. She walked faster and faster, then just as she reached it, she suddenly hit the brakes, twisting her body and promptly sitting down.

Her keen eyes caught the flash of a coat tail awkwardly stop and turn in behind a pillar across the road. *There you are, you bastard,* she thought. She sat back and waited, knowing that there was nowhere for him to go. He would have to step back out.

Sure enough, a few seconds later a young man in a dark parka nonchalantly stepped out into the crowded stream of people on the pavement. He didn't look her way, instead walking casually off in the other direction.

Thea drank deeply from her coffee, watching until he was completely out of sight. She pulled her phone out of her pocket and dialled Freddie's number.

'Alright? What's 'appening?' Freddie greeted her as he picked up.

'There are noises in the roof. We've got squirrels again,' she said.

There was a pause as Freddie registered the code.

'I'm in Club CoCo. Meet me here and we'll sort out pest control,' Freddie replied.

'On my way.' Thea ended the call and chucked her empty coffee cup in the bin next to the bench.

*

Half an hour later, Thea walked into Freddie's office and closed the door behind her. Freddie held his hand out and Thea passed over her phone. He handed her a new one.

'Thanks,' she said, turning it on. They used burners as a precaution already, but now Thea had rooted out a tail they would swap them even more regularly for a while.

'The main numbers are programmed in,' he replied, pulling the sim out of her old handset. He cut it up and threw the two tiny halves and the old handset into the bin. 'So, catch me up.'

Thea sat down in the seat opposite him and unbuttoned her coat. 'I suspected I had a tail on me for the last couple of days, but I wasn't completely sure. Thought I might just be paranoid.'

Freddie nodded. He often felt the same way; it was natural in their line of work.

'But I caught sight of him today. No one I've seen before, but then it wouldn't be, would it?' She pulled her dark hair to the side and smoothed it down. 'Thirties, dark hair, average height, boring clothes. He don't stand out.'

'They never do.' Freddie sighed heavily and rubbed the bridge of his nose.

'Do you think it's about the farm?' Thea asked.

'I'm not sure. I don't think so. This is about the time I'd ask Fraser to dig around, but we've got no one else at his level.'

Thea nodded solemnly. Fraser's death had left a big gap in the security of the Tyler business. They had no one on the payroll high-ranking enough to look into most police operations without being noticed.

'We need to think about grooming another one,' Thea said eventually.

'That's easier said than done, Thea,' Freddie replied. 'It's all about the connection, knowing someone who knows someone in that position. It took me years to find Fraser.'

'What do you want to do then?' Thea asked.

'I'll ask about. We might not have a DI anymore, but one of the plods might have heard something anyway.'

Thea nodded.

Freddie fiddled with the pen in his hand. It wasn't the first time they'd had the police looking into them, nor would it be the last, but he was still surprised. They hadn't sniffed around for a long time now. The police knew who they were, knew the family was underworld royalty, but without a specific charge to lay they left well alone. They were cautious of pestering the Tylers too much, at the risk of ever impeding a case that might truly bring them down. Freddie knew this and it didn't bother him. He was careful never to let one of those cases come about. He was an expert at covering their tracks.

'Don't worry about it. Just keep me updated and be careful where they follow you,' Freddie said eventually.

''Course. I weren't born yesterday,' Thea replied with a short laugh. She shook her head. She might be kept away from the main action, but she had still been part of the family business for years. She was the one who fiddled the books, who hid their money where the authorities couldn't find it, who organised the legalities and the day-to-day running of most of their money-laundering fronts. There was no way she would be stupid enough to draw police attention anywhere that could cause the Tylers harm.

'I know.' Freddie shot her a fond smile.

'Look, while I'm here' – Thea shifted in her seat and changed the subject – 'we need to talk. You've got too much cash built up again.' It was all well and good making the sort of money Freddie did, but keeping it under the radar was another problem entirely; one Thea battled with on a regular basis.

'Oh no,' Freddie protested sarcastically.

'Yeah, joke all you want but you won't be laughing when you get caught with it. It needs laundering but you're at capacity on all fronts.' Thea held her arms out in defeat. 'What do you want to do? It can't sit there much longer, especially now. It's too much of a risk.'

'Where is it?' Freddie asked.

'At the lock-up by Hanger Lane.'

'OK. Well, as it happens' – Freddie rolled his chair back and opened one of the desk drawers – 'I was aware of that and I've already come up with a solution.' He pulled out some papers that were folded over and slightly crumpled. He tried to flatten them out on the desk in front of him. 'We've just acquired a restaurant over in Hackney, near Vicky Park. Here, take a look.' He slid the papers across the desk and Thea leaned forward.

Casting her eyes over the legalities, Thea nodded. Everything was in order and above board. 'How much did we buy it for?'

'Nothing,' Freddie replied without elaboration.

Thea raised her eyebrows. 'Right. I won't ask,' she said. 'OK, well' – she screwed her lips to one side – 'that should work. What needs doing with it? We could do with sinking some money straight away, so—'

'So give it an overhaul. It's a tired old place, needs doing up,' Freddie replied. 'If you could go over there and sort out the staff, get a manager in place, kit it all out with new stuff and rebrand it. Then we'll have a grand opening.'

'Are you serious?' Thea sounded annoyed. 'You want me to just take over a restaurant and do everything myself? You realise I already have a full-time job with all our bloody accounts?'

'I'll put it in your name and you can keep fifty per cent of the profits,' Freddie replied.

'I – well—' Thea pulled her rant up short as she registered what Freddie was saying. 'Hmph.' She narrowed her eyes. 'I didn't want to work in a restaurant, Freddie.'

'And you don't have to. Once it's up and running you can leave it to the management and just watch the money roll in.'

'I already watch the money roll in,' she replied sarcastically. 'Too much of it. That's the problem.' She rolled her eyes. It was a good deal, she knew Freddie was giving her a lot – but still, she wished he had at least asked first. She tutted. 'Fine. I'll project manage it until it's up and running and get a decent manager on board.'

Thea knew she'd have to keep a regular eye on it and run the books, like she did for many of their other fronts. She had a portfolio of small businesses under her management now. If things got much bigger she'd need a full-time assistant. The problem was though, who else could they really trust to work alongside her and see into the core of their family business? The only people they could trust in this life were family. Especially now, with the threat of the police right behind them. True loyalty was the only thing standing between them and a life behind bars.

Saying goodbye, Thea put her coat back on and left the office preoccupied. Taking out her phone, she began typing a message to two of their men. The money in the lock-up was making her feel antsy now. It had been there too long. She'd have it moved today and split it up.

Her message sent, she locked her phone and checked her surroundings. She hoped Freddie found out why the police were tailing her and found a solution soon. Because suddenly she felt as though there was a dark and dangerous shadow hovering over them all.

CHAPTER FOURTEEN

Anna's phone screen lit up and she pulled her attention away from the paperwork she'd been frowning at. It was Tanya texting her to ask how things were going. Anna smiled and wrote out a reply. Tanya was clearly missing being involved in their work, especially here at Club Anya. It was their sanctuary, their baby. They'd built it together from nothing and no matter what else they did, it would always be their most special venture.

Anna was missing Tanya's presence too. It wasn't the same running the place without her vivacious best friend around. And it wasn't just having an extra pair of hands; she had help available whenever she needed it. Carl was an excellent manager and many of the other staff members stepped up when needed. It was more than that; it was Tanya's unique personality that was missing from the busy club.

Glancing up at the clock Anna raised her eyebrows in surprise. It was nearly 1 a.m. already. She had stayed much later than she'd planned to. Switching off the laptop in front of her, she stood up and stretched. Her back cracked from being hunched over the desk for so long. As she stretched, she glanced at the CCTV screens in the corner of the room. The monitor was tucked away so as not to distract, but something caught her eye in one of the darker pictures.

She frowned and walked over to get a better look. It was the camera outside the back door. There was an illuminated circle from the light above the door then darkness further out towards the small car park at the rear. No one went down there really, other than to put out the bins or after locking up for the night.

There was another grainy flash of something white in the darkness. Anna clicked the mouse on that camera, bringing the small screen to full size. She squinted. There was definitely something down there, but she couldn't make out what.

Remembering that this was where Tanya had been taken by one of Michael's men just a couple of months ago, her heart began to beat rapidly.

Making a decision, Anna marched out of the office and through the busy club to the front, her heels tapping out a sharp rhythm on the hard floor. She sidestepped a drunk man who looked as though he was about to try to talk to her and made a beeline for the two heavyset bouncers at the front door. She stopped by one of them.

'Ricky, can you come with me a sec? There's something going on out the back; I'm not sure what it is.'

''Course.' Ricky frowned, his large deep-set face looking concerned. He followed Anna back through the club, the crowd parting to let the six-foot bodybuilder through.

Anna bit her lip as they reached the end of the hallway at the back and paused to let him pass. Ricky looked down at her and noticed her pale face. He understood that the situation must be making her anxious after what Tanya had been through. They'd all been told that she'd been mugged and shot out there, just out of sight of the camera.

The door swung open silently and he stepped out with caution. He peered into the darkness around him and his gaze landed on the culprits halfway down the building. His eyebrows shot up and his cheeks flushed red. He looked down to his feet, stepping back so that Anna could pass. She came out and caught sight of the same thing Ricky had.

'Ahhh, I'm coming!' The podgy man leaning back against the wall with his eyes closed in rapture shuddered as he exploded into the mouth of the scantily clad girl on her knees in front of him. She gagged, but he had her by the hair and pushed himself further in until he'd finished releasing his load.

'Eugh,' Anna exclaimed in disgust. 'Are you fucking serious?'

The now spent man was startled at the intrusion and quickly pushed the girl away, exposing himself. With the white noise of central London buzzing around them and the blood roaring in his ears as he'd reached maximum excitement, he hadn't heard the two of them approach. He quickly covered himself up with his hand and ran past them, pulling up his trousers, back into the club.

The young girl on her knees spat to one side and wiped her mouth with the back of her hand, her eyes widening in horror at the sight of her boss's thunderous expression. She swiftly stood up and glanced from Anna to Ricky with a worried expression.

'What the *fuck* do you think you're doing, Chloe?' Anna demanded. 'Why the *fuck* are you blowing one of our customers in the back alley like some cheap whore?' she screeched. She couldn't believe what she had just witnessed. All the girls knew that this wasn't that kind of place.

Chloe reddened at Anna's words. 'Because I *am* some cheap whore,' she replied with attitude. 'On the side. I need the extra money to make ends meet, OK?' Her words were defiant but she looked away as Anna bristled.

'No, it's not OK. You know damn well that it isn't acceptable here; this isn't a whorehouse; this is a fucking club,' Anna roared. She was furious. Deep, hot anger coursed through her veins. This was *not* going to be a whorehouse – not now, not ever. They'd worked too hard to make it what it was.

'Well, I figured there was a little room for interpretation on that, considering Tanya's one of the bosses. We all know where she came from,' Chloe retorted.

The resounding slap that hit her across the face took them all by surprise. Anna stared at her hand in shock for a moment before dropping it. She hadn't planned on hitting the girl and certainly not so forcefully, but what she'd said about Tanya had made a red mist descend and it had just happened.

Chloe held her burning cheek and gasped. It had hurt. She stood there silent, not sure what to do or say next. Anna was clearly stronger than she looked and the dangerous glint in her eyes convinced Chloe it was not wise to retaliate. That and the six-foot bouncer standing over her shoulder, of course.

'Get out,' Anna growled through gritted teeth. 'And do not come back. You're fired, effective immediately.'

'What?' she retorted uncertainly.

'You heard me,' Anna replied, her voice shaking with anger.

Chloe blinked away the tears of pain, embarrassment and frustration that threatened to spill over. She took a deep breath and began to walk around them to go back into the club to collect her belongings. She paused by the door and glared back at Anna resentfully.

'You know, you might feel all high and mighty with your morals, but you don't have a clue what life's like for people like me. No one wakes up one morning and decides to suck cock for a living.'

Anna snorted and cast her eyes away.

'I have two kids at home whose dad fucked off with someone else while I was pregnant with the second. He never looks after them and don't give me a penny. You ain't got a clue what kids cost. My wage from dancing covers the basics, nothing else. My kids get nothing. Hand-me-down clothes and second-hand toys – *if* I've had a good month for tips. And because I earn full-time, I don't get any help from the government either. No benefits for us,' Chloe spat. 'I get no maintenance, no benefits and no help from anyone. So, excuse me, Miss Fucking Princess over there, for doing what I have to to give my kids a decent childhood.'

Lifting her chin, Chloe turned and marched into the building.

Anna shook her head. She was furious and reeling from the shock of what was going on in the shadows of her club. The comment about not knowing what kids cost had struck a nerve too. No, she didn't know what they cost. And she likely never would, if what the doctors had said were true.

'With the damage caused by the violent situation surrounding your first miscarriage, although you can fall pregnant, there is a significantly reduced chance of you being able to carry to full term. That is likely the reason you miscarried this time too.'

The doctor's words rang through her head and she closed her eyes, trying to push them away.

'Anna?' The concern in Ricky's tone brought her back to the present.

'I'm fine,' she said automatically. 'Please follow her and make sure she leaves. She's not welcome in here again.'

'Yes, boss.' Ricky left and Anna was left outside alone.

She tilted her head back and looked up into the sky. Taking a deep breath, she stared at the stars. There were no clouds tonight, nothing covering their beauty. Her anger was subsiding and her heart rate was slowing back to normal.

She rubbed her hand thoughtfully. It still stung a little, but she welcomed the feeling. Strangely, although she wasn't proud of hitting Chloe, lashing out like that had given her a little bit of release. It was like she had dispelled some of the pent-up mess of emotions that were constantly raging inside of her. It was the first thing that had actually slightly helped.

Perhaps that was something she needed to think about. She watched her breath as it curled up into the cold air. *What does that make me though?* she wondered. *If I need to hurt someone to feel human again?*

CHAPTER FIFTEEN

Freddie took one last deep drag on his cigarette and flicked it away. He entered the small workman's caff and closed the door behind him against the cold. The smell of grease and bacon made his stomach rumble but he ignored it. He wasn't here to eat.

He scanned the room and headed for a table in the back corner where a slight man sat alone, looking tense. He rubbed his short auburn beard and smiled in greeting as Freddie sat down.

'Hello, can I get you a coffee?' he asked politely.

'No thanks, Tim, I can't stay long,' Freddie replied.

'OK. Well, what's up?' Tim asked.

Tim was one of the beat officers on Freddie's payroll. He didn't have the clearance to go searching through a lot of files unnoticed, but his naturally friendly nature meant that he had a particularly large number of friends within the force. Freddie was hoping that with Tim's broad social circle and keen observation skills, he might have come across the information he needed.

'I think my family is under observation,' Freddie said quietly, watching Tim's expression. 'I need to know for certain and if so, why. I need as much info as I can get, whatever you know.'

'Oh,' Tim said, looking surprised. 'You think that…' He trailed off and Freddie could almost see the cogs turning in his brain. 'It is possible,' he said eventually, nodding slowly. 'A friend of mine, Adam, he's been moved over to a new taskforce. It's a' – he gestured with his hands as he searched for the words – 'like, an organised crime unit. The Secretary of State for Justice gave an internal speech a few months ago about wanting to crack down on the people who held the monopoly on the crime in London. It was nothing out of the ordinary; he gives little pep talks now and then. Except this time funding's been found to put this unit together. It's been up and running for a month or two now. That's all I know though. It could be them. Your family could be on their radar.' He pulled a face.

Freddie sighed and closed his eyes. Ben Hargreaves. The Secretary of State for Justice. The man who hated Freddie's family and all they stood for more than anyone else on the planet. Everything suddenly fell into place.

Just over a year ago, Ben's daughter had been taken outside one of Freddie's clubs. He'd forced Freddie to find her, threatening Anna's life if he didn't. In the end, it had been Thea who'd found her by chance, having followed their brother Michael to an abandoned house. He'd taken the girl in some twisted vendetta against her brother, who'd bullied him as a teen. Freddie had had no choice but to come clean to Ben, who had then ordered him to kill Michael in return for the family being left in peace. He'd staged a fake death for Michael and Ben had been none the wiser.

Now, though, it appeared their deal was off. Done with threatening Freddie directly, he was back to using the army of police officers at his command to bring the Tylers down for him. Clearly, he was no longer satisfied with just Michael.

'Thank you, Tim. That actually makes sense now.' He rubbed his forehead. 'I need to go. I'll be in touch.'

Standing up, he left the small café with a dark expression.

Ben Hargreaves was never going to stop. But at least this time he had an advantage. Ben didn't know that he knew about the taskforce or who was behind it. And while it remained that way he would stay out of Freddie's way. This was something he could use. He just had to work out how.

*

Anna curled her legs up underneath her on the large, comfy sofa facing the balcony in their lounge. The weak afternoon light made its way into the room and she stared moodily out of the window at the London skyline. She took a deep drink from the wine glass in her hands and felt a pang of longing for some time with Tanya. She missed her best friend so much. She wished they were sat here together now, sharing a bottle of Pinot and sharing their laughs and woes together, like they always used to.

Keys jangled in the hallway and Anna turned expectantly to the door. Freddie walked in with a tired smile.

'Alright?' he greeted her with a kiss.

'Yes, you?' she replied. 'Fancy a drink?'

'Go on then, I'll get a glass.' Freddie disappeared and came back with another glass. He sat down next to her and reached forward for the open bottle on the table. It was already more than half-gone. He raised an eyebrow. 'Bad day?'

'Very,' she replied darkly. She drained her glass and held it out to Freddie for a refill.

'Want to talk about it?' he asked as he poured. He didn't expect her to say yes; she rarely wanted to talk these days. He was surprised when she turned towards him, her expression open and engaged.

'Go on then. Get this…' Anna told him about her encounter the previous night with Chloe. Freddie sat and listened without comment, only widening his eyes in surprise when she relayed the part where she'd slapped the other girl around the face.

'Well.' Freddie paused to drink some of his wine as he tried to frame his response. He expelled a long breath and sat back, placing his arm along the top of the sofa behind her. 'The thing you've got to remember is that with your club, you reinvented the wheel.'

'Hardly!'

Freddie held his hand up to stem her protest. 'I know you think you didn't, but you did. The club scene to you is black and white, but in London, for these girls who strip and dance the way they do, that's part and parcel of the life. That's the way it's always been.' His hazel-green eyes locked on to hers intently.

'Well, that's not how my clubs work and I'm very clear on that point,' Anna replied strongly.

'And a lot of the girls are very grateful for that opportunity to separate the two, I'm sure. But not everyone. You have to remember – most places officially state that it's not on offer because it's illegal. The girls get told one thing but get tipped the wink that really that ain't the case. Surely you can see how it might be a grey area.'

'Well, still.' Anna folded her arms. This conversation wasn't going as she had expected. 'Throwing her kids in my face wasn't the way to gain favour. I'm sure they do just fine on her dancing wage. I did pay her decent full-time rates; I'm hardly a stingy employer.'

Freddie put his wine glass down with a frown and looked at her. 'Anna, you don't know how hard it is being a single mum with no other income and no family around.'

'Excuse me?' Anna bristled. 'What's that supposed to mean?'

Freddie held her stare. 'It's not meant as an insult, but you forget that you had the luxury of growing up in a family with two parents on good wages. I can remember times my old mum cried herself to sleep with worry because Paul or Thea needed new shoes and there weren't no money for it. I remember freezing cold nights where we piled up coats on the beds and bunked up for body warmth because we couldn't afford to have the heating on. Now I'd bet my last penny you don't have one memory like that.'

He watched Anna's gaze turn down to her glass. 'Luckily I was able to start earning when I reached my teens and things weren't so hard from then on. But not everyone has that option.'

He picked his glass back up and bit his lip. He didn't want to get Anna's back up, but he had to be honest with her. 'It's your club and your staff have to respect that things are done your way. But she probably wasn't trying to take the royal piss; she probably just thought that was how things were done.'

Anna nodded, the sting of Freddie's previous words subsiding. Perhaps she had been too harsh with Chloe. It had been such a shock that she'd acted without properly thinking it through. In fact, she hadn't stopped to put herself in the other woman's shoes at all. As Freddie said, Chloe had been doing what she knew, what she needed to. Wasn't that what everyone did, at the end of the day? That being said, she still didn't want stuff like that happening in her club. She rubbed her head. She needed to spend some time thinking about the situation.

'Listen, there's something you should know.' Freddie tactfully changed the subject. 'A couple of things actually. Hargreaves has put together an organised crime unit and we're in the limelight.'

Anna gasped. 'Hargreaves?' she repeated.

'Yeah. Seems he ain't content with just Michael after all.'

They stared at each other in silence for a moment.

'Don't worry about it for now, but just be aware. Thea's being followed, which means we probably all are. Keep an eye out and be careful what you say,' Freddie warned.

Anna nodded. 'OK.' She trusted Freddie knew what he was doing. He'd escaped Hargreaves' threats before; he could do it again. 'What's the other thing?'

'The other thing is about Frank.' He watched the fear flash across her face at the mention of Frank's name. Anything related to the mess that had led her to the shell of a person she was at present always caused her to flinch, and he hated himself for bringing it up. But he had to. He needed her help.

'A man called Joe Luciano has just arrived in London. He's a Mafia head and he's looking for answers. At the moment he has none, but he does know that Frank had a meeting with me. If the trail leads him to you' – he took Anna's cold hand in his – 'all you need to say is how well we all got on and how charming Frank was to you. I don't think they know about him wanting your club, but if they do, you need to tell them you were just in the first stage of discussion about that. Don't say you turned him down. Keep it vague.'

Anna felt her heart thudding violently in her chest, so much she thought it might rise up out of her mouth. She swallowed and nodded. 'Jesus, Freddie,' she breathed. 'How are we going to get out of this one?'

Anna knew enough about the Mafia to know that if they found out the truth, it wouldn't just be Freddie who suffered, but everyone he cared about. The whole family. Her breathing spiked and she suddenly felt claustrophobic. She felt like she was in that room at the farm again.

The room around her began to spin and the walls of the farmhouse began to form around her. *The wooden slats at the locked window barring her only means of escape. He was there watching her, always watching…*

'Anna? Anna?' Freddie reached forward and grabbed her arms. Her lounge reappeared and she realised she'd done it again. She'd disappeared into her own screwed-up mind. The worry and fear in Freddie's face was quickly hidden, but not quickly enough. Anna had seen it.

'Don't worry. I'm going to make it OK, alright? I have a plan. Half a plan anyway. And I promise you' – his intense gaze bored into hers – 'if I can make it work, we will never have to worry about anything again.'

CHAPTER SIXTEEN

Paul and Freddie exchanged glances, as they reached the front steps of the tall, grand hotel.

'Well, best get on with it then,' Freddie said, with more bravado than he felt. Paul nodded, his expression sober.

They had just received an invitation from Joe Luciano to join him for afternoon tea in his suite at the Dorchester. It seemed polite enough, but they all knew that there was no real choice involved.

They walked through the foyer and stepped into the lift. The doors closed and they were alone. As they moved up through the floors, Paul glanced at his brother.

'I suppose it's good that we're meeting in his hotel. I mean, it's not likely he'd kill us in here, if he did know,' Paul said.

Freddie stared at him and raised his eyebrows in disbelief as he waited for his brother to remember that this was *exactly* where they had killed Frank's men and abducted Frank himself.

A few moments passed and then the light dawned in Paul's eyes. 'Oh. Yeah…' He turned red and cast his gaze down.

Freddie shook his head and turned to face the closed doors in front of him. He was pretty sure Joe was still in the dark. They'd managed to get a clean-up team in to dispose of the bodies and evidence before anyone noticed. Thankfully the silencers they'd used on the guns had stopped the guests in neighbouring rooms making any concerned calls about the noise. It had been a tense operation, but they'd managed to ensure the room was left as though nothing had happened.

Still, the fact Joe had called them in had Freddie's stomach churning.

The doors opened and a heavyset man with dark slicked-back hair was waiting for them.

'This way, gents,' he said in a thick New York drawl.

They walked into the suite and through to the spacious lounge, where afternoon tea was already set out on the table. Two more men sat watching from the sides of the room, and Joe himself sat on the large cream sofa in the middle. He stood to greet his guests. Freddie plastered a smile on his face as he stepped forward to shake his hand.

'Joe, it's great to meet you. I'm Freddie; this is my brother Paul.'

Joe shook both their hands and pointed them towards the sofa. 'Please, take a seat. This is Tino.' He gestured towards the man who had escorted them in. 'And over there is Johnny Smarts and Big Al. That one's smart and that one's big.'

Freddie glanced at Tino and ignored the temptation to ask what his defining feature was. Instead he sat on the sofa opposite Joe, and Paul followed suit. Tino stepped forward and poured out two more cups of tea, handing them over.

Joe took his time, sizing each of them up before he spoke. 'Do you know the reason I'm in town, right now? Why I've invited you here?' he eventually asked.

Freddie sipped his tea. 'Lovely cuppa,' he said, nodding at Tino. 'Yes, I'm well aware. You're looking for information on Frank's whereabouts.'

Joe narrowed his eyes. 'And how exactly do you know that? I haven't yet put the word out.'

'I'm aware of that too. You see this is my city, Joe. I have eyes and ears everywhere,' Freddie replied calmly. 'I heard you were coming to town through one of my men. He didn't know why though because as you said, you haven't put the word out yet. But then you started asking questions to the girls at the front desk.' He grinned and tilted his head. 'Come on, Joe. Do you really think I wouldn't have them reporting to me already? You'd return the favour if I was visiting your city, I'm sure.'

Joe nodded with a glint of amusement in his eye. He poured himself some more tea. 'So, what do you know about Frank?'

'Not as much as I'd like to, to be honest,' he answered, his clear gaze unwavering. 'The last time I saw Frank he mentioned he'd soon be heading back home, that he had business to attend to but he'd return. So, I thought nothing of his absence. I was surprised to hear nothing further though. We'd been discussing terms for my new casino.'

'Really?' Joe asked, rubbing his chin.

'Yeah. That was the reason we met.' Freddie studied the other man carefully, watching for any changes that might indicate he knew more than he was letting on. It appeared he didn't though, as he nodded and seemed to accept the information.

'That sounds about right. He had mentioned he was meeting with your firm; I had assumed it was something like that. The casinos were always Frank's side of the business.'

Freddie nodded. 'So, what's happened? And what do you know so far?'

Joe pursed his lips and a small frown appeared on his forehead.

'Look, I liked Frank and we were about to embark on a *very* lucrative deal before he disappeared off the face of the earth. I want to find him just as much as you do,' Freddie said. 'So let us help you. We'll put the word out through my network, see if there are any whispers.'

Joe studied the two men in front of him. He kept tabs on the Tylers, had done ever since they had taken over London from Vince and Big Dom. The Mafia kept tabs on all the large firms in major cities where they still held any criminal monopoly. They had always had a good relationship with London, and there was no reason to doubt that they still did. But right now, Joe didn't trust anyone. And he wouldn't until they found out what had happened to Frank. As his father always used to say, *Keep your friends close and your enemies closer.*

'The last place anyone saw Frank was here. The staff said he never physically checked out on the last day of his booking but that this wasn't unusual. He, his men and their bags were gone.' Joe shifted his weight and sat back on the comfortable sofa. 'The next thing we heard he was in South America. Texts came through from a burner phone, but we soon began to suspect it wasn't him. Once we realised, we traced him back to England. His passport was never used to leave the country.'

'Shit,' Freddie murmured, shaking his head. 'What about the burner? Did you trace it to anyone?' he asked.

'No. It went dark. Not registered, of course,' Joe replied.

'And what about here? Have you looked through the CCTV footage to see when he left?' Freddie asked with a concerned frown.

'The cameras get wiped every month. There's nothing to view.' Joe's tone was tinged with frustration.

'Right.' Freddie shook his head. 'Not a lot to go on then.'

'No.'

Freddie reached sideways to the complimentary pen and pad that sat neatly on the side table nearest him. He scribbled something down, ripped it off and handed it to Joe. 'This is the number to my main club; you can reach me or leave a message there any time. I'm probably tapped, just so you're aware.'

Joe nodded his understanding.

'I'll look into it. If I hear anything I'll come back to you. I can't have a good man like Frank go missing in my city. It's not right.'

Standing up, Freddie straightened his jacket.

'It most certainly isn't. We'll find this bastard, whatever it takes. And I can assure you' – Joe's expression darkened and his voice lowered to a growl – 'whether Frank is alive or dead, they're gonna pay. No one touches one of the Five Families and lives to tell the tale. I'll personally make sure they die in the most excruciating pain possible but not until they've watched the same happen to all those they care about.' His cold smile didn't reach his eyes. 'Whoever did this has made the biggest mistake of their lives.'

A chill ran down Freddie's spine. He nodded. 'Good. That's no more than they deserve,' he said strongly. Checking Paul was with him, Freddie walked back out the way they'd come in.

He waited until the lift doors closed before he let out a long, heavy breath and closed his eyes. 'What did you see?' he asked, rubbing his forehead.

'Al and Johnny seemed to be on board, but I don't think Tino was convinced,' Paul replied quietly. 'He sharpened up when you asked about the CCTV. Probably wondered why you didn't know it was wiped every month if we've got staff on the payroll. That's what I'd wonder, anyway.'

'Hmm. What do you think about Joe?'

'I think he's undecided but using us as he has no other option,' Paul replied. He could see Joe had been warring with himself continuously throughout their meeting. The Tylers had shown no reason to be their enemy, but Joe was a smart man, and smart men never took a situation like this at face value. 'He is one dangerous fucker, Fred.' Paul shivered. There wasn't a lot that spooked him, but Joe Luciano was one person he really didn't want to cross. The fact they already had now sat in his stomach like a cold hard rock of worry.

'I know,' Freddie replied.

'And what's all that about everyone the person knows and loves dying? That's not how things are done,' Paul continued with a concerned frown.

'That's not how things are done here, Paul, but they ain't from here.'

The doors pinged open and the brothers marched forward through the foyer. 'So we'd better hope and pray my plan comes off. Because if it don't, we've just sealed the fate of the whole family.'

CHAPTER SEVENTEEN

Anna let herself into Tanya's flat with her spare key and closed the door behind her. She'd spoken to her best friend the night before and the hospital were releasing her today. Anna had arranged to collect her in a couple of hours, but she wanted to make sure the flat was all set up perfectly before then.

Walking through to the kitchen, she plonked the bags of food shopping down on the side, before switching the central heating on. Anna rubbed her hands together to warm them up as the boiler groaned and slowly came to life. Turning on the kettle, she packed away the food, filling the fridge and cupboards with goodies.

Princess came trotting through from one of the bedrooms where she'd been taking her nap and purred as she wound herself around Anna's legs. 'Hello, you,' Anna crooned as she leaned down to stroke her. 'You want feeding, don't you?'

Straightening up, Anna picked up the empty bowl and emptied the contents of a food pouch into it, as she had done every day while Tanya had been away. The fluffy white feline purred loudly in appreciation as she tucked into her lunch.

Next, Anna headed for the bathroom to place the spa set and candles she'd bought Tanya by the bath. As she placed the candles artfully around the gift box, a sudden noise made her jump. She paused. It sounded again, like keys being used on the door.

Anna frowned and looked out into the hall hesitantly. She wasn't aware that anyone else but her and Tanya had a key. The hairs on her neck prickled. Who was trying to get in?

As she was about to reach for her phone, the door swung open and revealed Rosie and Tanya. She sagged back with relief. 'Christ, you scared the life out of me,' she said, laughing. 'What are you doing here?'

'They let me out early,' Tanya said with a grin. 'Said I was too much trouble to keep any longer.'

'That much I can believe,' Anna replied. 'Why didn't you call me? I said I'd pick you up.'

'Oh, Mum tried but she couldn't get through, so she got us a taxi instead. It's fine,' she said, seeing the frown form on Anna's face, 'it was no hassle.'

'I didn't have any missed calls,' Anna said, looking at Rosie suspiciously.

'I called the club phone,' Rosie replied, setting Tanya's bag down on the sofa. 'You weren't there, but I left a message.'

'Weird, they usually call me—'

'Oh, look Tanya, isn't that nice? Anna's brought you some bits.' Rosie gestured towards the bread and the eggs in the basket on the kitchen side.

'Ah, thanks, mate,' Tanya said. 'You're a diamond. I honestly don't have the energy to get out and do anything right now; I'm pooped.' She flopped down into the large comfortable armchair and curled her legs under.

Anna studied her. She still looked extremely pale and had lost weight. 'You need to rest and eat some decent food. I've put all your favourites in the fridge. Why don't I make you something now? I bet you're starving—'

'No need for that,' Rosie interrupted. 'That's what I'm here for. Isn't it, love?' She shot a winning smile at Tanya. 'I'm going to be staying for a little while to help out, just till Tanya's back on her feet properly.'

'Oh, right,' Anna replied. Tanya hadn't mentioned that to her in any of their conversations. A stab of annoyance shot through her. She'd wanted to spend a bit of time with Tanya on her own, without Rosie constantly hovering and adding tension to the atmosphere. Anna didn't know what it was that made her feel so awkward, but there was definitely something off. She just couldn't quite put her finger on it. 'Well, how about a glass of wine and a catch-up then, eh? While your mum cooks.'

Tanya opened her mouth to respond but Rosie butted in again.

'Oh no, that's not a good idea, not when she's so tired. The doctor did say you needed to take things slow, Tanya,' she said, turning to her daughter. 'He said you shouldn't push it when you're tired and you're about done in from travelling home, I can see that.'

'Well, I guess—' Tanya's voice trailed off a little resentfully. Anna could tell she wanted to say yes, but it appeared she was too exhausted to argue. 'It has been a long day,' she admitted. 'Though it would be good to hear about—'

'Why don't you have a lie-down while I make some dinner and then you girls have a catch-up together tomorrow when you're settled back in properly, hmm?' Rosie suggested. 'She really does need to rest now that we're home, Anna.'

Anna bit back the stinging retort on the tip of her tongue and studied Rosie. She did not like how bossy she was being with Tanya. This was a woman who had ruined her daughter's childhood and who'd been absent for all the years afterwards. Who was she to start telling her what to do now? She turned away from Rosie pointedly and addressed Tanya.

'Tell me what you'd like to do and we'll do that,' she said. Out of the corner of her eye she saw Rosie raise her eyebrows.

Tanya's gaze flicked from one to the other and her forehead creased in a small frown. 'Well, I don't mind really,' she answered tactfully. Truthfully, she wanted Anna to stay, and if it had been anyone else trying to boss her around, she'd have told them to do one. But Rosie was just trying to help, and she had to give her a chance. Tanya didn't want to go against her at the first hurdle.

Anna nodded. She didn't want to be the cause of any further friction; it was the last thing Tanya needed. 'I'll go, hun, leave you to just chill out for a bit. I'll come back tomorrow and we can catch up then.'

Standing up, she walked over and leaned down to give Tanya a long warm hug. 'Love you to bits, woman,' she murmured.

Giving her one last squeeze, she smiled and walked out into the hall. 'Bye, Rosie,' she called back over her shoulder, as politely as she could manage.

Tanya watched Anna go and felt disappointment settle in her stomach. But she had to admit, Rosie was right about how tired she was. It had been a long day. She'd been longing for the comfort of her own pillows and her deep, super king-size mattress. The hospital bed had left a lot to be desired.

'I think I will go and lie down, Mum,' she said, standing up.

'Yeah, you do that, love,' Rosie said. 'I'll cook us some grub and wake you up when it's ready. Then maybe later you can have a nice big glass of this wine, I'll whip up a mocktail and we can have a girly one ourselves.' Rosie brandished the bottle of Pinot Grigio that Anna had so thoughtfully left to chill in the fridge and wiggled her eyebrows up and down.

'Oh, I thought you said it wasn't a good idea,' Tanya said. She tried to hide the annoyance in her tone.

'Well, no, not right now, but maybe later,' Rosie responded with a shrug. 'And you know, it might be nice to spend a bit of time just us, you know?' she said, accusation in her tone. 'You see Anna every day, you girls work together and go out together and everything. I've just got you back.' Rosie gave her a sad look. 'I only want the opportunity to catch up on some of the time we've lost. There's so much still to talk about.'

Tanya immediately felt guilty. Rosie had done nothing but help her since they'd reconnected and no matter what, she'd been by her side at the hospital every day. She'd even insisted on staying with her in the flat until she was fully back on her feet. Of course Tanya should spare her some one-on-one time.

'That sounds great,' she said. With a tired smile, Tanya padded off to her room and the long-anticipated comfort of her bed.

Rosie's smile was smug as she tied the apron around her waist and pulled out one of the meat joints Anna had placed in the fridge.

*

Anna stepped out onto the pavement and stared up at the high-rise building, resting her gaze on the light coming from Tanya's windows. She narrowed her eyes and pulled her coat around herself more securely against the cold. Rosie was up to something, that much she was sure of. And whatever it was, it wasn't good.

Setting off towards her car, Anna walked at a brisk pace. Whatever dark motive was behind Rosie's sudden appearance and her strange actions, Anna was going to find it. Because after everything they had been through, together or apart, Anna wasn't going to let anyone hurt her best friend ever again.

CHAPTER EIGHTEEN

Amy opened the door of the neat three-bedroomed semi-detached home she shared with Bill and grinned broadly when she saw who the visitor was.

'Freddie Tyler, you ain't paid me a visit in forever,' she said with an easy laugh. She stood aside to let him in.

'I know; it's a disgrace.' He leaned over and kissed her cheek on his way in. 'How've you been?'

'Good, thanks. You're 'ere for that husband of mine, I take it?' Amy led the way down the homely hallway and Freddie followed.

'I am indeed,' he replied.

They entered the large kitchen at the back of the house. Bill was just finishing up a sandwich and he quickly wiped the crumbs from the front of his shirt.

'Have you eaten, Fred?' Amy asked. 'Want me to make you one?'

'Nah, I'm alright, mate. Thanks for the offer though,' he replied.

'OK, well, call if you need anything.' With a bright smile, Amy turned and left them to it.

'Alright, Fred?' Bill greeted him and stood up.

'Good, mate. Yourself?'

'Pukka,' Bill answered. 'Got something to show ya. Come through to the office.'

Not one to beat around the bush, Bill got straight to the point and led the way through to a small study, shutting the door behind them.

Unlike the rest of the warmly decorated home, this room was all business. Several computer screens sat on a wide desk, underneath shelf upon shelf of technical equipment that Freddie couldn't identify. Filing cabinets sat to the side and one large leather office chair was neatly pushed under the desk. Bill gestured for Freddie to sit in this, then pulled a small stool forward for himself.

He hit the keyboard and two of the screens lit up. 'They came in the back door again last night, about two in the morning.'

'The game fixer?' Freddie asked, peering forward.

'Yeah. Here.' Bill pointed at a screen full of code and Freddie pulled a face.

'You realise I ain't got a Scooby Doo what I'm looking at, right?' Freddie raised an eyebrow.

'OK. So this is essentially the outside wall around the website. Like on a house it's there to protect and conceal from outsiders. There's a login area that's user-friendly if you have the passcodes – that's the front door, if you like. Then there's the client area where Joe Public can have a look around and place their bets. They're the windows. Then here' – Bill tapped the screen gently – 'is a very well-hidden back door. They've broken through themselves; it weren't put there by the designers. When it's closed it don't leave any trace – it's only visible when someone's holding it open.'

'While the buggers are robbing the house,' Freddie added.

'Exactly,' Bill replied. 'So last night they came in and placed a rogue game. I've already sent the details to Sammy; he's putting a block on the payout.'

'But surely that will tip them off to the fact they've been caught out,' Freddie said with a frown.

'Don't matter,' Bill replied, shaking his head. 'I've got all the info I can get on them. While they were busy putting the bets in, I traced their IP. They're using a VPN. This much I expected.' He shrugged. 'But that's OK. I managed to trace which VPN software they're using and that we can work with.'

'How so?' Freddie asked. He understood how VPNs worked: they bounced your IP address around the world from location to location so that anyone tracking them couldn't locate the true source and therefore the user's identity was hidden. This didn't sound like such good news.

'Well, now I know what software he's using, it's a case of hacking into the company mainframe and plucking out his details. This is obviously illegal in itself, which is why hackers think they're safe from the law. Pigs can't get access – it's a whole mess of data protection. But of course, you and I don't have to worry about all that. He'll have had to use a credit card, register his name and address—'

'And you can do that?' Freddie asked, surprised. 'You can hack a VPN company?'

'Me? Nah.' Bill shook his head and laughed. 'If I could hack at that level I'd have more money than God right now. The Bank of England would be scratching their heads wondering why all the coffers are bloody empty.' He chuckled. 'No, I can't. But I know someone who can. He's expensive, but he can hack anything, completely untraceable.'

'Yeah? Well, who's to say it ain't him that's laying the games on?' Freddie asked, his tone uncertain.

'If it was him, I'd never have caught him. And he certainly wouldn't be using a standard VPN like this.' Bill gestured towards the screen. 'Whoever this is, they might be smart enough to have pulled this off, but they ain't in the big leagues.'

'So, we're fighting fire with fire.' Freddie rubbed his chin thoughtfully. 'OK. Tell him to get me everything he can on this guy. I'll pay whatever his rate is.'

'It won't be cheap,' Bill warned.

'The money isn't important.' Freddie stared at the rows of code on the screens in front of him. 'Finding the fucker who's stealing from me is. And making sure that he understands *exactly* who he's dealing with.'

CHAPTER NINETEEN

'And without further ado, I declare Heaven Above open!' The small crowd cheered as Freddie popped the cork on the first bottle of champagne. They were in the bar area of Heaven Above, the new elite floor above the Heaven Sent massage parlour. It was a Monday night so technically they were closed to the public but as was custom, Freddie threw a small opening party for everyone involved.

Linda and Carla stood to the side together looking pleased as punch and Freddie offered them the first two glasses. 'A toast to the manager and assistant manager. I have every faith in you both,' Freddie said. 'And to you girls, who will outshine the rest of Soho, I'm sure.'

There was a loud cheer from the girls. A couple of them tried to catch Freddie's eye, fancying their chances with their handsome, powerful boss, but apparently oblivious, he turned his attention towards Thea.

Linda took over the floor. 'Right, girls, drink and enjoy the evening, because tomorrow the real work begins.' She turned on the music and a babble of excited chatter began to sweep through the room.

Thea looked around and smiled. 'You've done a bang-up job in here, Freddie – it looks lush.'

Freddie grinned. 'Fine praise indeed.'

'Clearly Anna's good taste has finally rubbed off on you,' Thea joked, nudging him with her shoulder.

'Oh thanks!' Freddie rolled his eyes. 'I do have pretty good taste myself, you know.'

'Yeah, I guess. In women maybe.' Thea laughed. 'Where is she anyway?'

'This ain't exactly her thing, is it?' Freddie replied.

'Nah, I guess not.'

'Even you're only here to see how you can creep money through the books,' Freddie reminded her.

'Well, yeah, I'm hardly looking for a job, am I?' Thea replied with a chortle. She spoke quietly, not wanting to offend any of the girls.

James walked over with a smile. 'This is fantastic, Freddie. You know I always wondered what the inside of one of these places looked like.' He peered around with interest, fascinated by the whole experience. Paul hid a grin. 'I mean, just look at these girls.' He admired one of the blondes near him openly. She turned to him, blinking at the sudden interest. 'I mean, darling, you're stunning.' His eager tone was sincere and she grinned.

'Thanks, babe,' she said with a throaty giggle.

'Seriously, Paul, I'm surprised you don't get tempted back over to the other side, hanging around beauties like this all day,' James continued, thoroughly captivated.

'OK, I think someone's had too much champagne,' Paul said with a deep laugh.

'I might have had one or two before I came over,' James admitted. 'But you wouldn't blame me if you knew the day I'd had,' he said, his previously happy tone deflating like a balloon.

Paul gave him a sympathetic look and looped an arm around his shoulders in support.

Thea frowned. 'Why, what's up?' she asked.

'Oh, just my bitch of a boss.' James waved dismissively. 'Don't mind me, I'm just being a Debbie Downer.'

'I thought you loved your job,' Thea said. She looked up at Paul for clarification.

'He did. Until his new boss took over. She don't like him, causes trouble.'

'Why doesn't she like you?' Thea asked, frowning. Everyone liked James. He was one of the nicest people she'd ever met.

'It was between her and me for the promotion. She got it and that was fine with me.' James held his hands up. 'But she's shit at her job and I'm not. I think she feels threatened. So she keeps doing her best to make me quit. She's close to winning too.' James sighed unhappily. 'As soon as I find something else decent, I'm going to hand my notice in. But I've not found the right place yet.'

'That's crap,' Thea replied angrily. 'Why don't we just' – she glanced up at Paul meaningfully – 'I don't know. Teach her a lesson…'

James shook his head. 'I don't want anyone to get involved. Honestly, she's not worth it,' he said firmly. 'Anyway. That's boring. Let's just enjoy tonight.'

James took a deep breath and smiled again. Catching Carla's eye, he walked away to talk to her. Thea stood beside Paul and watched him, biting the inside of her cheek as her mind wandered.

Freddie pulled her attention back to the room. 'Hey, can you come with me a minute? I want your thoughts on something.'

'Sure,' she replied.

Following her brother through to the newly decorated office, she sat down at the desk and glanced at the file he placed in front of her.

'Take a look at the expenses. How much more do you think we can get away with for the renovations? If you can mock up some invoices and tie them to the building company with Ralph, then I'll clear that the other end, and—'

'Freddie,' Thea cut him off and shook her head. 'I can't keep taking on projects like this. I physically can't handle everything we've got all by myself anymore. I'm stretched too far and if I take my eye off even one small ball, I could make a mistake – and that mistake could be what takes us all down.' She rubbed her face tiredly. 'I'm just one person, Freddie. I need help.'

'I don't know what to suggest, Thea.' Freddie rocked back on one foot and rubbed his head. 'This kind of position isn't exactly something we can place an ad for. Maybe I could take some of the load back myself. Some of the bigger ones are straightforward, aren't they? Perhaps—'

Thea tuned out as all the partial ideas running around her mind suddenly came together. 'What about James?' she said.

'Eh? What about James?' Freddie asked with a frown.

'He's literally just been stood talking to me about how much he hates his job, not five minutes ago,' she replied. 'He's looking for any excuse to leave. He's family and he already knows what we do. OK, so his background isn't accounting, but I could teach him what he needs to know. He's extremely intelligent. If he was interested, he'd be a great asset.' Thea's eyes took on an excited, determined gleam.

Freddie bit his lip. 'I don't know Thea. I mean… he ain't blood.'

'He may as well be,' she argued with a frown. 'He and Paul are like you and Anna – they're set for good. Why don't you ask Paul what he thinks?' Thea could see Freddie was beginning to come around to the idea and pressed forward. 'I really need someone, Fred. I'm serious,' she said, her face opening up in honesty. 'I can't carry on doing this by myself.'

Freddie nodded. Thea had a point. If he really was looking for a new position like Thea said, this could be a perfect opportunity all around. 'OK. I'll speak to Paul and if he's happy with the idea then he can put it to James.'

Thea let out a heavy breath of relief. It was the perfect solution to her problems. She just hoped that now Freddie had agreed, Paul and James would too.

CHAPTER TWENTY

Tanya laughed hard as Anna relayed some of the funnier moments in the club that had happened while she was in a coma.

'Honestly, it didn't seem funny at the time with you being in hospital and everyone so tense, but now it cracks me up looking back.' Anna laughed again. 'You should have seen her face! She was running around the stage back and forth, trying to warn Ellen that the rope was on fire, but Ellen was so engrossed on the rings it took ages for her to notice.'

Tears of mirth streamed down her face and Tanya roared with laughter.

'Even the customers were trying to warn her, but she just thought they were cheering her on!' Anna covered her face with her hands.

Tanya slapped her leg and shook her head, trying to catch her breath through the laughs. 'Oh Christ, I wish I'd been there to see that.'

'I wish I'd filmed it,' Anna said, shaking her head and wiping her eyes.

Tanya sat back suddenly, drawing air in sharply through her teeth and pulled an expression of pain.

'Tan? Are you OK?' Anna quickly put her glass of wine down on the coffee table and crossed the room.

'Yeah, yeah, I'm fine. Honestly, don't worry. It's just all the laughing. It pulls the muscles that the bullet ripped through.' She grimaced and touched her stomach. 'It's still tender. It's getting easier as I get stronger, but… well, it takes time I guess.'

Anna stared down at Tanya's hands. The room went dark around her and suddenly she was back in the barn, Michael restraining her and Tanya running towards them with a wrench in her hand.

Tanya's expression was angry, strong like a warrior. She was trying to protect her, trying to get her away from Michael. But he had a gun. The light shone on the cold, hard metal as he lifted it. Anna froze and tried to call out but it was too late. A loud crack rang out into the air and the bullet left the chamber. It hit Tanya with a dull thump and time seemed to stand still. Tanya's eyes locked with hers. Confusion, shock and then pain. Michael dragged her backward as Tanya slumped to the ground, blood running down her front, staining her clothes. There had been so much blood. She strained but he held her tight; she couldn't get away. She couldn't get to Tanya.

'Anna? Babe, you OK?' Tanya's voice cut through and pulled Anna out of the waking nightmare.

'Yeah… Yes, I'm fine.' Anna shook her head to dispel the last of the dark memory.

'You're white as a sheet.' Tanya frowned. She studied Anna and bit her lip. Her friend's gaze kept flickering towards her wound. 'You do know I'm OK, don't you?'

'What? Yeah, of course.' Anna brushed it off and looked away.

'I mean…' Tanya struggled to find the right words. 'Physically I'm fine. It's shit' – she gestured towards her stomach – 'but it's healing and that's just life sometimes, you know?'

'What, getting shot by a psycho?' Anna asked with a snort.

'No, I mean, just shit. Life throws it at you and you have to deal with it and move on. This was a big one, sure.' Tanya took a deep breath. 'But I'm just trying to focus on getting back to normal. I didn't die.' She held her arms out and shrugged. 'But that's me. What about you, Anna?'

'What about me?' Anna asked, her tone defensive.

'Well, you haven't really talked about everything,' Tanya replied gently. 'To anyone. It must have been awful for you. What you had to do, and losing the—'

Anna stood up abruptly. Tanya fell silent and bit her lip. Anna cleared her throat and walked back to where her wine glass stood on the coffee table. 'I think we need a top-up.' She gazed off into the distance. 'And then I'll tell you about the new act Sophie's working with. They're really good. You'll like them, I think.'

Tanya nodded slowly. 'I'm sure I will.' That was clearly the end of their previous conversation. She knew she had been pushing it, but she'd had to try. She was worried about Anna, and she knew that Freddie was too. She wanted to reach out and beg her friend to talk to her and to come back to them. But Tanya knew she couldn't. It would only serve to push Anna further away. They all just had to give her space and time and hope that she made it back on her own.

Tanya watched Anna walk to the kitchen and grab the half-drunk bottle of wine. As she came back through, her stance relaxed and she offered a genuine smile.

'Another?' Anna asked, holding the bottle up.

'As if you need to ask.' Tanya grinned and held her glass out.

As Anna topped it up, there was a sound in the hallway. Anna's heart dropped and a flash of irritation shot through her. Rosie was back. So much for quality time with Tanya.

'Oh hello, Anna, I hadn't realised you were coming over tonight,' Rosie said as she came through the doorway to the lounge.

Anna forced a smile. *Yes, you did.* 'Rosie, hi. Yes, we were just having a catch-up.'

'Oh lovely.' Rosie shrugged her coat off and sat down on the sofa where Anna had previously been sitting. 'What are we catching up on then? I'd love a sparkling grape juice to join in with, thank you.' She nodded towards the glass in Anna's hand.

Anna swallowed the retort that was bubbling to the surface and instead went to pour Rosie a drink. Princess poked her head up from her bed above the kitchen radiator and glared at Rosie. Anna heard the small growl that came from the cat and gave her a secret smirk.

'How was your evening, Mum? You're back early,' Tanya said with a polite smile. She could sense Anna's annoyance and although she wished relations weren't so strained between her friend and her mother, she could well understand it in this instance. They'd barely had any time together just the two of them since she had come out of the coma. She hadn't been expecting Rosie to be home so soon.

'There was hardly anyone at group tonight so it didn't take very long. When there's only a few, we just sort of talk more individually,' Rosie said. 'So, what have I missed then, girls?'

'Nothing much, just club talk,' Tanya replied.

'Where did you say your group was again?' Anna asked as she walked over with Rosie's grape juice. She handed it over to the older woman and sat at the other end of the couch.

'It's in a church, isn't it, Mum?' Tanya replied.

'Yeah, that's right.' Rosie nodded with a smile.

'Which one?' Anna asked, tilted her head in interest.

'Well, it's over Barbican way, you probably wouldn't know it.'

'Actually I'm quite familiar with the area; I have a friend who lives there. Which church?' Anna's gaze pierced Rosie's intently.

'Well…' Rosie hesitated. 'It's actually in an old monastery. The church got a bit busy, so the vicar, he sorted us out a room over there.'

'What, the Charterhouse?' Anna frowned. 'I didn't know they hired rooms out.'

'They don't to the general public,' Rosie came back, sounding defensive. 'But as the vicar asked them personally and it's for the church, they made an exception.'

'I see.' Anna sounded sceptical and Rosie bristled.

'Well, that sounds lovely,' Tanya quickly interjected. 'I bet there's much more room there. Good on the old vicar, eh?' She smiled encouragingly.

'We'll have to come to one of your groups sometime,' Anna continued. 'It's a beautiful building.'

'That sounds fun.' Tanya's face lit up with a big smile.

Rosie frowned. 'I'm sorry but no,' she said forcefully. 'My groups are serious; they're not some social club you can drop into when you fancy it. It's a safe place for people who struggle with addiction issues and hardship. A couple of young women with money to burn, who make their living selling alcohol, are not the kind of people my group need thrown in their faces.' She turned to Tanya with an apologetic look. 'I'm sorry, love, I don't mean that to be rude, but put yourself in their shoes.'

'Yeah, you're right. 'Course.' Tanya nodded. 'We get that, don't we, Anna?'

Anna smiled wryly. *Well sewn-up, Rosie*, she thought. 'Yes, of course.' She wasn't convinced at all by this martyr act Rosie was laying on. She downed the rest of the wine in her glass and placed it down on the coffee table. 'I'd best be off, Tanya. I promised Freddie I'd pop by and see him tonight,' she lied. 'He'd been so busy lately we've just been like ships passing in the night.' This part was true, though it was mainly down to her own engineering.

'Oh, OK. Well, I'll call you tomorrow?' Tanya was disappointed to see her best friend leave so soon.

'Great, talk to you then.' Anna waved goodbye to the pair of them and left.

*

Rosie screwed her mouth to the side and shook her head as Anna closed the front door.

'What?' Tanya asked.

'Nothing, nothing,' Rosie replied.

'No, go on.'

'Well, it's just a shame she can't be happy for you really, isn't it?'

'What do you mean?' Tanya frowned.

'She hates that I'm here; we both know that,' Rosie said, pursing her lips and raising her eyebrows. 'Even though she knows how happy we both are to have got this second chance. But then I guess that's what her type do.'

'What do you mean, *her type*?' Tanya took a deep breath, getting annoyed. She was happy her mother was here, yes, but that didn't mean she was going to let her badmouth Anna.

'Oh, I don't mean it nasty, Tanya,' Rosie said in a placating tone. 'I just mean, well, look at her. Since you've known each other she's always been the one with everything, right? The golden child of the two of you.'

'When I met her, Mum, she had nothing but a suitcase in the back of an old car,' Tanya replied flatly.

'Yeah, but she had a sob story, didn't she? She had the means for people to feel sorry for her, the spot in the limelight with you and with Freddie.' Rosie let that sink in for a moment. 'And she was the one with the perfect family, who then got the boyfriend and all of his family, while you were just the tag-along.'

'That's not how it was at all,' Tanya snapped hotly. 'You don't know how it was.'

'Well, why weren't it you who ended up with Freddie then?' Rosie hid a smile as Tanya's cheeks flooded crimson. She'd hit a nerve. 'I mean, you're all friends and that, why weren't it you two who hooked up? What was wrong with you, eh, that was right with her?'

'Oh Mum, you're being ridiculous,' Tanya scoffed. *Why would she say that?* she wondered.

'I'm not.' Rosie shook her head. 'And there's nothing wrong with all that, not at all. But I bet all that time when things were going so right for her, you were happy for her, weren't you?'

'Of course – she's my best friend,' Tanya exclaimed, exasperated. 'I always will be happy for her.'

'So then why, when for *once* something brilliant is happening for you that ain't happening to her, is she not happy for you?' Rosie sat back and stared at her daughter.

'W-well,' Tanya stuttered. 'She's just being protective.'

'Is she? Or is she really just pissed off that it ain't her in the limelight for once? That you've finally got something happening that she can't outshine you on?' Rosie crossed her arms and gave Tanya a smug, knowing look.

'Mum, you don't know Anna.' Tanya shook her head with a tired frown. 'She isn't like that at all. She's my best friend and she's *always* been there for me.'

'Yeah, when the chips are down and she can be the benevolent friend helping you up.' Rosie took a sip of her grape juice and waited, but Tanya just shook her head and didn't reply. She backed off. She'd sown the seed – that was enough for now.

'Anyway, maybe I'm wrong. But it just seems a little coincidental, this behaviour. Hopefully you're right. I am just an outsider looking in, after all.'

Rosie took another sip and dropped the subject altogether.

Tanya stared unhappily out of the window. Her mother didn't know what she was talking about. Anna was family, the only real family she had. Or at least she had been, until now. Now her family seemed to be expanding. Everything was changing. She rubbed her head, stressed.

'I'm going to bed,' Tanya said.

'Yes, you go, love – get some beauty sleep.'

Rosie watched her daughter's retreating back over the top of her glass. Glancing down at the bubbles fizzing harmlessly in her glass, she pulled a face then walked over to the sink where she poured it away and watched it disappear down the drain.

CHAPTER TWENTY-ONE

The black Mercedes screeched to a halt at the top of the path that led down to the docks. Freddie slammed the door and marched down towards Damien's Portakabin without waiting for Paul. Paul hurried after him. They crossed the distance quickly and entered without stopping to knock.

'What happened?' Freddie demanded without ceremony.

'It didn't even make it to shore before they raided it. They were waiting in the water.' Damien's face was flushed from the stress of the situation. 'They knew exactly which container to hit, went straight there. This weren't no random raid – they had intel. Armed to the hilt apparently. Jacob watched the whole thing, got to me as fast as he could.'

'Was it a big one?'

'Largest one for the month. More than half the orders were in there,' Damien confirmed, wincing.

'Fuck.' Freddie closed his eyes and put his hands to his head with a pained groan. 'How did they know?'

Paul sat down and rubbed his face, stressed. 'They couldn't have. There's been no one new on there for nearly two years. Has there?' he double-checked with Damien.

Damien shook his head. 'It's been the same crew for ages – none of them would give up information.'

'Then how the fuck did they know what container it was all in?' Freddie was completely dumbfounded. It made no sense.

It had been just over half an hour since he'd received the news that their latest shipment of knock-off alcohol had been raided by the police. That was shocking enough, but to learn that they had been lying in wait for it armed with all the information they needed was another level altogether. Freddie sat down next to Paul.

'Who's been arrested?' he asked.

'At the moment, it just looks like Stanley and the captain, who isn't one of ours. They'll have to let him go eventually and hopefully Stanley too, but even if they do pin him, he's a good lad. He knows the score,' Damien replied.

Freddie nodded. 'Have you called his wife?'

'Yeah. She's alright, he's teed her up in case this ever happened.'

'Good.' Freddie reached into his pocket and took out a wedge of cash. He peeled off a few fifties and handed them over to Damien. 'Pass this on to her, for her inconvenience. And keep me updated.'

'Will do.' Damien took the money and put it away in his desk drawer.

'How many orders were on there and whose were they?' Paul asked, his craggy voice heavy with worry.

'I've got a list here.' Damien slid a sheet of paper across the desk and Paul picked it up. His eyes scanned the list of codes and numbers and he sighed.

'Fred, this is a problem. We might just be able to make it up with the reserves, but it's a big one. We'll have to substitute a few things that the clients might not accept, and even if they do, we'll have nothing left if we get hit again.'

Freddie bit his bottom lip as he tried to think of any other options. There were none. 'Then we're just going to have to make sure we don't get hit again. And we'll have to convince the bastards to take what we have for now. Damien.' He switched his attention. 'Spread the shipments thinner and wider for a bit. I know it'll up costs but just do it for the short term. Up the orders by twenty per cent too. We'll need to refill the reserves. Keep your ear to the ground, and if you start feeling twitchy about anything, let me know straight away.'

'Will do, Freddie.' Damien nodded, his expression sombre. In all the years they had been running this operation, they had never lost a load. They'd come close once or twice and had other problems to deal with, but they'd never actually been caught. This was the first time, and even though it was something he couldn't have controlled, Damien felt like he'd let the Tylers down.

'We need to go,' Paul said, looking at his watch.

'Yeah.' Freddie stood up. 'Don't worry about it,' he said sincerely. 'It's one of those things. It might still have been a random raid and they just got lucky.' He held his arms out. 'Or it might not. We just need to be careful and watch our backs. Keep in touch.' Freddie turned to leave. Paul followed him out.

As they walked back up to the car, Paul glanced at his brother's face. 'Do you think it's that task force? The one Hargreaves is running,' he asked quietly.

Freddie shook his head. 'I don't see how it could be. They seem to be focusing on us and we haven't been near the ships. None of that crew would sell out, and there's no one new on board.'

'It's peculiar.' Paul frowned.

'It certainly is.'

They fell into silence as they reached the car and Freddie pulled off quickly. There was much to be done and now this on top of everything else. It was the last thing either of them needed.

*

James watched the world whizz past as he sat in the back of the black cab on his way to meet Thea. He was hugely excited and slightly nervous. Paul had made a few comments in passing over the last few months about bringing him into the family business, but he'd always assumed he was joking. Now it was all about to become a very real possibility indeed. Paul had taken him aside the night before, laying the offer on the table. He'd told James that if he wanted to take it, he'd need to spend a week with Thea first to see if it would work out. After that, if both of them were happy to continue, he could hand in his notice.

James had practically bitten his hand off at the wrist and promptly called in sick first thing that morning. It was the perfect opportunity. He just hoped he was able to live up to Thea's expectations.

Smoothing down the front of his crisp white shirt, he double-checked that his shoes were still in pristine condition. Even though he was way past first impressions with Thea, he still wanted to turn up looking the part and show her how seriously he was taking things.

''Ere we are, mate,' the cabby called over his shoulder as they pulled up outside a shabby-looking restaurant. Workmen were walking in and out and dustsheets spilled out onto the pavement from within.

'Oh, OK. Thanks.' James passed his fare forward as he opened the door. 'Keep the change.'

The cab pulled away and James paused, suddenly feeling awkward. He was definitely not in the correct attire for what appeared to be a building site. Taking a deep breath, he stepped inside and looked around to see if he could find Thea. His gaze landed on the petite brunette giving orders to two burly men in overalls at the other end of the room.

'… with the bar over here to the side, but leave the back end open to get through to the door. Oh hey, how's it going?' Thea paused to kiss James on the cheek.

'So, we good, yeah?' Thea checked back with the two men and they nodded their agreement. 'Great, let me know if you need me.'

The two men walked away and Thea grinned up at James. 'You look nice. I like your shirt.'

‘Thanks. Feel like a bit of a wally though, to be honest. Paul didn’t tell me to dress down.’

‘Oh, he didn’t know – it’s my fault, sorry.’ Thea pulled an awkwardly apologetic face. ‘I’m just all over the place these days, there’s so much on. Freddie just er… let’s say acquired this place about a week ago. It needs a total makeover, so these guys have been ripping everything out the last couple of days and soon they’ll start rebuilding it.’

‘Wow.’ James looked around. ‘I didn’t realise Freddie was in the restaurant game.’

‘He’s not,’ Thea replied drily. ‘And there’s a lot of things you don’t yet know about Freddie.’ She glanced at him critically. ‘Come on. I’ll buy you a coffee and we can talk. I have a *lot* to fill you in on before we can even get started.’

CHAPTER TWENTY-TWO

The cab swept past Old Spitalfields Market and pulled up outside the restaurant they were meeting Joe Luciano in for dinner. Anna stared at the building through the window with troubled eyes. Freddie's hand hovered over the door handle, then dropped.

'Listen, I know you aren't feeling like yourself right now,' he said, 'but I need you tonight. The real you. The strong, charming, knock 'em dead side of you.' He held her hand and locked gazes with her. 'We're in deep here, Anna,' he said honestly and sighed. 'If this is going to work, we have to be convincing, at every point. These people won't stop until retribution has been delivered. And their reach…' He dropped his gaze. 'Well, there's no escaping it. There is nowhere in the world that any of us will ever be safe again if we don't pull this off. So, this plan, it has to work.'

Anna nodded. 'I know,' she whispered. 'I know,' she repeated in a stronger voice. She cleared her throat and sat up straighter. 'OK, let's do this.' She reached forward and opened the door herself.

Freddie nodded, satisfied that her head was in the game. He paid the cabby and followed her to the front of the building.

'Welcome to Galvin La Chapelle. Do you have a reservation?'

'Yes, I believe…' Freddie glanced into the restaurant behind the maître d' and saw Joe raise his hand from the table he and Tino occupied. 'Yeah, we're with them.' He gestured towards the table.

'Ah, of course. Mr Luciano. May I take your coats?'

'Yes, thank you,' Anna replied, shrugging off her jacket into his hands.

As they approached the table, the two men stood and Joe held his hand out to Anna. 'Miss Davis, how lovely to meet you.'

Anna smiled widely and shook his hand. 'And you, Mr Luciano, though please do call me Anna.'

'And you must call me Joe.' He smiled back warmly. 'This is Tino.'

They all took their seats and a waiter subtly began pouring wine into their glasses.

'I hope you don't mind,' Joe said. 'But I ordered us drinks already. You do like red?'

'Yes, of course,' Anna replied taking a sip. 'Mm, bold.'

'Argentinian Malbec, 2012. It was a very good year,' Joe replied.

'So I've heard.' Anna smiled again, extending her attention to Tino. She looked around in appreciation at the restaurant. With high ceilings, archways and pillars, it was an impressive building and the classic décor fitted it perfectly. She noted some of the features and mentally filed it away in her business brain for future reference. She realised they had begun talking and tuned back into the conversation.

'... in the southern areas, but no one seems to have heard anything. It's been nothing but dead ends. I mean' – Joe sighed with frustration – 'he can't have just disappeared into thin air.'

Freddie shook his head. 'It's a terrible business. Like you I'm hitting brick walls. I've had every man on my payroll looking around and asking questions, but I've got nothing. But that isn't to say there isn't something to be found. There is, Joe.' Freddie tapped his finger on the table to emphasise his point. 'And we're going to find it. Because I cannot let something like this go unchecked in my city. Christ, I can't let something like this happen to a man I respect and like.'

'You're talking about Frank,' Anna joined in. She gave them all a sad look and grasped Freddie's hand on the table. 'Freddie told me that he's disappeared. I can't believe it, and here of all places. Frank had no enemies in London, or at least not that we knew of.'

'You met Frank?' Joe asked her, with a steady look.

'Oh yes. Only a couple of times. I liked him greatly,' she lied. 'We had dinner at one of your casinos in Mayfair, didn't we, Freddie? And then he and his men visited my club the next night. Of course, I gave them the VIP table.' Anna shot Joe a winning smile. 'Nothing but the best for our American friends.'

'Huh.' Joe and Tino exchanged a look. 'What made him come to your club, I wonder…' Joe studied Anna. It seemed unusual for someone like Frank to bother visiting a mere girlfriend of one of their associates.

Anna laughed. 'Oh, that would be for my girls,' she said with a twinkle in her eye.

'Your girls?' Joe questioned with a confused smile.

'Anna's club is a burlesque club,' Freddie interjected. 'She has showgirls performing all evening. Very talented girls. Club Anya is noted as the best show club in London,' he said proudly.

'Well, that makes sense,' Joe said with a chuckle. 'Frank does like the ladies.'

Anna forced herself not to pull a face as she remembered her past encounters with Frank. She recalled their meeting in her office when she'd shown him the proof that the club was owned by Tanya. He'd grabbed her by the throat and told her to stop trying to play in a man's world, spit flying out of his mouth as he raged in her face. *Sure,* she thought sarcastically, *he loves women.*

'I'll have to swing by myself sometime,' Joe continued.

Anna stiffened. What if he recognised the address and put two and two together? What if he knew that Frank had been after the property all along? Chances were that he didn't, but if he did, it would throw doubt over their whole story so far. She reminded herself to breathe. 'Of course.' She smiled again. 'I would be honoured. Just let Freddie know when you want to come and I'll set the VIP area aside for you.'

'Sounds like fun,' Tino piped up. He clicked his fingers loudly at the waiter and Anna cringed internally at his rudeness. 'Hey, garçon, we're ready to order our food.'

Anna glanced over at Freddie while the others relayed their order. He gave her a small nod and she forced herself to relax. Things were going OK. Right now, Joe was buying everything they were selling.

The true test was yet to come though. Freddie still needed to get them off their backs. The whole Frank dilemma needed to be buried once and for all.

CHAPTER TWENTY-THREE

Tanya pulled the purple knee-length dress over her head and down over her slim body. She twisted around and checked herself out in the mirror. She'd lost some weight recently, but the dress still fitted well enough, hugging her figure in a flattering matter. Stepping into the matching heels, she walked in a slow circle to make sure she was happy with her outfit choice.

Rosie knocked on the half-open door and walked in with a mug of tea. 'Here you go. Wow, that's a nice dress.' She stared at it enviously. 'Is it new?'

'Nah, it's an old one. Thought I'd wear it for my first day back at the club,' Tanya replied, taking the mug of tea.

'The club?' Rosie said, raising her eyebrows in surprise. 'You want to go back already?'

'Yeah.' Tanya sipped at the tea. 'That's pukka, thanks, Mum. I've been itching to get back. I can't just sit around here moping for the rest of my life.'

'It's hardly moping; it's healing, Tanya,' Rosie replied. 'You're still not quite back to yourself really, are you?'

'I'm pretty much there. I won't go full-time straight away, but I need to get back out there. I really am doing my own head in here,' Tanya said with a grimace.

'What do you mean?' Rosie asked, sitting down on Tanya's bed.

Tanya kicked off the heels she'd been trying on and sat down next to her, nursing the mug in her hands. 'I just mean that it ain't just the physical side of things that need to heal. My memory is slowly getting better now and that's great, but there's still a lot of other stuff I need to get over and I can't do that locked up in here.' Tanya sighed. 'Remember I told you about my ex?'

'Yeah, I remember. The one who left you to die when you'd been shot,' Rosie said bluntly.

Tanya winced. 'Yeah, him.'

'You still need to get over him, do you?' Rosie stared at her daughter intently.

'I think…' Tanya fiddled with a loose thread on her bedspread. 'It's not so much him. It's more the betrayal. I trusted him, you know? Like, even though we had been going through a rocky patch, I never expected him to betray me like that. What he did was really low.' She shook her head. 'And the thing is, he isn't the first to betray me. The one before that, Daniel, he was a scumbag too. I thought he was nice, a decent bloke, you know? But it turns out he wasn't. He had a wife and two kids at home.' She sighed. 'For some reason, I keep ending up with blokes who have no qualms about fucking me over. And you know what, it all adds up and takes its toll. I'm not a bloody robot; I have feelings.'

Rosie gave her a sympathetic look. 'Men are funny creatures. It's hard to work out what they really want and if you're even able to give it.'

Tanya frowned at her. 'If I'm able to give it? Mum, they were both liars and total scumbags. That's not a case of me not giving them what they want; that's a case of me attracting the wrong kind of guy.'

'Yeah, yeah, you're right.' Rosie squeezed her arm. 'Well, it sounds like you're better off without either of them, and you know what, now you can get out there and meet someone new, can't you?' She smiled encouragingly. 'In fact, I think it's a great idea, you going back to work. You can meet some nice new guys and get your sparkle back.'

Tanya stared at her mother. Rosie really didn't understand what she was trying to tell her. She smiled sadly and squeezed her mother's arm back. 'Yeah. Sounds good.'

'You know what else?' Rosie continued. 'I'm going to help you.'

'What do you mean?' Tanya silently prayed Rosie didn't mean that she was about to play matchmaker. The last thing she needed right now was another bloke. She just wanted to get back to work and back to normality.

'You ain't strong enough to do all your work yourself yet,' Rosie said. 'So I'll come with you and help you. You can give me some of your jobs to do. I'll be your assistant. It will be fun, you and me.' She grinned.

'Oh.' Tanya was taken by surprise. 'You don't need to do that, honestly—'

'No, I insist.' Rosie's tone was adamant.

'Thing is, Mum, there's so much that I'd have to explain and Anna has her ways of—'

'Oh, Anna-schmanna,' Rosie cut her off and waved dismissively. 'You've been shot and spent two months in a coma. I'm your mum. I promised that I would be here to help you and I meant it. I am coming,' she bossed. 'Plus, I've been dying to see your clubs, Tanya,' she admitted. 'I've heard so much about them all this time I've been cooped up here with you. I'd love to actually see them.'

Tanya immediately felt guilty. Rosie had been there for her the whole way. She'd cooked and cleaned and helped her do whatever she needed to without a word of complaint. The least she could do was include her now.

''Course, Mum,' she gave in. 'Let's do that then.'

'Oh brilliant.' Rosie clapped her hands together in glee. 'Right, well I'd best get dressed.' She shot a sideways look at her daughter. 'Only thing is, I ain't got anything smart like you. My clothes are all a bit dowdy really. I'll look a right mess in there, won't I?'

'No, not at all,' Tanya argued. But seeing the look on her mother's face, she glanced back towards her own wardrobe. 'But if you want, you can borrow something of mine. I think we're about the same size.'

Rosie shot up off the bed and over to the wardrobe immediately. 'Oh, can I? Thanks, Tanya,' she said, excited. 'You've got such nice stuff. Well, I guess you would with the sort of money you make,' she added.

Tanya felt her cheeks warm at the crass comment. She hadn't always had money; she'd worked hard to get to the position she was in now.

'Can I wear this?' Rosie had pulled out a chic black dress in a similar style to the one Tanya wore.

'Knock yourself out. I'll be in the lounge. Let me know when you're ready to leave.'

Tanya left Rosie to it and escaped to the quiet calm of the living room. Taking her phone out of her bag, she sent a quick text to Anna, giving her the heads-up. As it sent, she bit her lip. Anna wasn't going to like this one bit.

An hour later Tanya walked through the front door of Club Anya and felt a warmth wash over her. She was home. She breathed in the familiar smell of the club and her smile sparkled as Carl greeted her at the bar.

'Oh my God, the prodigal daughter returns!' Carl grabbed her in a big bear hug. 'We have missed you so much. I can't even begin to tell you how much. I mean, I love Anna, but she is a *shit* cocktail taster.' He let her go and looked her up and down with deep fondness in his eyes.

Tanya laughed heartily. 'Yes, she told me you weren't impressed with her on that front.'

'I certainly was not,' Carl joked. 'Nah, but seriously though, it's good to see you back. And well. How are you doing?'

'I'm good. Bit tired, but glad to be back.'

'Tired? You've been asleep for two months, how can you be tired?' Carl winked.

Tanya swatted his arm. 'Oh, come off it, you joker. Anyway, this is me mum, Rosie.' Tanya stepped sideways slightly to include Rosie, who had been quietly waiting a step behind her.

Carl tipped his head in a respectful greeting. 'Nice to meet ya, Rosie.' He studied her. There would have been no doubt about who she was, even if Tanya hadn't introduced her. It was like looking at an older clone of his vivacious boss. Rosie had the same bright, piercing green eyes and the same thick auburn hair – though it was slightly duller. As she smiled now, Carl could see the same twinkle in her face, despite the extra lines that showed her age. She was an attractive woman, just like her daughter. He idly wondered if she was single.

'Mum's going to help out around here for a while, just while I'm getting back to normal,' Tanya informed him.

'Oh, right. OK.' Carl was surprised but not unhappy about this new development. If Rosie was anything like Tanya, she would be a pleasure to have around. 'So what are you thinking?'

'Well—' Before Tanya could say any more, Rosie cut in.

'Mainly the running of things, helping Tanya out. She tires very easy, you know, Carl. She needs all the help she can get.' Rosie gave him a serious look.

'Oh yeah, of course,' Carl replied.

Tanya forced a smile. 'OK, well, let's get you through to the office then, Mum, and start showing you how we do things.' She took a deep breath. 'Is Anna in?'

'No, she left about half an hour ago. Said something about some errands,' Carl replied with a shrug.

'Right.' Tanya swallowed her disappointment. She had half-hoped Anna would be here so that she could confirm that this new situation was going to be OK. Now she'd have to wait and worry about it. On the other hand, she was also half-relieved. At least she could show Rosie the club without worrying about Anna's disapproval. She glanced sideways at her mother and felt a tug of longing for her vindication. It was not a feeling she was used to. Tanya Smith had never sought approval from anyone. Yet here she was now, wanting nothing more than to impress her mother and make her proud.

'Here we are. This is where we basically run things and sort out all the paperwork.' Tanya stepped aside to let her mother in. Rosie walked in and looked around the small space with a smile.

'My, my,' she mused, 'you have done well for yourself, haven't you?' Turning to her daughter, she saw the hope in her eyes. 'It's a fantastic-looking club, Tanya. You done well, girl.'

Tanya's heart soared, and she took a deep breath to stem the emotions that threatened to bubble to the surface. Memories of her unhappy childhood flashed through her brain. All the times she'd done well at school, or cleaned the house without being asked, or just tried to be really well-behaved so that her mother might offer her one kind word. She never had. Resentment stabbed her in the gut, but she brushed it away. Those days were gone. They were in the past, and nothing could alter what had happened. But Rosie was here now and she'd changed. She was finally the mother Tanya had always wanted.

CHAPTER TWENTY-FOUR

Freddie picked up the filthy sock by the tips of his leather-clad fingers in the dark room and pulled an unimpressed face at Bill.

'Really?' he asked quietly. 'This place is like a dosshouse. What grown man lives like this?' He dropped the sock and carried on looking around.

They were standing in the bedroom of a one-bedroomed flat in Tooting, lying in wait for the man who'd ghosted the betting system at the bookies. Bill's contact had come up trumps and provided them with a name and address, for a hefty price.

The furnishings throughout the small abode were simple but practical, mostly IKEA. Upon inspection, Freddie had found the fridge to be empty other than a few cans of Red Bull and an old block of cheese, and the sink was full of filthy plates and mugs. The overflowing bin gave off a repugnant smell, which competed only with the odour that wafted up from the moulding boxes of half-eaten pizza, thrown carelessly on the floor nearby.

The bedroom wasn't much better with an unmade, grubby-looking bed in the midst of piles of unwashed clothes. Socks and pants were strewn about everywhere, to the point that Freddie was having a hard time finding somewhere clear to stand.

The only part of the entire flat that seemed remotely organised was the huge desk to one side of the bedroom. No mess littered the area in front of the three screens that sat together behind the keyboard. Two shelves sported a collection of pristine comic figurines still in their original boxes, and several signed comics adorned the walls, protected in plastic casing.

'Nerd,' Freddie muttered, glancing up at them. *How has this geek ended up a thief?* he wondered.

Bill gave a short laugh and turned to look out through the blinds to the street below. It was a busy high street, buses and people passing constantly. Eventually a slight young man slowed to a stop outside the front of the building.

''Ere, this might be him,' Bill said quietly. Freddie walked over and they watched him enter. After a couple of minutes, the sound of keys jangled through the silence. They waited until they heard the front door close and the squeak of the settee indicating that he'd sat down before they revealed themselves.

Freddie walked out first and stepped into the young man's line of sight.

'Oh my God,' he squealed, jumping in his seat and spilling the cardboard carton of chips he'd been holding. 'Who are you?'

Big, scared eyes stared up at Freddie through thick glasses in a thin, pale face. They knew him to be twenty-one years old, but he looked barely sixteen. He began to shake, cowering back into the couch in his oversized Marvel jumper and skinny jeans. Freddie watched his jaw bob up and down as he tried to find some words but couldn't. He was terrified.

Freddie had been surprised to learn that the culprit of such an organised job had been so young, but he was even more shocked now by the thin excuse of a man in front of him. He looked at Bill, who was staring down at him with an expression of pure confusion. Freddie was glad to see it wasn't just him.

'My name's Freddie, Zack. Freddie Tyler. And this here is Bill.'

'Oh God.' Zack turned even paler. 'Why did you tell me your names? Are you going to kill me now? They never say their names unless they're going to kill who they've abducted.' His voice rose an octave as he spoke, and he gripped the arm of the sofa tightly.

'Well, honestly I haven't decided yet,' Freddie answered simply. 'But as it happens I haven't actually abducted you, have I?'

'Oh. No,' Zack replied. 'But you're in my flat.'

Freddie sighed and pinched the bridge of his nose. 'Right,' he snapped, 'firstly, you watch too much TV. Secondly, we need to have a little chat. Because you've stolen a lot of money from me and that ain't something I take kindly to.'

'Wh-what?' Zack whimpered. He tried to look surprised by Freddie's words, but Freddie could see the guilt colouring his expression.

'Don't bullshit me, mate. The bookies. You know exactly what I'm talking about. I can see it in your face. Get up,' Freddie ordered.

When he didn't immediately move, Bill grabbed him by the arm and yanked him upright.

'Please, I'm sorry. I do know what you're talking about,' Zack began to bluster, visibly panicking. 'It's literally the only thing I have ever done like this, and… and…'

'Oh come on,' Bill chided, still holding his arm. 'There's no way that was the dry run. You're too smooth. You've pulled other jobs before.'

'N-n— Well…' Zack swallowed and floundered. He didn't know what to say. He hadn't been expecting these two men to be here. How had they even found him? He was always so careful.

Freddie's gaze was cold and hard as he stared at the whimpering man in front of him. 'Where's my money?'

'I don't have it anymore,' he cringed. 'I-I spent it. It's just, I had debts and my rent was behind… Look, I have about two hundred quid in my account. I can get it out for you, pay you back in instalments.'

Freddie snorted. 'I'm not a fucking debt collector, mate. I don't make repayment deals with wankers like you, who – by the way – didn't officially borrow it in the first place. I want my money now. And if you ain't got it, then there is a very big problem here.'

'I'm sorry. Maybe I can take it from somewhere else to get it back to you, but it will take time to set up...' Zack replied with a whimper.

'Where did you get your tech skills?' Freddie asked, curious.

'I taught myself, learned from other people online. I don't know, I'm just interested in this stuff,' Zack answered, his gaze darting warily between Bill and Freddie.

'And you decided to use it to line your pockets.' Freddie said flatly.

'Well, wouldn't you?' Zack asked. 'I mean, we all have to make a living.'

'I get that, I really do. But unfortunately, Zack, you chose the wrong person to steal from,' Freddie said.

'I didn't know it was a person,' Zack said. 'Look, I targeted a betting shop because it was a business and I thought no one would get hurt. I only ever go for businesses. I don't want to cause anyone harm – please, you have to believe me,' he whined.

Freddie tilted his head to the side and considered this, watching the younger man's expressions. 'I actually do believe you. But you still stole seventeen grand from me. And you have to pay for that. You see, there are a lot of people watching what I do.'

Leaving Bill holding Zack upright, Freddie wandered through to the kitchen area. He opened the top drawer and found that it was empty. 'I run a lot of high-risk businesses and that comes with its own unique set of issues. One of those being' – he tried the second and third drawers – 'that people are always watching out for any sign of weakness. And I can't let them think I have any. If I were to just accept your apology and let you be on your way, I'd be open season for all those people. I'd have them running all over me, trying to take advantage.' Eventually Freddie sighed and pulled a large dirty knife and chopping board out of the sink.

'Oh please, no.' Zack started to cry – deep wracking sobs. He strained against Bill, but Bill held tight. 'Please don't hurt me.

I'll do anything. You – you want phones tapped? I can do that. I can even listen in on conversations when people aren't even using the phone. That would help you, right? Please…' He screwed his face up in despair. Zack knew he'd messed up big time here. He suddenly wished he'd just gone into that apprenticeship his dad had organised for him. How had life come to this?

'Bring him over here,' Freddie instructed.

'No, please, no!' Zack began to scream.

Freddie threw a dirty tea towel over and Bill stuffed it into his mouth. The screams became muffled but the tears of terror continued to run down his face unchecked. Bill dragged him over to Freddie without difficulty. Even though Zack was trying to fight his way out, he was small and weak and no match for Bill.

Zack squeezed his eyes closed and waited for the worst to happen. Suddenly a thudding sound registered in his brain and his head flew back, his body swiftly following as Bill let go. He found himself flying, the air whooshing past his ears in a surreal manner, and he wondered what had happened. A painful crack to the back of his skull jarred his senses for a moment as he hit the wall. He slumped to the floor, the pain exploding throughout his head from both the back and the front. Zack realised as his senses settled again that it had been a punch to the face that had flung him across the room. He touched his nose and cried out at the sharp pain. Blood dripped down into his mouth and he blinked his eyes open.

'Wh— I can't see,' he spluttered. 'My glasses! You broke my glasses. Oh, my head…'

'You're lucky it was only your glasses I broke, you fucking tea leaf,' Freddie responded, amazed at the balls Zack had, complaining about his glasses.

'I don't think it was just my glasses,' he whimpered. 'I think you broke my nose.'

'Good,' Freddie replied.

'Fred?' Bill gestured to Freddie to go over and he did so.

The two men began murmuring quietly, but Zack couldn't make out what they were saying. He held his head in his hands and groaned. It hurt like hell. Eventually Freddie walked back over and stood above him, seemingly contemplating something.

'Those figures in the other room. You collect them?' he asked brusquely.

'Yeah,' Zack replied warily. They were his most prized possessions, the only thing he really cared about in the world. He'd spent years and thousands of pounds collecting them.

'Which is the most valuable one?' Freddie asked.

'Well…' Zack tried to work out which one was worth the least to him. They were clearly going to take it from him as part of his punishment.

'Don't bullshit me either, because we'll check,' Freddie said sharply, reading his mind.

Zack sighed unhappily. 'Darth Vader. It's an original; there's only about five left in this condition in the whole world.'

Freddie disappeared and came back with the box. 'This one?'

Zack tensed and squinted to try to make it out without his glasses. 'Yes,' he answered grudgingly.

'Right.' Freddie picked up the dirty knife, laid the box down and set about violently stabbing it with all his strength. The knife popped through the flimsy plastic and into the figurine over and over.

'Oh my God, what are you doing?' Zack screeched, aghast. 'That's worth about ten grand – it's rare!' His heart broke into pieces as he watched Freddie decimate it.

'How could you?' he whispered when Freddie was done. He wiped the tears and blood from his face with his sleeve, still sitting on the floor where he had fallen.

Bill took a seat on the sofa and Freddie paced around the room, irritated. He wanted to teach this kid a lesson the old-fashioned way, not by breaking his toys like a child – but today's excursion was not turning out how they had planned at all.

'I'm going to give you a choice. Bill seems to think your skills, like this figurine was, are pretty rare. And that they could be useful.' Freddie clenched his jaw. It went against everything he usually adhered to, hiring someone who had stolen from him, but this wasn't a typical situation. Zack could be an asset he wouldn't be able to acquire anywhere else. It was an opportunity. Bill had pointed this out and seemed very excited about it, which in itself was not an everyday occurrence. And that aside, the boy hadn't purposely targeted him, so it wasn't like he was a genuine threat.

'So what I suggest is this. You will work for me, exclusively, until your debt has been repaid. I don't give a shit how it's repaid, whether through service or selling off your crap – that's your choice. But you will work for me. Once your debt is paid, I will begin to pay you for your services. If you accept this offer, we'll leave you in peace to get cleaned up and you'll start work tomorrow.'

'And the other option?' Zack asked.

'You decline, I break both your arms and dump the rest of your little toys in the Thames. You will still have to pay me back the seventeen grand.'

Freddie leaned back on the breakfast bar and crossed his arms, waiting for a response.

Zack swallowed hard. 'What makes you think you can trust me?' He kicked himself as soon as the words left his mouth.

Freddie stepped forward and leaned into his face. 'Because,' he said in a deadly voice, 'I know that you know that I can track you down anywhere, VPN or not. And if you betray me on any level, either I or one of my many, *many* men will find you and slit your throat while you sleep.'

Zack could barely breathe through his fright. At this close range, he could see the dark, murderous steel behind the other man's eyes and he knew without doubt that Freddie meant every word.

'I accept,' he gulped.

Freddie stood upright and straightened his jacket. 'Good,' he replied. 'You start tomorrow. Be ready.'

Without another word, the two men left the small flat. As they reached the end of the hallway, Freddie gave a small growl of annoyance. 'He'd better be worth it, Bill.'

Whatever happened next and whether Zack liked it or not, Freddie Tyler now owned him.

CHAPTER TWENTY-FIVE

Freddie woke with a start and quickly turned to grab Anna, who was thrashing around in the bed. She was making a loud strangled noise that sounded as though she was struggling to get away from something, but her garbled words were incoherent. She cried out Tanya's name and Freddie immediately knew that in her head she was back in that barn, watching her best friend bleed out on the floor.

'Anna, come on.' He wrapped his strong arms around her and tried to pull her up into a sitting position in the darkness of their bedroom. At the feeling of restraint, she began to scream louder, her voice even more panicked.

'Anna, wake up.' Freddie closed his eyes helplessly as he held her to him. She scratched at his bare arms and chest, and he grimaced but he didn't drop her. Instead he grasped her head with both hands and spoke calmly into her face, wiping her hair back out of her eyes.

'Anna, please, it's me. You're OK. I'm here. It's Freddie. You're at home.'

Her struggles lessened and her cries turned to whimpers of confusion as she began to wake from her nightmare.

'You're safe. Tanya's safe. I've got you.'

Her eyes opened and they looked into his, terrified. 'You're OK,' he repeated softly. 'I've got you.'

'Freddie,' she said in barely more than a high-pitched whisper as the tears began to fall.

'I've got you,' he crooned, pulling her back into his broad chest. 'I've got you.'

They sat like that for several minutes in the dark, listening to the sounds of London outside. Anna drew comfort from the warm strength of Freddie's embrace, but the memory was still there, lingering like a cancerous shadow. The dreams that haunted her felt as real as the day it had happened. They wouldn't stop, no matter how tired she was, no matter what she did to try to forget.

Gently pulling herself away from Freddie, Anna sat up and righted her thin nightie where it had twisted around her body. She wiped her face and pushed her hair back behind her ears. She hated herself for doing this to Freddie night after night, and she hated that she couldn't free herself from the trauma that always lay just under the surface. She felt weak and stupid.

'I'm fine,' she said in a faraway voice. 'Sorry I woke you. Go back to sleep.'

Slipping out from under the covers, Anna left the room and drifted through the hallway to the study. Picking up a book from the shelf she'd left it on previously, she sat down in the big leather chair behind the desk and turned on the lamp. Curling her legs up under her, she tried to open the book, but she couldn't. It was an Angela Marsons book. The fourth in a series that usually completely captivated her, but not tonight. Her brain was too foggy, and she was too exhausted to read it, even knowing that it would help distract her. Instead she lay it down on the desk in front of her, defeated. Staring off into space, she gave in to the ghosts and demons and replayed the memories that wouldn't let her go. She was too tired to fight them anymore. At least while she was awake it was easier to not get so completely lost in them.

Freddie heard her sit at the desk and dropped his head into his hands. He rubbed his face, trying to wipe away the sleep that still had hold of him, then stood up. Throwing on a dressing gown, he padded tiredly through to the kitchen and began making a hot toddy. It was all he could think to do, something his mother had sometimes done for him when he couldn't sleep. Hot milk and whisky with a little sugar. A good old Irish recipe to help dispel a cold, or to bring peace to those who were restless.

Freddie watched the milk bubble as it started to simmer. Anna wouldn't drink it, he knew, but he had to try. He'd made these before, but each time they were still where he'd left them in the morning. But what else could he do? He couldn't just leave her without at least trying to help, and practical things like this were the only way he knew how.

Once the hot toddy was mixed, Freddie poured it into a mug and took it through to her. He paused at the doorway and stared at the shell of a woman that was curled up in the chair. Anna's eyes were wide and haunted in her pale face. She looked drawn and beaten by the world around her, the life and strength that usually held her together nowhere to be seen.

'Here, try this.' He had no idea how many times he had uttered the same words to the same end. 'It will help you sleep.'

Anna stared blankly ahead, her eyes vacant. She hadn't heard him. There were times like this now where Freddie knew she was no longer completely there. Usually at night. It pierced his heart, as it always did, and he swallowed. He placed the drink in front of her gently and laid a hand on her shoulder. It seemed to jolt her and her head moved towards him, but still she didn't turn.

'I'll leave it here then.' Freddie waited to see if she would answer, but there was nothing. She may have been awake, but the nightmares still claimed her.

Freddie pulled a folded blanket off the back of the armchair in the corner. He laid it over her legs and left the room. Making his way back to bed, Freddie felt as though the weight of the world was on his shoulders. He was juggling some dangerous things right now and they worried him greatly – but not nearly as much as Anna's mental state did. How could he help her? Would she ever be the happy, strong woman he knew again?

CHAPTER TWENTY-SIX

Anna marched into Club Anya with her head held high and her war face on. It had been another bad night, but she wasn't about to let that get her down. She'd spent an hour in the shower washing away the cobwebs, put on her favourite black pencil dress, cracked out the red lipstick and made her way out for the day.

The bar area was empty and she paused, looking around for Carl. She knew he was in there somewhere and was surprised not to find him in his usual spot. A muffled thump came from one of the large storage cupboards near the toilets, followed by a curse. Anna walked over and opened the door.

'Come on, put your back into it,' Rosie bossed, standing with her hands on her hips. She was talking to Carl, who was trying his hardest to manoeuvre one of the large spare tables out on its side.

'What's going on?' Anna asked. She quickly stepped forward and took the weight of the other side of the table. It was heavy, not something that one person should be trying to move alone.

'I'm putting some extra tables out for tonight,' Rosie replied.

'What?' Anna replied with a frown. 'Why would you do that?' *Had they been overbooked?* Anna began to worry, thinking she'd missed something.

'Because you have a lot of unused space that's sitting there going to waste every night,' Rosie answered, her tone condescending. 'You could easily fit two or even three more large tables on the floor, but for some reason you haven't been using what you've got. I'm fixing that.'

'Excuse me?' Anna replied, her eyebrows shooting up in disbelief.

'Come on, Carl, let's get moving,' Rosie ignored her and tried to carry on.

'Er, no, Carl,' Anna interjected, her tone brooking no nonsense. 'Please leave it. Don't worry about this; you get back to your stuff.'

Carl pulled the table against the wall and glanced at the two women. They were each standing stubbornly with their hands on their hips and their chins jutting out. He felt awkward, in the middle of two such strong characters, each trying to assert their will. It wasn't something he was used to. Tanya and Anna were both strong women, but they worked as a team and didn't clash. He had a feeling Rosie's involvement in the club was going to cause a lot of trouble. Giving the older woman a quick smile, Carl skirted round the pair of them and retreated to the safety of his bar.

'What is your problem?' Rosie demanded. 'I'm trying to help you, you silly girl.'

'Firstly,' Anna snapped, 'I'm not a girl, and I would appreciate if you didn't speak to me with such little respect in my own club. Secondly, there is a reason we don't have more tables out, which, if you had asked, you would know.'

'Oh really,' Rosie scoffed. 'What's that then, your majesty?'

Anna narrowed her eyes and seethed. 'This club hosts all sorts of people,' she said through gritted teeth. 'It isn't just your normal strip club. We have acts, very talented ones. So our clients are not just horny, middle-aged men who want to sit down with their eyes glued to the girls. We have women too. We have parties, corporate dos, tourists…' She reeled them off one by one. 'During the course of any evening people mill around, walk to and from the bar, socialise with others in here. They stand and they dance to the music. This club is a hybrid. We keep those open areas because after months of watching how the space is used in here, we found that these are the areas people gather in and walk through.'

Rosie gave her a scathing sneer. 'Well, you just had to say. There was no need to be so uppity about it.' She turned and waltzed off, leaving Anna boiling with frustrated anger.

Anna slammed the door to the storage cupboard and stalked through to her office. She was fuming. Who did Rosie think she was, coming into their club, one they'd both worked so hard to build up, giving orders and changing things? She had no experience doing the things she and Tanya did, yet she was acting like she owned the place!

Opening her laptop, Anna started on the pile of paperwork that awaited her on the desk. Pursing her red lips, she made the decision to talk to Tanya. It wasn't working out, Rosie being here. She was nothing but a hindrance. Rosie Smith would have to go.

*

Freddie ended the call and hid a small smile. Rosie had riled Anna up a treat. Usually this wouldn't be amusing, but this time Freddie was delighted that someone had evoked such a reaction in his girlfriend, even if it was a negative one. Anna had been so absent and shut-off, an emotional outburst of any kind was welcome right now. Perhaps a new problem such as Rosie was what she needed to take her mind away from the darker events of their recent past.

He walked into the arched entrance to Club CoCo and through the glass front doors. The low beats of chilled house music sounded from the main area, where his staff were having a meeting. He gave them a wave as he passed and saw Holly, his new promotions manager, stand up and hurry after him. Freddie waited in the hallway for her to catch up to him.

'Hi, Holly, how's it going?' he asked.

'It's good, Freddie, really good,' she replied in her soft northern accent. She smiled brightly, her big blue eyes twinkling with life. 'I've got a couple of things to run by you – are you free to talk?'

''Course, go for it.'

Hiring Holly had been a good decision. She was intelligent and energetic and seemed to know exactly how to entice more and more people in every week. A blonde bombshell, Freddie was sure she was one of the attractions for many of the young men about town, but with a shrewd head on her shoulders this wasn't something that she let get in the way of doing things properly.

'I tendered for the club to be the location for the anniversary bash of *Time Out* magazine and we're getting the final decision tomorrow.' Holly grinned widely, her cherry-red lip gloss parting to show white even teeth. 'This is big. Huge. If they have it here, the club will be plastered all over the internet.' She painted a picture in the air with her hands. 'We'll never have to advertise again; we'll be turning crowds away.'

'That's brilliant. Well done.' Freddie was pleased but he wasn't sure why she was bothering him with this. His staff knew that he paid them over the odds to look after the club without troubling him. He was a busy man.

Freddie made his way up the back stairs towards his office and Holly climbed up after him.

'So, the thing is, if we do win the tender, they want to do a big piece on the club itself,' she continued, pulling her long blonde hair forward over one shoulder in a subconscious gesture.

'OK, that's great. They'll bring their own photographer, I take it?' Freddie asked, wondering if it was extra budget she was after.

'Yes, they will. And that brings me to the second part.' They reached the top of the stairs. 'The interview will include a section on you as the club owner. Who you are, why you started it up, what you're into, all that sort of stuff. They'll want a picture of you to put with it as well.'

'No,' Freddie answered straight away and shook his head.

Holly bit her lip, trying – not very successfully – to hide her frustration. 'I know you don't like being in the limelight, but it's for the good of the business. It's good PR to be seen by the people you want to come in and spend money here,' Holly stressed.

'Holly, I can't have my face splashed about in *Time Out*, or all over the internet,' Freddie replied with a sigh.

'Why not?' she asked. 'Look, sometimes we have to do things we don't want to, because it's for the greater good. Like, look' – she tried to lighten the mood – 'my nail tech went on holiday and I had to go to a really crappy little salon booth in a shopping centre to have these done.' She held up her long, shiny coral nails. 'It was bad times, but it was for the greater good. No one wants to see ugly hands.' She winked and tilted her head, trying to get a laugh out of him.

Freddie forced a smile. 'I know you're just trying to do your job. I appreciate that. But the answer is no. If we win the tender, you do the interview. Or Gavin. But I don't want anything other than basic details mentioned about me. OK?' He raised his eyebrows in question.

Holly sighed loudly. She knew when she had been defeated. 'OK then, well…' She lingered for a moment, trying to think of a better argument, but she had none. 'I'll let you know if we get it anyway. Catch you later.' She waved and retreated down the stairs to rejoin the team meeting.

Freddie shook his head. It wasn't her fault; she didn't know who he was, not really. She thought he was just a club owner, a playboy who was never around to run his business. Taking the keys out of his pocket, Freddie unlocked the door to his office and stepped inside.

He shrugged off his jacket and settled in behind his desk before dialling Thea's number. She answered straight away.

'Hey, how's everything? James getting on OK?'

'Swimmingly,' Thea replied. 'He's hit the ground running. It was a good decision all round, I think. Just don't hand me any new surprises for a while, OK? Give him a chance to get to grips with what we already have.'

'Sure thing. And how are the squirrels?' he asked.

'Not seen any for a few days but that ain't to say they've gone. They might just be getting clever.'

Freddie exhaled heavily through his nose. The task force that was following them and gaining intel was very much active, but they still hadn't made any bold moves. It was putting Freddie on edge. He needed them to show their hand so that he could work out how to deal with them properly.

'OK, well, keep me updated. Speak to you later.' Freddie ended the call and rubbed his face thoughtfully. What were they planning?

CHAPTER TWENTY-SEVEN

Anna marched through the long bar in The Last Laugh and past the stage. She raised a quick hand to Drew in greeting as she passed him but didn't stop when he began talking.

'Oh hi, Anna, I was thinking— Oh, OK then. Maybe later…' He trailed off as he saw the grim look on his boss's face. He raised his eyebrows and turned back to the drink he'd been making himself before the rest of the staff arrived to open up. 'Hi, Drew,' he muttered to himself sarcastically as she disappeared into the office. 'How's it going, Drew? Have I mentioned you're the best comedian I've ever seen, Drew? Oh, thank you so much…'

Anna closed the door of the office and forced a friendly smile as she saw Tanya was already sitting behind the desk waiting for her. 'Ah, you're here already. Thanks for meeting me before opening. I just needed to talk to you about something.'

'Yeah, you know I was already coming into Club Anya tonight?' Tanya queried with a small frown.

'I know, but it just couldn't wait, and actually I need to talk to you on your own,' Anna said pointedly.

She saw Tanya register what she meant and settle in to hear what Anna had to say. She took a deep breath. 'Listen, I know she's your mum and you want to spend time with her, but she has to go from the club. This isn't working. She's trying to change all sorts of things that she knows nothing about and she's running around acting like she owns the place.' The exasperation rose in Anna's tone as she was finally able to get it off her chest. 'She's ordering Carl around like he's some sort of skivvy, and she has absolutely no respect for the way we do things.'

'Anna.' Tanya shifted in her seat irritably, a deep frown forming. 'I need her right now, and her helping at the club means I'm able to stay a lot more involved.'

'But *why* do you need her?' Anna burst. 'You have *me*. You have always had me, and I can keep you updated with everything—'

'I don't want to just be updated, Anna,' Tanya shot back. 'I'm sick of being sat at home like a fucking lemon and feeling like I'm not part of anything.'

'Of course you're part of everything!'

'No, I'm not!' Tanya shouted, snapping. 'I'm the invalid who's been in a coma for two months and now needs to sleep all the time, while you run the clubs. *Our* clubs. And that feels shit.' The two women stared at each other for a long moment and Tanya took a deep breath. She lowered her voice again. 'My mum is just doing the things I've asked her to do. I'll speak to her about checking any changes with you first, but she's staying.'

Anna swallowed hard. She wanted Rosie gone, but it wasn't worth falling out with Tanya over. She would just have to deal with it for a while. It wouldn't be forever, she reminded herself. This was a temporary arrangement until Tanya was back to full strength. She forced a conciliatory smile.

'OK. Well, I appreciate you having a word. And I really am here for you, you know. If you need anything at all.'

'What I need is for you to start accepting my mum,' Tanya replied, still annoyed.

Anna nodded.

For the first time in their entire friendship there was an awkward silence, as neither of them knew what to say.

CHAPTER TWENTY-EIGHT

Diving out of the ground-floor window into the overgrown shrubs underneath, Marco rolled and picked himself up as quickly as he could. The sound of gunfire behind him spurred him on as he ran full pelt towards the high fence surrounding the old cordoned-off warehouse. There was a hole in the fence, hidden by this bush. The police wouldn't know about it and therefore probably wouldn't have officers stationed on this back corner.

Panting from the exertion, he glanced back over his shoulder. They had been caught red-handed, right in the middle of their whole cocaine operation. He couldn't believe it had come to this. How had they found out?

Reaching the fence, he slid to the ground, dust billowing up around his feet as he scrambled to get the larger branches out of his way. He quickly pushed through the small opening. Sweat dripped down his brow and his heart thudded in fear at the thought of being caught himself.

Running into the trees, he melted out of sight of the warehouse and tried to remember exactly which direction the old dirt track was. When he set up this operation, one of the first things he'd done was make sure an escape plan was in place, just in case. He was thankful now that he'd had the sense to do that.

Marco ran and ran without stopping for what seemed an age. He developed a stitch in one side and slowed to a jog, holding his hand over the pain. There were no sounds behind him, no shouts or the barks of police dogs, so he didn't think they were following him.

Eventually Marco stopped and looked up to the skies above the dark, towering trees. He caught his breath and closed his eyes. Birds tweeted nearby and for a moment Marco envied them their simple lives. Aware that he was still in a vulnerable position, he started forward again, looking on the trees for markers.

A few minutes later he found the marks he'd carved all that time before. Counting the trees, he reached the correct one and dropped to his knees. With both his hands, he shovelled the earth and twigs and dead leaves out of the way until, under the raised roots, his hand connected with the thick strap of a dark green backpack. He yanked it out and dusted off most of the mud.

Not stopping to open it, Marco went in search of the bike. He needed to get out of these woods fast and get in touch with someone who could help him get out of this place for good. His card had been marked. He was no longer safe anywhere in this country.

*

The darkness of night had finally fallen as Freddie steered his car around the back of the remote country pub. He ignored the entrance to the car park entirely, knowing that there was likely to be CCTV. He didn't need his number plates pinging up anywhere out here. As he pulled to a stop, a figure darted out from the bushes and quickly got into the driver's seat. Freddie moved straight off again, swinging the big car out onto the narrow road.

'What happened?' Freddie asked as he drove.

Marco looked a state, his face haggard and drawn in a way Freddie had never seen before. His clothes were clean, a simple tracksuit, but his bag was filthy. He guessed correctly that this was a getaway stash. He'd never seen Marco in anything less than one of his usual flamboyant designer suits.

'We were raided. No warning, nothing out of the ordinary, just a full-on armed raid. I was lucky enough to be in the very back. Stephen ran through warning us and the rest of my men held them off. They didn't see me; I got out. But everyone else…' He dropped his head into his hands.

'Hey, everyone did what they were paid to do.' Freddie knew the guilt Marco must be feeling, but these were the risks they took in their business. And the men were paid well to protect both the business and their boss. 'You'll see them right.'

Marco nodded and sighed heavily. 'Yes, I will. But in the meantime, I need to get out of here. I need your help.'

'Where do you need to go?' Freddie asked, turning a corner onto another deserted country road.

'I need to get back to Spain, to my hometown. I have much more sway there.'

Freddie nodded in the dark. That made sense. Once they had tied the cocaine operation to Marco – and chances were that they already had – there would be no safe place here for him. His face would be on every police station wall and every TV news station.

'I can sort out a boat to get you across to Calais. It won't be comfortable; it will be a container crossing, but I don't think you'll get past the UK border even with a fake passport,' Freddie said.

'I think you're right,' Marco admitted.

'And I can arrange a fake passport for when you get to the other side, but it will take a few days. And it won't be cheap,' he added.

'I understand. Thank you, my friend. I appreciate this more than you know,' Marco replied sincerely. He was indeed grateful that Freddie was helping him. Of all his clients, the Tylers were the biggest, and the ones he liked and trusted the most. He was glad he'd made the right choice.

Freddie bit his lip as he tried to work out where to take Marco to lie low. He couldn't keep him too close – with the task force tailing them it was too risky. But Marco needed to stay somewhere for the next few days, somewhere Freddie could guarantee that anyone who saw him would be loyal to him.

The idea dawned and he set course back into central London. 'Here…' Freddie opened the glove box and pulled out a thick scarf. 'Wrap this around your bonce and cover your face. I know where we can go.'

Twenty minutes later Freddie hustled Marco through the door of Heaven Sent. It was heaving with customers, but none of them were particularly interested in looking up to see who had walked in. They were more concerned with keeping their own heads down, hoping that no one would recognise them. He hurried Marco past the reception desk and through the hallway to Linda's office at the back. The door opened and Carla began to walk out. She stopped and quickly moved out of the way when she saw her boss charging through in such a hurry.

'Freddie?' She closed the door behind the two men and turned to him in concern. 'Everything OK?'

'Yeah, well no, sort of.' Freddie scratched the back of his head, on edge. It had been a risk taking Marco here where so many cameras would have picked up their approach, but it was the best option he could think of. 'This is Marco.'

Marco had taken his scarf off and extended his hand to shake Carla's. 'Lovely to meet you,' he said politely in his melodic Spanish accent.

'And you.' Carla looked back to Freddie in question.

'I need you to keep him here, out of sight,' Freddie said, his expression serious. 'You can't tell anyone he's here, other than Linda and the girls, and they need to stay quiet too, OK?'

'Yeah, sure, anything you need, Freddie,' Carla answered, bewildered.

'He'll need to stay in one of the bedrooms, so can you get one cleaned up and move the bookings around for the next few days?'

'Days!' Carla exclaimed. 'We're booked solid.'

'Well, move the dates or cancel them,' Freddie replied. 'It should only be for a few days. Got it?'

'Got it.' Carla pursed her lips. Freddie was the boss. It was his business at the end of the day; she just helped run it.

'Marco, you'll be safe here. Carla will organise anything you need.' He glanced over to her. 'Just take it out of the till and make a note.' He turned back to Marco. 'Then I'll send word as soon as I've sorted it all out, OK?'

Marco nodded. 'OK.'

Freddie clapped his hands around the other man's arm. 'I won't come back; it's too much of a risk, so I'll bid you farewell now. It's been an honour, mate. I'm going to miss working with you.' It was the truth. Marco had been an excellent supplier and someone he and Paul both genuinely liked. 'Good luck getting home, and once you're back up and running, let me know if there's anything you need from here.'

'You're a good man, Freddie,' Marco said with feeling. There weren't many truly decent men left in the criminal underworld, not like the old days. But Freddie was one of the best.

With one last nod, Freddie turned and left the building.

As he switched on the ignition in his car, he made a strangled sound of exasperation. He hit his hands against the steering wheel twice and then pulled in a deep breath. Calming himself down, he backed out onto the busy Soho street. This was going to hit his business hard. For a long time, they had been ordering all of their cocaine through Marco. They had no reserves and a hell of a lot of orders to fill.

First the alcohol shipment and now this. Things couldn't get much worse on the supply front.

'You must really fucking hate me, big man,' Freddie called up to the heavens. He shook his head. His luck seemed to be all cashed out. Or *was* it luck? He paused his train of thought. Maybe he'd been missing the wood for the trees. Perhaps this was the information that the organised crime task force had been collating all along. But if that was the case, how exactly were they getting it? And what was going to get hit next?

CHAPTER TWENTY-NINE

Tapping her pen on the table in irritation, Anna looked over the shift patterns again. It was no good. However she looked at it, she was one showgirl short. She couldn't stretch any of the others any further than she already had; they were already filling up Chloe's spaces as much as they could. She needed to find a replacement, but every time she thought about running auditions, Freddie's words came back to her and she felt a stab of guilt.

Had she acted too harshly with the girl? It's not like she hadn't been clear on the rules here – this place was a clean, above-board club. But if she had misunderstood that there was no so-called 'room for interpretation', like in other clubs, maybe Anna should have given her the benefit of the doubt. She needed to talk things over with Tanya. Except things were still strained between the two of them, so she wasn't sure what to do.

Anna looked up from the laptop at the sound of a soft tapping on the door.

'Come in,' she called.

The door opened and Sophie popped her head round with a smile. 'Hey, how are you?' she asked sunnily.

'I've been better,' Anna answered with a roll of her eyes.

'Would that be something to do with a certain someone out there in the bar?' Sophie questioned casually but with a smile creeping up on her face.

'You've met her then?' Anna replied, pulling a face.

'Oh yes,' Sophie said with a polite but heavy laugh. 'She's a real delight.' Sophie fiddled with the sleeve of her jumper as she sat in the chair opposite Anna. 'I've just been informed that I need to spend more time training the performers, because their sets aren't tight enough.' She pulled a face to shrug it off, but Anna could see the comment had made her friend anxious.

Her blood boiled. How dare Rosie speak to Sophie that way? Rosie didn't know her or the dancing business at all. That woman was getting far too big for her boots.

'I'm really sorry, Sophie,' she said with a frustrated sigh. 'Please just ignore her. The shows are fantastic. She's an absolute menace.'

'OK. As long as you're sure.' Sophie's open expression was still slightly anxious. 'Because if there are any areas you want me to particularly work on with the girls, I can work it into the schedule. You just have to let me know. I won't take offence.'

'Honestly, there is nothing that needs doing that you aren't already doing brilliantly. I promise,' stressed Anna. 'She literally has no clue whatsoever when it comes to what we do here. I've tried to speak to Tanya about it, but—' She sighed. 'Rosie's apparently just trying to help her out and bond with her, and Tanya wants her around. So, the rest of us are just going to have to deal with it for a while.'

'I see.' Sophie shot Anna a sympathetic look. 'Well, if you need any help with anything she messes up,' she said with a laugh, 'you know where I am.'

'Thanks, Soph.' Anna gave her a warm smile. Sophie was a good friend to her and Tanya. She had been with them since the start.

'Anyway.' Sophie stood up. 'I actually have to go. I was just popping in to say hi. Only here to pick up my coat. I'm starting a new class down the road shortly so I don't want to be late.'

'Oh really? What's the class?' Anna asked.

'Fire breathing,' Sophie said with excitement. 'I see Rhonda do it in her shows all the time and it looks so cool. I fancied giving it a go.'

'Oh wow!' Anna laughed. 'I look forward to seeing you do it up on the stage.'

'Fingers crossed!' Sophie waved goodbye and left.

Anna pursed her lips. It was about time she had more words with Rosie. The woman had never worked in this sort of environment before – why did she suddenly feel that it was OK for her to put her two pence in? Standing up, she marched out to the main bar. Carl was busy changing the optics, but she couldn't see Rosie.

'Where's Rosie, Carl?' she asked.

'Oh, literally just walked out the front door.' He pointed and the door banged shut. 'She's off to her church group.'

'Right.' Anna resisted the urge to roll her eyes. 'The church group.'

As she turned to go back in the office, an idea dawned. She paused. 'Carl?'

'Yeah?'

'Can you open up tonight?'

'Sure, no problem,' he replied over his shoulder.

'Thank you.' Anna smiled grimly to herself as she ran to get her coat. Something about these church stories didn't add up and she was about to find out exactly what.

Peering around the corner at the end of the street, Anna checked to see that Rosie was still in sight. She was. It had started raining and the older woman pulled her coat collar further up her neck and sped up towards the glowing sign of the Leicester Square Tube station in the distance.

Anna blended into the busy crowd of tourists also making their way to the Tube and calculated the route in her head. If Rosie was telling the truth and she really was going to the Charterhouse then she'd need to change at Kings Cross and go over to Barbican.

Sure she was on to something, Anna clenched her jaw in determination and entered the station. She tapped her Oyster and sped through, looking around wildly for any sign of Rosie. Eventually she clocked the back of Rosie's head as it disappeared down the escalator. Anna swiftly followed, making sure to stay behind someone bigger than her at all times, so that she could hide if Rosie turned around.

Rosie didn't turn around, however, and carried on down to the platform and onto the waiting train. Anna jumped into the next carriage. She positioned herself so that she could just about see Rosie through the window and waited as the train set off to the next station.

When the doors opened again, a horde of people surged in, pushing everyone back. Anna tutted in annoyance as she was forced up against two people and body-locked in. Rush-hour commuter traffic was in full swing. She could no longer see Rosie and her heart sped up. *What if she gets off?* she panicked. *I'll lose her.* The doors closed and the train set off again.

A bump on the tracks sent everyone lurching to one side and something cold and hard touched against Anna's neck.

'No!' she cried, twisting round in fear and knocking a man flying.

His arm was wrapped around her chest like a vice as he forced her forward down the steps, one by one. The pressure of the blade against her neck was getting harder and the pain intensified as eventually the sharp metal bit through her skin. She could feel the blood dripping down her neck. He was going to do it. He was going to kill her.

Anna suddenly remembered that she was in a packed train and looked around, her eyes wide with mortification. She gasped for breath, feeling like she had no air in her lungs.

'Hey, you OK?' a middle-aged man nearby asked tentatively, concern on his face.

She looked around and saw a sea of confused faces. 'Yes, I'm sorry. I just… I'm sorry. I'm fine.'

Swallowing hard, Anna forced herself to stand still and breathe at a normal pace. She looked away, her cheeks burning red. As she had hoped he would, the man shrugged and dropped it. Anna silently thanked the unspoken rules of British engagement. Londoners were busy, introverted people when it came to interactions on public transport. No one wanted to waste their time on some crazy lady who'd had a strange outburst.

Anna spotted Rosie again at Kings Cross and sure enough she boarded the next train towards Barbican. The rest of the journey was pleasantly uneventful, and as they alighted at the other end, Anna's energy was renewed. Surely Rosie wasn't actually going to this meeting? Anna was convinced she was right and that she was close to uncovering Rosie's big secret.

They turned one corner and then cut through a small park and Anna's hopes fell as the imposing building of the Charterhouse came into view. She hung back by the entrance to the park as Rosie crossed the road and entered via the front gate. Making her way through the door into the building, she disappeared from view.

Anna turned and ran her hands through her thick dark hair. She shook her head and closed her eyes, feeling foolish. What was she doing? Why had she followed Rosie all this way like a complete stalker? Was she going mad? Perhaps she was. And in doing all this with no justified reason, she was completely undermining Tanya, her best friend in the world. This suddenly became starkly clear. Maybe Rosie wasn't the problem after all. Maybe it was her.

Feeling utterly deflated and stressed, she looked around. Noting the Malmaison just down the street, she made her way over in search of their bar. She needed a strong drink and not in her own club for once. This time she needed to be alone to gather her – clearly demented – thoughts.

CHAPTER THIRTY

Freddie locked the front door of the Portakabin at the docks and slipped the key into his inside pocket. He looked up at the stars in the clear night sky and breathed in deeply. Most people didn't appreciate the scent of the city, citing the pollution levels and moaning about the cars and the soot while they rode the Tube and created the traffic. The hypocrisy was hilarious and something Freddie could never understand. London was a great big beautiful mess of dirty history and modern promise. This incredible city that he called home was a product of both the good and the bad, the clean and the dirty. Much like himself. Perhaps this was why he loved it so much.

As Freddie began to walk down the docks towards the path that would lead him back up to the road, he realised he had stayed much later than he'd intended. It was dark, the moon being the only thing lighting up the cobbled path ahead of him. He frowned. There was usually a street light on. Freddie glanced up at the tall lamp post as he approached it, wondering why it was off. As he paused underneath, his foot stepped on something that made a sharp crunching sound. Looking down, Freddie realised it was glass, the glass from the large bulb above. Someone had knocked it out.

Too late Freddie realised his vulnerable position and tensed, all his senses on high alert. He turned around and cursed as he laid eyes on two dark figures lumbering up the path behind him. They didn't seem in much of a hurry, so Freddie calculated that they were probably just the muscle. But whose muscle?

Turning back towards the top of the path, Freddie saw two more figures walking down towards him. They had been waiting for him to leave, ready to corner him here. It was a smart move, he had to admit. There was no way out from here and no cameras. There was no phone service down here either; it was a drawback of this location that he often complained about. Freddie glanced up to the railings on the street above. It was too sheer to climb and no one could even see this stretch of path from the road. Unless he fancied his chances in the river – which he did not – he had no choice but to stand and await whatever was coming. His heart rate sped up and he took a couple of deep breaths.

The two figures behind him came to a stop a few feet away and the two in front finally got close enough for Freddie to identify them. It was Joe Luciano and Tino, which he swiftly realised meant that Big Al and Johnny Smarts must be the ones behind him.

Freddie's blood began to boil at Joe's audacity, but he kept his head. Not only were they the most dangerous men around right now, he was severely outnumbered and well cornered. They were flexing their muscles, and all Freddie could do was swallow it.

'Joe,' Freddie greeted him in a casual tone and with a polite smile. 'I wasn't expecting you down here.'

'Oh, I was counting on that,' Joe answered. His eyes glinted dangerously in the dark. 'I feel like you've been avoiding me these last few days.'

'Avoiding you?' Freddie tried to sound genuinely surprised. 'Why on earth would I do that? We're friends, aren't we?' He held Joe's gaze.

Joe smirked and stepped closer. 'Yeah, this is what I keep hearing. Yet here you are, the most powerful man in this city and you can't seem to find out a damn thing. That smells fishy to me. Don't you agree, boys?'

There was a murmur of agreement around him and Freddie exhaled slowly.

'Listen, Joe.' Freddie stepped forward to stand face to face with the Mafia boss. 'I'm as pissed off by that as you are. But all that leads me to believe is that Frank didn't go under suspicious circumstances. For all we know he could have decided to do a runner himself or drunkenly walked into the river. If there's nothing to be found then it's either something bizarrely accidental or incredibly well planned by someone not within my city limits. I mean, it's not like you haven't got enemies all over the world, let's be honest here.'

'This guy.' One of the men behind Freddie made a sound of offended disgust.

'Hey.' Freddie held his arms out. 'I'm just speaking the truth. You've got no enemies here, but there are wannabes all over the place. And you know it.' Staring intently at Joe, Freddie fought to keep his poker face. He wasn't too big to admit to himself that he was getting worried. These guys were brutal and ruthless, even by his standards. And he was cornered alone in the dark by the river. It wasn't looking great.

'Are you a wannabe, Freddie?' Joe asked, eying him with suspicion. 'Did you off Frank in some crazy attempt to become one of us, I wonder?'

'Not fucking likely, mate,' Freddie said through gritted teeth. 'I earned my own position and my own turf; I don't need to kill anyone or steal jack shit.' If Joe wasn't so heavily backed, Freddie would have happily torn him a new one for that suggestion. Freddie was a proud man; he had earned that right. Not many men would get away with saying something like that to him.

Joe's eyes flickered up for a moment and the next thing Freddie knew, the two men behind him had pulled his arms back and lifted him so that he was barely touching the floor.

'What the fuck do you think you're doing?' he demanded, trying to fight his way out of their grip. It was no use however. Either of them on their own was fairly evenly matched against him but there were two of them. 'Get off me!'

They dragged Freddie to the water's edge and hung him over it. This forced Freddie to stop struggling in case he was dropped, and he seethed with anger, breathing heavily through his tightly clamped teeth. Joe wandered over and stood next to him, looking down into the black depths of the Thames.

'I hear if you fall in around here the weeds at the bottom wrap themselves around your legs and pull you down. So easy to drown, even for the strongest swimmer,' he said.

Freddie continued to breathe heavily through his nose but kept his mouth shut. His position was more than a little precarious and he'd learned many years before that at certain times it was better to wait and listen than to fight your corner with all guns blazing. He needed to know what he was up against before he could attempt to regain control of the situation.

'Personally, I'd still make sure they were wearing their concrete boots before they went down. Do you do that around here?' Joe asked, as though they were engaged in nothing more than polite conversation. He shook his head when Freddie didn't respond. 'I mean, I could fit you a pair right now, drop you over this edge and no one would ever find you. Well, other than the fishes. They like a good feast. But no, your friends and family, the cops, they could be right here discussing your case and never know that you were just a few feet away. Isn't that crazy?'

Leaning into Freddie's ear, Joe whispered quietly, 'Between you and me, the Hudson is full of my old friends. That's where they go, back home, when we find out they aren't such good friends after all.' He straightened up and nodded to the men holding Freddie. They pulled him back and stood him straight.

Freddie ripped his arms back from them as they loosened their grip and turned on them with a low growl of anger.

'But of course, it's not often we have to do that. Most of our friends are just that – friends. Like you.' He glanced back at the river and gestured towards it. 'You should make more use of this outlet, if you haven't already.'

Freddie made a tight fist with each of his hands, itching to let his anger fly. But he kept it contained. His expression was icy as he glared at Joe. 'We treat our friends with respect here,' he said coldly. 'And we expect the same in return. There's no need to threaten me, Joe. I'm not exactly hiding.'

'Of course,' Joe said with a sly smile. 'And we wouldn't dream of threatening you, Freddie. I merely wanted to share a good burial tip with you. And to touch base, remind you we're still here. I look forward to you getting us some information soon.'

Joe clicked his fingers and his men walked away, back up the path towards the road without a further word. 'I'll be seeing ya,' he said. He nodded and turned away himself.

Freddie waited until they were out of sight before he turned and punched the nearest crate with all his frustrated might.

CHAPTER THIRTY-ONE

The next morning Freddie took one last deep drag on his cigarette and flicked it away. He'd barely slept, both Anna's nightmares and his fury and frustration at Joe's threats keeping him up. Life was getting very dark on all fronts.

Reaching the front door of the greasy caff, he opened it and made a beeline for Sammy and Paul, who were already there waiting. Mentally he filed the stress of the Mafia and Anna away to worry about later. Right now, he had other problems that needed addressing. Paul signalled to the waitress behind the counter and she came over as Freddie sat down.

'What can I get you?' she asked, pulling the little notebook out of her apron pocket.

'Three teas, love,' Paul replied. He frowned. Dark circles ringed Freddie's eyes and he seemed irate.

'Coming up.' She bustled off to get their order.

'So, what's up?' Sammy asked once they were alone.

Freddie's expression was grim. 'I think we might have a leak. The raid on the shipment, that was unexpected, and Damien seems to think they knew exactly where to look.'

'That could have just been luck,' Sammy offered.

'Which is what I initially thought too,' Freddie replied. 'But yesterday our cocaine supplier was raided. Armed response, the lot. There had been no signs, nothing out of the ordinary.' Freddie pulled a face. 'A bit coincidental don't you think?'

'How would they have got that information though? It's not like we give out the details to many people, and none of ours would nark,' Paul said, shifting his weight in his chair.

'That's what I can't work out. But both of our biggest supply chains hit in such a short space of time? It's too precise to be an accident.' He sat back in his chair.

They were silent for a few minutes, each lost in their own thoughts. The waitress came back with their teas.

'Here you go, guys. Let me know if you need anything else.'

'Thanks,' Paul muttered absently. 'What do you want to do then, Fred? Got any ideas?'

'At this point the only thing we can do…' Freddie paused, loathe to continue. He trusted his men; they had more than earned it over the years. To start testing that trust again now went against the grain, but it was the only logical move to make. 'I don't like it one bit, but I think the first thing we need to do is pull everyone from the inner circle together, everyone in the know, and lay a trap. A test.'

Paul made a sound of dislike and shook his head, and Sammy pursed his lips with a frown.

'I don't like it either, but have you got any better ideas?' Freddie glanced from one to the other. 'The three of us grew up together from kids. The only thing I'm sure of right now is that it ain't going to be one of us.'

'Well, who could it be then, Fred? Bill? Dean?' Paul exclaimed. 'Come on, all our guys are loyal to the bone – you know that.'

'I do know that. But this information is coming from somewhere and we have to check ourselves. It's not personal; it's business,' Freddie stressed.

Eventually Paul nodded, seeing the sense behind his brother's words.

Sammy blew out a long breath. 'You're the boss, Fred. But I hope for their sakes they don't ever find out about this test, whatever it will be. It would crush any one of them to think you doubt them.'

'I know, and that's why it's going to stay between us,' Freddie replied. He took a deep drink from the hot tea. Even suggesting this lay on his conscience like a heavy weight of deceit.

'Paul, I want you to get the core crew to meet me tonight at CoCo. All of them. Tell them I have a big job on the cards.' He took another sip of his tea and stared at his brother intently. 'Tonight we're going to set the cheese in the rat trap. And then we'll know for sure whether or not we really can trust our own men.'

*

'Hey, I was hoping you'd be in today. How are you feeling?' Anna gave Tanya a warm smile as she set down her handbag on the desk.

'I'm fine. Honestly, I'm looking forward to the point when that stops being the first thing people ask me,' Tanya said with a laugh.

'Oh, sorry.' Anna held her hands up in surrender.

'Nah, don't be. It's natural. I'd still be asking too if it was the other way round.' Tanya grinned. 'How have you been anyway? Feel like we haven't properly caught up in ages.'

We haven't. Your mother sees to that, Anna thought wryly. This wasn't something she could voice though, unless she wanted to rile Tanya up again. 'Yeah, I know what you mean,' she said brightly. 'I'm OK. Just been really busy. Actually, I wanted to talk to you about something...'

Anna relayed the story about how she had found Chloe and their subsequent conversation.

'You?' asked Tanya, her tone incredulous. 'You slapped someone around the face?' She put her hand over her mouth as she guffawed. 'That's hilarious.'

'Really?' Anna raised her eyebrows. 'That's what you just got from this story?'

'Oh come on, put yourself in my position.' Tanya was still laughing. 'I don't think you've ever even swatted a fly before and suddenly you've full-on smacked a bitch. You'd be laughing too, if you were me right now.'

Despite herself, Anna couldn't help the grin that forced its way onto her face. It did seem a little funny when she looked at it from Tanya's point of view.

'Well, look…' She tried to take the conversation back to a serious level. 'After what she said about you, I just saw red. And then I fired her.'

'Oh.' Tanya's tone sobered.

'And Freddie seemed to think I was a bit hasty.'

Tanya swayed her head from side to side as she weighed it up. 'I know why you did it. But these girls…' She twisted her mouth as she decided how to word it. 'The clubs they've worked in before – the ones that *I* worked in before, they were very different. And the line is hazy. The bosses tell you one thing to cover their backs, but they expect another. And a club like ours is pretty rare. It's the white rhino of clubs. Rather than the Spearmint Rhino, if you get my drift.' She chuckled at her own joke.

Anna smirked. 'Maybe that's what we should have called it.'

'Look, I'm not being rude, but you can't understand how things are for them. You've never been there. It's not an easy decision to start doing all that but it just becomes a way of life. The norm.'

'Well, that doesn't make it OK, Tan,' Anna objected. 'And she has no right being so disrespectful about you either. You're her boss.'

Tanya shook her head. 'I don't love the reminder, but I'm actually not offended by her bringing up my past.' She shrugged. 'It's true. I was on the circuit, and she was only trying to explain why she thought the rules were up for interpretation.'

Anna sighed and bit her lip. Tanya disagreed with her too. That was both her business partner and her boyfriend, the two people whose opinions she valued the most.

'What do you suggest then? Because I'm not having it here; this club can't go downhill and get a rep for being seedy,' Anna said, folding her arms. 'But perhaps I could talk to Chloe,' she added grudgingly. 'We could do with bringing her back, to be honest.'

'I think that would be a good start,' Tanya replied frankly. 'But this is going to keep happening, unless we work out a better arrangement.'

'What do you mean?' Anna asked, curious.

'Well...' Tanya thought about it. She studied Anna, not sure whether she was going to be open to hearing her idea. 'We can stop it happening onsite, but some of them are going to find a way to do it somewhere.' She studied one of her long, shiny red nails casually. 'What if we came to some arrangement and found suitable premises nearby where – after their shifts, of course – they could take their client, if they had discreetly arranged something? Somewhere safe and clean that we control, but that has no ties to the club, making sure that the clubs reputation stays intact.'

'Are you serious? You want us to be their pimps?' Anna frowned deeply and she began to pace the room.

'Well, you work with what you have, Anna. When life hands you lemons...'

'You make pimp lemonade? Is that what you're trying to tell me?'

Tanya relaxed back in her chair and waited for Anna to process the idea. She knew it wasn't one her friend was going to like, but the opportunity was there begging to be taken, and if they didn't do it, it would just end up serving to line someone else's pockets.

Anna's mind raced. She couldn't believe what Tanya was suggesting. But then again, a large part of her brain kept annoyingly insisting that she had a point. She thought back to the night she found Chloe in the side alley. It was dirty and cold out there and not safe in the slightest. What if the guy had been a psycho? Lord knows there were enough of them around. Anna shivered as the faces of Michael and Tony flashed through her mind.

If she was to consider this, at least they could keep it away from the club and the girls would be a lot safer. The whole thing could be regulated. She began to tip towards agreeing but then an alarm bell rang in her head.

This was illegal! They could both end up in jail if they were caught. But then again, Freddie had never been caught and neither had Tanya back in her days on the scene. It was known to be a rife industry in Soho; the police were hardly going to suddenly knock down the door.

Anna rubbed her forehead as she paced. A few months ago, she wouldn't even be considering this. She'd have told Tanya no, straight away. But things had changed recently. *She* had changed. After everything that had happened, something had shifted inside of her. The darkness that had become a part of who she was during her difficult past had grown and overtaken her insides, like some sort of cancer. She felt it every day now, hard and cold, locked inside her chest. When she gazed into the mirror, there was a new, haunted look behind her eyes that she realised was a mirror of Freddie's. Now that she recognised it, she realised it had always been there in him. The mark of someone who had crossed that last line into the void of the underworld's horrors. And somehow it changed the way she looked at everything now. The thought of opening up this house that Tanya was suggesting no longer seemed like such a shocking and horrendous idea. It was just good business sense. There were worse things in the world…

Slowly, Anna nodded. 'OK,' she said. 'I think that may be the best plan.'

'What?' Tanya sat up sharply. 'Really?' She hadn't genuinely been expecting Anna to agree to it, but she'd thought it worth a try. 'Er, OK then.' Tanya blinked, still shocked and opened up the laptop in front of her. 'I'll start looking at what's up for rent.'

'Let me know what you find,' Anna replied. 'I need to get off to The Last Laugh. Have you got those rotas?'

'Yeah, they're on the printer.' Tanya pointed towards them.

'Thanks. Listen, what do you think about making Drew assistant manager officially? He helped out a lot while you were in hospital. He did a good job too. And living upstairs, he keeps an eye on the place.'

Tanya considered it. 'Yeah, go on then. He's a good egg, that one.'

'He is. I'll catch up with you later then.' Anna leaned over to kiss Tanya on the cheek, then left to get over to the other club.

Tapping away on the keyboard, Tanya began her search for the property for their next venture. The Last Laugh was a weight around her neck and she regretted stepping out of her comfort zone and opening something that she had so little interest in. This, however, she could get excited about. This was going to be a *lot* of fun.

CHAPTER THIRTY-TWO

Freddie looked around his office at the group of men who had gathered. Bill and Sammy sat together to one side, along with Seamus. Paul stood against the wall near Dean, Reggie and Simon. Freddie had a lot of men on his payroll, but these were the core few who knew about and oversaw all of the Tyler operations. It was with a heavy heart that he sat there about to set them all up for a possible fall. But it had to be done. He prayed that he was wrong and that this would all come to nothing.

'Glad you could all make it,' he said brusquely. Picking up his packet of cigarettes from the desk, Freddie lit one and took a deep drag before going any further. 'Paul and I have been planning a big job that's likely going to take all of us to pull off.' He exhaled, blowing a long plume of smoke into the air. 'There's an antiques dealer in an old church off Leonard Street.'

'That's Old Street way, right?' Reggie piped up.

'It is indeed,' Freddie answered. 'It's called Westland London.' He exchanged a look with Paul across the room. 'They're getting a delivery over the next few days from someone who's trying to bring a shit ton of cocaine into London. The coke will be hidden within some sort of antique object. I'm not sure what this will be exactly or what name it will come in under, but whatever it is, it'll be sold through auction on Saturday. It will then be taken on to be broken down and the cocaine extracted. Now' – Freddie flicked his ash in the crystal ashtray on his desk – 'the first problem we have is that this is obviously taking the absolute piss. The cocaine business along the central belt has never been a free for all – there are rules. The second problem we have at the moment is that we are currently out of stock ourselves, due to recent unforeseen circumstances. So what we're going to do is this.'

Freddie rolled out a map of Greater London and everyone leaned forward to have a look. 'We're going to steal it late Friday night before the auction and use the product ourselves. Two birds with one stone. Here is the church and here are all the cameras in the streets surrounding it.' He pointed to the red dots that he'd drawn on earlier to indicate the right spots. 'Now, we can't escape the ANPRs; it's just impossible, so I've come up with a solution.'

All eyes and ears were on him and Freddie felt the weight of what he was doing bear down on him. Was this the last time he was going to be able to truly trust his men? Was one of them disloyal? Had they sold out? Family and loyalty meant everything to him. If this was the case, he'd have to dole out maximum retribution, but he couldn't bear to think about it.

'Paul, Sammy and I are going to pull the heist alone onsite using a van with fake plates. We'll break in and load up, then drive out west, to here.' Freddie used a pen to show them where he meant. 'This spot is blind for a stretch, meaning we can get another van in there to move the goods over. Bill, you and Seamus will be waiting for us with that second van. When that's swapped, Paul, Sammy and I will drive on in this direction' – he followed the road with the pen – 'ditch the van here and scarper. You'll drive the goods on up here' – he moved it back again – 'to this point, where Dean, Reggie and Simon will be waiting with the third van and you'll repeat the process. Bill, you dump the van here then you and Seamus get off the map and back home. Dean, you three will take the goods out to the Fairfield barn. Do you remember that place?'

'Yeah, sure do,' Dean answered.

'Good. You leave the third van and all the goods there and get back into town. We'll let the dust settle for a few days and then start circulating,' Freddie finished.

'Nice.' Dean high-fived Simon with a broad grin. 'Our dealers have been getting itchy already. We were due that last load before Marco got hit. I tell you, I'm glad we've got some product coming.'

'Yeah, well' – Freddie stubbed the dying end of his cigarette out – 'don't promise them anything yet. Just in case this doesn't pan out. It's their first try; they might get cold feet or change the date or something.'

Bill frowned. 'How are you going to be able to tell which shipment it is? You can't take their whole inventory.'

'They have a log of when things came in. I'm going to take everything that comes in over the next few days, to be sure.' Freddie busied himself rolling the map back up. He hated lying to his men, especially Bill. They were such close friends. But he couldn't rule anyone out at this stage other than his brother and Sammy.

'OK.' Bill frowned and narrowed his eyes as he studied Freddie.

'Go on then, get on with your nights. I'm sure you've all got better things to do than hang around here.'

Freddie watched as they filed out one by one, all calling goodbyes to their boss.

He looked up to see that Bill was still lingering. 'Alright, mate?' he asked.

'Yeah,' Bill replied in a suspicious tone. 'Are you?'

''Course.'

Bill frowned and pursed his lips. 'You sure, Fred? Because you just don't seem yourself tonight. Is there something going on?'

Freddie groaned internally and the guilt he felt intensified. Bill was sharp; another lie wasn't going to throw him off. He sighed.

'Look, I've got a lot on my plate at the moment. Anna's still not coping with things as well as I'd hoped.' This was the truth, even if it wasn't actually related to this situation. 'Honestly, I don't know if she'll ever get back to how she was before. And that's worrying me more than I can tell you. Because you know as well as I do that she was something truly special. And that ain't to say she isn't still; of course she is. But she's lost that spark of hers.' A feeling of unbridled sadness stabbed Freddie through the heart as he voiced how he really felt for the first time. 'And I just can't imagine a world where she never finds that again.'

Bill nodded sombrely. He felt for Freddie. He couldn't imagine how helpless he'd feel if it was his Amy who'd gone through what Anna had.

'She'll find her way back, Fred. Sometimes it just takes a bit more time. Old hands like me and you' – he pulled a face and shook his head – 'well, we forget what it's like the first time you turn out someone's lights. And she had a lot of other bad things happen that day too.' Bill purposely didn't mention her miscarriage. Everyone knew it was a raw subject for Freddie.

Freddie sniffed and cleared his throat, suddenly embarrassed to be talking about things so deeply. He had only meant to throw Bill off, not treat him like an agony aunt from the local paper. 'Yeah, yeah,' he said, his tone brisk. 'I know.' He smiled tightly. 'She'll get there.'

Bill took the hint and picked up his jacket. 'Let me know when you have any more details. Oh, and that Zack kid—' Freddie had placed Zack under Bill's management for the time being. 'He's actually shaping up quite well.' He tilted his head. 'He'll definitely open up some doors on new jobs.'

'Good to hear. 'Night, Bill.'

Freddie waited until the door had closed behind him, then slumped back in his chair and rubbed his temples. He reached for the cut-crystal whisky decanter on the desk and poured himself a generous measure.

For better or worse, the trap had been laid. Now all Freddie had to do was wait to see if someone would fall into it.

CHAPTER THIRTY-THREE

Rosie tilted her head to listen and heard the sound of the shower turning on. Checking that the bathroom door was shut, she tiptoed through to Tanya's bedroom. Princess was sprawled out at the end of Tanya's bed and gave a low growl of annoyance at the intrusion. Rosie narrowed her eyes at the fluffy white feline.

''Orrible little thing,' she muttered under her breath.

Princess turned back to her grooming and Rosie walked past her to the large built-in wardrobe at the other side of the room. She slid the door open and ran her fingers across the array of coats inside. She had been borrowing Tanya's clothes to wear to the club every day and was enjoying every second of looking so good. She hated putting on her old shabby coat over the top though. It was about time that daughter of hers let her go through these too. She did owe her after all. Rosie was her mother, the one who'd brought her into this world and suffered the strain of having to bring her up. Tanya owed her everything.

Rosie thought back to her memories of Tanya as a child and her lip curled in disgust. She had hated the little brat from the second she had been dragged from her body, screaming and crying for attention, her little face red and blotchy. The crying hadn't stopped; she'd been the most difficult baby Rosie had ever had. Tanya's brothers had not been such a problem, years before. As Tanya had grown, she was always moving, always making noise. She was the devil's child right from the off.

Rosie's useless husband had adored that little girl however, which just increased her hatred towards her even more. Her husband didn't have any love left for his wife by then, always cheating and leaving her alone. And it was all Tanya's fault. All those years of hardship and loneliness, the reason she'd ended up turning to drink – it was all the fault of that red-haired little bitch.

Rosie felt the bitterness rise up inside of her again and she pushed it down. She breathed through her nose slowly and closed her eyes. It would do her no good to rile herself up. There was a time and place for those feelings and this wasn't either. She brought her thoughts back to the present and looked back into the wardrobe.

Pulling a long fitted black coat from its hanger, she tried it on. Turning in the full-length mirror to see from all angles, a wide smile spread across her face.

Tanya padded into the room, a towel around her body and wet straggly hair around her shoulders. 'Oh, hey. That looks nice on you,' she said kindly. 'You want to wear it?'

So eager to please, the voice in Rosie's head spat sarcastically. *As she bloody well should be.* 'If you don't mind, love.' Her casual tone did not betray the bitter thoughts. 'Only if it doesn't put you out.'

'Not at all,' Tanya replied picking up a second towel from the ottoman to dry her hair with. 'Knock yourself out.'

'Thanks.' Rosie smiled sweetly and turned back to the mirror, her green eyes greedily drinking in her smart, sophisticated reflection. She nodded. *Yes,* she thought. *The coat would do very nicely indeed.*

*

Anna stared up at the block of council flats just off Finchley Road and wondered again at how peculiar London was. Not a stone's throw away were houses worth millions of pounds and these tired, ugly buildings stood right next door. The pale bricks were filthy from years of soot and rain where they hadn't been cleaned and the white paint around the door and window frames were peeling away.

Peering at the sign, she carried on walking down to the next identical block. Elm House, that was the one she was looking for. Pushing the main entrance door, Anna found it to be already open. She took a deep breath and walked in, sidestepping the muddy boots that were flung outside the first front door and the bike missing a wheel by the bottom of the stairs.

Climbing the stairs, Anna rapped on the door of the flat she'd been looking for and waited. She could hear *Jeremy Kyle* blaring away in the background somewhere within. It took a couple of minutes before her knock was answered and Anna straightened up, waiting to see what sort of reception she'd get.

With stained, faded tracksuit bottoms and a vest top on, Chloe clearly hadn't been expecting any visitors. Her brunette to blonde ombre hair that always looked so fabulous up on stage was scraped up into a dull, untidy bun and there were dark circles under her eyes. Her expression quickly turned from surprise to hostility.

'What the hell do you want?' she asked, folding her arms.

'Can I come in?' Anna asked.

'Why?'

'Because I'd like to talk to you.' There was a long silence. Anna realised she was going to have to do better than that. 'I also want to apologise to you. Not that it was OK to be doing that at the club,' she quickly added, 'but I shouldn't have reacted quite the way I did. Can I please come in and talk to you for a minute?'

Chloe considered it and then stepped aside, grudgingly nodding for Anna to pass her.

'Thank you,' Anna said, walking in.

Chloe shut the door behind them and Anna looked around. It was a small space, everything cramped up closely together in the tiny flat. Two small children sat playing with their toys in front of the TV.

On the table, there was a still-steaming cup of coffee next to the job paper and a pen. Chloe quickly closed the paper and shoved it under the table onto one of the chairs.

'Want one?' she gestured towards the cup.

Anna shook her head. 'No, thank you. I can't stay long.'

'OK, well, go on then.' Chloe sat at the table and picked up her coffee, waiting to hear whatever Anna had to say.

Anna sat opposite her and clasped her hands together on the table. 'I'm sorry for chucking you out. That was unfair. I was just shocked. Whatever you might have assumed, we really meant it when we said that there was to be no side action. We aren't that kind of club. But that being said, this whole incident has made Tanya and I think about things.'

'Oh?' Chloe questioned, her expression interested.

'You were right about Tanya; she did used to be on the scene. And because of that she understands the need that a lot of you have to supplement your income.'

'Yeah.' Chloe put her coffee down and nodded towards her children. 'Those two need things all the time. And childcare is expensive. And when you're single and working, you don't get no help. This place' – she gave a short humourless laugh – 'it's a shithole. But it's the only thing I can afford as a private renter. I'm not stupid; I don't have any fancy hopes of moving somewhere nice. I can't afford that on my own in London whatever I do. But I do want to be able to afford the things my kids want. Football boots, dance lessons, toys that come from an actual toy shop. And those things don't come from my official salary. Not once the tax man and the landlord have had their share. So yeah, I do need to supplement it. And I'm not the only one.'

Anna nodded. 'I can see that now. And that's why Tanya and I have come up with a solution that should suit everyone.'

'I'm listening.'

Jeremy Kyle was still on and an angry wife started attacking a cheating husband. Chloe picked up the remote and muted it.

'We're opening up a house nearby. Somewhere that the girls can work shifts in – around or after their other shifts, of course. Anyone who wants to pay for personal services can book in to see their girl there. It's somewhere safe and comfortable, and it's away from the club entirely.'

'So what's the catch?' Chloe asked.

'The catch is that this is all structured. There will be set prices, fair rotas for those who want to be involved and we would take fifty per cent of the proceeds.' Anna sat back and waited to see what Chloe thought of it.

Chloe considered it. Fifty per cent was a lot but it was about right. That was what most pimps took, though most pimps were complete assholes and made you do the deed in crappy, horrible places. She'd had one in the past and had eventually walked away as he'd done nothing for her. Anna, however, was promising an actual house, somewhere that would be run properly. No more freezing outside with gravel cutting up your knees, worrying that this punter might be the one who kills you. That seemed like a pretty fair deal.

'That all sounds great. The girls are lucky,' she said with a sad smile.

'I want you to come back to work,' Anna replied frankly. 'If you want to, that is.'

Chloe's face flooded with relief and the deep frown of worry that had been set in her forehead since Anna arrived suddenly disappeared. 'Oh, thank God, I was about to apply to McDonald's.'

They both laughed and Anna was glad she had listened to Tanya and Freddie. She might not love the situation, but it was how things were, and Chloe was a good dancer. They needed her.

'Now that's settled, I'll see you tomorrow night. You're on at eight.' Anna stood up and waved goodbye to the children playing quietly on the floor. A pang of grief shot through her and she pulled in a sharp breath. Swallowing, Anna forced the thoughts away. She didn't have time for all of that. Right now, she had a whorehouse to open and that would take a lot of planning.

Her next port of call was to tell Freddie. Or did she have to ask him? It was his turf after all. She shivered in partial excitement and partial dread as she wondered what his reaction would be. She was looking forward to her first step into the underworld. But what was Freddie going to make of it?

CHAPTER THIRTY-FOUR

Freddie sipped at the cup of tea the lady of the house had kindly brought through and smiled at her politely. 'Lovely cuppa, thank you.'

Pleased, she nodded with a smile and scurried back out of the room. She didn't speak much English, just enough to get by. His friend Nigel had met her over in Thailand on a holiday, years before, and had brought her back to England and married her within six months.

Freddie knew Nigel from school. They had always got on as kids and occasionally caught up over a beer still. His father had run a newsagent's and owned the flat above it. When he reached retirement age, he had moved to a villa in Spain and handed everything over to Nigel. This was where Freddie was now, sitting in the lounge of the flat above the high-street shop. It overlooked Westland London, the old church with the antiques where they were supposedly pulling the big job later that night.

He'd been seated at the window, behind the thin organza curtain which ensured him a good view without being seen for just over an hour. It was still a few hours until he was supposed to arrive with Paul and Sammy to take the goods, but Freddie knew that if the police had been tipped off, they would position themselves early. He wanted to be here to see them arrive, if they were going to. The rest of the men had their instructions and were set to be at the points Freddie had stated. He would cancel them all at the last minute, once he knew for certain either way.

Freddie looked down once more at the goings-on below. The busy street was teeming with life. A small smile crept onto his face as he watched the people going about their days. He loved London with a deep passion. It was his home, but more than that, it was filled with an energy that seemed to burst from every seam. There was nowhere else in the world he would rather be.

As he watched a young mother pull a hat onto a protesting toddler, the glint of blue and yellow on white caught the corner of his eye. His heart thumped in his chest, so hard that he thought it might burst out. He followed the police car's journey, his gaze intense. When it didn't stop outside the front he heaved a huge sigh of relief. He sent silent thanks up to the heavens.

Freddie's relief was short-lived however, as the car slowed down to a brief stop a little further down the road. The passenger doors opened and three armed officers stepped out. The three officers hurried in through the church doors and disappeared.

As that door closed, another car arrived and dropped a second lot of armed officers off. The third car was unmarked and parked further down the street, the plain clothes detectives inside watching from afar. They were subtle, but not so subtle that Freddie didn't spot them from his lofty vantage point. He tried to get a look at them, but he was too high up; the angle of the room obstructed his view.

His heart sank like a lump of lead. Closing his eyes, he leaned forward and rested his head in his hands. He couldn't believe it. They hadn't told another soul of this plan, only those few men, his most trusted men of all. Which meant that one of them had turned informant.

Freddie blinked rapidly to dispel the mist of grief and disappointment that was clouding over his eyes. Most of those men had been with him from pretty much the beginning. They had been through everything together, built up the empire that they now ran and benefited from under Freddie's rule. And now one of them had betrayed him; had betrayed them all.

Picking up his phone wearily, Freddie sent out a blanket text.

Job's off. Disband.

Slipping it back into his pocket Freddie thought about his next move. This was something he had never in a million years thought could happen. It shocked and saddened him to the core. He felt as though he'd been punched in the gut. Taking a deep breath, he made a difficult decision.

They had discovered the presence of a rat. Now they had to find out just who of his oldest and closest friends it actually was. And it was time to bring in someone who could do exactly that.

CHAPTER THIRTY-FIVE

Tino, Johnny and Al walked behind their boss as he made his way through Hyde Park. The three men were tense and glanced at each other from time to time. They were not there to take a leisurely stroll; one of the other bosses had landed and everyone around them was angry right now. The disappearance of Frank Gambino was an outrage to say the least, and although Joe had been trying to keep a lid on things until he knew more, time had gone on long enough and now the news was spreading.

Vito Lucchese had arrived with a handful of men to help out and he was not well known for his patience. Although a dangerous man in his own right, Joe Luciano was logical. If a goal could be reached without issue or injury then he would always try that route first. Vito was clever but hot-headed and cared little for any destruction that he left in his wake. Both Tino and Al had been witness to him losing the plot on more than one occasion, and Johnny had heard the tales. He was a loose cannon, though none of them would ever dare to voice this.

Joe pulled the collar of his long woollen coat up around his neck as he marched ahead of his men. The wind was picking up and dead leaves swirled around his feet. The moody grey skies seemed to mirror his own emotions as he walked towards the place he'd told Vito to meet.

As Joe approached the bench he could see Vito already seated, a grim expression on his hard-weathered face. Vito's men loitered nearby, smoking and watching for any intrusion. They nodded in respect as Joe reached the bench. He sat down next to Vito.

'Welcome, Vito,' Joe greeted him. 'I hope the journey was not too stressful.'

'Not at all, my friend. It is the dire situation we find our comrade in which is stressful,' Vito answered. He spoke quietly, yet his deep nasal voice seemed to hold a natural authority.

'Indeed,' Joe agreed, nodding.

They stared out over the park and Joe studied a young man holding a newspaper as he took a seat further down the long, wide path.

'He's following you?' Vito asked, following Joe's gaze.

'He's one of them. They're tame enough. They watch from a distance, keeping tabs. From what I understand from our contacts that's all they're there to do. We get flagged up at the airports.'

'Huh,' Vito grunted. 'Maybe we need to look into alternative means of travel.'

'Perhaps.' Joe waited as a couple strolled by. 'So what are you here for, Vito?'

'I'm here to help you find the sick fucks who took Frank.' He paused to light a cigarette. 'I think we can safely assume at this point that he's dead. If he was taken two months ago here and we've had no ransom, no blackmail, and they've tried to pretend he was alive and well in South America, well…' He shrugged and shook his head. 'They ain't after our money.'

'I agree, but I don't know how much you can do out here. I've been talking to everyone I can, looked into hospitals, mortuaries – Christ, I've even gone round the patients with amnesia. But I've found nothing. The police who were tailing him, their files just say that he disappeared. I talked to his casino managers, his business contacts – there's not been a whisper. He had no enemies here; there was no one who could benefit from his death.'

'You're wrong,' Vito cut in sharply. 'Someone *did* benefit from his death, otherwise he would still be here. There's foul play in the air, Joe, and we need to find out where and who and why.' Taking a deep drag on his cigarette, Vito glanced at Joe sideways. 'The talk has been that you aren't looking hard enough. The families are questioning your abilities. That's why I'm here.'

'What?' Joe growled. His face clouded over with thunder. 'You have no idea how hard we've been looking, the pressure we've put on.'

'Hey, I'm not saying that's me.' Vito held his hands up in surrender. 'Don't shoot the messenger. I'm just telling you how it is. But maybe together we can make some headway. Put this all to rest.'

Joe narrowed his eyes. 'I want to get the son of a bitch who took Frank as much as you do. But he's a ghost.'

'Yeah, well.' Vito flicked the cigarette away. 'Even ghosts leave trails, Joe. So you and me, we gotta get ourselves on a ghost hunt. And when we find that son of a bitch, we need to leave a trail of bloodbaths so bad that London will remember it for years to come. Because no one messes with one of ours and gets away with it. Not now, not ever.' His lip curled into an ugly sneer. 'We need to step things up a notch, starting now, and remind these British bastards exactly who they're dealing with.'

CHAPTER THIRTY-SIX

Freddie drove down the tired-looking high street of Potters Bar and turned off after spotting a sign for parking. As he manoeuvred, another car passed him and the driver did a double take. It was a split second and Freddie didn't have time to register exactly who it was, but he guessed it was one of Cos's men. He wondered if Cos knew he was here yet.

Cos was an old friend and head of one of the Greek firms that ran North London. Technically Potters Bar was outside of London, a stone's throw from the M25, but the turf still fell under his jurisdiction. He made a mental note to pop in on his old friend out of courtesy before heading back into the city.

Leaving the car, he walked back out onto the main street and down the road until he reached a door with a sign in the small dirty window that read 'London Central Private Investigations'. Opening this, Freddie stepped off the street into a small hallway which immediately gave way to a steep set of stairs. He climbed them and knocked on the only door at the top.

'Come in,' a curt voice commanded.

Freddie walked in and smiled coldly at the woman sat behind the desk in front of him.

'Hello, Sarah. Long time no see.'

*

Anna narrowed her eyes hatefully. Rosie had been causing all sorts of trouble again in the club and according to the phone call she was currently on with Drew, had been attempting to do the same at The Last Laugh.

'She tried moving the stock around, telling the barmaids they weren't organised enough. I had no idea who she even was. Well, actually I thought it was a creepy version of Tanya to begin with. I pinched myself. Thought I'd fallen through some sort of time warp or something and woken up a few decades in the future.'

'So what happened then?' Anna gently steered him back towards the point.

'Well, once I'd established that this wasn't the case and that she also wasn't Tanya's older, evil twin, I told her to get the hell out of my bar. Honestly, it was a real Peggy Mitchell moment. I felt fabulously empowered.'

Anna rolled her eyes and waited for Drew to continue. Usually she found his banter amusing, but not today – not when it was about Rosie. There was nothing she found funny about that woman; she was like a poisonous thorn that was lodged in her side.

'She tried to argue with me but I wasn't having any of it. Jokes aside, I can't have her at The Last Laugh, Anna. She's upsetting everyone and it's not for the greater good.'

'No, I understand completely, Drew, I do. I'll talk to Tanya. Don't worry about it. Just get back to sorting the bar out for tonight.'

'Thanks.' The relief in Drew's voice was palpable.

Anna ended the call and rubbed her eyes with a groan. Her last conversation with Tanya about Rosie hadn't gone well, so she wasn't looking forward to bringing this up. It was a tense time. She and Tanya had been through hell and back together on more than one occasion, but nothing had ever threatened the bond between them before. Tanya used to joke that it was so strong they could give No More Nails a run for its money. But Rosie's interference had shifted things and now matters were not so simple.

Whether she liked it or not though, Tanya was going to have to listen this time. She had to compromise somewhere and if that meant stopping Rosie from trying to stick her oar into The Last Laugh, then she was just going to have to lump it. Tanya couldn't have it all ways.

Hearing a noise in the empty club beyond her office walls, Anna stood up. Hopefully that was Tanya and she could talk to her about it now, get it over with. Opening the door, she paused as she caught sight of Rosie stepping around the end of the bar. She wasn't sure what made her stay and watch rather than revealing herself, but she did. Silently pushing the door almost shut, she watched through the crack.

Rosie glanced back towards the closed front entrance and tilted her head as if listening. Anna held her breath. Quickly – so quickly that for a second Anna wasn't sure if she had just imagined it – Rosie pulled up a bottle of gin from under the bar and took a big swig from the open top. Her hands went back down below the bar again and Anna could no longer see them. She blinked and her jaw dropped in horror. Flinging the door open, she marched through.

'I knew it!' she cried. 'You're no recovered addict; you're still drinking!'

Rosie jumped and clasped her hand to her chest. 'Jesus Christ,' she yelled back. 'You nearly gave me a bloody heart attack. What the hell are you doing sneaking up on people like that?'

'What do you mean, *what am I doing*?' Anna retorted angrily. 'I've just caught you red-handed. You've been lying to Tanya all this time.'

'What exactly do you think you've caught me doing, hmm?' Rosie asked, holding her hands up for Anna to see. 'I haven't touched a drop of alcohol, thank you very much. All I'm guilty of is grabbing a quick swig of water, because I'm bloody thirsty after running around all day,' she shouted.

'Gin isn't water,' Anna shot back.

'Oh, I see, this is gin, is it?' Rosie picked up a large bottle of water from under the bar in front of her and held it up with a look of contempt on her face.

Anna frowned. 'No, that's not—'

'Exactly,' Rosie cut her off in a scathing tone. 'No, it's fucking not.' She shook her head and shot daggers at the younger woman. 'You have a real problem with me, don't you, Anna? Come on, admit it. You liked having Tanya all to yourself all these years and now it don't suit you that someone else who cares about her has come along.'

'That's not it at all,' Anna replied. 'I'm the least possessive person in the world; she'll tell you that.' Her eyes darted back to the bar. That bottle was definitely not the one she'd seen Rosie drink from. She knew her stock.

'Would she though?' Rosie asked, with a cruel smirk.

Anna narrowed her eyes. 'My problem, Rosie, is that you didn't give a shit about her all these years and yet suddenly you want to play mother of the year. It doesn't add up. Why? Why now? And I *knew* this whole sober act was a con. It's all to draw her in and make her trust you again. Well, I've caught you now, because I know damn well what I just saw and that was you drinking gin from the bar when you thought no one was watching.'

'Oh, Anna.' Rosie shook her head and gave her a pitying look. 'I get it. You've been through a lot. Tanya told me about you being kidnapped.' Her voice was as silken as a snake. 'And about losing the baby.' She looked her up and down. 'I know you had to… well, let's just say that you've had to do some dark things, shall we?'

Anna heard herself gasp. Surely Tanya hadn't told her all that? Tanya would know that at the very least discussing what had happened with Michael was a complete no-no, even when it came to family. *Especially* when it came to new family who had never been connected to them before. She felt herself tremble and she hoped it wasn't visible.

'I don't know what you think you know, Rosie—'

'I think I know a lot,' she said flatly. 'But I think above all that you've been through so much that it has clearly damaged you mentally. I think you see things that aren't there and your mind plays tricks. I think you're paranoid and angry and don't like change.'

Anger surged through Anna and her eyes flashed. She'd heard enough. 'Just stop,' she commanded. She raised her chin and looked down on Rosie with disgust. 'I hoped more than anyone that you were the real deal for Tanya, but you're not. I will be telling her about this and you can explain yourself to her. You are not my problem, and I will not be drawn into your games.'

Anna turned on her heel and left before Rosie could try to argue with her further. This had gone far enough and she wasn't sure that she could hear any more without either breaking down or attacking the woman. She needed to work tonight, but tomorrow she was going to out Rosie for the fraud she really was.

CHAPTER THIRTY-SEVEN

Sarah Riley stared up at Freddie with a look of pure shock on her face. It was several seconds before she found her tongue.

'What the hell are you doing here?' she asked in an uncertain tone. She glanced at the door behind him, wondering if he was alone.

Freddie watched the fear and confusion flash across her face, fighting with the anger and defiance that begged to come to the surface but daren't. He had buried her career and any chance that she'd had of going against him eighteen months before, when she'd worked with the Secretary of State for Justice in his search for his daughter. Up against Freddie, she had threatened to take him down at the first available opportunity. He got there first.

Freddie had known from the start that she wasn't quite as straight as she made out. It was little things that gave her away, things that only someone like him would notice. He'd done some digging and discovered her dirty little secret. She'd lied to the force and stolen a bag of money from a bank when she'd been first on the scene of a robbery. It had been lying there abandoned, all ready to go. But the robbers had already scarpered. She'd seen the opportunity and taken it. Luckily for Freddie, it had created one for him too. He'd given Sarah an ultimatum – leave the force and disappear quietly or he would out her. She'd had no choice.

'Don't worry, I'm not here to cause you harm. I have a proposition for you.'

Sarah snorted in disbelief. 'You really think I'd be interested in what you have to say, after what you've done to me?' she asked.

'Firstly' – Freddie walked over and made himself comfortable in the chair opposite hers – 'you did that to yourself. You challenged me and lost; you can't be a sore loser forever. And secondly, yes. I do think you'll be interested, if you can get over yourself long enough to listen to what I have to say.'

Sarah glared at him hatefully. There was only one person she truly despised in this world, one person who made her blood boil with bitterness, and he was sitting directly opposite her. What was he doing here? Hadn't he done enough already?

'Whatever you have to say, I'm not interested,' she said curtly. Her dark eyes blazed defiantly and her jaw set in a stubborn line.

Freddie picked up a pen and began to twiddle it between his fingers. 'How's the private investigator game working out for you?'

'Very well, thank you. Now, the door's that way—'

'But that's a lie, isn't it?' Freddie ignored the icy dismissal. 'I saw your accounts for last year. You barely cleared eighteen grand, and most of that went on the running costs. How are you even paying your rent?'

Sarah's face turned red and she couldn't stop her eyes from flickering to the side of the room. Freddie turned to look and noticed a door through to what could only be another tiny room, judging by the footprint of the narrow building.

'Oh. Really?' Freddie frowned. Despite his general dislike for Sarah Riley, he didn't take pleasure in seeing just how bad things had got for her. 'You're sleeping here?'

'Oh, why don't you just fuck off, Freddie,' she burst, standing up. Her Amazonian figure loomed over him and the desk. 'I don't know why you're here but I don't need you sticking your nose into my life. Whatever I do is no one's business but mine. Now please get out, I have a client due any minute.'

Freddie didn't move from his seat. 'Listen, you're right. It ain't my business. But I *am* going to tell you what I came here for.'

'Oh for crying out loud!' Sarah exclaimed, rolling her eyes. She sat back down in her seat with an aggressive stance. 'Fine. Get it out, and then *you* get out.'

'I have a job opening that's come up. As you probably know, my brother and I run a successful private security company. It's mainly for clubs but we have personal protection contracts too. I need a manager to run the day-to-day operations. Someone who understands the game.'

'And someone who's willing to turn a blind eye at times, I would imagine,' Sarah replied wryly.

'Well, yeah,' Freddie replied with a shrug. 'I'm not going to sugar-coat it – you know who I am. But for the main part, this business is legit. The basic salary would be fifty-five a year.'

Sarah's attention sharpened and Freddie let that sink in. He knew she needed the money badly.

'And that would be all above board?' she asked. 'PAYE?'

'Yeah. Including thirty days' holiday.'

'And what about the rest of it? You aren't just after me for that. I wasn't born yesterday; you need my skills for something else. What?' she queried, the distrust clear on her face.

'Well, that's a little more private. The details of that would have to stay between you and me. OK?' Freddie waited until she nodded her agreement. 'Alright then. I recently found out that there's a rat in my house.' The lines on his face deepened and he looked weary as he spoke. 'Information has been leaking out about my less legal operations. It's caused me a lot of hassle.'

Sarah hid a smirk and her eyes glinted in amusement, but she didn't say anything. She knew better than to wind Freddie up. She'd been down that road before.

'I set a trap, laid a fake job out on the table to my closest men. I gave a gag order. When the time came, I was watching from a distance. The pigs turned up a couple of hours before we were due, armed to the teeth. They knew.'

Sarah whistled and raised her dark eyebrows. She was far from Freddie's biggest fan but one of his own men setting him up like that? That was cold.

'I want you to work for me directly and follow them, each one, as though they were a suspect. I need you to find out who it was. And for your troubles there will be a hefty wedge on top of your salary, in cash.' Freddie studied her. 'What do you say? Are you in?'

Sarah bit her lip. Working for Freddie went against the grain at the very core of her being. He was the reason she was in such dire straits in the first place. If it wasn't for him, she would still be on the force. She'd still be in the revered position that she had worked so hard to get to.

But then again, the deal he was offering was extremely tempting. She would be great at running the security firm; it would utilise her many skills. It would keep her busy too. There was nothing Sarah hated more than being idle; she just wasn't built that way. Though she hated to admit to it, Freddie was right. The private investigating hadn't gone well at all. It seemed no one was putting money into things like that these days, with social media giving them the opportunity to stalk people so well on their own. So here she sat, day after day, with nothing to do but stare at the wall and worry about money.

Sarah glanced towards the door to the next room. It was barely more than a cupboard and it currently housed all her worldly possessions and an old sleeping bag laid across two lumpy suitcases in lieu of a mattress.

She sighed. He had her by the balls. There was no way she could refuse and he knew it. 'What are your suspicions so far?' she asked grudgingly. 'Any probable culprits?'

'So we have a deal?' Freddie asked.

'We have a deal, Tyler,' Sarah said flatly.

'Good. Then no, no probable culprits. I can't see any of them doing this – that's the problem. Either I'm missing something—'

'Or you're too close,' Sarah finished.

'Exactly.'

Leaning forward, Freddie pulled the notepad next to Sarah's laptop over. He began writing something down. 'These are the list of my men who were in on the job. Paul and Sammy knew I was setting it up; they're the only ones I completely trust right now. I'll let them know of your involvement, so you can talk to them if you need to.'

He pushed the notepad back across to Sarah and she checked it over with a nod.

'OK. I'll get on it.' She ripped off the top sheet and folded it neatly, before slipping it into her pocket.

Freddie stood up and reached into his suit-jacket pocket. He pulled out a thick brown envelope and dropped it onto the desk in front of her.

'There's five grand upfront. Get yourself sorted out and be ready to start at the security firm on Monday. This extra business I need you to start straight away. Got it?' Freddie held her gaze.

'Got it.' Sarah put the envelope into her top drawer casually. Much as she hated to admit it, she was excited about this new challenge already and spurred on by the fact that her money troubles were starting to melt away – but she didn't want Freddie to see any of that. She still despised him and always would. She knew that he also felt the same way about her. He must have been down to very limited options to have asked her for help, she realised.

'Oh, and Sarah?' Freddie was about to walk out of the door when he paused and turned around. He met her gaze with a cold expression. 'Screw me over and I will fucking bury you.'

CHAPTER THIRTY-EIGHT

James practically skipped down the street in the cold winter sun, holding the two coffees in his hand with a beaming smile on his face. He'd been working with Thea for almost two weeks now and was loving every second of it. The more he learned about the Tyler family businesses, the more amazed he became. He had known who Paul was, but he'd never delved into anything under the surface. It wasn't his business. Or rather, it hadn't been up until recently. The extent of the Tyler portfolio, both legal and illegal, was impressive by any standard. When Thea told him how Freddie had built it up from nothing and from such a young age, his respect for the man grew tenfold.

With his little finger, and being careful not to spill the frothy drink, James pushed a floppy lock of dark hair back off his forehead into place.

Working alongside Thea had turned out to be a delight too. He had been worried to begin with that it might put strain on their close friendship, but it had not. James worked hard and made sure that he always listened to Thea with eagerness and respect. They had settled down together nicely, and from what Thea said she was happy with his progress so far. He had already taken over one set of accounts as his own and Thea was divvying up more and more responsibilities by the day.

He walked up the garden path to the front door and was settling the coffees on top of each other to free his hand when it swung open.

'Oh, hello, Mollie,' James greeted her with a warm smile.

The smile was returned but immediately faded when she clocked the cardboard cups in his hand. Her eyebrows shot up so high they almost joined her hairline and she placed her hands on her hips.

'James Waters, I cannot believe you would do this to me,' she declared.

'Oh, er, sorry, Thea said you were going out so I didn't bring you one. Here, you can have mine.' He held his own cup out to her and the look of outrage on her face heightened.

'I do not want your American pisswater, thank you very much.' Her voice rose an octave and James blinked. 'I am not upset that you didn't bring me one. I'm upset that you've come to my home with this rubbish in your hands when you could have had *decent* coffee in my kitchen.'

'Oh.' James laughed in relief. Mollie was pulling his leg. Wasn't she?

'Oh, it's funny now, is it? Well' – Mollie lifted her nose in the air indignantly – 'that's just lovely, isn't it. All my sons go off and leave me in me old age. They fly away to little flats instead of their lovely big family home and then this happens. They drink pisswater from an American chain. An American businessman has replaced their mother.' Her chin wobbled. 'And you might not have lived here, but you're one of mine these days too and now you're at it. I'm not needed by nobody, it seems.'

The speed and volume of her dramatic rant rose steadily and James's mouth flapped like a fish out of water as he tried to work out how to stop her.

'No one needs Mollie Tyler anymore, oh no, not now that—'

She was cut short as Thea quickly ran through from the back of the house. 'Oh, Mum, there you are,' she said with exaggerated relief. James's eyes widened and he watched in silence. 'Could you get me some of that cake you made?' Thea asked in a soothing voice. 'You know, that really rich fruit cake? I've been *dying* for a taste all morning. Those accounts have given me a right hunger for it and I have no idea where you hid the damn thing.'

'Oooh yes, of course, love.' The wobble immediately disappeared and Mollie's eyes twinkled as she smiled pleasantly at her daughter. She nodded, her head bobbing up and down with purpose. 'I knew there was a reason I made that one this week.' She bustled off. 'It's just what you need, isn't it—'

Thea rolled her eyes at James with a grin, and he had to put his fist to his mouth to stop the laughter.

'Sorry, I should have warned you.' Thea gestured towards the cups. 'Starbucks is the enemy in this house. In fact, food or drink of any kind that Mum hasn't prepared herself is the enemy. She's basically Hitler and all foods outside her domain are threatening her empire.' Thea pulled a comically horrified face and James burst out laughing.

'James?' Mollie's voice wafted through from the back. 'Do you want some as well?'

'For the love of God, say yes,' Thea whispered.

'I'd love some,' James immediately called back, in an enthusiastic tone. He stepped inside and Thea closed the front door behind him.

'Come on through then. And chuck that crap in the bin; I've got the good stuff on.'

James looked longingly at his caramel macchiato and pulled a sad face. Thea gently took it from his grasp with a sympathetic pat on the hand.

'It's for the greater good, trust me.' They walked through the lounge towards the kitchen. 'Anyone who thinks Freddie runs this family is severely mistaken,' Thea muttered to James quietly.

'What's that, love?' Mollie asked as they entered the large kitchen cum dining room.

'Just saying to James here that anyone who thinks their fruit cake gives yours a run for its money is severely mistaken,' Thea said, more loudly and with an innocent smile.

'Ahh, thanks, love.' Mollie smiled smugly as she placed two side plates with thick slices of fruit cake down on the table.

They sat down and James glanced at the pile of notebooks next to them.

'So, what are we doing today?' he asked, taking a bite.

'Well…' Thea glanced at her mother.

Mollie caught the look and wiped her hands on her apron before taking it off. 'I'll be off then; leave you to it.' Folding the apron, she put it on the side and left the room.

Mollie knew exactly what her sons did and more recently about Thea's involvement with the accounts, but further than that she turned a blind eye. The small amount she had been privy to over the years had already been enough to keep her up nights, worrying. So she routinely excused herself.

'So we need to hide some extra money that's built up,' Thea said, picking up one of the files nearby. 'And we need to work out where's best to do this without a noticeable surge.'

'How much are we talking?' James asked.

'Thirty thousand this month, around the same next.'

James whistled. 'OK, so where do we start?'

'Have a look through the files, see what we can put as profit and then we'll have to make a trip to the casino with the rest,' she instructed.

'The casino?' James frowned.

'It's a last resort way of laundering the money,' Thea explained. 'But we try not to do it too often or it becomes obvious and the casino puts you on a watch list.'

'So how does it work?' James asked, intrigued.

'We go in and change, say, ten grand's worth of cash into chips. We have a drink then lose fifty quid or so on a table, playing safe. After a couple of hours, we take the chips back to the cashier. Anything above two grand in chips can be transferred into a bank account. It's a legitimate deposit, and if it's looked into by the tax man, it was a lucky night on the tables. Winnings are winnings – they're tax free and above board and the money then has a paper trail.'

'Wow, that's really clever,' James replied.

'It is, but like I said we can't take the piss, so I only do it when we're stretched.' Thea tucked her dark hair behind her ear and passed half of the pile of notebooks over to James. 'So let's get started.'

James opened up the first notebook. It was for the gymnasium. 'Oh, that reminds me!' His head shot up. 'You're coming tonight, aren't you?'

'To Seamus's fight? I wasn't going to,' Thea replied.

'Paul told me to ask if you can join us. Apparently, some big Mafia bosses are in town and they're coming as guests,' he said, his eyes twinkling. 'How exciting is that? I bet they're super scary but, like, in a thrilling sort of way, you know?' He giggled, finding the whole idea very daring. He'd never even thought about people like the Mafia as being real before he'd met Paul. But now here he was, about to go to a boxing fight with them. It was all very dramatic.

Thea's blood froze in her veins as James's words registered in her brain. She stared at him, not really seeing as she processed what this meant. James didn't know everything that had happened when Michael had taken Anna. He knew the basics, but Thea knew Paul had never told him about Frank. Why would he? Thea was kept abreast of everything, but James had not been part of the business at the time and had never met Frank.

He didn't know about Frank's disagreement with Anna, or that it was he who'd poisoned Seamus. He had no idea that Freddie and Paul had tortured the man in a warehouse, certain that it had been he who'd abducted Freddie's pregnant girlfriend. And most importantly of all, Thea knew that James had no idea that they'd doused Frank in petrol and set him alight, watching until he died and burned down to nothing. It wasn't the sort of thing you went home and told your partner about over a glass of wine. It was dark and gritty and kept only between those who needed to know and who could be trusted implicitly with that sort of knowledge.

James was completely unaware that any member of the Mafia on their doorstep was very bad news indeed. Because it meant that they were getting close.

Thea looked at his bright open face, alight with interest and amusement. *Oh how blissful your ignorance must be,* she thought wistfully. She needed to speak to Freddie before they all went tonight. Now that she understood the weight the Tylers were under, there was no question about it – she had to be there. She just hoped and prayed that the Mafia were still in the dark and that Freddie had a plan. Because if not, they were all dead men walking.

CHAPTER THIRTY-NINE

The gymnasium was full to the brim with hyped-up spectators going wild with feverish, carnal cries as the two men in the ring hit out at each other again and again. Sweat exuded from every pore in their bodies as they fought with all their strength and intelligence, trying to outwit their opponent at every turn.

Seamus surged forward again, focusing his punches on the other boxer's lower right side. He had an old injury there, a piece of information Sammy had passed on to him. It was working; he sagged and an expression of pain formed on the man's face. Seamus lunged again. He was close, but he needed to keep his opponent going a little longer. The bell rang to signal the end of the round and he pulled back. Cries of frustration sounded from the crowd. As he walked to his corner, he glanced at Freddie.

Freddie nodded and gave him a meaningful stare. This was the one. He was to win in the next round, at all costs. He sat down and took the break, gathering what was left of his strength.

Anna stood next to Freddie, dressed to the nines and acting her part as the dutiful partner. She was tense, but no one who did not know her as intimately as Freddie would notice that underneath her easy smile. Both Joe and Vito stood the other side of Freddie, between him and Paul. Their men were sprinkled among the rest of the family and Sammy.

Freddie had not told Anna of Joe's visit to the docks. He wasn't sure she would be able to cope with the information right now and had been trying to avoid all mention of them altogether. They themselves had become unavoidable though, inviting themselves along to the match this evening, sending word that they wanted to see Freddie's prize fighter. The Tylers had had no choice but to courteously extend their hospitality and offer them front-row seats. It would have been a snub not to.

Joe had been polite and jovial, acting as though this was nothing but a fun pastime with friends. Vito was clearly not feeling up to acting so light-hearted. His gaze had been cold and hard as he was introduced, and Anna could sense the burning anger beneath the surface just waiting to be unleashed. She was worried. Was he angry because he knew? Or was it all a show to try to root out the truth? The suspense was painful, and she could tell by the tight grip Freddie had on her hand that he felt it too. She took a deep breath and gave Seamus an encouraging smile.

The next round began and everyone cheered, standing up to watch. Seamus held back, conserving his energy and letting his opponent tire himself out. As his blows became slower, Seamus stepped back and took his chance. With everything he had, he rained hard punches onto the other man. He was a powerful, unstoppable force as he pushed back over and over, landing blows on the injured side with aggressive precision.

The last blow finally pushed him over the edge and the man crumpled to the floor in a defeated heap. The ref ran forward and slammed his hand to the floor, counting. The room held its breath until the final slam confirmed the end to the match. Seamus had won. The ref raised Seamus's hand, acknowledging him as the victor. The excitement in the room reached fever pitch as the crowd roared.

Freddie and Paul exchanged a satisfied look. Seamus had executed the fight perfectly. They had made a lot of money tonight.

'Joe, Vito, let me take you through to the changing rooms to meet Seamus and show you around. We had a refit last year and are quite proud of what we've achieved with the place.' Freddie urged them to follow him. 'Anna, why don't you stay with Thea and the others? We won't be long.'

'Of course.' She smiled politely as Freddie and Paul guided the two men off.

Joe clicked his fingers and Tino followed, as did two of Vito's men, who looked distinctly unfriendly. Anna wanted to stop them but knew that she couldn't. She wished Freddie would turn around so that she could subtly alert him to her fears, but he didn't. Something felt very wrong. Vito definitely wasn't falling for their act of friendship. Biting her lip, she reminded herself that Freddie already knew the score. He'd be watching them.

She forced herself to turn around and join the conversation that was taking place behind her between Thea and James. Sammy caught her eye as she turned and gave her a look that told her not to worry. She hoped he was right.

CHAPTER FORTY

Freddie took the men down through the narrow hallway that led off the back side of the ring. It opened out to a small rabbit warren of rooms, including the changing rooms, medical centre and general offices.

Something big was brewing with Vito and Freddie could tell he was a live wire. He could read him like a book. There was a feral need for violence lurking under the surface and that made him extremely dangerous. It was better to give him the opportunity to launch at him back here in private, rather than in front of a crowd.

'... smaller group activities led by one of our trainers. It's aimed at the youths on the nearby estate, to give them skills and a way to vent their pent-up aggression without turning to violence.' Freddie spoke casually, giving them the usual spiel about what they did at the gym, but he was fully aware when Vito turned deadly quiet behind him.

BANG.

Freddie was pushed forward violently against the wall and his head connected with the plasterboard. He reeled and turned, only to be grabbed by the scruff of his shirt and pushed back again by Vito.

Paul cried out and jumped forward instinctively to fight his brother's attackers, but one of Vito's men turned a gun on him, forcing him into submission. He held his hands up and cursed under his breath.

Joe stepped back to watch. He wasn't at all surprised by Vito's actions, Freddie realised. They had clearly planned it before they came.

'Freddie Tyler, out to save the world, huh? Well, ain't you just a saint?' Vito sneered. 'All those *youths* must kiss your feet to receive such charity.'

Freddie ignored the sarcastic jibe and stared back into the other man's eyes, his gaze level and cold. 'What do you think you're doing, Vito?' he asked, his voice dangerously low. 'Is this really how you treat your hosts, after we've been so accommodating?' He watched the gun out of the corner of his eye. *Fucking cowards,* he thought.

Vito pulled back and slammed him against the wall again. 'I want answers,' he yelled, spit flying from his mouth. 'Where is Frank, huh? Because I don't buy it, this whole pally-pally bullshit. I don't think you and Frank were friends at all. What would he want from you? You might be a big fish in this small pond, but we're fucking sharks, and we eat people like you for breakfast.'

'Frank didn't want anything from me,' Freddie spat back angrily through gritted teeth. 'It was me who wanted something from him, to open up a new casino. I asked for his blessing and his advice, and in return we negotiated a sizeable percentage that would be paid to him. He was set to make a lot of profit for nothing. *That's* what I offered. And yeah' – Freddie forced his face forward into the furious one in front of him – 'we *were* friends. Because Frank understood the value of alliances. However small we fish might be to you.'

Seamus walked out of the changing room down the hallway, still naked from the waist up. He did a double take before pelting full speed towards them. 'Freddie!'

Freddie held a hand up to stop him in his tracks. 'It's OK, Seamus,' he quickly called. 'We're just having a little discussion. Go back inside.'

'But…' His worried gaze flickered between Freddie and Paul, who was still on the wrong end of a barrel.

'Now,' Freddie ordered. His tone brooked no nonsense.

Against his better judgement, Seamus did as he was bid. He knew that whatever happened, he was always to do as his boss commanded. He cursed the fact that there was no back way out. There wasn't even a window in the changing rooms. If there was, he could have run to get Sammy. But now he was just going to have to sit and wait and hope that Freddie had it under control.

As the door shut, Freddie surged forward against Vito. There was a short battle as he made slow headway, but eventually he pushed himself away from the wall. Vito still clung to his shirt and was pushing back against him with all his might. The muscles strained in Freddie's neck.

'I don't trust you, you fucking nobody,' Vito spat.

'And I don't trust you, coming here into my gym, holding a gun to my brother in our own hallway. But here we are, both as equally in the dark as each other,' Freddie shouted in his face. 'So here's how I see it.' He gripped Vito's hand and forced it off his shirt. 'You can either keep attacking us and make an enemy for no good reason, or we can work together to find him. That's what I *thought* we were doing already,' he yelled at Joe across Vito's shoulder.

Joe sighed. 'Vito…' He shot him a meaningful look. 'I think he needs a little extra motivation.'

Vito placed his hands on Freddie's chest and shoved him back against the wall. 'I think you're lying.' He sniffed. 'I think you had something to do with it. I don't believe someone could rule as much as you do here, have the power and connections that you have and not be able to find out what happened to a man as notorious as Frank.' He shook his head and spat on the floor before snapping his fingers at his men.

The man who wasn't busy pointing the gun at Paul stepped forward and grabbed him roughly by the arm.

'Hey,' Paul yelled. 'What the fuck?' He tried to pull away but the man holding the gun cocked it and held it closer to his face. Paul looked over to Freddie, a furious but helpless look in his eyes.

'What do you think you're doing?' Freddie roared. 'Get off my brother right now.'

'I don't think so.' Joe stepped forward. 'You've been so gracious this evening with your hospitality, we're going to extend our own hospitality to your brother for a while. When you bring us news of Frank you can pick him up.'

Vito and the man holding Paul's arm began pushing him back out of the hallway. The man with the gun moved closely behind and lowered the gun to his back, hiding it under a jacket. 'One sound out there and you're meat,' he said menacingly.

Freddie started after them but Joe barred his way. 'I don't think so. One wrong move and your brother is toast, so you'd be wise to stay here where you belong.' He eyed Freddie hard before turning around to follow Vito and the other men. 'I'd hurry up with that information if I were you. We're hospitable hosts for a while, but you don't want to leave Paul with Vito for too long. He isn't known for his patience with people once they've outstayed their welcome.'

Leaving Freddie with that threat he exited the hall and Freddie was alone once more.

'Fuck!' Freddie shouted in frustration as he turned and punched the wall.

He crouched down and took a deep breath in, running his hands through his hair. Closing his eyes, Freddie tried to think. They had Paul now. This changed things and definitely not for the better. If only there was another way out, a way to solve this problem quicker, but there wasn't.

The one plan they had formed to get the Mafia off their backs for good wasn't ready. Freddie needed time and now it appeared that he had even less of that than he'd thought. With the Mafia here in town, with how suspicious they already were and how sharply they looked into things, their options were severely limited. It had come down to just one possible option of full escape with all loose ends tied up. And even then, the plan would only work if it was executed at exactly the right time.

Freddie wasn't sure that he could pull this off anymore, not without Paul's help. 'Fuck!' he exclaimed again, leaning back to sit against the wall. He looked up to the ceiling. What was he going to do?

A noise by the door caught Freddie's attention and he stifled a groan as James poked his head in, followed swiftly by the rest of his body when he clocked Freddie sat alone on the floor.

'Freddie? What are you doing?' His brow furrowed uncertainly. 'Where's Paul gone? He just left without saying a word. Is everything OK?'

Freddie stood up and walked over to James, his heart sinking heavily. 'No, mate. Everything isn't OK.' He grasped James's shoulder in a gesture of comfort. He wasn't going to take this well, Freddie already knew. 'I'm going to take you home with me and Anna tonight. We'll chat there, OK? We've got a lot to talk about and this isn't the place.'

They re-entered the gym, and the general noise of happy, excited people that had been dampened behind the door became full volume again. Freddie locked eyes with Anna and saw the dread behind her expression. He didn't try to smile and pretend things were OK. They weren't. But somehow he had to find a way out. Because if he didn't, it wouldn't just be Paul who was murdered; it would be all of them. Anna, James, Thea, Mollie… anyone closely associated to him. No amount of fake papers or money would be able to save them this time. There would be no remote corner of the world that would be safe for any of them anymore.

CHAPTER FORTY-ONE

Sarah Riley pulled the ridged crisp out of the packet and crunched it loudly as she sat in her car watching the front door of the greasy café across the street. From where she'd parked, she could see the table that Dean was sitting at with the mousey-looking blonde woman he'd met up with. As she watched, Dean tentatively reached his hand over towards where hers lay on the table as she talked away animatedly. Her hand flew up in an unconscious gesture, exaggerating her words, and he pulled his back as if he'd been stung. Sarah rolled her eyes and crunched another crisp.

Dean might be a good enough criminal, but he was useless when it came to women. She'd only been following him for a couple of days and already she could see that the one thing he cared about was getting his leg over whoever this blonde was. She looked her up and down critically. The woman was quite attractive in a quiet, girl-next-door kind of way. But she was a cut above Dean. Her outfit was subtly flattering and expensive, and her hair was softly styled. The way she sat upright in her chair and held her head gave off an air of sophistication. Dean was soaking it all up as he listened, but even from here, Sarah could tell he didn't stand a chance.

She idly wondered what this woman was doing with Dean. It wasn't an affair; there was none of the body language on her side. She was definitely not with the police either. From a mile off, Sarah could tell those who'd ever been in the force. The woman also didn't seem particularly interested in whatever Dean had to say either, having not stopped talking for about half an hour. She shrugged. It wasn't her business. Her job was tracking down Freddie's rat and she was already ninety-five per cent sure it wasn't Dean. He didn't have any motive and was clearly much more distracted by his personal life than anything else.

Starting the engine, Sarah sighed and pulled away. It was time to see what Bill Hanlon was up to. Bill was the last person Freddie would expect to cross him, and in fact Sarah couldn't really see it either. But if there was one valuable thing she'd learned in her years on the force, it was not to trust anything except for the proven facts. Everyone was a suspect until proven innocent.

Pulling her indicator down, she waited for the traffic lights to turn green. It had been a shock initially, Freddie's arrival. She hadn't ever expected to see him again after their last encounter. It had been even more of a surprise when he'd offered her a well-paid job – a legal one too. Well, for the most part.

She was enjoying this job. She needed something to challenge her sharp brain. But still, something told her that Freddie's information didn't quite fill out the whole story. He was adamant that no one else knew of their plan, but she wasn't so sure. Pillow talk was a killer; it had taken down many a man throughout history. And what about Anna? She didn't believe for a second that Freddie wouldn't discuss his worries with his partner. And what if the leak wasn't one of those men, but Paul or Sammy, who had been made fully aware of his plan? It would have provided them with the perfect opportunity to stay off the suspect list. They could have reported it to the police as true information and let Freddie pitch the blame somewhere within his inner circle. Blame shifted. There was so much to consider.

Reaching her destination, she slowed down and turned in. By sheer luck someone was just exiting the end spot next to the house. She pulled in, cut the engine and reached into her handbag, rummaging around until her hand connected with a small black box.

'Gotcha,' she hissed.

Stepping outside, she peered through a small gap in the hedge. It looked like someone was home, but that was OK. She'd cased the front already and knew where the cameras were. Bill was tech savvy, so she'd known there would be some sort of protection around his house. There was one camera below the bedroom window on the roof which covered the front drive and the area around the front door, and there was another on the top of the roof, pointing down at the garage.

One area he hadn't thought to cover though was the small side alley that ran between the hedge and the house through to the back garden. There was a fence panel in the way, but she could scale it easily. All she had to do was get through the hedge behind the camera's view and she'd be on her way. Once inside the garden, she would have to assess the area. Hopefully there would be an opportunity to sneak in through the back and plant the listening device somewhere. The kitchens were at the rear of these houses and it was nowhere near a meal time, so if luck was on her side, Bill and his wife wouldn't be in there. And if they were, she'd just bide her time out of sight. It wasn't like she needed to be anywhere. She could wait them out.

Grimacing as she eyed the prickly hedge in front of her, Sarah pulled the sleeves of her leather jacket down and used her arms as a shield to cover her face so that she could push through. Biting her lip so as not to cry out when a particularly sharp piece of wood caught her in the neck, Sarah carefully stepped over the roots and twisted around the unyielding branches, not stopping until she reached the other side.

Brushing the dead leaves off the front of her clothes, Sarah shook her head from side to side to make sure there was nothing she'd missed. With cat-like moves, she silently scaled the fence and pulled herself over to the other side. It was at times like these that she was glad of her unusually tall, lithe figure. It may have been the source of the bullying she'd endured all throughout her childhood, but it made breaking into places that much easier.

Creeping forward, she crouched as she passed the window to the downstairs toilet, in case someone was in there. Reaching the end of the wall, Sarah took a slow, calm breath and listened for any sign of life in the garden beyond. There appeared to be no activity, so making sure she had a good grip on the listening device, she stepped forward and turned the corner.

Nearly jumping out of her own skin, Sarah yelped and dropped the box with a clatter as she found herself face to face with none other than Bill Hanlon himself. He stood just inches away, leaning sideways against the wall with folded arms and an expression that would make the hardest of men quiver in their boots.

'And what exactly do you think you're doing in my back garden, DCI Riley?' he asked with no trace of amusement in his voice.

Sarah swallowed. 'I'm not a DCI anymore,' she said, trying to work out what to do. The device was on the floor between them. 'How did you know I was here?'

'Sensors. You really think I'd leave my gaff that open?' He shook his head as though disappointed. 'Sloppy.'

Sarah silently cursed herself. Of course he'd have motion sensors. This was Bill Hanlon. The guy had pulled off more bank jobs than she could shake a stick at. He'd even been known by the moniker 'Billy the Banker' for several years. He would never be so stupid as to leave a back door unprotected like that. It was something she should have thought of. She could have kicked herself.

'You need to tell me what's going on – right now,' Bill demanded.

'I can't do that,' Sarah replied, jutting her chin out stubbornly. 'So either you can let me go and I'll leave you in peace or I can fight my way past you.'

'Huh.' Bill laughed without humour at her audacity. He leaned forward and, despite herself, Sarah took a step back. 'I'd like to take this opportunity to remind you of a little tape I have stored in my safe, in which you're the star. I don't need to fight you, Sarah; I've got you by the short and curlies for life.'

Sarah swallowed again, the lump in her throat not disappearing. She pulled at the collar of her jacket as the heat of panic began to flow through her. Bill was right. He didn't have to do as she said; it was the complete opposite. She'd fucked up royally here.

'So are you going to start talking, or do you fancy that little stretch behind bars?' Bill asked. His gaze didn't waver as he waited for her response.

Sarah slumped in defeat. There was no other way around it; she was going to have to tell him. On the plus side, she was pretty certain it wasn't him anyway. But Freddie wasn't going to like this one bit. The last time they'd spoken he had made it explicitly clear that none of his men were ever to find out what they were doing. He didn't want to break their trust. And now here she was, about to tell one of his closest friends that Freddie had set him up and was having him followed to see if he was a police informant. It wasn't going to go down well.

'Fine. I'll tell you,' she said. 'But do you have something strong to drink? I think we're both going to need it.'

CHAPTER FORTY-TWO

Anna set the platter of nibbles down on the coffee table and ran her eyes critically over the spread.

Tonight was the first time since Tanya had been home that she'd arranged to come over to Anna's for a girls' night. Anna hadn't pushed, happy to travel to see Tanya instead, knowing how easily she still tired. But when Anna had texted to ask if they could meet up, Tanya had suggested this arrangement. Anna was thrilled. Not only had she missed having her friend over for girls' night, but it meant that there was no way Rosie could butt in and get in the way of their catch-up.

The thought of Rosie cast a cloud over Anna's happiness for a moment. She hadn't seen Tanya the previous day to tell her about Rosie's drinking. She'd been swamped at work and then, of course, Paul had been taken. Times were becoming darker than ever. Tonight was the night she was going to tell her, but it wasn't something she was looking forward to.

She stretched and looked out of the window at the views of the city, her thoughts circling Rosie as they always seemed to these days. Over the years, Anna's heart had bled for her friend every time she'd caught Tanya staring wistfully at Leslie, her own mother. She'd wished so many times that Tanya had a mother who cared about her, that she had *any family* who cared about her. And now here she was, the wonderful Rosie who wanted to make amends. But it was all just a lie. More than anyone, Anna had wanted it to be true, but it wasn't.

The doorbell sounded and Anna skipped through to open it. Tanya stood there with a big smile on her face and a bottle of wine in her hand. She was dressed down in jeans and a fitted jumper as they were staying in, but she still sported a full face of make-up and wavy, voluminous hair. Anna smiled and shook her head. Only Tanya would get dolled up for a night in.

'You look rather fabulous,' she said with a laugh.

'Well, don't want to get caught out, do I?' Tanya responded, kissing Anna on the cheek as she swept inside, leaving a cloud of Chanel Mademoiselle in her wake. 'We might just be chilling here, but I still had to travel over. What if I was walking along and suddenly poof!' She spread her hands out in front of her, painting a picture. 'There he is.'

'There who is?' Anna asked.

'Mr Right!' Tanya exclaimed, rolling her eyes. 'Good make-up could be the difference between Mr Right stopping in his tracks, falling in love with me at first sight and us riding off into the sunset with a bottle of cherry vodka, or,' she said with a serious expression, 'him taking one look at the bags under me eyes and running off in the other direction, yelling *fuck no* as he goes.'

Anna threw her head back and laughed. 'So those are the only two options?'

Tanya tilted her head as she considered it. 'Yes,' she confirmed.

Anna shook her head. 'You're bonkers, woman. Even with bags under your eyes, you're stunning, and you know it.'

'That's all very well you thinking that, but you don't have an eight inch and a six pack, so that ain't going to do me much good, is it?'

Anna snorted in amusement. Tanya sighed and wandered through to the kitchen.

'I've already put the glasses out,' Anna called, as she walked back through to the lounge and curled up on one end of the sofa.

Tanya came through and clocked the food displayed so prettily on the coffee table. 'Aw, Anna!' She smiled and leaned over to hug her best friend. 'You're a diamond, you are.'

Anna took the bottle from her, unscrewed the cap and poured them a glass each. Tanya took hers and made herself comfortable at the other end of the sofa.

'So how are you feeling? Good day today?' Anna asked.

'I'm right as rain, me,' Tanya replied with a tight grin. 'Feeling more like myself every day. Thank the lord and Lucifer…' She rolled her eyes. She was sick of feeling like an invalid now. It was time life went back to normal so that she could focus on forgetting the past.

'Good; I'm glad,' Anna replied.

'Where's James?' Tanya looked around, as if expecting to find him.

'He went home. I asked him to stay, hoped we could distract him for a while, but he just wanted to be in his own home.' Anna shrugged sadly.

James had been almost inconsolable when they got him home the night before and explained the situation. Freddie had told James the truth about Frank, though he was careful not to go into the gory details surrounding his death. He'd told James that now he was part of the family business, he had a right to know things like this. James had turned white as a sheet, but to his credit, he accepted the information bravely. He was one of the Tylers now, and as such he needed to understand exactly who they were and how dangerous Paul's predicament was.

In the end, he had calmly told Freddie that he didn't care what had happened or why, just begged him to bring Paul home. Anna had stayed up with him late into the night. He had eventually fallen asleep as the dawn crept through the windows and exhaustion could no longer be kept at bay.

'I get that. I'd want to be on my own for a bit if I were him right now,' Tanya replied. 'Poor thing. Poor Paul,' she added, shaking her head. 'It's a bad business, all this. What's Freddie doing about it?'

Anna rubbed her face with her hands. 'I don't know. He says they have a plan but he won't talk about it. The only thing I can gather is that whatever it is, it's a gamble. Which is worrying.' She sighed. 'Freddie never gambles. Not when it's life and death. Which means he's in a corner.'

Tanya looked down to her glass, her expression sombre. 'You know what they do, the Mafia, don't you?' she said quietly. 'They ain't like Freddie. If Freddie loses this, it won't just be them they go after.' She glanced up at Anna.

Anna nodded. 'I know.' The pair sat in silence for a moment, then Tanya took a deep breath and shook off her dark thoughts.

'It's going to be fine,' she said, her tone resolute. 'Freddie has always got himself and us out of bad situations before. I mean, look at when Michael took us. There was a time then where I thought we weren't going to make it.' She swallowed. 'I said my goodbyes to this world in a dark barn in the middle of nowhere, bleeding out. I didn't think there was any way I was coming back from that. But Freddie pulled through. Somehow he got there and he saved us. So we just have to trust that he'll do it again. If there's one thing we know about him, it's that he'll do anything to protect those he cares about.' She smiled and Anna tilted her head in agreement. 'Anyway, aside from that, how are you? Have you spoken to Chloe yet?' Tanya reached over to the table and popped a mini quiche into her mouth.

'I have, yes.' Anna shifted her weight, shaking off the cloak of dread that had been sitting on her shoulders. 'She's happy with her new shift rota and is looking forward to starting at the house, once we've got everything set up.'

Tanya nodded. 'Good. There are a couple of places I thought we could have a look at, but I'm not sure they're exactly what we're looking for. Have you spoken to Freddie yet?'

Anna grimaced. 'No,' she admitted. 'He's been so under it with everything lately.'

'Anna, you know we can't make one move without knowing he's on board. From a business point of view and for you personally,' Tanya stressed. The last thing she wanted to do was cause relationship problems between the two of them. God knew they'd been through their fair share of those already.

'I know, I know.' Anna nodded her understanding. 'I'll talk to him. I promise. Anyway,' she changed the subject. 'How's everything at home? How's your mum?'

Tanya immediately tensed. 'She's OK thanks, really good. It's been nice having her there with me lately.'

Anna smiled politely and took a sip of her wine. There was a long silence. Eventually Anna spoke, deciding to just rip off the plaster and come out with it. 'Listen, there's something I need to talk to you about. And it's not something I take any pleasure in telling you.' She took a deep breath.

'Anna, don't.' Tanya cut her off before she could begin. 'I know what you're about to say and there's no need. Mum already told me.'

'She already told you what?' Anna asked warily.

'About the misunderstanding at the club. You thinking you saw her drinking gin when it was really just her water.' Tanya's level gaze met Anna's.

Anna shook her head and laughed, a humourless laugh. 'Of course she did. Of course that's what she's told you.' She made a sound of frustration. 'Tanya, I *did* see her drink the gin. It was one hundred per cent the gin bottle and not the water bottle. That just happened to be nearby and she tried to use it as an excuse.'

Tanya shook her head solemnly. 'You were over by the office from what I heard – that's quite a way away. It could easily have looked like the gin bottle—'

'Tanya, it was *not* water!' Anna exploded, the thought of Rosie twisting things so that she looked like a victim sending her over the edge. 'I swear to you on my *life*, Rosie is drinking again. She probably never stopped; it was just a story she made up to make you trust her. She *knows* you wouldn't trust her drunk in a million years – she isn't stupid.'

'Anna, that's enough,' Tanya replied sternly.

'No, Tanya, it isn't enough.' Anna's eyes beseeched her. 'Can't you see what she's doing? She's playing you like a fiddle right now, playing on all the things that she *knows* you crave from her. She's not here for you, she just needs you onside so that – so that…' Anna floundered, not knowing how to finish. She hadn't planned on saying this much and now she'd backed herself into a corner.

'So that what, Anna?' Tanya snapped, sitting forward. 'Come on, so that what? You sit there telling me she's some sort of shady creature, yet you can't back it up. What would she have to gain? She's spent all this time looking after me, getting to know me again and she hasn't asked me for a *thing*, Anna. I even had to insist that I pay her for the hours she puts in at the club. She tried to do that for free. For *me*.' Tanya poked her chest to emphasise her point. 'To help *me* out with my responsibilities. Because that's what a mum does.'

'Tanya, I don't know why, but I swear to you I'm telling the truth,' Anna replied, her open expression pleading with Tanya to believe her. 'You have to admit, something doesn't add up. Why now? Why the sudden turnaround after all this time?' Anna rubbed the bridge of her nose. 'She is *not* sober, and these meetings she apparently goes to, you can't tell me you don't feel like something's off about that.'

'Are you serious?' Tanya's eyes flashed. 'So, are you telling me you also don't think she goes to group?'

'Well…' Anna thought back to the night she'd followed Rosie to Barbican and faltered. Rosie had gone exactly where she'd said she was going. Anna couldn't argue with that. 'No, it's just—'

'Exactly,' Tanya said, her tone hard. 'Honestly, this is a joke, Anna. How dare you attack her like this? You know what, she was right.' Seething with hurt anger, Tanya stood up and slipped on her shoes, which she had discarded on the floor. Her cheeks burned hotly. 'She said to me you were jealous and she was right.'

'What?' Anna's jaw dropped. She couldn't believe what she was hearing.

'You've always been the one who got everything. From the second we met. You were the one with the sob story and the drama where everyone had to save you. Then you were the one who rode off into the sunset with the white knight.' Tanya reeled off all the points Rosie had made. 'You were always the one with the perfect family while poor little Tanya looked on in the background. You have *always* been the golden swan in the centre of the picture and now, finally, *I'm* the one who's got something special and incredible happening to me. I'm the one with the mum who's going the extra mile and helping out – and you can't stand it. Because it's not *your* drama and you aren't the only one with great parents anymore. And maybe even because you aren't the only one I have around to rely on anymore.'

Tanya came to the end of her emotional rant and took a deep breath, misery and anger etched into her face.

Anna felt like she'd been slapped. She couldn't believe the words coming out of Tanya's mouth. In all the years that they had been friends, lived together, worked together, they had never had an argument. Rosie had been around for five minutes and suddenly it was like the world was falling apart.

'You don't mean that,' Anna said, her voice quivering. 'That is *her*, poisoning you.'

'She's not poisoning me, Anna, she's just being a mum,' Tanya shouted. 'And maybe she's finally just pointing out the things that I've been too blind to see myself over the years. Because even now you're doing it.' Tears filled Tanya's eyes and threatened to spill over. Anna's betrayal hurt more than she had ever thought possible. And it was betrayal. Why else would she be trying to sabotage something so good? 'Why can't you just be happy for me?' she asked. 'You've had love and family all these years, and sure, Rosie isn't the perfect mum, but she's *my* mum. And she's *here,* and she's *trying.* That is all I have ever wanted.'

Sniffing and blinking away the tears, Tanya suddenly turned and walked out of the room. She needed to get out of here. Of all the people in her life, she'd thought Anna would have been happy for her and supportive of this latest development.

'Tanya?' Anna called after her. 'Tan, please, come back. Can we just talk—'

The front door slammed and Anna's words trailed off. She stared at the doorway through to the hall for a moment in shock. She couldn't believe it. After everything they'd been through and the steel-like bond that they shared, suddenly they were arguing like enemies.

The tears began to fall and she hugged herself. She felt as though she'd been shot in the stomach by a cannonball. What was she going to do now?

She took a deep breath and wiped away her tears. They both needed some space to calm down, but then she needed to fix things with Tanya as soon as possible. The longer she left it, the deeper Rosie would drive the wedge between them.

She felt a fresh surge of hatred for Rosie as Tanya's words came back to her. That wasn't Tanya, not really. Tanya would never think that of her. Rosie had manipulated her. Tanya knew more than anyone how fiercely Anna loved her. She also knew that Anna hated being in the spotlight, so all that rubbish about having to be at the centre of drama made no sense at all.

Rosie Smith had a lot to answer for. Anna narrowed her eyes as the anger bubbled harder and harder inside of her. Rosie had taken this way too far now and Anna was going to make her pay for that. She was going to uncover that manipulative bitch once and for all and expose her for what she truly was, if it was the last thing she ever did.

CHAPTER FORTY-THREE

The door to Freddie's Portakabin flew open and he looked up with a frown of annoyance. He hadn't been expecting anyone at this time of the night and everybody knew to knock before they entered one of his private domains. He blinked in surprise as he registered that the intruder was Bill, his heavy frame bowling from side to side as he marched towards the desk, a thunderous expression on his face.

'Bill, what's happened?' he asked, immediately concerned.

'I'll tell you what's happened, Freddie,' Bill snapped. 'I was enjoying a nice cup of tea with my missus when my perimeter alarm went off. At first, I thought it might have been a cat that had chosen to ignore the high-pitched sound waves in my garden designed to keep them away, but I figured I'd check it out anyway. Imagine my surprise' – the sound of feet running down the cobbles reached Freddie's ears and Bill turned to allow him a clear view of the open door – 'when I found *this* instead.'

Sarah Riley bowled into view and nearly bypassed the door completely in her haste, stopping herself by grabbing the door-frame. 'Freddie,' she puffed, catching her breath after running to try to keep up with Bill. 'It's – I can explain...'

Freddie held his hand up to silence her and focused on Bill, waiting for him to continue. This was bad – very bad. It was exactly what he had hoped to avoid. Trust between men was important to anyone, but especially in their world. In a life without law, morals were everything. He just hoped there was still a chance to salvage their friendship, because losing Bill would hurt him both personally and professionally.

'She was skulking around, carrying this.' Bill threw the little black box on the desk in front of Freddie. 'Was about to plant it in my house.' His lip curled.

Freddie took a deep breath and let it out slowly. 'I know what it looks like, and I'm not going to sit here and tell you—'

'What it looks like,' Bill cut him off, 'is that you were testing my loyalty to you after years of already proving it time and again.' His deep voice was hard and angry. 'Which at first I couldn't believe. Surely not, I thought. Surely Freddie would never in a million years question that. If I'd had to lay my life down on the fact you'd never do that to me, I would have done. I was about to come over here and tell you where you could fucking stick it, that we were *done*.' He stared at Freddie, hard, but his tone calmed down slightly as he continued. 'But then Sarah told me about the pigs turning up at the antiques place and how no one outside our circle had a clue.' He sighed. 'And I realised on the way over here that whether I like it or not – and I don't,' he added, 'you did have good grounds for your suspicions. In your position, I'd have had to do the same thing.'

Bill walked forward and sat down. He looked behind him at Sarah who remained tensely in the doorway.

'For fuck's sake, woman, close the door and sit down. We've got a lot to discuss and I haven't got all day,' Bill demanded.

Freddie visibly sagged in relief as he realised that although Bill was angry, he hadn't turned against him. Sarah closed the door and sat down next to Bill, alert and wary. Bill and Freddie stared at each other for a long moment, their expressions serious.

'There was no part of me that at any point questioned your loyalty, Bill,' Freddie said frankly, spreading his arms out to the sides. 'But there is also no part of me that questions any of the others either.' He shrugged and rubbed his forehead, stressed. 'I've gone round and round and I don't believe it could be any of you, but it *is* one of you. And I couldn't choose which one if my life fucking depended on it. Which it may well do,' he added. 'My life out here anyway. Whoever it is, they're trying to have me put away. I'm guessing they're probably working with this task force too, seeing as the timing is pretty coincidental. But I can't see the wood for the trees. That's why I've brought in Sarah.'

Bill turned to Sarah and looked her up and down, unimpressed. Sarah bristled but bit back her scathing remark. She had messed up today, and though her respect for her new employer was around the same level as her respect for dog shit, she understood very well on which side her bread was buttered. It wouldn't do her any favours to piss him off further by offending Bill.

Freddie watched the silent exchange. 'I know she might seem an odd choice, but she's good at what she does. And she can't betray me without hurting herself.'

Sarah's face flushed and she held her head up higher, turning her gaze away. She couldn't stand being talked about as though she wasn't in the room. It was disrespectful, especially to someone like her. Up until Freddie had ousted her from her well-earned position in the force, she had always been treated with respect. People moved out of her way, bought her coffee, called her 'Ma'am'. Now here she was in a tin box by the river with a couple of criminals who looked down on her as if *she* were the parasite. It was a joke. But it was a joke that she was the butt of, and that was a fact that she couldn't escape. She'd made her bed all those years ago when she'd taken the money from the robbery site. And now she had to lie in it.

Bill sighed. 'She's going to need help, going against our lot. They ain't stupid. We haven't stayed out of handcuffs this long by luck. She might be good but our guys are better – you know that. I caught her before she even got in the house and I'm not sure some of the others would take the news as well as I have.'

'What do you suggest?' Freddie asked, leaning forward.

Bill shifted his weight in the chair and sighed again, much more irritably this time. 'Well, I'll have to help, won't I?' he said grudgingly. It didn't sit right with him at all, what they were doing. But he knew Freddie had no choice but to carry on, and he didn't want to see the shit hit the fan. At least with him there to guide her, Sarah couldn't mess up quite so spectacularly again. 'I'll give you some information and some better gear to work with. That shit's outdated and bulky.' He pointed to the black box on the table. 'It don't work well either; half the time it don't even record. I'm guessing you ordered it off some spy website?'

Sarah rolled her eyes but didn't answer. Bill nodded. He'd thought as much. People like Sarah might be good sniffer dogs but they had no clue where to get decent equipment. The good stuff was only available on the black market or the dark web, to people who weren't officially security cleared.

Although he already had a few sources for things like this, Zack, the new kid, had been teaching him a lot. He was glad Freddie had agreed to take him on. He was proving to be a valuable asset already.

'We have a new guy who can get hold of good equipment for you. She got a budget?' Bill directed this question at Freddie.

'Get whatever you think she needs; money's no issue.' He didn't care how much it cost; he just wanted it sorted.

'Right.' Bill nodded and stood up. 'Meet me at The Black Bear tomorrow lunchtime. I'll have your stuff then.'

Sarah nodded and Bill turned to Freddie. 'Nothing else I need to know while we're here?' He lifted one thick eyebrow.

'No. You know everything now. And thanks for understanding. I'm in a real tight corner here.' Freddie nodded, his tone sincere.

Bill nodded slowly. He thought back over the years and he shook his head sadly. 'We've been friends a long time, Fred. Nothing's going to change that.'

Bill walked out and closed the door behind him.

There was a long silence as Sarah waited for Freddie to address her. He stared at the door after Bill, his eyes cold, his expression unreadable. When it appeared as though he had forgotten she was there, she cleared her throat.

'Listen—'

'Shut up.' Freddie's words were quiet but the hard authority behind them made her think twice. She closed her mouth. There was another long silence. Eventually Freddie began to talk, his eyes still locked on the door in front of him.

'You're here to do a job. One I'm paying you very well for.' Freddie's tone was soft and deadly and a chill ran up Sarah's spine. 'If I begin to suspect for one second that you are trying to undermine me and break things down from within, I won't just send that tape of you to the police; I'll make sure that word goes around whatever prison you end up in that I want you dead. Do you understand me?'

Sarah blinked. 'It was a genuine mistake, Freddie,' she answered in a voice much more confident than she actually felt. 'I'm not trying to do anything but get on with it. I didn't see the perimeter trigger.' She clamped her mouth shut. There was no point trying to tell Freddie that she had accepted her position and was enjoying the challenge. That was something he would only believe through watching her actions.

'It better have been,' he answered eventually. 'Now get out.'

Sarah stood up and left with a scowl of annoyance on her face. Freddie was pretty certain that she was annoyed at herself rather than at him, but he couldn't be sure. He didn't have the luxury of being able to give anybody blind trust anymore, especially someone like Sarah.

He sat back and reached for his cigarettes. Lighting one, he took a deep drag and blew out a plume of smoke, watching it curl up into the air like some sort of ethereal dancer. There was beauty in this world, even in the darkest of places. But the darkness held nothing but horrors for Freddie at the moment. Threats were all around and things that used to make sense no longer did. Paul was the Mafia's prisoner, living on borrowed time. Out there somewhere one of his closest companions was whispering all of his deepest secrets to the police. Was Sarah just another threat? Was he stupid bringing her here, at such a vulnerable time? Or would her involvement pay off in the way he was hoping?

There was no way to know for sure, and for once, Freddie wasn't certain what lay around the next corner.

CHAPTER FORTY-FOUR

It was cold – freezing in fact. The tips of the long blades of grass around her bare legs were edged with glistening white crystals of frost. Her teeth chattered and her bones shook through the thin nightie she'd been wearing when her mother had thrown her outside. She hugged herself in an attempt to warm up but her skinny arms were no match against the merciless winter.

'M-m-mum, please…' Her reedy voice sounded pathetically desperate even to her own ears, and she knew that her pleas would only serve to fuel Rosie's anger further, but she had to try. It hurt everywhere that she could feel, the harshness of the cold December night unyielding.

Her bare foot began to cramp in complaint and she doubled over, trying to warm it between her hands. Hot tears stung her eyes at the pain.

'M-mummy,' she begged, beginning to sob. Only ten minutes before, she had been tucked up warm and fast asleep in her bed. She had woken up suddenly as Rosie grabbed a fistful of her hair and dragged her down the stairs. Before she could even ask what she had done wrong, she'd been thrown out of the kitchen door into the small garden behind the house.

The door flew open, and for a second Tanya thought her mother had taken pity on her, but her hopes swiftly faded as she looked up into Rosie's thunderous expression.

'Shut your scheming little mouth,' Rosie screamed in her face, before lowering her voice to a hiss. 'You are a disgusting little brat

who doesn't deserve to live in this house. All you have ever brought me is destruction. Your father's gone again, run away to greener pastures, leaving me here to deal with you.' The snarl on Rosie's face was full of hatred. 'So you'll stay out here and you'll sit there quietly until I decide you're allowed back in. I don't want to hear one sound out of you, do you hear?' Her arm shot forward and she grasped Tanya's face in her hand. 'I said, do you hear?'

Tanya's tears fell faster as her mother's bony fingers dug painfully into the soft flesh of her cheeks. She tried to nod. 'Yes, yes,' she squeaked in fear.

'Good.' Rosie pushed Tanya away from her forcefully and the young girl fell to the ground, unable to steady herself in time.

The door slammed shut again and Tanya picked herself back up, shaking even more violently than she had been before. She looked around the small garden for anything that she could wrap around her, before she froze to death. There was nothing.

Wiping away her tears with the back of her hand, she stumbled back to the small brick step under the door. She sat down and pulled her knees up to her chest, squeezing her eyes shut. She had to be good and quiet, then maybe Rosie might let her back in. She tried to think of anything else but the cold.

Replaying Rosie's words in her head she wondered where 'greener pastures' was. She had no idea. She was only four.

*

Gasping for air, Tanya woke with a start and sat upright in bed. She gulped in a deep breath, then another and another. She turned the bedside light on and looked around. She was in her bedroom at home. *Her* home. The one she had worked hard for and bought herself. No one could throw her out of it. It was just a dream, a bad nightmare.

She put her hand to her chest and took a deep slow breath trying to calm down her racing heart. Shaking her head, she ran her hands through her long, wild hair. It had been years since she had last had a nightmare, especially one like that. Her childhood was not something she liked to remember, but clearly Rosie's presence was dredging up old memories.

Tanya rested her head on one hand and rubbed the last remnant of the bad dream out of her eyes with the other. Sitting back upright, she reached for the water bottle by her bed and took a sip.

The bedroom door opened and Rosie's face appeared, concern written all over it. 'Are you OK?'

'Yeah, what's up?' Tanya replied.

'I thought I heard you crying,' Rosie said, pulling a confused face.

'Nah, I heard that too. Not sure what it was. Probably the cat,' Tanya lied.

'Oh.' Rosie rolled her eyes. 'Damn bloody thing…' She shuffled off, closing the door again behind her.

Tanya stared at the door for a few seconds. The mixture of love and fear she'd felt for Rosie as a child was still fresh in her mind. The memory of the bitter hatred it had grown into was creeping up on her and she pushed it away, reminding herself that all she should feel now was renewed love and friendship. This Rosie was a completely different person to the one she'd known back then. This Rosie wanted to make amends and build a better future for their relationship. This Rosie had looked after her every step of the way since she'd left hospital. She was the mum she'd never been before.

Sliding back down under the warm covers, Tanya shook off the memory of that cold night. It was just one of many, but she refused to let it haunt her anymore. No one could move forward in life when they were clinging to the past. She had watched so many people make that mistake and she refused to be one of them. The past was the past, and it could stay that way. Tanya Smith was moving forward, and this time her mother was coming with her. She just hoped that at some point her subconscious would realise that too.

CHAPTER FORTY-FIVE

It had been two days since Tanya had walked out of Anna's flat and she'd not seen hide nor hair of her. She had tried to call her, texted to ask if they could meet up to talk, but Tanya had ignored all of her attempts at contact. It had put Anna in the darkest of moods, to the point that even Freddie had been treading carefully. She was lost without her best friend and could not seem to find the light in anything while things weren't right between them.

She stalked into Club Anya, checking her watch with a frown. She'd been tied up at The Last Laugh for much longer than expected after one of the comedians decided he didn't want to go up on stage on the same night as one of the others. It had taken Anna a painstaking hour of ego stroking to convince him to perform, which was no mean feat when her patience was already worn so thin.

'Is that supplier here yet?' Anna barked at Carl as she walked past the bar.

He raised his eyebrows. 'Well, hello to you too. And no.' He turned back to stocking the shelves.

Anna paused and looked over. 'Sorry, not myself today. He should be arriving soon; can you point him my way?'

''Course,' Carl replied with a smile.

'Thanks.' Anna carried on and marched into her office. As the door swung open, Rosie dropped the files she'd been holding in surprise. Anna blinked and took a step back. 'What the hell are you doing in here?' she demanded with a frown. 'And what are they?'

Rosie bent down and picked them up hurriedly, her cheeks turning crimson at being caught out. 'I'm looking for the petty cash breakdown. I told Tanya I'd sort it out this month, but I need to look at the old ones to make sure I'm doing it right.'

Anna stepped forward and snatched the files out of Rosie's hands.

'Hey!' she protested, trying to swipe it back.

Anna stepped deftly out of the way and opened it up. Her eyebrows shot up. 'These are our end-of-year accounts from two years ago. This is nothing to do with petty cash. Why are you *really* looking at these?' She held them up and stared Rosie down challengingly. Rosie may have been allowed to help out here, but it didn't mean she was suddenly privy to their private files.

Rosie put her hands on her hip and looked offended. 'Well, I didn't know that, did I? I'm just trying to find what I need. Everything's a right mess in here; you can't tell the club's arse from its ear'ole the way you keep your paperwork.'

It was Anna's turn to look offended. 'Are you serious? Every single piece of paperwork in this office is filed properly, in date or alphabetic order, depending on what it is.' She stepped forward menacingly, her pent-up anger getting the better of her. 'Tanya and I have been running this place for years. We created it from nothing. Its ongoing success and popularity are because the way we do things *works*.' She stepped forward again, forcing Rosie back. 'And you think you can swan in here, into *my* club and *my* office, and tell me our methods stink?'

'Well, it's not actually your club, is it, Anna?' Rosie shot back sharply.

Anna blinked, taken aback. What did Rosie mean by that? Surely Tanya wouldn't have told her about the secret papers that placed it all in her name? That was private information; no one knew about those except for herself and Tanya. Even Freddie didn't know.

'I mean, you can't exactly sit there claiming all this is yours. It's half Tanya's and let's face it, this was all *her* dream initially, wasn't it? You just jumped on the bandwagon; you'd never even worked in a club before,' Rosie continued spitefully.

Anna let out a long breath. 'You have no idea what you're talking about, Rosie. You turn up like a bad penny after all these years and suddenly have opinions on everything? Give me a break,' Anna scoffed. 'I doubt even Tanya is going to be thrilled to hear I've found you snooping around our accounts. Bit suspect, I'd say, wouldn't you?'

Rosie narrowed her eyes with a smile and pushed her face closer to Anna's. 'Trouble is though, Anna,' she said softly, 'she ain't speaking to you right now, is she? She's pissed off at you for trying to turn her against me, isn't she? So how you gonna tell her that?'

Anna fought the urge to punch the older woman in the face. Her anger bubbled and her hand twitched, but she forced it to stay still. It would do her no favours to hurt the woman, however badly she was asking for it. Rosie was right about one thing. Tanya was already angry at Anna for what she'd said; this would cross a line that they wouldn't be able to return from.

Rosie smiled like a snake as the silence lengthened. 'That's what I thought,' she said smugly. Turning around, she stuck her nose in the air and waltzed out of the small office.

The hammering inside Anna's head grew louder and louder with each breath that she took until eventually it seemed to burst out of her with a rumbling growl.

'Gaaahhhh!' She twisted to the side and, with all her might, punched the wall. The solid surface connected with her fist and the pain immediately gave her a moment of relief. It disappeared almost instantly and so she drew back her arm and, in quick succession, smashed it back into the wall again and again, the explosion of pain that travelled up her limb each time slowly eroding the frustration and fury that had taken root inside of her.

In a frenzied trance, Anna poured all of her energy into the action. It wasn't just the pain of falling out with Tanya that was melting away, it was everything. The farm, killing Michael, watching Tanya get shot, losing the baby – all of it flashed through her mind as she continued to pummel the wall with her now bloody fist.

As the blood smeared over the magnolia paint, Anna's mind seemed to register what she was doing and logic returned. She pulled her arm back and stared at her red swelling knuckles. What was she doing? She shook with adrenaline still, but suddenly the pain stopped feeling so good and it began to really hurt.

'Oh my God,' she uttered, shaking her head in disbelief. 'What's wrong with me?'

Her gaze shot back to the wall and she groaned internally. Thankful that they had chosen to use gloss paint throughout, Anna opened a drawer in one of the filing cabinets. She pulled out some easy-clean wipes and quickly rubbed the blood smears away with her good hand. When that was done and she was sure the wipes were well hidden in the bin, Anna looked back to her hand.

The bruising was already beginning to show, dark purple patches filling the spaces between the bleeding cuts. *What had she been thinking?* She hadn't been thinking, she realised. She had just done it. Biting her lip, Anna stared at the door. There was a first aid kit in the bar, but there was no way on earth she was going to let Carl know what had just happened. He'd think she'd gone crazy. Maybe she had.

Shrugging her jacket off, Anna gingerly laid it over her injured hand as though she was too warm and wanted to carry it. Taking a deep breath, she shook her dark hair back over her shoulders and checked that she looked composed in the mirror before opening the door and walking out.

'Carl, something's come up. It can't wait. Can you please apologise to the supplier, give him some free drinks and tell him

I'll rearrange?' Anna asked as she walked past, her stilettos tapping a fast rhythm as she tried to leave as swiftly as possible.

'Oh.' Carl frowned. 'Of course. Everything OK?'

'Yes, fine,' Anna replied with a bright smile. Too bright she realised, as Carl's frown turned into one of suspicion.

'OK then, catch you later.'

But Anna didn't hear. She'd already gone.

CHAPTER FORTY-SIX

Anna stepped out into the bright sunlight and joined the throng of tourists hurrying through the noisy streets of Soho. She shivered and wished she could put her jacket on, but she couldn't – not yet. Pausing to gather her thoughts, Anna turned and stared down towards Shaftesbury Avenue. Remembering that there was a Boots in Piccadilly Circus, she decided to head there to buy what she needed to patch her hand up. Turning around to walk through the back streets, she immediately collided with someone walking the other way.

Blinking in surprise, she found herself staring into a broad, hard chest and quickly stepped back. 'Sorry…' she began but then frowned as she realised she knew who it was. 'Seamus! What are you doing here?'

'I was just on my way to drop this at your club.' He held up a scarf that Anna immediately recognised. 'You left it at the match the other night. I didn't want you to miss it. Hey.' He frowned. 'What have you done to your hand?'

Anna swiftly drew her arm back under the jacket and her cheeks burned red. 'Nothing.'

Seamus raised one eyebrow and waited for the truth.

Anna sighed. What was the point in trying to hide it? Freddie would see it anyway. As long as Carl didn't know to worry and Rosie didn't know to gloat, it didn't really matter. 'I hit a wall,' she admitted in a matter-of-fact tone. 'Really hard.'

Seamus reached for her hand. 'May I?'

They moved away from passing pedestrians, and Anna let him take her palm. He turned it over from side to side, checking out the damage. He gave a low whistle. 'I feel sorry for the wall.'

Despite how she was feeling, the smile crept up on her face and Anna laughed. 'It had it coming,' she joked.

Seamus shook his head with a grin. 'Come on, we need to get this sorted out,' he said easily, in his melodic Irish accent. 'I've got a kit in the car. Luckily it doesn't look like you've broken any bones.'

Anna fell into step beside Seamus and let him lead her through the busy streets to his car. Now that she was no longer hiding her wounds, she shrugged her jacket on, careful not to touch the injured hand any more than necessary.

'Do you always have a kit in the car?' Anna asked, curious.

'I got into the habit when I used to fight in the underground rings,' Seamus replied. 'They didn't always have the best facilities. More often than not, me da would patch me up in the car park. Figured there was no good reason to stop being cautious. You never know when you're going to need it.' He glanced down at her. 'What did the wall do, anyhow?'

Anna thought about it. It had been Rosie who'd pushed her over the edge, but was that all it was? She was certain that it wasn't. Before she'd slapped Chloe, she'd never resorted to violence when she was angry. It just wasn't her way. But here she was, having her second physical outburst in a matter of weeks. It was most definitely about more than just Rosie.

'I don't really know,' she answered quietly. 'It was just there.'

Seamus looked down at Anna again and saw the sadness wash back over her. His heart felt for the woman. He'd heard people talking about her: Freddie, Bill, Paul. They talked in whispers and behind closed doors about how Anna had changed, how she'd closed off from the world and how they couldn't seem to bring her back. Everyone was worried, but no one seemed to know what to do.

He had been there that night too, seen the horrors that she'd faced and faced a few of his own. In a strange way, he understood exactly how she felt.

They reached Seamus's car and he opened the passenger door, gesturing for her to sit down. Anna sat on the edge of the seat, still facing outwards as Seamus grabbed a rucksack from the boot. He knelt down by her feet and pulled out some supplies.

'Here.' He took her hand. 'This will sting.'

Anna drew in a sharp breath as he cleansed the wounds but held still and let him get on with it. Seamus glanced up at her face and then back down to her hand.

'You know, I still think about it all the time. At night, when my da is asleep and the world has stopped with its distractions for a few hours.' Seamus took a deep breath. 'It was his eyes. That's what I see. The image that haunts me. It was a split second; he had a gun and it was shoot or be shot.'

Anna had visibly tensed and the blood drained from her face, but she hadn't stopped him, so he carried on. 'I had no choice, but of course that doesn't matter later on when your demons won't let you rest. It doesn't make it any easier. I'd never done that before.'

The wounds clean, Seamus reached for the antiseptic cream and unscrewed the lid. Anna remained silent. 'The only thing that holds my demons at bay is fighting. When I fight in the ring, when I fight alone with a bag, I'm fighting them. I fight the guilt and the memory and the anger that burns inside of me. It releases it all, sends it away from my body through my fists.' He stopped and looked up into her eyes. 'If it's a fight you want, don't fight a wall – fight me. Let me teach you how to fight your demons properly. Because – and forgive me if I'm overstepping – but I think you need it. And I think I understand probably more than anyone else what you're going through right now.'

Anna stared into his eyes, her own filling with tears. After a few seconds, she blinked them away.

Seamus picked up the dressing and placed it over her knuckles, wrapping gauze tightly around her hand. 'We don't have to talk about anything. We can just fight. And you don't have to answer me now. The offer is there – you can take it up whenever you choose.'

Fixing the end of the dressing with a safety pin, Seamus gently placed her hand back on her lap. 'There you go. All patched up. I'd better get off; I have some errands to run for Freddie.'

Straightening up, Seamus passed Anna the scarf he had been about to drop off when he bumped into her.

'Yes, of course. You must be busy.' Anna cleared her throat and stood up. 'Thank you,' she said and smiled sadly. Seamus was just eighteen and already he'd been through so much. Underground boxing rings and gun fights were supposed to be the things of films, not a young boy's history. But despite all that, this young man had a quiet strength and a knowing way about him that most men twice his age hadn't yet developed. 'You're wise well beyond your young years, Seamus. Has anyone ever told you that?'

'I've heard it said once or twice.' Seamus grinned. 'Well.' He locked the car back up as Anna stepped away from it. 'I'll be seeing ya.' He paused as if just realising something and pulled an awkward expression. 'Er, you'll be telling Freddie about the wall, won't you? Only I'll see him later and I don't like to keep secrets.'

'Don't worry, Seamus, there's no need to hide anything,' Anna reassured him, not wanting to cause him stress after he'd been so kind to her. She waved him off with a smile and began to wander slowly back towards the club.

As she walked, Anna thought over Seamus's words. Perhaps he was right. Perhaps she did need to face her demons and fight them. The memory of the relief that came from hitting the wall crept back into her mind. Maybe she should get into the ring and learn to do it properly. She'd heard of women who'd been abused and attacked taking self-defence classes to help themselves heal mentally. This wasn't that different really.

Pushing her hair back behind her ear, she made the decision to try it out. What harm could it do anyway?

CHAPTER FORTY-SEVEN

Sarah sat at the bar in Club CoCo nursing the gin and tonic in front of her as she observed the people around her. Freddie's main club was actually a pretty nice place, she had to grudgingly admit. With dark, atmospheric tones and modern, expensive-looking furniture, it practically oozed sex appeal. Which of course was exactly the sort of thing a club needed to ooze, in order for the rich and beautiful to grace it with their presence.

The staff were pleasing to the eye. Gavin, the bar manager was a real looker, not someone she'd turn down given half a chance. The female clients must love him, she realised shrewdly. But of course it was the women who worked here that truly dazzled. The people who spent the most money were large groups of men and therefore the focus would be on drawing them in.

The barmaids were stunning, their ample assets on subtle display, and standing at the door every weekend come rain or shine was the PR manager, Holly. Strikingly beautiful with long, silky platinum locks and big blue eyes, she knew exactly what she was doing placing herself on the front line to draw them in. She was a modern-day siren. It wasn't exactly in her job description to stand there with the doormen, but she knew what her strengths were and she played them to the max. It was a smart move, Sarah had to admit. The hot-blooded young men on the door saw her as a sexy challenge, but all Holly gave them was a smile and the most direct route to the bar.

Sarah idly wondered whether Holly had ever tried her luck with her broodingly good-looking boss. It wouldn't be the first story of its kind. She wouldn't get far though; Sarah knew that. Even after all these years, Freddie was still besotted with his girlfriend Anna. No other woman could compare to her. It would almost be sweet, were it not so sickening, Sarah thought with a sneer. She took another sip of her gin. The thought of Anna reminded her of her suspicions of pillow talk.

She'd hit dead ends with everyone she'd followed so far. Nothing seemed out of the ordinary, no red flags had popped up. That wasn't to say that Freddie's men were in the clear, not yet. But it did mean she needed to start looking at other options. It was time to think outside the box. Could it have been a wife or girlfriend? Or was there another explanation that she hadn't yet thought of?

Lost in thought, Sarah began tapping her fingernail against her glass. *Chink, chink, chink.* The noise fell into the same rhythm as the music. As Gavin passed, he glanced down at her hand to see what the new noise was. He winked at her and carried on mixing his customer's cocktail. *Chink, chink, chink.*

She stopped and sat upright. That was it! Could it be? She picked up the phone. There was only one way to test her theory.

'Hey, I'm in CoCo – can you come meet me?' She paused. 'Great, oh and could you bring Zack? I have an idea.'

*

Freddie walked in the front door of his and Anna's apartment and closed it softly behind him. He could hear the noise of the TV coming from the lounge and so made his way through, undoing the top two buttons of his shirt as he went. It had been a long day. Anna sat in the dark, curled up on the sofa with a glass of wine in her hand, watching a film. The bandaged hand lay loosely in her lap.

'Hey,' she greeted him tiredly. It was late even by their standards, but she'd wanted to stay up to see him. She'd missed him.

'Hey,' he responded quietly, walking through and sitting down on the coffee table in front of her. 'Let me see?' he asked. Anna passed her hand over and he began to gently undo the gauze.

They sat in silence in the dark room as he removed all the bandages, the only light coming from the flickering TV screen. When they were off, Anna stretched out her hand and pulled in a sharp breath of pain. Freddie stilled it with his own and checked it over with a critical eye.

'Seamus did well wrapping it tight like that. It's kept most of the swelling at bay. You should be OK to keep this off now, if you'd rather,' he said.

'Yes, I think I will,' Anna replied, pulling it back and studying it herself. She'd certainly done a number on it; it looked terrible. Purple and red, it didn't look like her hand at all.

Freddie leaned forward and rubbed the tops of Anna's arms. She leaned into him and gave him a lingering kiss on the lips. Freddie rested his forehead against hers and Anna breathed him in. He smelt like home. This was exactly what she had been craving all evening. With everything going on and without Tanya to bounce off, she had never felt so deflated.

'Seamus mentioned that he'd offered to teach you to box,' Freddie murmured.

'Yes, he did,' Anna replied.

'Do you want to take him up on it?'

'Maybe.' She relaxed back into the sofa and took a sip of her wine, reaching her good hand out towards Freddie. He took it and held it. 'Only if it doesn't interfere with his work though; I know you have him on a lot of jobs.'

Freddie shook his head. 'Not at all. He still has plenty of time to train you.' He didn't add that he thought it was a good idea. This had to be Anna's choice; he couldn't sway her either way. But the idea had given Freddie renewed hope. It could be a step towards getting Anna back to her full self again. Or at the very least take her mind off all this business with Tanya.

'It's not exactly my sort of hobby,' she said with a small laugh, 'but maybe Seamus is onto something. I don't know what's got into me lately, but going round hitting people and punching walls is *not* my usual style.' She shook her head, ashamed of her behaviour. She must seem like some attention-seeking scumbag. 'I need to work it out.'

Freddie nodded. He rubbed his thumb across the back of her soft pale hand. She meant the world to him. He just wished he could reach in and take away all the darkness and confusion that was dampening her soul. But he couldn't. And he wasn't able to express that to her either. It just wasn't their way.

Anna watched his thumb trail over her hand and suddenly wondered if he would still be so caring towards her if he knew what she was planning? She still hadn't asked him for permission to open the whorehouse. It would technically be in competition with his own business, and he had spent a lifetime earning the right to be the underworld ruler of this area. He'd shed blood, sweat and tears to get to where he was. No other players had been allowed to open up houses on his patch, so why would he let her? Tanya seemed confident that he would, but at the end of the day it was business. And it made no business sense to give her permission. If she was in his position, she'd decline him on the spot. But she had promised Tanya she would try, so she would.

If Freddie said no, as she was sure he would, they'd just have to open it outside the central belt. It wouldn't be ideal; the punters would have to travel, but that was the deal they had made with the girls. No funny business in the club and in return they would provide a safe alternative place to go afterwards. She'd made a promise, and she wouldn't go back on that now. And if this was the case, then Freddie would have no grounds to be angry with her about it. She would respect the rules, but that did not stop her from working around them.

Nervous that her next words were going to ruin the quiet moment between them, Anna took a deep breath. There was no perfect time to open up this discussion, so it may as well be now.

'Listen, I need to talk to you about something.'

'What is it?' Freddie asked, looking up into her eyes.

She paused for a moment, mesmerised as she always was by his intense gaze. His hazel-green eyes bored into her, and for a moment she considered forgetting about the conversation entirely. All she wanted to do was unbutton the rest of his shirt and seek comfort in the sculpted body she knew she'd find beneath. His musky scent filled her nostrils and she breathed him in deeply.

'Do you remember when I found Chloe out the back of the club?' she asked, forcing her business hat back on.

'Yeah, what about her?'

She cut to the chase. 'Tanya and I want to open up a house for the girls. Somewhere they can take their clients.' She tilted her head up. 'They're doing it anyway and I'd rather it be somewhere safe and regulated than in the back alley. And I'd also rather it wasn't connected to the club. If we open up a house, we can keep the two totally separate. And at least make something from it ourselves. Everybody would win. If we're allowed to go ahead with it, that is.'

Coming to a stop on her pitch, she clamped her mouth shut and waited tensely for Freddie's response. He stared at her, his expression unreadable.

'You're asking for my permission,' he stated flatly. He exhaled slowly.

Anna's stomach flipped. She'd known it wouldn't go down well. He looked annoyed. 'If it's a no that's fine,' she said defensively. 'Say no more; we'll look at doing it outside the boundaries. We—'

'I didn't say no, Anna,' he interrupted her, his tone irritated. 'Christ.' He sat back and rubbed his face. 'You don't have to ask my permission for anything. Ever,' he stressed. 'Why would you even think that you did?'

Anna was confused. 'Because this is your turf, Freddie. You are the head of the firm and these types of businesses are under your jurisdiction. I'm well aware of that.'

Freddie shook his head in disbelief. 'Yeah, OK, that's basically true. But you aren't just anyone. You're family.' He paused to catch her eye. 'Our businesses have always been separate, yes. But that doesn't mean our interests are. Family is family. You want to open up a whorehouse – and honestly' – his eyes widened – 'I never thought I'd live to see the day that those words came out of *your* mouth – but that's fine. Fuck, if you came home one day and told me you wanted to sell Arabian horse cock out of the living room that would be fine.'

Anna immediately burst out laughing, and it was so infectious that Freddie couldn't help but join in, despite how serious he was trying to come across.

'Arabian horse cock?' she asked, tears of mirth beginning to run down her face. 'Tell me that's not a thing.'

'Yeah, well, you never know. Seriously though.' He sobered up. 'You don't have to answer to me for anything. In this family, we support and help each other. Whatever we want to do. I mean' – he shook his head with a small smile – 'look at all we've been through. Remember that time we nearly had to run away to South America? You were willing to up and leave your whole life to come with me. And you really think I'd let that level of support go just one way?'

'I never really thought about it,' Anna admitted.

'I don't ever want you to think that I wouldn't support you in the same way you support me,' Freddie said, with meaning. 'No, I wouldn't allow that from a competitor. But family isn't competition. Family is… well, it's what it's all for.'

Anna felt a stab of grief as Freddie unwittingly reminded her of her miscarriage. She hid her feelings, not wanting him to realise and feel guilty.

'I would do anything for you, Anna. *Anything.*' Freddie stopped there, not wanting to push too far. Anna was still fragile, and the last thing he wanted to do was get too close to her troubles and for her to pull away again.

She felt stupid. How could she have questioned Freddie's response? How could she have looked at the situation so coldly, all business? A small voice in the back of her head answered, *Because you're dead inside. You died that day at the farmhouse.* She closed her eyes and pushed the internal demon away. She wasn't dead inside, at least not completely. She might struggle with the past, but she still loved people. Freddie was the love of her life, and right now all she wanted to do was curl up in his arms and forget that she had been so blind.

She reached forward and wrapped her arms around him, kissing him hungrily. Freddie tensed momentarily, surprised, but quickly recovered and grasped her to him. He took the wine from her hand and placed it on the table before picking her up and carrying her through to the bedroom.

Anna melted into his strong embrace and let herself go. Her demons were still lurking, but for tonight they could wait.

CHAPTER FORTY-EIGHT

Paul woke to the morning light coming through the hotel window. He grimaced as the cuffs that chained him to the bedpost cut into his wrist painfully. This was the fifth day he'd been here chained up like this. Four nights of pure discomfort. Shifting slightly, he tried to lie less awkwardly, but it was difficult. With his free hand, he rubbed the sleep from his eyes. He was desperate for a piss, but he already knew that there was no point asking. They came through every few hours to take him to the loo and feed him, but other than this he was ignored. On the first day he had kicked up, demanding to be uncuffed, and all that had earned him was a punch to the face and a closed door.

Voices wafted through from the other room and he tilted his head to listen.

'… and what if he's telling the truth? What if he really is that useless?' Paul couldn't work out whose voice it was.

'Then we still kill the bastard anyway. Him, his brother, all of them. If we don't find out who it was, at least that will serve as a warning of what we can do.' This voice was Vito's, he was sure of that. 'And as far as holding off much longer goes, I'm losing patience. We've all got pressing business back home. If he doesn't come up with something soon, then it's time to clear up and move out.'

An icy trickle of fear crept up Paul's neck and he swallowed hard. Closing his eyes, he wished there was some way he could get out of here and get to Freddie. Freddie needed all the help he could get if he was going to pull this plan off and Paul was no longer sure he would manage it in time. He shuffled back down the bed, laying his head down on the pillow tiredly.

Was this the end of the line for the Tyler brothers? Was it the end of the line for them all?

*

Anna's hand was starting to heal up. She'd stayed away from the club until now, texting Tanya to ask her to cover. Tanya had actually replied to this text, though it had been curt and all business. The lack of any emotion in her response had both hurt and worried Anna greatly. She had considered going over to apologise and withdraw her comments about Rosie, but when it came down to it, she just couldn't. She couldn't lie to her best friend and neither could she dispel her concerns about Rosie. Something bad was brewing, something to do with Rosie, but she just couldn't put her finger on what. The problem was, now that Tanya had her defences up, Anna couldn't be there to help her when it all eventually came out. This was what was worrying her the most.

She greeted Carl as she walked through towards the back office and he grinned widely.

'You're back! How are you feeling? Tanya said you had a cold,' he said.

'Oh, I'm fine.' Anna cast her eyes away. 'Just needed a couple of days to rest.'

'Drink?' Carl asked, holding up an empty wine glass.

Anna bit her lip as she considered. There was no doubt a whole pile of paperwork on her desk to be done, but it could wait for a while. 'Sure, go on then.' She slipped onto an empty bar stool and waited as Carl poured her a glass of Pinot. Taking the glass from him with a grateful smile, she saw him register her bruised hand with its grazed knuckles.

'Christ, what you done?' His brow furrowed into a look of concern.

'Fell down the stairs in my building,' she lied with a roll of her eyes. 'This hand took the brunt of it.'

Carls frown deepened. 'You don't take the stairs in your building,' he replied sceptically. 'You have a lift.'

Shit, Anna thought. 'It broke down.'

'Well, that must have been a bugger, from all the way up there.' Carl eyed her suspiciously.

'Yep. It was. Luckily it's all fixed now though.' Anna smiled brightly and took a sip of her wine. This was why she didn't like to lie. If you told one lie, you usually had to tell a few more just to back it up. But it was still better than admitting the truth. Carl thought the world of her and Tanya, and he'd be upset to find out she'd been in such a state that she'd attacked a wall.

Eventually Carl shrugged, accepting the information. 'So, what's going on between you and Tanya at the moment anyway?' he asked, picking up a glass to polish.

'What do you mean?' Anna tried to sound casual.

'Oh, come off it, you know exactly what I mean,' Carl chided. 'What's happened?'

Anna sighed and tried to work out where to begin.

'Is it about Rosie?' he asked, lowering his voice.

'Well, yes, it is actually. Wait.' Anna lowered her voice too. 'Is she here?'

Carl nodded and tilted his head towards the stockroom.

Anna pulled a face. 'I'll tell you later then,' she murmured.

As if knowing she was the focus of their conversation, Rosie appeared, shrugging on her borrowed coat. Anna hid her annoyance at seeing it on her. Rosie was all over everything of Tanya's these days, it seemed.

'I'm off then, Carl, can't be late for the meeting,' she said, with an air of self-importance. 'Oh.' she caught sight of Anna. 'Hello.'

Anna raised her eyebrows at the other woman coolly and didn't respond. She was tired of playing nice with her after all the shit-stirring she'd been doing.

Ignoring the icy response, Rosie swept past and disappeared out of the front door. Carl waited a few more seconds before he resumed their conversation.

'Go on then, spill.' He placed the spotless shiny glass back in its space and picked up another one.

Anna tilted her head to one side thoughtfully. 'It's Thursday, right?'

'Right,' Carl confirmed.

'She doesn't hold a meeting on Thursdays.'

They looked at each other for a moment and Carl thought about it. 'No, she doesn't usually,' he replied.

Without another word, Anna stood up and shrugged her jacket back on. 'I'm going to see what she's up to,' she said as she marched towards the exit. 'I'll be back. Oh, and don't tell Tanya,' she shot over her shoulder.

'I won't, don't you worry,' Carl said, widening his eyes at the thought. Whatever these two were going through, he certainly wasn't going to get involved. Neither of them needed any further fuel added to the fire right now.

The door slammed behind Anna and Carl shrugged. He hoped whatever it was she was looking for that she found it soon. Because both girls were utterly miserable at the moment. They needed each other more than they realised.

CHAPTER FORTY-NINE

Sarah crouched down behind the bins at the end of the road as Sammy turned to look over his shoulder. He'd done so a couple of times on his journey from the local shop back to the bookies, but Sarah didn't think it was because of her. He seemed to check behind himself habitually, wherever he went.

As Sammy reached the door to the bookies, Sarah pulled a stick of gum from her pocket and put it in her mouth. Chewing, she narrowed her eyes at the nondescript car parked down at the other end of the road. She knew for a fact that this was a police car. There was a loose tail on Sammy, one she had been dodging successfully so far. Freddie had told her all about the task force. She had listened with mixed feelings. Once upon a time, she would have headed such a team, especially with Ben Hargreaves putting it together. A pang of longing had stabbed through her stomach, but she was fully aware that her loyalties lay on the other side now, whether she liked it or not. It was her job to keep off the radar, and any information she gained on their strategy she needed to feed straight back to Freddie.

Turning away, she pushed her hands down into the pockets of her leather jacket and walked briskly back the way she had come, towards her own parked car. Sammy didn't appear to be the rat from what she could tell, but she'd had to check. His routine was fairly rigid, only changing whenever Freddie called him in to do something. There were no serious women on the scene and no family or friends, other than those within the Tyler firm.

Unlocking her car, Sarah glanced over her shoulder then slid into the driver's seat. Reaching into the bag next to her, she pulled out a small iPad and pressed the button that brought the screen to life. Now that Bill was helping her, she had access to all sorts of equipment that she hadn't before. Even when she'd been working in the force, they hadn't had some of this tech. Some of it was because it would breach regulations, but some of it just hadn't been made available to them. Now though, she just needed to look at the CCTV outside Club CoCo.

Bill had helped her set up all the camera feeds to connect to her iPad so that wherever she was, she could access them. She had both Freddie's clubs and access to the traffic cams near Freddie's home. Bill had found a back door into this system, so although she couldn't move the cameras or zoom in, she had access to the city council's surveillance.

With a touch of the screen she was back to the live feed outside CoCo and she peered at the busy street scene. What she wanted to know was whether or not there was a tail car on Freddie at the moment. It was a priority of hers to stay off their radar. If any one of them saw her and took a photo back to the task force, there were several people who she was sure could identify her immediately.

Squinting and pulling the screen closer, she could just about make out the nose of one of the cars she had logged.

'Damn,' she cursed. That ruled out going over there. About to switch it off, something else caught Sarah's eye. She frowned. There was a woman across the road loitering outside one of the shops. This was the second time in two days she'd seen the same woman at the same point. As she watched, the woman glanced across the road towards the club. She didn't seem particularly interested in the shopfront at all. In fact, this was why Sarah had picked up on her presence last time too. Her behaviour was out of place.

Taking a screenshot, Sarah made a mental note to show it to Freddie and ask if he recognised her. Though the chances would be slim – the photo was grainy at best. As Sarah watched, a young child ran out of the shop and put his hand in hers. They walked off together out of sight of the cameras. She shrugged and put the iPad away. Perhaps it was just coincidence after all.

Starting the ignition, Sarah bit her lip and pondered who to follow next. As her thoughts landed on one person, she pursed her lips and pulled out into the road. This one she'd been curious about from the start.

CHAPTER FIFTY

Anna hunched into the collar of her jacket, careful to make sure her footsteps were silent as she followed Rosie down the street towards the Charterhouse.

She slowed down when she got to the green, making sure she didn't gain on Rosie too quickly as she passed through the gates. On the way over, Anna found herself wondering again if she was just mad. It wasn't like she'd actually found any evidence that these meetings were fake; if anything, the last time had confirmed that Rosie was telling the truth. But something kept niggling her and she had to be sure.

Rosie unlocked the front door and disappeared inside, into the darkness. Anna sighed. Rosie was exactly where she said she'd be, yet again. There were probably a bunch of people inside waiting for her guidance. About to turn away, Anna paused. If there were a bunch of people inside, then why was it so dark?

Ignoring her better judgement, which was screaming at her to go home, Anna crossed the road and went in through the gates. The chapel loomed above her to the right and tall dark windows stared down at her from in front. Hurrying to the front door, she tried the handle and breathed a small sigh of relief as she found it was unlocked. She stepped inside, squinting as her eyes adjusted to the dark. Rosie was nowhere to be seen.

Looking around, Anna found herself in what appeared to be a small shop with a reception desk at the front. To her right, there was some sort of long hallway leading to the chapel and a small museum which curved around the back of the hallway. Behind her were some sort of educational meeting rooms, and to the left, there was a passage that led to the living areas of the old monastery.

Creeping down the short hallway to the door behind her, which led to the main educational room, she peered in through the window. It was in darkness.

Next, she headed towards the chapel, walking down a long, creepy-looking hallway. The tall ceiling and ancient crooked walls gave off a distinctly eerie feeling. She took a deep breath to calm her racing heart.

'Stop being a wimp,' she whispered to herself.

The shadows moved as she walked on, slow enough to stay quiet but fast enough to get to the chapel doors quickly. A small stone carving glared down at her from its nook in the wall as she passed, daring her to give in to her fear. She reached the carved stone archway that led through to the chapel and allowed herself a momentary pause of relief.

Creeping forward, Anna began to circle around the back of the old chapel. Suddenly the sound of whispers hit her ears and she froze, tilting her head to listen. It was Rosie. Her heart began to pound as all her senses tingled. What was she up to?

Following the sounds, Anna hid behind a wooden pillar. As she peered around it and looked up to a small balcony, she could make out two shadowy figures in the dark. The one half-facing her was Rosie; she could tell by her size and shape. The second figure was much bigger, a man, but that was all she could make out as he had his back to her.

Their frantic whispers became clearer but still not quite clear enough, so she crept forward, being painfully careful not to make a sound.

'… it's there, I tell you, in her personal safe,' Rosie said. 'It can't be anywhere else; I've been through everything.'

What was she talking about? Anna frowned. What had Rosie been looking for?

'The bitch is there every time I turn a corner, but I've still had a thorough look. It's the only place I can't get into. The only place she'd keep something like that too, if you think about it. She'd be paranoid about it falling into the wrong hands if she left it anywhere else.'

Anna's eyes widened as suspicion crept in. Was Rosie talking about the deeds that signed everything over to Tanya? How would she even know about that? Surely Tanya wouldn't have told her. But the memory of their argument in the office came back to her. She had wondered back then if she knew too.

'I know that's the only place I'd keep a document that took my business away from me,' Rosie continued. 'But I can't find the key for love nor money. She must keep it on her.'

Anna's jaw dropped and her breathing quickened. It *was* that. Rosie did know. But what did that have to do with the man up there with her?

'That's not a problem,' the man whispered back dismissively. 'If you can get me in after closing tomorrow night, I'll bring the tools to break into it. Stage it so it looks like a general break-in to the club.'

Anna blinked and stopped breathing for a moment as something niggled at the back of her mind. Her brain was trying to tell her something, but she couldn't quite reach it. It was his voice – there was something familiar about the way…

The moonlight shone across his face as he turned in a frustrated circle on the balcony above and Anna put both hands over her mouth to stifle a gasp as the realisation of who the voice belonged to finally hit home.

Why on earth was he here with Rosie? How did they even know each other? Her breathing became more ragged as she suddenly realised the danger she was in. She needed to get out of here right now. She shook her head in disbelief. *How was this happening?*

'As soon as we get our hands on it, we'll wait for the hype to die down, make sure Tanya's ownership becomes public knowledge and then' – he turned back to face Rosie again – 'we'll kill her. Make it look like an accident.'

Anna's jaw dropped in horror and her heart fell through her stomach like a ball of ice. His words seemed to reverberate around her brain until they became a jumble of white noise that threatened to overwhelm her. They were planning to murder Tanya. She had to get out of here, warn her before it was too late – warn everyone!

Still caught up in these horrifying revelations, Anna stepped back without looking first. It was only a small sound, but it was enough to alert them to her presence as her foot sent a loose stone chip hurtling down the stone hallway off into the dark void beyond.

'Who's there?' he roared, running along the balcony towards the set of stairs that Anna knew came out just behind her. In a panic, she set off running full pelt back the way she came, through the old stone archway into the hallway beyond.

Her heart leaped into her mouth as she heard the heavy treads of his feet behind her. She turned to look fearfully over her shoulder as she reached the end of the hallway and saw him bowl into view just as she exited. Terrified as she was, she gave silent thanks for the cover of darkness. At least he hadn't yet seen her face. If he saw her face, she was dead. No one even knew where she was. She hadn't even really told Carl; all she had told him was to stay quiet, to not tell Tanya. She could have happily kicked herself for that decision now.

'Where are you?' he shouted from behind her. She nearly jumped out of her skin. He was close, but he hadn't yet seen which way she'd run. Whirling around, Anna quickly weighed up the options. There was a set of stairs, but if she went up, she would be trapped. There were a few doors. She chose the one at the other end of the hall and ran straight for it. As she dashed through the door, it creaked, its hinges old and weary. Straight away, she heard the heavy thuds of his feet heading her way.

'Shit,' she squeaked under her breath, cringing.

Not stopping to think, she ran through the large, grand room beyond to another doorway and the ground seemed to give way as she found herself falling. It took every ounce of her self-discipline not to cry out as she rolled down the steps and onto the unforgiving flagstones.

Ignoring the searing pain that shot through her knee, she forced herself up and tried to run. Looking around wildly, she realised she was now trapped in some sort of old enclosed walkway. It reminded her of a dungeon. The only light came from the row of windows on her right. Her fear intensified. There was nowhere to go but forward and the hallway was long. She wasn't going to make it.

Gritting her teeth, Anna began to run.

The heavy footfalls grew louder. He was just the other side of the door. She was only a few feet ahead, her only saving grace the door that barred his view. Any second he'd jump through and reach her. Anna braced herself.

Out of nowhere, a pair of hands suddenly shot out from the wall and grabbed her roughly, dragging her back into a hidden crevice beside a sealed-off doorway. The arms that held her were strong and unyielding as they swallowed her into the darkness. Anna instinctively screamed out in terror, but a hand quickly covered her mouth, muffling the sound.

Her pursuer burst through, and she heard his feet hit the ground as he vaulted down the steps. Anna froze. Her captor froze too, both of them silent as ghosts in the wall.

He stopped just yards away and Anna held her breath. All he had to do was turn and peer into the doorway properly and he'd catch sight of their little hidey hole. If he did that, there was nowhere else to go; he'd have her.

Another set of feet came pattering down the stairs, smaller lighter ones. 'Where've they gone?' Anna heard Rosie ask.

'I dunno. I thought they came down here, but there's nowhere to go,' he replied, doubt colouring his tone.

'Maybe they went through the kitchens,' Rosie replied. There was a pause before she continued. 'It was probably one of the old blokes going for a late-night prayer.'

'But why would they run?'

'Well, you probably scared him, didn't ya?' Rosie chided. 'You did shout pretty aggressive. Poor bloke probably had a heart attack.'

'I guess.' The man didn't sound convinced, but Anna heard the sounds of Rosie pulling him away.

'Ahh come on, it were nothing. What could it be? You're getting paranoid.'

'Yeah, well, you would be too if you'd been through what I have.'

Their conversation died off as they walked back to the chapel to continue their plans. When the sounds had faded to nothing, the arms around Anna's body and the hand on her mouth loosened. She immediately jumped out into the light of the tunnel and backed away from the person who had grabbed and held her, panting still from the fright.

Her saviour stepped out of the shadows and Anna frowned, blinking to make sure she was seeing correctly. 'What the hell?' she exclaimed, shaking her head in pure disbelief. 'Well, this really is quite a night.'

CHAPTER FIFTY-ONE

Anna stepped behind the busy bar and poured herself a glass of wine. Carl and the barmen were all busy with customers and she didn't want to disturb them. The twins were up on stage performing their act for the excited crowd, accompanied by loud, upbeat music. It was Friday night and the club was packed out, just like always. Anna smiled serenely as she looked around, keeping up the pretence that tonight was just a normal night. They couldn't do anything to spook Rosie, not now.

Sarah Riley sat on a stool further down the bar. She had a drink in her hand and to anyone who didn't know her, she was just another customer enjoying the entertainment. When she had stepped out of the shadows and revealed herself to Anna the night before, Anna had never been more surprised or grateful to see her. As they snuck back out of the Charterhouse, Sarah had confessed that she had been following her but didn't elaborate on why.

'All you need to know,' she'd said, 'is that I'm looking into something for Freddie. I was merely eliminating you from the process.'

Despite her curiosity, Anna had accepted this and questioned no further. There were more pressing things at hand, and she had just been glad that Sarah had been there to save her. A few more seconds and he would have caught her, and if he had, she wouldn't have lived to tell the tale. But he didn't catch her, and she certainly *had* told the tale. Now their counter plan was in motion and all she had to do was wait.

Rosie wandered through to the bar and cast an eye over to the clock. It was only another half hour or so until closing. She sidled up to Anna casually. 'I've got some things Tanya asked me to take care of for her, so I'll be here late. I can close up,' she said.

'Really?' Anna forced herself to sound natural. 'Surely whatever it is can wait until tomorrow? You must be tired.'

'No, I'm fine,' Rosie responded quickly. 'I'd rather get it done and have it out the way.'

Yeah, I bet you would, Anna thought darkly. She pushed down the bitter anger she felt towards the snake the stood beside her and instead shrugged. 'Suit yourself.' Unable to stand her closeness a moment longer, Anna walked back into the office. She shut the door and leaned back against it, closing her eyes.

Taking a deep breath, she grabbed her jacket from the hook and strode back out to find Rosie. She was standing at the reception stand, nosing through the bookings for the following night.

'Ah, here you are,' Anna said. 'If you're sure you're OK to lock up, I'm going to head off.'

'Yeah, yeah.' Rosie waved her away dismissively, not making eye contact. 'You go.'

'OK, see you later then.'

'Mmm.'

Walking past the bar, Anna began heading down the passageway that led to the back. Glancing over her shoulder to make sure no one was watching, she paused by the basement door. Rosie was engrossed in the book and Carl was busy with a customer. Opening the door, she slipped inside and made her way down to the stockroom.

*

'Tan, please. Just come with me, yeah?' Freddie pleaded impatiently. They were in Tanya's flat, and although she had grudgingly let him in, she now stood stubbornly with her arms folded and a stony face.

'But where to, Freddie? If you can't even tell me that, then why on earth would I just blindly follow you out somewhere in the middle of the night?' Tanya asked. 'Would you if you were me?'

Freddie hesitated. 'Fair point. But you have to trust me on this one, Tan. There's something you need to see.'

Freddie had wanted to tell Tanya, but Anna had insisted that he couldn't. Given how strained their relationship had become, especially since their previous argument, there was no way Tanya would believe it. She had to see things unfold for herself. It was the only way. But now it seemed that Anna's plan wasn't all it was cracked up to be. And Tanya had a point – why would she blindly follow him when he was acting so shadily?

'This is clearly some big plan to get me to speak to Anna, and I get it, Freddie, really I do, but—'

'Tanya,' Freddie cut her off as he glanced at the clock on the wall. He was running out of time. 'Look…' He stepped forward and grasped her arms. 'We've known each other a long time. We've been friends – family even – for a long time, and in the last few years I've never given you any reason not to trust me, have I?'

'Well, no, I guess not…' Tanya's resolve began to wane. 'But—'

'I've never tried to tell you how to live your life, have I? Even that time when Anna was gone and you went off the rails, shoving coke up your nose every two seconds, making big life changes. I told you I was concerned, but I didn't try to push you to do anything you didn't want. So why would I get involved in your little spat, eh?'

'Because you'd do anything for Anna,' Tanya replied flatly.

'I would. But this isn't about her,' Freddie replied, his tone determined. 'You need to come with me, and I can't tell you why because you have to see it for yourself.'

Tanya bit her lip as she considered going. He pressed forward.

'Please? I'll bring you straight back here, and I promise I'll never turn up at this time of the night asking for anything ever again.'

Tanya snorted and raised an eyebrow.

'OK, well, unless I really need to. I realise this isn't the first time.' Freddie rolled his eyes.

Tanya sighed and dropped her arms. 'Freddie, you can always turn up if you need to. That's what family's for.' She reached for a jacket and shrugged it on over the yoga pants and jumper she'd been chilling in. 'But I swear to God if I find out you haven't got a bloody good reason for making me leave the house like this, I'll fucking murder you, Freddie Tyler,' she threatened.

If he hadn't been about to tear her whole life apart once more, Freddie would have laughed. Instead all he managed to conjure up was a sad smile as he followed her out.

CHAPTER FIFTY-TWO

It was pitch black in the small basement and the three figures waited in silence. They could have turned on the light, but it would have been seen through the door cracks and Anna didn't want to give anyone reason to check it out. Closing time had been and gone, the partygoers leaving to find somewhere nearby that would serve them something hot and greasy to soak up the alcohol. The bar staff had chatted as they'd cleaned down for the night and split up their tips. Carl had eventually gone home, after checking that all was as it should be and now there was only Rosie, still hiding out in the office, waiting for her accomplice.

Anna still couldn't figure out how the two had even become connected. It was an odd situation, and she hoped to find answers when everything came to a head. It wouldn't be long now. She'd given the key to the cleaning cupboard by the toilets to Sarah, and she was currently there, lying in wait. She would have it open just a crack, enough to hear and see Rosie bringing him through to the office from the back door when he arrived. Once he was in the office, Sarah would come to get them and they would have him surrounded.

Bill and Sammy sat on crates either side of her, both tooled up and ready for what was coming. Anna strained her ears but still couldn't hear anything. It was virtually soundproof down there, and the white noise from the water tank covered any small sounds which might otherwise have made it through. It would have been more convenient to have hidden somewhere upstairs, but the cleaning cupboard was the only place. It was small, only big enough to fit one person and nobody knew Sarah. If she had been unlucky enough to have been discovered by one of the bar staff, she could have feigned drunk misjudgement and texted Anna to let her know they would have to go in blind.

Luckily, this was not the case, and Anna looked up as light suddenly filtered down the stairs. Sarah beckoned silently for them to come up. Sammy darted forward and made his way up first, followed by Anna and Bill. They stood outside the office door and could hear the excited whispers from the traitors within. The sound of a drill came through the door and Anna decided that enough was enough. She pushed the door open hard and it hit the wall behind with a bang.

Rosie let out a small scream of shock and backed away towards her accomplice. He turned with a look of anger on his face at being interrupted.

'You,' he spat and went to make his way towards her menacingly.

'I don't fucking think so,' said Bill as he walked past Anna, pointing his gun directly at his head. The man faltered, a look of panic flooding over his face. 'Drop the drill. Now.'

He did as he was told, but his face twisted into a bitter mask and he snarled in frustration.

Now that the man in front of her was no longer an immediate threat, Anna stepped forward into her office, an icy expression on her face, the crack of her heels loud in the tense silence. Sammy slipped in the other side of her and pointed his gun at Rosie. Sarah waited by the door, leaning back on the frame to watch it all unravel.

Anna glared at the two intruders, trying to work out which one to address first. Her hatred towards each of them was equal in its might. She eventually decided on Rosie.

'I knew you were up to something,' she said quietly. 'I could feel it, from the second you arrived. *Why now?* I thought. You hadn't given one jot of thought to your daughter for all these years. You made her childhood hell. You hated her.' Anna's face twisted in disgust.

Rosie didn't answer. For once she wasn't sure what to say, how to get out of the corner she'd backed herself into.

Anna turned to him. 'And you.' She looked him up and down, still so confused. 'I don't even know where to start.' Anna stopped and swallowed hard, a flood of emotions threatening to engulf her as she stared into the hate-filled eyes that bored into hers. 'Yours was the last face I ever expected to see again.'

He opened his mouth to reply but Bill cocked the gun and pushed it closer. He stopped, eying it warily.

'There will be time for you to have your say,' Anna said. 'But not yet. There's someone else you need to explain yourself to first.'

CHAPTER FIFTY-THREE

The sound of Tanya's voice wafted down the hallway.

'What are we doing *here*, Freddie? Christ's sake, it's bleedin' closed. If you wanted a drink, I had some back at the flat.'

Tanya stepped into view and she stopped suddenly just outside the door, looking in. She blinked a couple of times in shock as she saw the guns and then eventually her gaze landed on the man standing next to her mother. Her hands shot to her mouth and she gasped in horror.

There in front of her was the one person she had never thought she would see again. The man who had loved her, slept in her bed and shared her life for a whole year. The man who had then turned on her and left her to die, bleeding out alone and scared in a cold dark barn. A million bittersweet memories flashed through her mind as she stared into the dark brown eyes of her ex, Tom.

'Oh my God,' she cried. 'What is he doing here?' She turned as white as a sheet and one of her hands instinctively moved down to her stomach, where she'd been shot. 'Freddie? Mum? What's going on?'

Rosie saw her chance and went for it, licking her lips before she spoke. 'I don't know. I was just here doing paperwork and then everyone just burst in. They turned a gun on me like I'm some sort of criminal, but—'

'Oh just stop,' Anna cried. She turned to her best friend, speaking urgently. 'Tanya, I knew that something was off about your mum. I know you didn't want to hear it and Christ, I don't blame you. I'd feel the same. But I knew. I could sense it from the moment she came back – she wanted something.'

'All I wanted was me daughter,' Rosie shot, her eyes pleading for Tanya to believe her.

Anna ignored her and carried on. Tanya just stood there, still in shock from seeing Tom.

'I followed her to the Charterhouse last night.'

It was Rosie's turn to gasp. Tom shot her a furious look.

'She wasn't holding a meeting, Tan – that was all a lie. There are no meetings. She was meeting Tom in secret. I overheard them talking. They know about the document. The one that puts the club in your name.' Freddie shot her a puzzled look. 'She's been searching for it and worked out that it must be in my personal safe. *That's* what she told Tom last night. She then let him in here tonight after closing. He's breaking into the safe – look.'

Anna pointed at the drill and then the beginnings of the hole he'd started on in the metal door. 'They were planning on making this public then killing you so it looked like an accident. Though I really can't work out why that would benefit them,' she added, coming to the end of her tale.

Tanya looked stunned, dragging her gaze away from Tom towards her mother. 'Mum? Is this true?' Her voice trembled with disbelief.

'No, of course not,' Rosie replied desperately. 'I told you, she's jealous. She'll do anything to discredit me, take this away from you.'

'Tanya, she's lying,' Anna pressed.

'Stop, just stop!' Tanya held her head; it was too much to take in. She took a couple of deep breaths, her face suddenly haggard. There was a long silence as everyone waited for Tanya to say something. Anna glanced unhappily at Freddie. She hated doing this to her best friend, but there was no other way she'd believe them.

'You know that…' Tanya tilted her head and frowned sadly. 'That you're my next of kin. Don't you, Mum?' she asked.

'Wh-what?' Rosie blustered.

'You know that you're my next of kin,' Tanya repeated, closing her eyes in anguish. 'If I die, everything I own goes to you. I don't have a husband or children, so you're the next relative. I never made a will to change that. Which you know, because you asked me about that not long ago. I didn't see anything strange in it at the time. I thought you were just curious, concerned for my wishes.' She groaned and rubbed her face. 'Oh God, tell me it's not true… I thought you loved me,' she said miserably, tears beginning to fall down her pale face. 'I thought that you were genuine. All this time, getting to know me again, spending quality time… It was all for this?'

Rosie looked around her at the sea of angry faces. She lifted her chin and dropped the act. It was over; she wasn't going to get out of this one now. She narrowed her eyes as she looked back at Tanya, her expression hard again.

'Loved you?' she scoffed. 'Did you really believe that, eh? Didn't I teach you enough when you were a child? No one could love you, Tanya.' Her lip curled as she finally voiced her true feelings and vented all her bitterness. 'I don't, Tom didn't, no one ever will. Not really. You were a demon of a child and you're a self-indulgent bitch as an adult. Just look at you,' she sneered.

Tanya laughed, a bitter humourless laugh through her tears. 'Well, look who's turned up to the party. Hello, Mother. Now *this* is who I remember. God, you're right! How could I ever have been so stupid as to believe you. Wow.'

Tanya put her hands on her hips and turned in a circle, trying to walk off the shock. The pain burned through her heart like a branding iron. All she wanted was to collapse and cry and die right there and then, but that wasn't an option. Life could throw what it wanted at her, but she was a fighter. Not even her mother could change that. *Especially* her mother.

'Tanya, I'm so sorry,' Anna said through her own tears. It killed her to see Tanya like this, to watch Rosie try to destroy her.

Tanya shook her head and put a hand up to ask Anna to stop. She couldn't cope with her pity right now. She wiped her eyes and stared sadly at the hardened face of her defiant mother. Her gaze flickered over to Tom, who was now sweating profusely and looking rather worried. 'I don't understand why you're here,' she stated. 'What have you got to do with her?'

Rosie barked out a short laugh, filled with glee. 'Oh, of course. You don't know that part, do you? He traded up, love. Sick of being with such a prissy little bitch like you, he came and found a real woman.' Rosie preened and gloated as Tanya frowned in confusion.

'Traded up? I don't understand,' Tanya replied.

'Then let Mummy make it clear for you,' Rosie replied sarcastically. 'When you screwed his life up and made it so that he couldn't even go back to his own home, because of your thug friends here' – Rosie glared around the room – 'he remembered you telling him about me and where you grew up. He came to find me to ask for my help. At first, I wasn't going to get involved. After all, I wanted nothing to do with you; I was happier pretending that you didn't exist.'

Tanya flinched.

'But then he came back with a bottle of wine, said he could use some company at least. One thing led to another' – she glanced up at Tom and giggled – 'and the next thing we know, we ended up in bed. Couldn't get enough of each other.'

Anna's jaw dropped and she swivelled to look at Tanya. Tanya looked as floored by this revelation as she was, her eyes wide, her mouth hanging slack.

'We started seeing each other. Tom couldn't believe his luck, getting with someone of substance for a change. Someone who actually made him happy, rather than someone who looked down on him. Isn't that right, babe?'

Tom had turned bright red and kept his mouth shut, but this didn't deter Rosie one bit.

'With things going so well, and after he told me what he had in mind, I decided I would help him after all. Because that's what you do for people you love. Ain't it, babe? That's what you told me.' She shot him a loving look, but nothing was retuned.

Her smile dropped and she began to look a little uncertain. *Why wasn't he standing with her, like he always did?* He'd always been so passionate, so intense about what they had between them. The last few months had been the romantic bliss that Rosie had craved for so many years. She hadn't believed her luck at first, that this young, handsome man had fallen for her. But he had. Twenty years wasn't that much difference if you kept yourself trim and fit like she did, she reasoned. And the fruit was all the juicier for being stolen out of her daughter's bowl.

Everyone in the room was stunned and there were a lot of confused glances being shared. Suddenly Tanya burst out into hysterical laughter.

'Oh my God,' she cried. 'You really think he loves you!' She bent over with another peal of laughter. 'You don't see what he's done, do you? Oh, Tom…' Tanya shook her head in amazement. 'That's low, even for you.'

Having recovered from the initial wave of shock and pain that her mother had caused, Tanya strode forward towards her now with renewed confidence. 'Tom doesn't love you. I bet he even struggled to keep it up long enough to bed you, you deluded, wrinkled old prune.' She turned to mock Tom. 'I'm guessing Viagra was needed for this one? Amazing.'

Turning back to her mother, she carried on driving it home. 'You just said it yourself – you refused him when he asked for your help. But he *needed* you. This wouldn't have worked with any other person on the planet. And our dear Tom here has been so intent on getting what he *thinks* are his dues that he'd even screw an old hag like you rather than give up. You've been played, Mum. You're so obvious in your desperation that all he had to do was follow the signs and give you what you so clearly wanted. The lonely old woman who blames everyone but herself for her problems. You were the easiest target going.'

'That's not true,' Rosie spat back. 'He loves me – you can't fake what we have. And he don't give a shit about you anymore, or his "dues", as you put it. He gave up on that when he met me, but when I told him all you'd done, all you'd taken away, we decided to go ahead with it. Because *I'm* owed something back from life; *I'm* owed a new start,' Rosie's anger spewed out. 'And *you're* the one who owes it to me. It was *me* he was doing this all for.'

Tanya shook her head in wonderment. 'You really believe that, don't you? I'm sorry to burst your bubble, *Mum,* but the moment you inherited all this, Tom would have married you and killed you off too. That was the plan from the start, wasn't it?' She aimed the question at Tom.

His dark gaze burned into hers and he jammed his jaw shut in a hard line. She nodded, ignoring the stab of heartache that shot through her as she looked at him. His silence was confirmation that she'd hit the nail on the head. After all he had already put her through, he had come back to finish the job. And now the extreme lengths he'd gone to were all coming out. Rosie wasn't done though. Her breathing spiked as she began to panic and she sidled up next to Tom, pulling on his arm.

'That's not true, is it, Tom? Go on, tell them. Tell them what a bunch of fucking idiots they are. They'll never understand what we have. Will they, Tom? Go on, tell them,' she urged.

Tom shoved her off his arm roughly. 'Get off me, Rosie. There's nothing to fucking tell. It's all gone to shit now – can't you see that?' he yelled. 'It was all for nothing. We're fucking dead.' His voice cracked on the last word as he looked out into the hallway into Freddie's eyes. The cold, hard eyes of a professional murderer.

They held a promise for him as he stared. There was going to be no mercy this time.

'Tom?' Rosie recoiled, stung by his words.

'Tom's done with you, Mother,' Tanya taunted coldly. 'You've outlived your purpose.'

'B-but—' Rosie's bottom lip quivered and her eyes filled with tears. It wasn't fair. Tanya was doing it to her again, taking away her happiness.

'Bill, could you please escort Rosie down to the basement?' Anna asked quietly. 'Tie her up near the boiler; we'll deal with her later. If that's OK with you, Tanya?' she added gently.

Tanya nodded, her drawn face looking weary of it all. 'Do what you want with her,' she said emotionlessly. 'I don't care anymore.'

'What? Tanya!' Rosie squeaked as Bill grabbed her by the arm and Sammy took over watching Tom. 'Wait, please. Tanya, you can't do this. You've put me through enough – you owe me!' Her complaints grew quieter as Bill took her away.

Freddie walked into the room and Anna retreated out of the way. He touched Tanya's arm in a gesture of comfort. 'I'm going to take Tom away now,' he said. 'And you won't see him again. So if there's anything you want to say, say it.'

Tanya looked up into the fearful, angry face of the man she'd once loved and her heart broke into a hundred pieces all over again. How could he have done what he did to her? The lies, the deceit, leaving her to die, and now here he was again, trying to dupe her out of what she had worked so hard to achieve and willing to end her life for it, as if she were worthless. Of all the things she'd been through over the years, Tom was the hardest thing she'd ever had to survive.

This was her last chance to speak to him, and there was so much left to say that she couldn't even begin to work out where to start. Her head whirled, a thousand emotions fighting each other to get through. Hatred warred with heartbreak, betrayal with disbelief. Then in a moment of resignation, she realised that sometimes when there is too much to say, it's better to say nothing at all. Slowly she shook her head.

'He's all yours,' she whispered.

Sarah and Freddie each grabbed an arm and Sammy moved with them, his gun still pointed at Tom's head. Tom didn't bother to try to fight his way out as they dragged him away. He already knew he'd lost.

CHAPTER FIFTY-FOUR

The car pulled up around the back of Freddie's newly refurbished restaurant. Tom frowned, wondering where they were. He was surprised when Freddie opened the door and pulled him out. He'd been expecting to be taken somewhere more remote. Maybe Freddie wasn't going to kill him after all. He stumbled as Freddie pushed him forward roughly.

'Move,' Freddie growled.

There was a weak light just above the back entrance that Tom assumed he was supposed to head for. Sammy fell into step beside him, the gun now hidden under a jacket but still pointed at him nonetheless. He heard Freddie pause behind him to address the woman, whoever she was. Tom hadn't seen her before.

'Go home, fix yourself an alibi and never speak of tonight again.' His tone was curt. Tom raised his eyebrows, intrigued as to their relationship, despite the fear he was feeling for himself.

'Sure,' the woman replied. She didn't seem fazed by Freddie's coldness. 'See you tomorrow.' She melted off into the shadows and Freddie caught up with them as they reached the door.

Reaching into his pocket, he pulled out a set of keys. Tom scanned the area, looking for any open windows or sign of life around him, but there was nothing. There appeared to be offices, bars and other restaurants spread around the building they were about to enter, but they were all closed, and from the back he couldn't seem to locate any residential properties at all.

Once the door was open, Sammy shoved him through into the pitch-black hallway. Low beeps sounded from a little glowing box by the door as Freddie typed in the code and, once the system was offline, he flicked on the switch.

'The good thing about this system,' he said as he led the way down a narrow hallway, 'is that it's linked to the CCTV as well. I can turn it all off from there. Handy, don't you think?'

Tom swallowed hard as the lump of fear in his throat grew bigger.

They reached a small door at the end of the hallway and Freddie unlocked it. There was a set of steep stairs just beyond and he proceeded up them, disappearing out of sight. Sammy prodded Tom with the barrel of the gun – hard. 'Go on – up you go,' he said.

He stumbled forward, following Freddie into the darkness. At the top, Tom found himself standing in what appeared to be a small living room. It was dark and dingy, the light bulb that hung from the ceiling not giving off much light. In the middle of the room, behind a small wooden coffee table was an old greying sofa that may have been green in a past life. A kitchenette ran along one wall, which consisted of a sink, a small work surface and a two-ringed hob with two wonky cupboards hanging off the wall. Looking to his right, Tom could see through the open door to the small bedroom which appeared to hold just a single bed with rumpled sheets. Freddie took Tom by the arm and led him through to the last door, which Tom guessed rightly was the bathroom.

'Get in,' Freddie ordered, pointing to the tall old-fashioned bathtub.

Tom did as he was told. Watching the steadiness with which Sammy's barrel remained pointed at him, he didn't try to resist when Freddie made him raise his arms up in the air. There was a whir and a click as the first handcuff shut over his wrist. He frowned. What were they doing?

Freddie wound the chain of the cuffs over the top of a metal ring he hadn't noticed was hanging above the tub, then clapped the second one over his other hand. As Freddie stepped backward, Tom pulled down on the ring, testing its strength. It didn't budge.

'When I acquired this place, the owner vacated this flat pretty quickly, didn't take much. Not that it seems he had much to take. Don't know how he lived like this; it's a fucking hovel.'

Freddie took off his jacket and threw it back into the living room. He started to unbutton his shirt. 'I had a proper look around after he'd gone and found this.' He gestured towards the big metal ring that Tom was now handcuffed to. 'It's obviously a shower rail, but it's the sturdiest fucking shower rail I've ever seen. I don't know what use the owner had for it when it was put in, but that thing's buried into the ceiling so deep a bloody bomb wouldn't dislodge it. Maybe that was it,' he added, the thought just occurring to him. 'Maybe it was some sort of weird bomb shelter. Or maybe not being upstairs, who knows.' He shrugged and pulled the shirt off, laying it neatly over the discarded jacket. He stood in his vest and flexed his muscles. 'All I know is, it's going to be of great use today.'

Pulling his arm back, he shot his fist into Tom's stomach with a hard punch. Tom cried out, the blow taking him by surprise. He gasped for air, winded. Freddie paced up and down, in no particular hurry just yet. Sammy leaned against the doorframe and watched, waiting until Freddie required his help again.

'I've been looking for you for a long time. You've cost me a lot of time and resources, Tom,' he said conversationally, rolling his neck from side to side. 'You did well staying off the grid, I must admit. Though we both know that was because you were living off the bag of cash you stole from Michael, don't we? Which, incidentally, he stole from me.'

He turned and struck another blow to Tom's stomach, sending his body rocking back until the handcuffs stopped him moving any further. 'That pissed me off,' he said in a hard voice, pointing his finger in Tom's face.

Walking back over to his jacket, he crouched down and searched for something in the pockets. 'Ah, there they are.' He pulled out his leather gloves and put them on, pushing each finger in neatly as he went. 'Don't want your face messing up my fingers, do we?'

He rocked back and smashed his fist into Tom's face as hard as he could.

Tom gave a strangled cry as his nose exploded, blood splattering all down his front. 'Jesus,' he moaned.

'Oh, he ain't gonna help ya,' Freddie replied. 'Not this time. You know I've been wondering.' His brow knotted in curiosity. 'What were you doing in the Charterhouse?'

Tom stayed silent and Freddie pulled his fist back again.

'OK, OK,' Tom said hurriedly. 'My grandad. He lives there. I was just staying there with him while Rosie was with Tanya. It was closer for her to meet me. She was a needy bitch.'

'Grandad? You don't have a living grandad – we checked,' Freddie replied, suspicion in his tone.

'He isn't my proper grandad. He was just married to my gran for a while when I was young. We got on. He helped me get my first job. We stayed in touch,' he told Freddie grudgingly.

'Huh...' Freddie and Sammy exchanged glances. They hadn't picked up on this piece of information. With him not being currently married into the family or related by blood, he hadn't come up in their findings. If he had, they might have found Tom sooner.

'He ain't done nothing wrong.' Tom sounded worried. 'He didn't know. I didn't tell him what happened.'

'Don't worry. I don't believe in hurting family, Tom. The only person I want to hurt is you.' His frown darkened and Tom was reminded again just how dangerous Freddie could be. Sammy walked out of the room, leaving them alone for a few moments.

'You tried to fuck me over with Michael, tried to help him put me under and take my businesses. You'd have seen me rot behind bars if I hadn't caught you.'

'Freddie, listen,' Tom began to plead.

'I don't think so, sunshine. The time for listening has passed.'

Sammy returned with a baseball bat and handed it to Freddie. Freddie didn't break eye contact with Tom, his angry gaze boring into his trussed-up captive.

'You already crossed the line by doing this much, you see. Just for that, you were already on my hit list. If it had just been that, I might have taken pity on you and put a bullet through your head, made it quick. I'm not sadistic; I don't usually take pleasure in hurting others. But then…' He weighed the bat in his hand and fixed his fingers around the handle in a good position. 'You went along with him kidnapping Anna. You allowed that to happen.'

'Freddie, please, that was nothing to— Argh!'

Freddie swung the bat hard into the front of his kneecap and Tom screamed, the veins in his neck protruding as he strained against the handcuffs.

'Anna was pregnant with my child. She had our baby growing inside of her, hers and mine. She should have been at home, safe and sound where she could rest and where her family could have taken any stress off her shoulders.' A look of grief passed through the anger on Freddie's face. 'But instead she was with my psychotic brother, watching her best friend get shot and waiting for the worst to happen. Instead, she lost our baby, terrified and alone – and while our child bled out of her onto the *fucking stairs*,' Freddie's voice rose into a shout, 'she had to pull the trigger on my brother's head just to get herself out. Can you imagine what that must have felt like?'

He swung the bat again and hit the same kneecap with a sickening crunch. Tom screamed out in agony and began to cry like a baby.

'Nah, me neither.' Freddie sniffed. 'But I still have to watch it play through, every day on her face. See the scars that run so deep that sometimes I'm not sure if she's even there anymore.'

The sound of Tom's sobs filled the small flat as Freddie rubbed his face tiredly. Thoughts of Anna ran through his mind, and his resentment towards Tom grew.

Sammy slowly put on his own gloves, his expression sombre. Like Freddie, he didn't usually take pleasure in the violent side of their world – it was just part of the job. This guy, however, deserved everything he got. This man had entered their world, albeit on the edges. He had spent time in their homes, broken bread and shared wine at their tables. He'd dated Tanya for a whole year. And he'd betrayed them all.

'After all that, after everything you did to myself and Anna…' Freddie hefted the bat up into the air again, ready to strike. 'You not only treated Tanya like a complete mug, but you left her bleeding on the floor like an animal in the road. This was your girlfriend, mate. I mean, I know you'd had an argument but Christ, that's a bit much, isn't it? I've never heard of something so cold.' He shook his head, disgusted and then smashed the bat down again on the same knee with great force. This time it completely shattered, and the lower half of Tom's leg hung at a strange angle as he bellowed in pain yet again.

His bloodcurdling scream echoed around the room. 'Help, someone, please, oh my God.' Wracking sobs obscured his words and bloody spittle flew from his mouth. 'Please, anybody, please…'

'Shut up,' Sammy ordered with a growl. 'Unless you want to make it even worse.'

With difficulty, Tom reigned in his cries, dulling them to muffled sobs.

'If you think this is your punishment for all you've done,' Freddie said, 'think again. This is just the beginning. I'm merely preparing you now for what's to come. Because believe it or not there are much worse creatures out there than me, Tom. And I'm about to introduce you to them.'

Tom's attention sharpened. A chill ran up his spine as he wondered what Freddie meant by this. 'Before we get to that point though, there's more to be done.'

Freddie pulled the bat back and, putting all of his strength behind it, whacked it around the side of Tom's head.

There was a high-pitched ringing in his ears as Tom came round. In reality, he'd only been out cold for a matter of seconds, but he felt groggy, as though waking from a deep sleep. Blinding pain seared through his skull as he tried to open his eyes. It hurt like nothing he'd ever felt before; not even his knee felt quite this bad right now. *Was his head broken? Had Freddie cracked his skull?* It felt like he had. He tried to cry but even that hurt too much and he stopped, a strange keening the only noise he was able to make. He forced his eyes open, despite the pain. The thought of not being able to see what they were about to do to him was too terrifying.

Tom flinched at the sight of Sammy standing close by. The movement sent a fresh wave of agony through his head and he nearly vomited. Freddie had disappeared, but through bleary eyes Tom could see him reappearing. There was something in his hand. Was it a gun? He prayed to God that it was a gun and that he was about to put him out of his misery.

As Freddie drew closer, he realised he wasn't that lucky. It wasn't a gun; it was what looked like a pair of garden shears. A feeling of dread rushed through him and he balled his fists. They were going to take his fingers. His breathing became fast and laboured as he went into full panic mode.

'Hold his nose,' Freddie said to Sammy.

Sammy grasped Tom's face with one hand, holding it still, and pinched his nose with the other. It took a millisecond for Tom to catch up with what they were planning to do and he clamped his mouth shut. He couldn't breathe with Sammy holding his nose and he fought against him, trying to move his head away from the man. But Sammy held on tight; there was no way out. He bucked and twisted and nearly passed out from the pain of his injuries, but it was to no avail. He couldn't fight it any longer; his body was crying out for oxygen, and with a shriek of horror, he opened his mouth to draw in the breath he so badly needed.

With lightning speed, Freddie shoved something in his mouth to keep it open and reached in. The leather gloves grasped onto his tongue and Tom began to screech with all his might, over and over again. He felt the leather pinch down hard to keep hold and then the touch of the cold metal as the shears made contact.

Lining them up as far down the tongue as possible, Freddie clamped down on the sheers as hard as he could, the heavy-duty metal blades cutting through the flesh and muscle. Tom's screams heightened to fever pitch as Freddie had to push harder to get through the toughest part of the muscle. Eventually the tongue fell to the floor and blood cascaded out of Tom's mouth, spraying all of them.

Large droplets of his own blood seeping into the white of Freddie's vest was the last thing he saw before he blacked out.

CHAPTER FIFTY-FIVE

Anna walked back through to the office with a steaming mug of tea. She gently placed it on the desk in front of Tanya, who hadn't moved or said a word since Freddie had left. Rosie was still down in the basement, kicking and screaming.

Tanya stared at the drill on the floor, her wide eyes seeing straight through it to some distant thought. Her eyes were red-rimmed where she had obviously been crying, but they were dry now, and although she looked as though she carried the weight of the world on her shoulders, she was calm and still. Anna hovered, not sure what to say.

'I'll just be out here, if you need me,' she said eventually. Opening the door, she was nearly through it when she heard Tanya reply in barely more than a whisper.

'I'm so sorry.' The three words were so full of heartbreak that Anna nearly cried, but she held it in. It wasn't what Tanya needed right now.

She shook her head and walked around the desk. 'Don't be,' she replied, her voice wobbling. She wrapped her arms around Tanya's thin shoulders and held her tightly. 'You shouldn't have to be. I should have been wrong. I wish I'd been wrong.'

Tanya broke down into silent tears, and Anna could no longer hold back her own as she felt the deep, wracking sobs pulse through Tanya's body under her arms. She squeezed harder and Tanya turned her head into Anna's shoulder.

They stayed like that until Anna's back ached from leaning over and the tea went cold, the bond between them flowing as strong as it ever had before.

*

Anna woke the next day and rubbed her eyes tiredly. She looked across to Tanya who was fast asleep, sadness still etched into her face. They were in Tanya's flat. Anna had eventually taken her home to get some rest and had fallen asleep on top of the covers next to her when Tanya had begged her to stay. It had been a long night for everyone but especially Tanya. She'd been through so much.

When they'd left the club, Tanya had hesitated, wondering aloud what they should do with Rosie. Anna had firmly insisted that she spend the rest of the night where she was, tied to a chair in the dark basement. It was only for a few hours, and it was the least Rosie deserved after everything that had come to light. As Anna lay in bed now, she hoped Rosie was terrified. She hoped the older woman was expecting the worst.

Sensing Anna awake next to her, Tanya stirred and turned over. 'Hey,' she said, her voice hoarse from all the crying she'd done the night before.

'Hey,' Anna whispered back. 'Fancy a coffee?'

'More than life itself,' Tanya replied. 'I'm knackered.'

'Well, that's to be expected,' Anna said, sitting up. She swung her legs down off the bed and walked heavily through to the kitchen to turn on the coffee machine. Princess was waiting for her on the kitchen side, purring as Anna walked in. She stopped to rub her under her chin.

'You knew, didn't you?' she asked quietly. 'You knew she was a mean old lady.'

Waiting for the water to heat up, she opened a pouch of food for the fluffy white feline and tipped the contents into her bowl.

By the time Tanya crawled out of her room, Anna had made two steaming coffees and was ladling poached eggs onto fresh toast.

'Ah, man, I really miss living with you,' Tanya declared as she slipped onto a stool at the breakfast bar. 'Remind me why we don't live together anymore?'

'Freddie,' Anna replied, laughing.

'Oh yeah, him. Well, tell him to piss off and come move in here. I'm much more fun than that moody old git.' Her eyes twinkled in good humour and Anna breathed an internal sigh of relief.

If Tanya was back to making jokes then she wasn't entirely broken. She still had her fighting spirit.

As Tanya cut into her breakfast, Anna took a deep breath.

'We need to decide what we're going to do with Rosie. We can't keep her in the basement, and we certainly can't let her just walk away. Reporting her is out, because that would implicate Tom, and we definitely don't need them looking in that direction.' Tanya raised her eyebrows and rolled her eyes in agreement. 'So it's down to us to dole out what we feel is appropriate. What *you* feel is appropriate.'

Tanya exhaled slowly and chewed her toast. It still hurt, everything that she had found out last night. She knew that it was going to hurt for a long time. There was a chance that she'd never get over it. Rosie had duped her, good and proper. She had held Tanya's heart in her hands, carefully peeled back all the protective layers that she'd spent a lifetime constructing and then crushed it in one cold, cruel move.

The things Rosie had done were unforgivable this time. They should have been unforgivable the first time. When Tanya had opened her eyes that day in the hospital and seen her face after all those years, she should have sent her away without audience. But she hadn't. She'd made a mistake, and she was never going to make a mistake like that again.

As she thought back to her lonely, unhappy childhood she had a thought. A cold smile crossed her lips and she looked up towards Anna. 'I've got an idea. But first we need to go shopping.'

CHAPTER FIFTY-SIX

The flame in the boiler somewhere nearby burst to life and Rosie cried out in fright. It was darker than hell down here; not one sliver of light came in from anywhere. The silence was almost overwhelming, but it wasn't as bad as the sudden sounds that kept her jumping out of her skin. She had no idea how long she'd been down here, but she judged that it must be at least somewhere near lunchtime by now. Her stomach growled for food, and her mouth felt as dry as a bone.

She had been so desperate for the toilet a few hours ago that eventually her pelvic muscles had failed her and she'd soiled herself. The rancid smell of her own urine still assailed her nostrils now, a continuous reminder of her own embarrassment.

Rosie had tried to escape the ropes that bound her so tightly to the hard-backed chair, but it was no use. There was no give in them whatsoever. Bill had been merciless as he tied her, ignoring her complaints. The scathing look he'd given her before he'd departed had left her in no doubt of his feelings towards her. Everybody seemed to hate her; not one person understood.

This was all *her* fault. That scheming, evil brat that she'd spawned. She'd only been trying to get back a little of what she was owed. She wouldn't have had to do that had Tanya not stolen so much from her in the first place. Her happiness, her marriage, her future. For the millionth time, Rosie wished that she'd drowned the little demon at birth. It would have saved her so much heartbreak.

Lost in her own little world of self-pity, it took Rosie a few moments to realise that the door was opening. She squinted against the sudden light and watched as the bane of her life descended the stairs, her viper of a friend Anna following closely behind. With difficulty, she smothered the bitter sneer that was fighting for its place on her face.

'Tanya? Is that you?' She tried to sound as feeble and vulnerable as possible. She had to play to Tanya's weaknesses.

She'd realised far too late that she'd been stupid the night before, showing her cards like that. In her mind, Tom was going to get them out of the predicament they'd landed themselves in. He was going to show Tanya how he really felt and when she crumbled into a heartbroken mess, he was going to take Rosie's hand and they'd march out together, heads held high. But that had not happened. All that bravado and passion he'd so readily displayed for the last few months had swiftly disappeared when she needed him to show it most.

But despite that, Tanya was wrong – Rosie knew she was. Tom had been telling the truth. He'd finally seen in her what all the other idiots over the years had been blind to. So he'd frozen up? That happened to people. She just needed to get out of here and find Tom so that they could come up with a new strategy for their life together. They could forget Tanya; she meant nothing to either of them at the end of the day. Rosie could forget about the money too. It had never been her idea to begin with; she'd only gone along with it because Tom had convinced her that she deserved it. They could start afresh somewhere new. But right now, she had to play her cards right to get out of this mess.

Tanya and Anna stood over her, united by the coldness in their eyes. A stab of annoyance shot through her. She'd thought that she'd put paid to this little friendship, but it appeared this was no longer the case. Ignoring Anna, she focused on Tanya.

'Tanya?' She forced a tear into her eye. 'I'm so sorry. I didn't realise that Tom was trying to turn me against you. When I came to you, it was out of love. I got so swept up with his lies that I didn't see.'

Her whiny tone made Anna's blood boil, and she had to turn away to stop herself from striking the woman.

'I'm going to untie you now,' Tanya said in a flat tone. 'I can see you've had an accident. I've bought you something to change into.' Tanya knelt down behind her mother and untied the ropes.

Rosie heaved a great sigh of relief as the blood rushed back to her hands. 'Ah, thank you. That man was rather rough with me,' she said indignantly. She reached for Tanya's hand and gave her a watery smile. 'Thank you for believing in me. I think that if we just—'

Tanya snatched her hand away and glared at her coldly. 'I said, change your clothes. Hurry up.' She walked over to stand with Anna and looked away as Rosie began to undress.

Rosie changed quickly, keeping her eye warily on the two women waiting for her. Something was up and it wasn't good. A prickle of warning crept up her neck. She needed to tread carefully.

Slipping on the thin dress that was in the bag, Rosie looked down at it properly for the first time. She frowned. It was some sort of flowery summer nightie. She opened her mouth to ask Tanya why she'd brought her this, but seeing the expression on her daughter's face, thought better of it and stayed quiet.

'Ready?' Anna barked over to her. 'Good. Let's go.'

Rosie narrowed her eyes hatefully at Anna's back as she began to mount the stairs but followed just the same. 'Oh, my clothes.' She turned to take them but Tanya blocked her way.

'No need; I'll grab them later,' she insisted.

'OK.' Rosie didn't feel entirely comfortable walking around in just a short floaty nighty and her underwear, but she pursed her lips. She'd no doubt be home soon and could change into something clean. If Tanya wanted to give her the cold treatment all the way back then so be it. Perhaps making her travel in this nightdress was her punishment for stealing Tanya's boyfriend. Even though technically they had already broken up. Rosie rolled her eyes. *Children*, she thought. *So dramatic.*

Shivering as she stepped out into the cold winter air, she hurried into the waiting car. She thanked God that she had thought to put her shoes back on. Tanya hadn't made her forgo those at least. As she slipped into the back and onto the cool leather seats, she looked around with interest.

'Nice car,' she said as the two women got in. 'Whose is it?'

'Freddie's,' Anna declared from the driver's seat.

Of course it is, Rosie thought spitefully. 'Lovely,' she said.

Tanya had got into the back with her and she tried again to engage her in conversation. 'I really am sorry, Tanya.' She kept her voice soft. 'I never wanted to hurt you. This is still so new to me, us being like this.' She paused but there was no response. The car had pulled away and was making its way down the road. 'You know all this time we've had together, me looking after you, caring for you, helping out with the club—'

'Just stop it,' Tanya said sharply. She turned to face her mother, anger and disgust in her eyes. 'I don't want to hear it. You're a dirty lying bitch who was planning to steal my business and end my life. Your own daughter.' She closed her eyes in grief and shook her head. 'Don't talk. Just be quiet or I'll change my mind about this trip and I'll just drop you off to Freddie instead, let him deal with you.'

Rosie turned as white as a sheet and sat back silently in her seat. Tom had told her all about Freddie. He was the last person she wanted in charge of her fate.

CHAPTER FIFTY-SEVEN

Half an hour later, Rosie peered out the window, looking for a sign. She had no idea where they were, but it certainly wasn't anywhere near Tanya's flat, this much she was sure of. When they eventually came to one, she was surprised to see it read 'Dagenham'.

Another five minutes passed and Tanya leaned forward to speak to Anna. 'Turn down here. About a mile up.'

A smile curled up the corners of Anna's mouth and Rosie's heart began to pound. Anna sped up the small A road and Rosie tried to see where they were heading. There was nothing but fields on either side of them, and not one car passed them as they continued on. Eventually Anna slowed to a stop and pulled into a small dirt siding. She twisted in her seat so that she could see them in the back.

Tanya pulled herself up to full height and looked down on Rosie in contempt. 'You know, you really had me going for a while. You did,' she admitted, nodding. 'But Anna saw right through you. I just wish I'd listened sooner. Because she's my real family.'

Rosie scoffed and Tanya's hand shot forward and grasped her face tightly. Rosie's eyes bulged in shock as her daughter leaned in close.

'Don't you ever laugh at her. You don't know the meaning of family, or love for that matter,' she spat. She let go and Rosie rubbed her face where an angry red mark was beginning to show. 'Family are the people you can count on, no matter what. No matter what you do, what your faults are, whether you argue and disagree, they *always* have your back. Blood means nothing if you don't have that.'

Anna nodded in agreement, her expression sombre.

Tanya shifted her weight and pulled a sad half-smile. 'Do you remember those nights when I was a little girl and something would go wrong in your life and whatever it was' – Tanya tilted her head to one side – 'you'd blame me. It wouldn't matter what it was, or why it had really happened, you would drag me from my bed and throw me outside in the cold.'

Anna stifled a gasp. Tanya had never told her about that.

'I was barely more than a toddler the first time I can remember you doing that. I'd be freezing, exhausted and scared but still you'd make me sit out there. It was like my suffering somehow made you feel better.'

Rosie coloured and she looked down. 'N-no, I don't remember…'

'Oh, but you do, Mum,' Tanya replied. 'I can see it in your face. And the thing is, I was willing to forgive you things like that. I gave you a second chance. And you screwed me over even more.'

Silence fell over the car as Rosie didn't answer.

'I can forgive a lot of things, but trying to kill me isn't one of them.'

Rosie fiddled with her hands in her lap and stared past Tanya out the window. 'Take me home now please,' she said. 'I get it, we're done. I just want to get my things and go. Tom and I won't bother you again.'

'Oh my God!' Anna's eyes widened in disbelief and she shook her head. 'Rosie, Tom isn't coming back. Even if he wanted to be with you – which he *doesn't*; he was using you to get to Tanya – he couldn't anymore. He's done. You're over,' Anna stressed.

'What do you mean he can't come back?' Rosie looked worried.

Tanya looked up to the heavens. 'He'll be dead by now, Mum,' she said bluntly, tired of pussyfooting around it. 'Don't you get it? He crossed Freddie. He did unspeakable things, which, to be fair, you probably don't know the half of. But he did, and they've finally caught up with him.'

Rosie made a sound of shock and fright and her hand shot to her mouth. Tanya leaned in with a cold look on her face. 'And if you ever mention a word of that to anyone else, you'll be next. I barely saved you from it this time. You're lucky the choice was mine. Now.' She sat back. 'Take off your shoes.'

'What?' Rosie asked, aghast.

'You heard me. Do it.' Tanya waited as Rosie did as she was told. 'Now get out of this car and start walking that way.' Tanya pointed out across the fields. 'The M25 is just a little walk away. When you get there, you can do what you like. Hitch-hike, walk around, throw yourself under a lorry – I don't care. But once you're out, don't you *ever* set foot inside Greater London again, do you hear me?' Tanya spat bitterly. 'It's about time you learned how it feels to be cold and alone and scared. Oh, and don't even think about waiting on this road. Anna and I are going to sit here and watch until you're out of sight, and if you don't go then all I have to do is put in *one* call and Freddie will have you picked up.'

'Tanya,' Rosie said, alarmed. 'What are you doing?'

'What I should have done a long time ago. Now *go on,*' she yelled. 'Get out! Go!' She leaned over and opened the door behind Rosie.

Tumbling backward, Rosie just stopped herself from falling out by grabbing the door. Shaking like a leaf, still stunned that this was even happening, she stepped outside. The intense cold hit her straight away, the bitter wind whipping her thin nightdress around her. 'Tanya, it's cold,' she whined.

Tanya smiled. 'I know,' she replied. 'Now start walking.'

Rosie looked at the hardness in her daughter's eyes and knew that there was no going back. They had her: game, set, match. She considered running back down the road to find help, but the threat of Freddie was too real to ignore. Tears stinging her eyes as she shivered violently, Rosie made her painful way into the first field, crying out as stones and thistles cut through the skin on her feet.

Anna and Tanya watched in silence from the car until Rosie's slow journey was well underway. Anna turned to her friend and saw the shine of tears in her eyes. She gripped her hand and held it fast, knowing that even though the revenge was poetic in its form, it must cut her to the bone that it had come to this. She had given all of her trust and forgiveness to the woman who had tortured her so much as a child. That took a strength that most people didn't possess. She deserved better.

As Rosie became nothing more than a speck in the distance, Anna turned back towards the steering wheel. 'Come on,' she said gently. 'Hop in the front. There's a little village up ahead. I'll bet you a tenner there's a restaurant nearby with a decent white wine selection.'

Tanya smiled at her, blinking the tears away. 'You're on,' she said as she slipped through the middle into the front passenger seat. 'Let's go.'

CHAPTER FIFTY-EIGHT

Paul jolted awake as someone marched through the door into the bedroom. It was the middle of the day, but he'd been catching a few moments of shut-eye after another restless night. The thought of how much James would be worrying had kept him up, night after night. He wished he could speak to him and just assure him that everything would be fine, but he couldn't. That wasn't how this worked.

His time under the captivity of Joe and Vito hadn't been too bad. The men weren't exactly friendly, but it could have been worse. Still, the threat of it all turning very ugly very quickly hung over his head like a ten-ton weight.

'Hey.' Tino whistled to get his attention. 'Come on, get moving. It sounds like your brother's finally come up with the goods.' He walked over and unlocked the cuff, holding Paul to the bed. The cuffs fell off away from his wrist and Tino disappeared again. Paul sat up, suddenly alert.

Freddie had the goods? Did that mean he had pulled it off? Or had he found another way? Swinging his legs off the bed, Paul quickly put on his shoes and walked out into the main room where all the men were buzzing around, excitedly preparing.

'Good news.' Joe clapped him on the shoulder in an almost friendly gesture. 'It appears he's caught the guy. We're all going over there now. And if everything is as it should be' – he shrugged – 'then you're free to go.'

Paul swallowed. His hopes had sky-rocketed but he didn't want to lose his head just yet. It might not be what he was thinking; it might just be a ruse to get Paul out into the open. He fervently prayed that it wasn't and that Freddie really had found the answer to all of their problems.

*

Sammy was waiting for them at the back door of the restaurant and held it open as they all filed in. 'Please go through to the bar. Freddie's waiting for you there.'

Paul noted Sammy's dishevelled appearance and gave him a questioning look as he passed. Sammy nodded, almost imperceptibly, and Paul took a deep breath, his hopes rising even further.

They passed through the dark hallway into the main restaurant and Paul clocked Freddie. He was sitting on his own in one of the new booths, drinking neat vodka from a small glass. The bottle was right next to it. It wasn't this that made Pauls eyebrows shoot up in surprise though; it was the complete state of him.

Freddie sat in his black suit trousers and a white vest top – or at least it had been white, at some point. Now it was splattered with blood, his usually neat hair a tangled mess, and a sheen of dried sweat coated his arms and face. There were very few times in their life that Paul had ever seen Freddie like this and each one of them had been very dark indeed.

Freddie didn't smile as the band of men reached him. 'Sit,' he said, unceremoniously. 'Grab a glass, have a drink. You're gonna need it.' He took another gulp of his own.

'You said you found the guy,' Vito said, his tone slightly less aggressive than usual as he too took in Freddie's appearance. 'So where is he? You kill him?'

'Nah, I thought I'd leave that honour to you.'

'But you've beat him to a bloody pulp, by the looks of you,' Vito said, frowning.

'And cut out his tongue, as promised,' Freddie replied darkly.

'Why?' Vito looked at him with suspicion.

'Because, Vito.' Freddie stood up. 'It weren't just your mate he killed. He also murdered my brother.'

'What?' Joe piped up. 'I thought your brother was in Rio?'

'You've done your research – congratulations.' Freddie turned to him. 'But you didn't go deep enough. Michael was living under the name Steven Munroe. I sorted out a passport, papers, everything. You can check it out, if you like.' Turning back to the table, Freddie leaned against it. 'We brought him back over here several months ago. Enough time had passed, the heat was off. We were slowly introducing him back into underworld society.'

Paul nodded gravely, backing up Freddie's story.

'He met Frank with us, was going to be involved in the new casino. It was a new venture, good ground for him to come in on after being away for so long. Or so we thought.' Freddie exhaled heavily. 'Tom was one of my foremen on a building site. He started dating one of Anna's friends, got some ideas and asked me for an in. We tried him out, but he was no good. He just didn't have what it took, you know?'

Joe nodded. He did know. He had wide boys approaching him all the time, thinking they had the balls, but they were nothing but showmen. It was a different breed of man altogether that lived the sort of life they did.

'Michael told him it was over. Perhaps it was harsh, but it had to be done. We couldn't have him working for us in that way. He was a liability. Had a temper that he couldn't control.'

Freddie held his hands out in a gesture of defeat. 'What could we do? Tom went off in a rage and we left him to calm down. Michael and a couple of his men had some business later that day at a farm he was looking to acquire. We didn't realise it at the time, but Tom followed them there. When he caught up with them, he pulled out a gun and shot them dead on the spot. They didn't even see it coming. One of our guys was a DI, Fraser, he had a gun on him, but Tom had anticipated that. Before he could even take aim, Tom took him out.'

Freddie paused and rubbed his face, the real memories of that day flooding back. He cleared his throat and pushed on. 'The others were unarmed. We don't carry guns unless we need to. With our laws, it's not worth being caught. One of them tried to call me. The phone connected but all I heard were the shots. By the time we'd got there, he was gone. We arranged the bodies so it no longer linked us to the situation and we've been looking for him ever since.'

'It was only last night that we found out the rest.' Sammy stepped forward, his face grim.

'What's the rest?' Joe asked, looking from Freddie to Sammy and back to Freddie again. All eyes were on Freddie as they waited to find out.

'We finally located Tom late last night, brought him here and began torturing him for what he did. Killing a member of our family certainly doesn't allow you a quick death,' Freddie said. 'He tried to barter for his life with extra information.'

Freddie reached into his trouser pocket for his cigarettes and lit one, throwing the packet on the table. He gestured towards it. 'Help yourself,' he said, blowing out a plume of smoke.

'He said he'd heard you were in town and looking for Frank. That he knew where he was and asked me to let him go in exchange for his location. Obviously we said no and then tortured him until he spilled all he knew.' He shrugged and took another deep drag, letting it out slowly.

Vito picked up a glass and poured himself some of the vodka on the table. 'Go on.' His tone was almost friendly now that they were getting somewhere.

Freddie looked around. Everyone was watching with bated breath, their defences down now that they were sure that they were on the same side. Freddie shot a look at Paul, a look that only he knew to be mocking their audience.

'What we didn't know was that Frank had also driven out to see Michael that day. I don't know why. I don't know if it had anything to do with the casino or if it was something else they were working on – nobody knew but them. But he and his men drove out there in some sort of black car. Tom had massacred the lot of them and was leaving when Frank pulled up. He took them by surprise and shot them too.'

'But what about *their* guns?' Joe asked, frowning. 'Surely three armed men against one had better chances than that.'

'The way Tom told it, they weren't armed. I don't know if they had packed the guns away so that they weren't caught – I did warn them this was a risk here – or whether they just didn't have time. I guess we'll never know. One thing I did find out was that Tom is ex-army. He's got a clean, fast shot on him.'

'Well, shit,' Joe said, looking round to Vito.

'What happened next? His body wasn't found, that's for sure. We'd know,' Vito said, with a deepening frown.

'That's because it's at the bottom of a lake. Tom knew he needed to run and that I'd be able to track his number plate, so he covered the bodies with sheets and drove off in their car. He drove for about an hour and then eventually dumped the whole lot in a lake. I can show you which one.' He took another drag on his cigarette, maintaining solid eye contact with Vito. 'It was a clever plan. We had no idea Frank was dead, so we didn't look out for any signs of him or see if any car was registered. We didn't know how Tom had got away, assumed he'd hitch-hiked his way out, or roughed it on foot. He threw us right off the scent.'

'How did you find him in the end?' Vito asked.

'The idiot tried to come back to steal money off his ex-girlfriend,' Sammy answered. 'She caught him red-handed and called us in. She's a good girl; her loyalty is in the right place.'

Paul looked on as Freddie elaborated on what had happened. He'd get the straight version later, but it sounded like a lot had gone on since he'd been held up with the Mafia bosses. He gazed round at each of them in turn. They all bought it. And why wouldn't they? It was the only thing that made reasonable sense, and the culprit was all tied up nicely in a bathtub waiting for them. The only thing missing was a bow.

Freddie led the procession through the back and up to the dingy, neglected little flat. Tom was vaguely lucid and he began to cry again as he saw everyone enter. He looked terrible, blood running all down his face and front, two black eyes and a nasty gash to the side of the head. Paul was amazed he was still holding on to life. Freddie had done a real number on him.

'You can use this flat to do what you will to him.' Freddie handed Joe the handcuff keys. 'Send word when you're done and I'll send my clean-up crew in. A gift, in the hope that we can form a much more trusting and friendly alliance going forward,' Freddie said, adding emphasis to his last few words.

Joe nodded. 'We accept with great gratitude.'

Freddie nodded back and turned to leave.

'And Freddie?'

Freddie paused.

'Those plans for the casino… Please, go ahead with them. Whatever deal you had with Frank, you now have with me. We can sort out the particulars later.'

'Thank you,' Freddie replied, his expression still cold. This was the best outcome considering the circumstances, but he was more than irked that his hands were tied against doling out retribution for taking Paul. However it was what it was, and they were lucky to have been able to shift the blame like this. The plan wouldn't have worked with anyone else. No one else in the world deserved the pain and suffering that Tom was about to be put through, and Freddie wasn't the kind to throw innocents to the wolves.

Freddie tipped his head and walked out of the room, Paul and Sammy falling into step behind him. They descended the stairs and left the dark bloodied flat full of Mafiosi behind them.

As they left the building and felt the fresh air hit their skin, a cold grin spread across Freddie's blood-spattered face. The back door swung shut and Sammy unlocked his car.

'And that, brother,' Freddie said to Paul, 'is how you tame the Mafia.'

CHAPTER FIFTY-NINE

Sarah Riley had pulled her chair round to the back of the desk, next to Freddie. She was going to enjoy this meeting more than she cared to admit. It had taken her a little while to figure it out, but she'd done it.

All this time, Freddie had been so sure it had to be one of his core band of men, even though he couldn't imagine any one of them being disloyal. There had seemed to be no other possible explanation. But Sarah had checked each one of them out in turn and there had been no way it could have been them. It wasn't any of their partners either. None of them seemed to talk much about private things, but even if they had, their partners all seemed to check out too.

It had been the day that Bill and Zack had sorted her out with more advanced tech that the suspicion had formed. She'd been mulling the possibilities over and over again until she realised that Freddie had told her that the meeting had taken place in his main office at Club CoCo. This was where he conducted most of his business. What if someone had managed to infiltrate his office and bug it?

The new task force that was targeting organised crime had hit him hard on his shipments and his cocaine supplier. He was still suffering greatly from that second blow, having to pay above the odds for small amounts of average product just to stay afloat until he could source a long-term supplier again. It was bad business indeed for someone like Freddie Tyler. But these were the sort of things that he would have been discussing in his office.

Sarah had taken her new bug detector and had scanned Freddie's office. Sure enough, she'd come across several closed-circuit devices. The fact they were closed circuit meant that whoever was managing them was having to come in every couple of days and switch them out. They didn't have great battery life and they couldn't transmit. Which led to another question. How were they getting in? Freddie kept the office locked at all times, and he was the only one with a key. It wasn't like he wasn't going to notice someone switching them up if he was sitting there watching. Even the cleaner wasn't allowed in unless he was present. He guarded his domain well.

With help from Zack and permission from Freddie, Sarah had planted tiny cameras just outside and inside the door to the office and had left Zack in charge of keeping watch. It had taken a couple of days, but the trap had worked, catching the snooper in the act.

Sarah had taken great pleasure in delivering the results to Freddie. He had been as surprised as she was, and she'd even noticed a glimmer of admiration in his eyes as she broke it all down for him. She had proven her worth and gained some grudging respect from her employer. This was something she was particularly pleased with. They might naturally loathe each other, but life would definitely be a lot easier going forward if they at least respected each other.

A knock sounded at the door and Sarah forced her face to not look quite so smug.

'Come in,' Freddie commanded.

Holly popped her head around the door, a friendly smile on her cherry-red lips. 'Did you want to see me?'

'Yes, I do. Come in. Take a seat.'

Holly stepped through and closed the door before taking a seat opposite them at the desk. She crossed her tanned, slender legs and twisted them to the side, the smile not leaving her lips. 'So, what's up?' she asked brightly.

'Oh, not much.' Freddie smiled back, a predatory smile. 'I'm just wondering how you're getting on with your investigation, DI Holly Miechowski?'

Holly visibly paled, and her neck bobbed as she swallowed. She shook her head, still smiling but with a slight frown. 'Sorry, I'm confused?' she said.

Sarah pulled the bag of bugs up from her lap and emptied them onto the table. There was a long silence as Holly stared at them, clearly weighing up whether to keep trying to hold her cover or not. Eventually she realised there was no point and the smile finally dropped.

'Well, I got what I could,' she said brazenly. 'It should be enough to put you away for a few years at least. It was good while it lasted.' She narrowed her eyes and smirked.

Freddie and Sarah exchanged looks.

'I wouldn't even try it if I were you,' she continued. 'The entire force knows I'm here, and if I disappear, you'll be picked up within five minutes. So I think we'll just part ways now.' She stood up to leave.

Sarah turned the laptop round to face her and Holly stopped in her tracks. The video played out on screen and she watched herself break into the office by picking the lock. The video showed her every movement, crystal clear.

'I've got a few more of those too.' It was a lie; she only had one, but Holly didn't need to know that.

'And what?' She shrugged, but Sarah saw the flash of devastation cross her face as she realised where they were going with it all.

'And you know as well as we do that while bugging an office is fairly legal, it immediately becomes clearly *illegal* if that officer has broken in unlawfully to plant said bugs. With all the proof we've collated, everything you have will be thrown out of court as useless. Every second you've spent here has been for nothing,' Sarah shot, letting all the smugness she felt flow out.

Holly stared at her, her face slowly turning red in hot rage and frustration. 'You fucker,' she growled in a low voice. 'You absolute fucker.'

Freddie stood up and walked around the desk. He stood over her, purposely close to intimidate. Reaching into his pocket, he pulled out an envelope. 'Here are your wages up to date along with your P45. Your employment is terminated, effective immediately.'

Holly snatched it out of his hand, fuming but not quite brave enough to say anything in her precarious position.

'Oh, and one more thing.' He bent down and shoved his face into hers, forcing her backward in surprise. 'You can walk out of here today, but I know everything about you. I have your address, the details of your family, I even know the route you run every morning,' he snarled. 'If I ever find you tailing me or mine again, or if you ever tell another soul that you've met my friend Sarah here today – *especially* if you talk about Sarah – I'll find you. And when I do, you'll never see the light of another day. Do we understand each other?'

Holly pursed her lips and cast her eyes down. 'Perfectly,' she replied, through gritted teeth.

'Good. Now get out.' Freddie stepped out of her way and Holly stormed out without another word.

'You think that's the last we'll see of her?' Sarah asked, walking round to join her boss.

'That's the last I'll see of her,' Freddie replied. 'But probably not you.'

'Oh?' Sarah asked, with a frown.

'I need you to go into another job for me. I'll still pay you well, but this one is a little more in your field again.' Freddie sat back down.

'What job?' Sarah asked warily.

'You're going to go back into the force. And more specifically, you're going to join the task force that's trying to take me down. They want to plant spies in my camp? Well, it's only fair that I repay the favour.'

CHAPTER SIXTY

Anna punched the pads that Seamus held up in front of him hard, all her pent-up energy and emotion going into every hit. There was no sound in the empty gym other than Seamus's voice and Anna's small cries of exertion. It was late at night, dark outside, the gym closed off to the outside world. Here the two of them came twice a week now to work out her frustrations and release her demons together.

It had been two weeks since the Mafia had finally left town and since Tom had disappeared for good and Rosie had last been seen walking towards the M25 in nothing but a nightdress. No one had heard a whisper from her after that. Tanya had scanned the news for a few days for any traffic accidents on the M25, but it seemed that her mother had escaped being run over by a lorry after all. She told Anna that the most likely bet was that Rosie had caught a lift back to her dismal home where Tanya had grown up and she still lived. She had never moved in all these years, so Tanya doubted she suddenly would now. Their threats seemed to be enough to keep her silent and at bay, which was all that really mattered.

Anna had been working on getting Tanya to stop trying to fight everything on her own, and to her surprise her words had hit home. Tanya had begun voluntarily going back to the psychotherapy sessions that had been offered to her. Her short-term memory was no longer a problem, but the trauma she had suffered was. She was convinced that had all the extra stuff with Rosie not happened that she would have been strong enough to get over the rest, but that final betrayal had pushed her over the edge. She couldn't be totally honest with her therapist, of course; a lot of what she spoke about in her sessions were the PG version of events, but she stuck to the truth as much as she was able.

'Left, right, right, come on, Anna, uppercut.' Seamus's instruction gave her a clear path towards the emotional relief she craved from the activity. 'Faster, come on. Again.'

Anna pulled back and wiped the sweat off her forehead with her arm, her hands encased in boxing gloves. She fixed her stance and focused on the pads. The pads were the enemy, Seamus told her. When they were in the ring, the pads and the bag were everyone who had ever hurt her, every nightmare that had ever stolen sleep, every memory that darkened her heart. It was all there in front of her, ready to be beaten.

'Come on, Anna,' Seamus barked at her. 'You've got more than this in you – pull it out. Formation. Left, left, right.'

With a roar, Anna pushed forward again, tensing her core and punching the pads with all her might. This time she didn't let up; she completed the rotation again and again, putting all of her energy into it. Seamus was right – she did have more in her and she needed to get it out. She needed to keep hitting and hitting until she was completely spent, until she was ready to collapse. Only then would she go home and sleep easy.

Already, after just a few sessions, she was beginning to feel a lot more in control. It didn't take away the pain, and it didn't make her losses and guilt any lighter, but it seemed to channel a lot of the anger she felt. When she was in the ring with Seamus, she could let it out and set it free. The club walls were safe once again, as were her knuckles now that she was forced to wear gloves.

She hit out again.

His eyes stared back at her, empty and cruel. He knew she was losing the baby and he was glad. He'd just shot Tanya and was about to try to kill Freddie too.

Her fists flew, Seamus stepping one foot back to steady himself.

Blood everywhere. Tanya's blood on the ground. Blood around her feet as the baby inside her died. Michael's blood on the walls as the echo of the gunshot reverberated around the walls.

She heard herself cry out a feral, strangled war cry as she attacked the pads. Her hits were no longer so controlled, and Seamus focused on moving the pads to accommodate her fury.

Tanya's face as Michael dragged her away. The doctor's face as he told her she would likely never carry a baby to full term. Damaged womb. Freddie asking her if they could try again, just two days ago.

Forcing herself to regain control, she tensed her muscles again and put her back into the punches, making them harder, stronger.

'That's it, keep going,' Seamus shouted.

Sweat dripped from every pore and her body ached as she pushed forward one last time. As her last punch connected, she dropped her arms and bent forward, gloves on her knees, to catch her breath.

Seamus took off the pads and threw them to one side. 'I think we're done for today. Any more and you'll throw up. Come on, sit down.'

Anna sat on the stool in the corner of the ring for a moment and Seamus passed her a bottle of water. He sat on the rubber floor next to her and leaned back against the ropes.

Anna grinned at him, exhausted. 'Thanks.'

'That was a good session. You're getting stronger,' he replied.

Anna nodded slowly and took another swig from the bottle. 'Yes,' she said eventually. 'I think I am.'

*

Freddie walked into the coffee shop near the office and ordered. As he waited by the side, his phone rang. Seeing it was Paul, he picked it up.

'Alright, mate?' He paused. 'Yeah, go ahead. I'll be at CoCo; meet me there when you're done.'

Ending the call, he slipped the phone back into his pocket and once again thanked the stars that he still had a brother to talk to. It had been touch and go with the Mafia, especially after they had taken Paul. Before that point, if things had gone tits up, they could have at least tried to run. They probably wouldn't have made it far before Joe and Vito tracked them down, but they could have tried. The second they had Paul though, that option had gone out of the window.

Freddie had spent months looking for Tom. He knew that the Mafia wouldn't leave without spilling blood, without getting their retribution on whoever was responsible for Frank's death. It just wasn't done. They hadn't become who they were today by letting things like this go, and someone had to be sacrificed if the Tylers were going to escape the blame. But whatever way they looked at it, there was only one person who genuinely deserved to be put in their place – Tom. Freddie had taken lives before; he had done a lot of things he wasn't proud of, but he had always lived by a code. And that code meant that he could never bring himself to set up an innocent person. It had to be done the right way. But Tom had evaded them for so long that towards the end, Freddie had begun to question if they could pull it off. In the end though, Tom had unwittingly delivered himself right into Freddie's hands and everything had fallen into place. It was almost poetic.

'Thanks,' Freddie said to the barista as he handed over the steaming coffee.

Freddie stepped out into the brisk morning air and began walking down the road towards the club. There was much to be done.

Freddie had never been so happy to see Paul the day they'd handed Tom over. When they'd left the restaurant that night, they had gone straight back to Paul's flat where James had crumpled to the floor and cried his eyes out in relief. Paul had comforted him and held him and Freddie had been touched to see the strength of the love between them. He was glad for his brother that he had found someone to share his life with. Happiness was all that he ever wanted for his family. It was what he worked for, killed for, lived on the edge for, every day.

There was still a lot of trouble to sort out on the work front. Freddie and Paul still needed a new cocaine supplier. Marco had arrived safely back in his home town thanks to their help, but he was nowhere near having his operation back up and running, and so the Tylers were still in the market for a new supplier. It made them vulnerable and it put Freddie on edge, but they had been through worse before and had always come out on top, so he had every faith they would be able to do that again.

He reached Club CoCo and looked up to the bright blue sky. It was cold, but it was a beautiful day and with the life they led, Freddie believed in embracing these moments. He closed his eyes, feeling the breeze on his face.

*

Sarah Riley smoothed down the front of her smart business suit and stared across the desk at her new boss.

'I'm glad to have you back, Riley. You'll be fully briefed shortly, but in summary the team I put on the Tylers fucked up royally. We had to drop the whole case. I've even had harassment accusations hit my desk.' Ben Hargreaves ran his hands through his hair in angry frustration. 'Can you believe that? From those utter scum,' he spat. Taking a deep breath, he pulled his emotions back in check.

Sarah watched as the vein in his temple throbbed, despite the renewed calmness in his tone.

'I want to bury them, Riley. I want to bury them all so deep they never see the outside of a prison cell again.' His dark eyes bored into hers. 'And now that you're back and I finally have someone competent to take the lead, that is *exactly* what we're going to do.'

Leaning forward, Sarah nodded, a cold determination flashing through her expression. 'You can count on me, sir. I can assure you, there is no one else in the world who wants to take down Freddie Tyler more than me.' She sat back and clenched her fist. 'No one.'

A LETTER FROM EMMA

To those of you who have just joined the series here, thank you so much for buying my book and I really hope you've enjoyed being introduced to the Tylers. To those of you who have been on this journey with me from the beginning, I hope you have enjoyed the latest instalment and watching our characters grow through experience and hardship. You probably feel as connected to these characters as I do now.

If you enjoyed *Fierce Girl* and want to keep up to date with all my latest releases, just sign up at the following link. Your email address will never be shared and you can unsubscribe at any time.

www.bookouture.com/emma-tallon

If you enjoy my books, I would really appreciate if you could leave me a review on Amazon. I read every single one and I love to hear what you liked, what you're looking forward to finding out, how you felt as you read it. It makes all the days and nights tied up in my office worth it.

Through this series we have seen Anna, Freddie, Tanya, Paul – all of them really – develop and change so much, but I think throughout *Fierce Girl* we have seen them move to a whole new level. These colourful, flawed people are absolute warriors. Even when we think they are about to break, somehow they pull it back, and even as the author, this sometimes really surprises me. As I write certain scenes, it's like they take over the keyboard and write their actions themselves. Honestly, Freddie and Tanya get so outrageous sometimes that I end up laughing out loud and my poor editor ends up having a small heart attack before it gets carefully edited back to what's acceptable!

I have to say, with the exception of *Runaway Girl,* which will always have the most special place in my literary heart, this has been my favourite book to write yet. Some books just flow from your fingertips and some fight you all the way. This one was a real pleasure to write and I am greatly looking forward to continuing the story on.

I hope to see you again on book five, but for now, wherever you are and whatever you're doing – have a great rest of your day!

Warm wishes,
Emma Xx

emmatallonofficial

EmmaEsj

@my.author.life

www.emmatallon.com

ACKNOWLEDGEMENTS

As always, a huge thanks to my amazing editor Helen. I might write the books, but she takes this raw, messy thing and turns it into something sleek and beautiful. I couldn't do this without her.

I also want to take a moment to acknowledge the incredible support I receive from my handsome husband. He isn't a reader, but all the little things he does to show his support and help me work every day makes such a big difference, and I'm so lucky to have such a fantastic man by my side as I travel this road.

Lastly, the biggest thank you goes out to you wonderful readers. As I write every emotion and every twist, I have you guys in the back of my mind. Thank you so much for all of your tremendous support, reviews, comments, shares – you guys mean the absolute world to me and I appreciate you more than you know.

Printed in Great Britain
by Amazon